A KILLER WITH A MISSION.

A DOG ON THE RUN

The dog heard the soft *click* of the lock in the darkness. The sound traveled under the door and into the tiny bedroom. It sniffed the heat. Rhythmic pulses of air pushed through its nostrils and excited its olfactory nerves. As it swiftly sorted the odors, it encountered a novel one, a human one. Despite the presence of this interloper, it refrained from barking. Zainah had taught it to do nothing to betray its presence here in the building. No dogs allowed . . .

A BREED APART

Pierre Davis

A Dell Book

A BREED APART
A Dell Book / June 2009

Published by Bantam Dell
A Division of Random House, Inc.
New York, New York

Dell is a registered trademark of Random House, Inc., and the colophon is a
trademark of Random House, Inc.

ISBN 978-0-440-24508-7

Printed in the United States of America
Published simultaneously in Canada

www.bantamdell.com

OPM 10 9 8 7 6 5 4 3 2 1

Dedicated to Rolo, the best dog ever

Acknowledgments

Most of this book was written during a time of great solitude. Nevertheless, a few individuals were extremely helpful in bringing it to life. These include my story editor, David Kelly, who brought his considerable intellect and intuition to bear. And my longtime friend and fellow writer Mark Christensen, who mounted a spirited defense of the work during critical moments. Anna Dudey, Dr. John Kingman, and William Piland were among the early manuscript readers who lent a big measure of enthusiasm and support when it was needed most. My agent, Richard Pine, came through with excellent creative insight and a large dose of faith in my ability to pull this thing off. Kate Miciak and her team at Bantam Dell delivered a truly magnificent editing performance. Finally, Patti Watkins has been beautifully supportive in bringing this work down the home stretch.

A Breed Apart

PART 1

Elliot

CHAPTER 1

Elliot slouched in the sad yellow stink of the aging van. He watched the rain smack the windshield as he listened to the muted squawk of the police band and wondered how many cigarettes it took to make something smell this awful. Next to him, Sparks sped the process along by lighting up. Carefully, of course. He didn't want to send a signal to the dope house down the block.

Elliot Elliot. E squared. Double E. Dubby when he was a kid. The legacy of an idiot father long gone in an old Toyota pickup. Took the tools of his trade with him. A pool cue. A maxed-out credit card. An empty beer cooler.

"Couldn't you step outside with that?" one of the guys asked from the back. A young guy, nonsmoker obviously. You saw that all the time these days.

Sparks ignored him. Sparks was top dog. Team leader. Sparks called the shots. He turned to Elliot, the greenest among them, recently yanked off desk duty, pushed through training and out onto the street. Sparks pointed through the windshield into the gloom and drizzle beyond. One crummy little house after another. Almost identical, especially at 5 a.m.

"Check out the ride."

A tricked-out Honda sat in the little driveway where Sparks pointed.

"Dead giveaway. They're never smart enough to drive something shitty. They gotta haul out their dick and wave it around."

Sparks referred to the residents of the house. A Mexican-Colombian conspiracy, intelligence said. Bad boys backed by combat-level armament. Dealers of meth, crack and coke. High-octane drugs only. Perfect for a customer base running on empty.

Sparks snorted. "Cool cars. Bad dudes. Crappy houses. It's always the fuckin' same. Always. I want out." He exhaled twin cones of pale blue. "Two more years. That's it. I'm outta here."

Sparks rubbed his beard. Sparks always rubbed his beard. He had amazing whiskers. His face went from nude to opaque in just a couple of hours. Elliot once asked him why he didn't just grow a beard. *Because I'd look like a fucking terrorist,* he replied. A career-limiting move, for sure. Right now, he just looked sleazy.

"I've heard some people don't deal so well with retirement," Elliot ventured.

"Not me," Sparks said. "I'm ready. I'm more than ready. You watch your ass out there. These guys won't go down easy."

Elliot nodded. At the briefing, they'd learned of six possible residents. Five murder raps and sixteen armed assaults among them. Elliot was fearful, but not frozen. Elliot was ex-military, sort of.

Sparks looked at his watch and stubbed the cigarette in the ashtray. "It's showtime."

He grabbed the radio mike and checked in with the support team tucked away in the next block, then turned to the rear. Six faces framed in blue helmets turned toward him. "Okay, you guys know the drill. Be cool."

They all spilled quickly and quietly out of the van. They formed up single file, then trotted up the street through the gloom, Elliot in the rear. The light thump of combat boots pushing through the drizzle.

_____

Elliot's Kevlar vest bobs slightly as he trots along. His M16 feels weightless. He rides high on the heat of the moment.

Sparks signals a halt as they pour into the front yard. No light seeps from anywhere in the house. A streetlight rakes the front and pushes the porch into shadow. Sparks points to the tactical light mounted under the barrel of his rifle. The signal is understood. When they crash in, they will go to tactical light so no time is lost hunting for a light switch.

They steal onto the porch. They split in two and bracket the front door. Sparks opens the screen door. Very carefully. Sims and Carter come up from opposite sides with the entry ram, a heavy metal tube with two handles.

The ram flies forward just as Elliot sees the tricycle out of the corner of his eye.

It sits out in the yard, small and pink. Plastic streamers hang limp off the handlebars. Not good, Elliot thinks. Intelligence said nothing about civilians. He turns to Sparks just as the door explodes into the darkness beyond.

"Police! Put down your weapons and hit the floor!"

Tactical lights on cocked rifles sweep the floors and walls. Spotlights from hell.

"I said police! Put 'em down and get down! Right now!"

Elliot's bad feeling gets worse. The beams rake over family pictures, flowers in vases, neatly stacked magazines. His light beam reaches the end of the living room wall. It spills down a little hallway. It approaches an open doorway, a black tunnel.

Pop! Pop! The tunnel spits two muzzle flashes. The tunnel hurls two concussive thuds, and two 40mm slugs streak toward the person of Elliot Elliot, sometimes known as Double E, other times as Dubby.

The first slug whistles by his ear. Its shock wave kisses his earlobe as it continues out the front window and buries itself in the wall of the house across the street.

The second slams into his Kevlar vest, high on the chest. Its kinetic energy balloons into a nasty punch that puts him on his back. His weapon flies loose.

He comes to rest just as the return fire starts. Rule of the game: Anyone shoots, everyone shoots. Sparks told him that. Sparks had it nailed. Above him, the muzzles flash and the rounds fly. The noise is unbearable. The shooting stops, but the ringing in his brain continues.

And through its silver fog, he begins to hear the screaming of children.

CHAPTER 2

Eighteen Months Later

T he air conditioning shoved the tropics back onto the streets of Kuala Lumpur, where it hung thick and wet. The speaker on the podium droned on. Her laser pointed to the complex diagram on the big flat panel behind her. A computer model of a neutrophil going on the offensive. The audience followed the bouncing red beam. The model might do many things. The model might evoke wonders. It might become a clerk in a molecular bureaucracy, one that permitted the selective immigration of foreigners into the human body and shut down autoimmune reactions in the process.

Dr. Richard Stennis scanned the audience. A few dozed, felled by jet lag. Others squirmed. Some paid rapt attention. So it went during the Seventh International Conference on Immune Response. Stennis had hoped to mine this session for useful technology. Didn't work. All this session would do is put the speaker on the path to her next grant.

The speaker concluded. The lights came up. Applause

rippled through Hall 5 of the city's new convention center. A very large room, ambitiously conceived. Plush seating, long tiers of decorative wood, spectacular display technology. The great cities of Asia instinctively understood that they were the future and planned accordingly. Singapore, Shanghai, Bangkok, Kuala Lumpur.

But Dr. Richard Stennis didn't care about geopolitics or the sweep of history. Stennis cared about pure information. He checked his watch as he headed for the door. Becker must never be kept waiting.

The two men came forward as he emerged into the main hallway outside. One Malay, one Vietnamese. Both in subdued sport shirts, black slacks and shiny loafers. Classic security types. The pair made Stennis uneasy. They reminded him of what might happen if he violated his nondisclosure. It would never even reach the courts.

"Dr. Stennis?" A nod. "This way, please."

They cut across the wave of humanity flowing out of the halls and merged into a stream of academic types shuffling toward their next meeting. Suddenly, there was Rudolph Becker, walking beside him. Security nowhere in sight. Stennis always marveled at this. It was just like the quantum shift of electrons to higher orbits. Instantaneous.

Becker. Early forties. Slight and small-boned, with slender arms protruding from his sport shirt. Fair skin and pale blue eyes. Eyes that blazed. Eyes that never slept.

"Has the conference been productive, Dr. Stennis?"

"A few things of interest, but not as much as I'd hoped."

"This won't impact our schedule, will it?"

Stennis tensed. "I don't like the word 'schedule,'" he countered. "It implies knowledge of the future. It suggests that we know exactly how things will unfold and can build a timeline to match. In this particular case, no such assumptions are warranted."

"Ah, yes," Becker replied. "But you see, I do have a schedule in mind. One that's pretty well mapped out. Which means that you too have a schedule, whether you like it or not."

"I understand," Stennis conceded.

Becker put his hand on Stennis's shoulder. "Think positive, Dr. Stennis. You also have a fantastic opportunity. Keep your eyes on the prize, as they say." He paused. "That is what they say, isn't it?"

"Yes, that is what they say." Of course it was. Becker was playing with him.

"Good. Are you ready for the test subject?"

"Yes, we are. Where do you stand on that?" Stennis asked.

"She's being processed for transport. There's been a slight delay, but we'll soon be back on track. It won't be long."

Stennis felt a hand touch his elbow. He turned. The Vietnamese security guy. He turned back. Becker had vanished.

The man currently called Victor Korvin beheld the motor scooter covered with cats. Scrawny, desperate cats. Cats draped off the fenders, the running board, the seat, maybe a dozen. Their master sat nearby, selling photo opportunities to passersby. The first drops of warm rain fell through the night and pelted Korvin's exposed head. He stepped into an Italian restaurant that opened onto the street and sat at a table by the bar.

He ordered a simple dinner salad and a glass of bottled

water. In front of him, the band worked its way through some elevator jazz. One of their friends sat at the bar and played the cowbell. Pitiful. Cheap, derivative music played by hacks. His salad came. As he ate, a squall soaked the street in a blaze of rose-colored light from all the brilliant signage along the avenue.

The squall ended. Victor Korvin paid the bill and left. Just in time. The press of people on the street and in the shops was starting to annoy him. Their collective lust for the material and the mundane showed how weak and vulnerable they truly were. He would leave this decadence as soon as possible and retreat to a place of greater purity.

He took a taxi and got out a quarter mile from his destination. He walked along a row of modest shops and mingled with the tourists. A neatly dressed man approached him. A Malaysian. The man fell in beside him and addressed him in fluent English. A man who might be of "assistance" once they got to know each other.

"Hi. How you doing tonight?"

Korvin understood him, but remained silent. The man pegged him as a westerner. The man pegged him wrong. The man demonstrated one of Victor's major assets. He was from nowhere. He possessed a bland and agreeable face, the mark of a man desirous of conformity. He wore his hair in the buzz cut made popular by American movie stars, so he left little impression of personal style. He was of medium build and possessed no physical distinctions. His age might have been anywhere between thirty and forty-five. Only his hands appeared powerful. For this reason, he displayed them sparingly.

Korvin stopped and turned to confront the man's relaxed smile. And for just a moment, he let his persona down. The man looked into Korvin's eyes and saw something indescribably awful. His smile collapsed. He spun and walked away, head hunched down, hands in pockets.

Korvin stepped into shadow when he reached the building. Public housing. Fifteen stories of subsidized despair. Twenty-five dollars a month, U.S. Laundry hung on lines across the little balconies, with hammocks pitched outside to escape the smothering heat. He pulled the little night scope from his pocket, counted up nine stories and over three. He found the girl asleep in her hammock, one leg pitched over the edge.

He dialed a local number on his cell phone. Three rings and a male voice said, "Clear." He did not respond. No need, no questions.

He crossed the street and entered the lobby, a concrete cave. A tarnished plaque extolled the virtues of public assistance. It failed to mention that the building would be demolished in a few months. He noted that the wire was snipped on the lone video camera that surveyed the scene. He pressed the button for the elevator, and scanned the graffiti in Malay scrawled on the door until the doors opened and he ascended to the ninth floor.

He got out and looked up and down an empty hallway bathed in naked fluorescent light. Cooking odors and body stink hung heavy in the confined heat. Gray metal doors with deadbolts ranged along each wall. He quickly oriented himself and went to the girl's door.

It would take him between twenty-five and thirty-five seconds to pick the lock. An acceptable interval of risk. In the early evening, the city hummed. By ten, it suddenly wilted, so he would most likely have the hall to himself.

The lock yielded in twenty-seven seconds, and he let himself inside.

The dog heard the soft *click* of the lock in the darkness. The sound traveled under the door and into the tiny bedroom. The dog sniffed the heat. Rhythmic pulses of air pushed through its nostrils and excited its olfactory nerves. As it swiftly sorted the odors, it encountered a novel one, a human one. Despite the presence of this interloper, it refrained from barking. Zainah had taught it to do nothing to betray its presence here in the building. No dogs allowed.

Korvin gently closed the door and remained absolutely still while his eyes adjusted. The room took shape. Tiny kitchen. Little dining table. Futon couch. The urban night drifted in through the open sliding door. The girl slept on the hammock. No blanket, just a loose-fitting cotton dress, colorless, in the shadows. He took the weapon from his pocket, a lead sphere the size of a golf ball, with a slender nylon cord attached. An ideal solution. No noise, no struggle. He measured out the required length of cord.

He stopped when he reached the girl. Beautiful skin and a peaceful mouth. The weapon dangled at his side. Her head was slightly cocked and sunk into the pillow. Her right temple was clearly accessible. Excellent. He swung the weapon in an expert and vicious arc.

The dog heard the impact—a low-pitched *crack*—and rose to its feet and sniffed the space under the door. A trace of the strange human scent, and then the tiny *snick* of the lock and the closing of the door. It smelled no more reason for alarm, so it lay back down.

Once outside, Korvin spotted the ambulance advancing as he walked down the street. He signaled with a raised index finger as it passed him. He was done. He knew nothing of the origin of the ambulance, but he could guess. It was not an ambulance at all. The two men inside would use it as a cover to remove the target without raising alarm.

With the job now done, Korvin thought back to the original briefing. They had been very opposed to giving him any background on the job, but he'd insisted. He never worked blind. The girl had worked as a technician in an anonymous lab facility. Her job put her in close daily contact with a test animal of some kind. For whatever reason, the girl conspired to kidnap the animal and go into hiding with it, probably to save it from the usual fate that befell such beasts. Three days ago, she pulled it off. Very stupid. Becker's intelligence network located her in less than twenty-four hours. Shortly thereafter, Korvin was contracted to perform the execution.

And now it was done.

He walked on through the hot haze of the polluted night. The city was poisoning itself, the product of human corruption expressed in chemical form.

He returned to his small hotel room, with its modest fixtures and spartan bed. After completing his daily exercise routine, he fell into a deep and righteous sleep.

CHAPTER 3

Hell is corporate," the bald man declared. "And Satan is the CEO. You know that, don't you?" He pointed to the double doors. "And the people out there are staff for him. I know this. I'm a professional."

"I think I'm beginning to get it," Elliot said, and leaned forward in his chair. "But who are the shareholders?"

The bald man glowed in a moment of supreme knowledge. "We are all the shareholders. Each and every one of us. One share of hell. One share of heaven. We get them at birth."

"Well now, if you've got a CEO and you've got shareholders, you've also got a board of directors, right?"

The bald man looked leery. "I don't know about that."

Elliot shrugged. "Standard corporate practice. The board looks out for the interests of the shareholders, people like you and me. And that means Satan has to report to the board. So, if you've got a problem with Satan or his staff, you go to the board. The board gets the problem fixed. It's as simple as that."

The bald man's eyes narrowed. "And who's on the board?"

"Well, among other people, I'm on the board. And that's why I'm here. They called me in because they said you had a problem."

The bald man relaxed slightly. "Yeah, I got a problem. Big-time problem. So what you gonna do about it?"

"I've got staff of my own," Elliot answered. "And if I bring them into this, they can take care of everything for you."

"You're sure about that?"

"Look, I took time out from an incredibly busy schedule to come over here and see you. And I don't waste my time on things that don't work."

The bald man seemed partially convinced by Elliot's exasperation. "How soon can I see them?"

"They're downstairs. I can have them up here in just a couple of minutes."

"Don't keep me waiting," the bald man warned.

Elliot rose from his chair. "I wouldn't think of it, especially with all that you've been through. They'll be right up."

The attendants looked expectant when Elliot entered the nurses' station. He pointed his thumb back toward the ward holding the bald man. "Has he ever seen any staff from the next floor up?"

"Don't think so," the head attendant said. A large black man with an easy smile. A long-term worker on the psychiatric ward. A person attuned to the warped humor of the place.

"Good. Get a couple of those people to come on down. Tell them he thinks they work for the board of directors of hell. Tell them that he expects they'll help him. Then medicate him right up to the max."

The head attendant grinned. "I like it. How come we haven't worked with you before?"

"Because we're short on bodies today. Three people phoned in sick this morning."

Elliot had responded to the call a half an hour ago. Acting up was handled locally. Assault mandated that security get involved. A large man on the loose, they said. A delusional man. One who had made a slingshot out of pilfered surgical tubing and then ricocheted a domino off the head of an attendant. Satan's staff was going down.

Elliot gave the attendant his card and the man's brow furrowed as he read it. Elliot winced. He knew what was coming.

"Hey, man, says here you're a detective. So now, what's that all about? Since when we got detectives up here?"

"Good question. But maybe we should tend to Mr. Bald Guy first."

"Oh. Yeah." The attendant shuffled off toward the phone. Elliot took it as his cue to leave.

Elliot looked out the window by the elevator. A dense cluster of new buildings perched on the wooded hillside. The Pearson Institute of Health Sciences. Multiple hospitals, a medical school, a dental school, a nursing school, numerous research facilities, many clinics, and everything required to support them 24/7.

Including a Department of Public Safety. Fifteen thousand people worked at Pearson. Several thousand more occupied hospital beds. Another few thousand came daily to visit them. And on any given day, several dozen came to prey on all of the above and the property in general. Hence, Elliot's job.

Fifty people worked within the department, including the director, better known as the Chief. It was, after all, a police department. The Pearson PR people played that down, but staff played it up. Ten bodies manned the desks and computers, thirty patrolled the campus in three shifts, and five more supervised them. Three lieutenants sat atop the org chart under the Chief. One ran the office. The second ran patrol operations. The third pretty much ran himself. That was Elliot. Lieutenant Detective Elliot Elliot, in charge of investigations.

"Hey!"

Elliot turned.

The attendant stood at the other end of the hall. He held the card up and pointed to it. "They got your name wrong. They used your first name twice."

"Yeah, I saw that. They'll have to fix it."

The elevator doors opened and Elliot entered. So here he was, a detective. Fallout from the raid. The big Chief down at the city police department took his exercise at the same athletic club as the little Chief up here. The little Chief thought it was cool to hang with the big Chief. So when big Chief said he needed a favor, the little Chief jumped.

The favor was Elliot.

Elliot walked out of the lobby and turned up the hill. Pearson's buildings followed the topography in a most clever manner, with ingenious walking bridges and stacking schemes. He reached the building housing his office, the Support Services Building. Nothing ingenious here. No sculptures and marble, unlike the lobby to the Biomedical Research Center, just linoleum tile floors and hanging fluorescents. Frayed posters with safety slogans. A dented coffee machine. Standard cop stuff, which was fine with Elliot.

Bobby Seifert looked up from his computer screen as Elliot settled into his cubicle. Young Bobby, chubby, redheaded and smart. The lone staffer under Elliot's dominion. Bobby ran the paperwork, checked the records, worked the network and thought the Chief was an asshole. Bobby was right.

"So, did you shoot the crazy guy?" Bobby asked in partial jest.

"Nope. Just hobbled him. Severed his Achilles tendon. What's come in since I left?"

Bobby turned back to his screen. "It seems that this woman up at the library had her laptop stolen."

"Her laptop, huh? Well, how about that."

Laptops. No murders. No heists. No kidnappings. No armed robberies. Just laptops. It took Elliot about a week on the job to realize that the "investigations" part of his detective title really meant stolen laptops. Dozens every month. A lucky day meant a purse lift in Emergency to buck the trend. Worse, every stolen laptop launched a mind-numbing slew of documentation. Victim interviews, property descriptions, insurance forms, inventory reports.

Elliot settled in and started a response report on the bald guy. At least he wasn't a laptop, even though he might think he was now and then. Elliot remembered the time he got a date because of a stolen laptop. It had seemed very promising. A cute physical therapist who had lost her laptop in the cafeteria. She'd put it down and headed to the food line, then discovered it gone when she came back. A big surprise to her, but not to Elliot, who wrote her up, and then asked her out.

On his way to meet her, he'd taken stock of himself. Mid-thirties, never married. Dark brown hair with just enough curl to make it permanently tousled. Blue eyes, always a little weary, set against dark features. A well-trimmed goatee, which he vowed to shear off at the first fleck of gray. A slightly crooked nose, broken while riding his BMX bike as a kid. All in all, a reasonable appearance. Not stellar, but good enough to survive a first date.

They met at a trendy little place with a quiet booth in the back. She was trim and blonde and even more attractive than he remembered. It all seemed just a shade short of perfect.

"I'm feeling a little anxious," she told him as she twisted the stem of her wineglass.

"Well, I mean, we don't know each other," Elliot suggested.

"I don't think that's it."

"Then what do you think it is?"

"I ran out of Xanax."

"That's some kind of tranquilizer, isn't it?"

"Yeah. I started taking it when I broke up with my boyfriend. I was feeling really weird. Know what I mean?"

"Kind of."

"I went to my doctor and told him I was upset and needed some Xanax because I was having problems at home. He said that maybe we should try some counseling before we went to drugs. I told him it was too late. That I was too freaked. Then he asked me to describe exactly how I felt. I told him that the night before, I went into the bedroom where my boyfriend was sleeping. And suddenly, I wanted to go to the garage and get the gas can, and bring it back, and pour it on him, and light him on fire, and watch him burn. It was all I could do to stop myself."

"And what did the doctor do?"

"He gave me a prescription for Xanax."

Elliot couldn't recall the balance of the conversation.

The vision of the burning boyfriend had yanked him back sixteen years and dropped him in the Gulf.

Sergeant Elliot Elliot. Twenty years of age. Firm of haunch, sound of mind. Instant veteran of the first Gulf War. Now in a Humvee on the road north out of Kuwait and sweating profusely under the desert sun. Baked by the heat, blinded by the light. Ordered to scout the "target area" on the road ahead, whatever that meant.

A four-lane divided highway cut through the hot haze. In the boiling air, a heap of wrecked vehicles took shape. Trucks, buses, campers, tanks, armored personnel carriers, dump trucks, station wagons, pickups. Scorched, riddled and pocked.

Elliot stopped the Humvee and got out. He could go no further on the clogged roadway, so he walked and sweated. It was utterly silent. Not even the buzz of a rogue insect. He entered the tangled mass of blackened metal. The desert wind fluttered the antenna on a jackknifed tanker truck. A carbonized body sprawled facedown just outside the cab. Life minus all its liquids.

Elliot continued on. For once, he thanked the desert wind. It cut through the silence. It countered the awful stillness, the kind that often settles into the wake of massive violence.

On it went. Hundreds of carbonized bodies. Only the teeth remained human. Ivory on black. Only the teeth echoed the screaming of the night gone by.

And each step took Elliot that much further from all that anchored his life. There had been no combat here. Only wanton slaughter. He wandered on through this horrible exhibition. And as he did, he felt the center of him shift in some inexplicable way.

After a quarter mile, he turned back. His pace quickened. He would have sprinted, but the heat would have put him down. He had to escape while still able to reclaim his former self. Elliot Elliot, a product of civilization, an attendee of picnics, a player of softball, an earnest student, an abider of the law of the land.

And he nearly made it.

But then he came upon the minivan. It stood upright and normal, a cheerful blue in color. Not a scratch on it. It pointed straight up the highway, as if immune to the lethal chaos around it. Except for the passenger.

Many products of extreme violence remain inexplicable in spite of the best forensics. And the more extreme the violence, the deeper the mystery. Such was the case with the passenger in the minivan. The body's gender had vaporized along with its water content, but Elliot assumed it to be male. Its carbonized elbow jutted leisurely out the open passenger window, as if on a weekend drive. It wore a short-sleeved yellow sport shirt sprinkled with little pictures of weightlifters, a shirt that showed no signs of flame. Its head of dull charcoal gazed on down the road out of sockets of the deepest black.

And as Elliot looked on, the ashen arm, the arm so comfortably posed, disintegrated. It fell into a light sprinkle on the desert sand. A little dark cloud of dust drifted out the empty yellow sleeve.

Elliot walked back to his vehicle at a furious pace. But it was too late. He was locked out. He would return to civilization, but view it from without. The dust cloud from that charcoal arm would forever darken his internal sky.

He returned from the Gulf. He went to school. He graduated. He worked for an accounting firm. No good. He needed to find a community much closer to the heart of darkness. He drifted toward police work. He felt no personal bent toward violence, but needed its proximity to feel a bond. He did well at the academy. He gravitated toward administration, toward desk duty. Then Sparks. Then the trouble. Afterward, they sent him to counseling, but it didn't seem to make much difference. He threw out his pills and replaced them with old cowboy movies. The kind with heroes in big hats climbing over enormous rocks somewhere in southern California in the fifties. He found a cable channel that ran this genre 24/7, and he'd plop down in front of them when he had trouble sleeping. The campfire scenes worked best. The steady strum of the old guitars and the smooth vocals tranquilized him every time. Who needed Ambien when you had Gene Autry?

So now Lieutenant Detective Elliot Elliot sat in his cubicle in the Support Services Building at the center of this vast medical empire. He wrote his report. He documented the disappearance and probable theft of the victim's laptop. He finished and leaned back in his chair. He envisioned a line of laptops spanning the entire length of his career here at Pearson.

In this, he was wrong.

CHAPTER 4

Korvin gripped the railing of the aging steamer with its Libyan registry, Filipino crew and Chinese captain. He couldn't see the coast through the darkness, but he could smell traces of it. Pine. Animals. Auto exhaust.

He checked his watch and pulled out his handheld with its global positioning system. The little display presented the soft glow of a miniature map. The ship ran north. It hugged the west coast of the United States, where it flirted with the twelve-mile limit.

He moved near the stern and looked up at the superstructure. Its portholes spewed yellow light. Its decks were empty. No one watched. Why should they?

He approached a shipping crate that sat alone on the empty deck. A prying bar rested on top. He opened the crate and pulled out the Zodiac and the electric pump, then plugged the pump into a utility socket and threw the switch. The motor whined. The pump shoved air into the Zodiac and the boat took its final shape.

He extracted a length of rope from the crate and attached it to the nose of the craft. A glance at his watch told him it was almost time. Moments later, he felt a change in the throb of the engine. The hiss of water sliding by the hull subsided. His cue.

He worked the boat over the railing and lowered it to the surface of the sea. It caught the ship's motion and glided along in tow. He took his pack from the crate, strapped it on, and pulled out a small outboard motor. After pitching the empty crate and the pump overboard, he looped a second line around his waist and attached the motor.

He took one last look up at the empty superstructure. Its occupants had been generously compensated. He was never here. He was never anywhere. He climbed over the railing and pulled the engine up and over. It dangled beneath him as he worked his way down the hull. His feet played over chipped paint and corroded metal.

When he reached the boat, he carefully guided the motor to rest on the floor, then let himself down and in. He pulled a knife from a scabbard on his belt and cut the craft free from the mother ship. Its looming hull surged off into the night. Within a few minutes, it would return to cruise speed. At first light, someone would remove the line still attached to the railing.

He mounted the little engine on the motor plate and paused. Stars studded the firmament. Water lapped at the hull. The boat bobbed and rolled gently. He let the moment linger. It reminded him of skies long ago, of an expanse of empty land instead of sea. Kyrgyzstan.

He fired up the motor and headed for the coast. Its small fuel tank held enough gas to get him there, but not much more. Lights already winked in the distance. The quarter moon revealed the coastal range of mountains. The little motor buzzed and whined.

Kyrgyzstan. Ugly and landlocked. A twisted confluence of peoples and cultures. He came from a village flush with weaponry and steeped in cruelty. A remote and brutal place unaffected by the advance of civilization. The males lived in a hierarchy based on their ability to injure or kill those beneath them. The women lived in misery and fear. He left the village as a young man and took its dark legacy with him to the city. He was intelligent, industrious. He joined the army and became an officer and polished and shaped the violence within him. Worked in intelligence and learned English at American University. Assassinated several wayward members of the so-called Parliament. Approached murder and torture as engineering problems. Caught the attention of the CIA. Did contract work in Afghanistan. Specialized in the unspeakable and unforgivable. Occasionally, he would stand on the precipice of the moral void within him and peer into a chasm of utter darkness and limitless depth. At such moments, the evil of his actions threatened to totally consume him, because he had no faith or ethical conviction to pull him back from the edge. But in time, he found a solution. He became an ascetic, devoted to self-denial, personal deprivation and unflinching self-discipline. He cast off the weakness and corruption of the mass of humanity. Purity of intent and singularity of action became the principle weapons of his trade. He came to understand that he who tortures himself grants himself license to torture others with impunity. He also came to understand that the market for his skills was global; he greatly expanded his scope of operations.

He approached the shore where there were few lights. A small town with a little forest of streetlights presented itself to the south. The surf was stronger and more chaotic than he expected. Several times, he nearly lost the boat when a wave crest collapsed under him.

One final surge put him up on the beach. He dragged the boat to where wet sand met dry sand, drew his knife and punctured the hull. After detaching the motor, he pulled out his pack. He gathered up the collapsed boat and hiked into the dunes, where he found a depression in the sand in a secluded spot. After going back to fetch the motor, he buried the entire assemblage in the loose sand, using his powerful hands as a shovel. His pack held a change of clothes, casual attire typical of the region. He changed into them and stuffed his wet garments into the pack, which he shouldered as he stood to leave.

After careful deliberation, he followed a path down a small creek to the wet sand near the surf and headed south. The dunes tapered off and he passed houses, some vacant, some occupied. A few of the big gas-guzzling vehicles favored by Americans presented themselves in a display of decadence and weakness, but none were correctly positioned for his use.

But then, as he approached the town, he saw an opportunity. He stood in the roar of the surf and assessed the situation. An SUV sat at the end of a block that terminated at the shore. The proper model.

He continued south in the wet sand toward town for a hundred meters. Then he turned north. If they traced his tracks in the dry sand, it would appear that he came up the beach from town.

He reached the vehicle and surveyed the layout. Three houses, comfortable little bungalows. Probably owned by comfortable, indulgent people. Then, a vacant lot where the SUV stood. A wind-swept pine put it partially in shadow from a security light, and he followed this shadow right up to the vehicle. He produced a small electronic apparatus. A product of car-theft rings in Beijing, where big cars fetched premium prices.

The apparatus not only let him in, it surrendered the vehicle's electronics to him. He started the engine and quietly turned the vehicle around and headed up the block. Within a minute, he was on the main coast highway. He glanced at the digital clock on the dashboard. Perfect. By the time the vehicle was missed, he would be through with it.

The SUV climbed up through the coastal range. The air grew cool and thinner. No moon, no buildings, no lights. Only darkness beyond the splash of the headlights. Korvin passed the time by devising investment strategies. Hedge funds, stocks, mutual funds, tax-exempt bonds. He mixed them in various combinations. He estimated the attendant risks. He projected the potential returns. The advance from this project had already been deposited in various banks around the world. Friendly, customer-oriented banks.

His briefing in Bangkok had been conducted by a third party that furnished all the necessary information in a PowerPoint presentation. The briefing was thorough and intelligently organized, but Korvin expected nothing less. It was the same group that handled his last assignment. Through careful observation, he'd deduced who had hired them. All the data pointed back to a financier named Becker, an illusive and paranoid banker obsessed with security. This time, the assignment was considerably more difficult. It involved a Dr. James Oakner, a renowned surgeon, a highly visible individual. But the compensation was nearly astronomical, so Korvin put aside his reservations and accepted.

He glanced down at the vehicle's GPS display. He was over the summit and descending toward the lowlands and the city beyond.

The headlights came up fast from behind. Twin beams flared across the rearview mirror. Korvin reached to the seat beside him and took up the pistol. He placed it in the door pocket to his left, handle facing forward.

Red and blue lights blossomed above the twin beams. They painted the interior of the SUV with a pleasant wash. Korvin gradually slowed and pulled over to the shoulder. He calmly assessed the situation. There was no municipality for miles. Must be state or provincial police of some kind. A solitary officer a long way from backup. Not a problem. He reached in his coat pocket and extracted a packet of documents. He did a quick sort and produced a driver's license. He opened the glove box and located the registration.

He watched the patrolman's approach in his side-view mirror. He processed the data. Overweight. Nonathletic gait. He rolled down the window as the officer came up. He smiled.

"Good evening, Officer."

"Good evening. Could I see your driver's license and registration?"

The man was soft. Addicted to ritual and lethargic routine. Korvin could sense it.

"Of course." He handed the documents to the officer, who cast his flashlight beam on them.

While the cop read, Korvin rehearsed. If asked to exit the car, he would open the door and draw the gun in a single, fluid motion. The officer would not have time to separate the two actions. This failure would cost him his life.

The patrolman looked up from the registration. "So you're not the owner of this vehicle?"

"It belongs to my brother-in-law. I borrowed it to haul some furniture."

The officer handed back the documents. "The reason I stopped you is that your left taillight is out. You'll want to get that fixed as soon as possible."

"Absolutely. Thanks, Officer. I'll take care of that as soon as I get to town."

"Alright then. Good night."

"Good night, Officer. Thanks." He watched the man head back to his patrol car. This man who would eat bacon and pancakes at dawn in some little café. This man who would return home and squabble with his wife and repair the kitchen sink. This man who lived on by the slimmest of margins.

━━━━━━

He drove on through the night. Highway became freeway. The city sprang up around him, full of streetlights and mini-malls. He crossed a bridge that spanned a big river. He continued east. He parked the SUV in a quiet neighborhood, grabbed his pack and walked a few blocks to a transit mall. The dawn peaked over some distant mountains as he stepped aboard the commuter train back to the central city.

He got off the train downtown and walked to a waterfront park. Sleeping bags infested the grass like giant larvae, their occupants hidden within. Two men were already awake, thick and muscular. They slouched sullenly on a wooden bench as he approached. They stared at him with contempt. At this time of day, they owned this place. He was an invader. They challenged him with their eyes.

Vicious eyes, hard as glass. He stared back. They wilted. They knew.

He continued on up the waterfront until he could see Pearson. A little city unto itself, perched on wooded slopes above downtown. Steel and glass blazing in the early morning light.

When he reached a parklike boulevard that wound along the bottom of the slopes beneath Pearson, he walked its edge until he came upon a small turnoff. Perfect. Here he stepped into the woods. A hint of trail took him the first ten meters up the slope, then died.

He continued on until the forest swallowed him completely. Then he stopped. He removed his pack, stretched, and took account of the world about him. Lush, green, damp. Drainage from above cut the hillside into a series of gullies. Fir trees and alders formed a thick canopy. Their foliage shredded the sunlight and preserved the wetness. Moss, ivy and ferns carpeted the slopes in a dense tangle. Signs of biological struggle abounded. Moss crept up the tree trunks, sucking sustenance from their bark. In turn, ivy used the moss as a substrate in its skyward grope.

He put his backpack on. This would be his base of operations. He would live in primitive isolation, free of the toxic effect of civilization at large. He would maintain the purity he needed to survive and succeed in this most perilous of trades.

He started on up the hill. The hospital was somewhere off to the north, but right now, that didn't matter. He would deal with the doctor and the hospital later.

———

"He's late," declared Clyde, who was Jimmy Page.

"He's early," countered Tanya, who was John Bonham.

"I've got an idea," suggested Elliot, who was John Paul Jones. "Let's split the difference and say I was right on."

Ian, of the golden locks, said nothing. He was too busy being Robert Plant.

The dispute centered on the timing of a passage in "Ramble On," one of Led Zeppelin's signature tunes. If you were going to be a Led Zeppelin cover band, you'd better have "Ramble On" nailed.

Clyde resolved the matter by looking at his watch. "Later. The noise curfew's now in effect." He took off his Epiphone double-neck guitar, a knockoff of Page's Gibson SG model from the seventies. The band practiced once a week in his garage and produced a megaton of sound that pounded through the adjoining residences. Protracted negotiations and local noise ordinances had produced the curfew.

Elliot took off his Fender Jazz bass, a contemporary version of Jones's 1961 model, which now went for around twenty-five thousand dollars. Clyde came over as he put the instrument in its case.

"So you're now a medical cop instead of city cop? Is that the way it works?"

"Something like that," Elliot replied.

Clyde wrote code for a living, the kind that went into things like pacemakers. At fifty-three, he was the oldest. Ian came in youngest at twenty-two. Elliot and Tanya, who was gay, were in the middle. Led Zeppelin spanned all generations. In the end, they might just possibly sail on into assisted living. Dementia and "Dazed and Confused" might become the ultimate geriatric partnership.

"You get the same pay, the same benefits up at Pearson?" Clyde asked. He liked quantitative information, like the kind you wrote into computers. He approached Jimmy

Page's guitar licks the same way. Note for note, each with a specific duration and value. His musical reach was bounded by the works of Led Zeppelin. The same was true of all of them. Elliot had become a Zeppelin addict years before, when he worked as a DJ on a cruise ship, long before his army years. He'd gravitated to the bass because it was the easiest point of entry into their music, and he eventually mastered their book. But ask him to play anything else, and he was dead in the water. In the end, he was a cop, not an artist. The band was a hobby, but a humanizing one, and that's what counted.

"Yeah, the pay and benefits are about the same up there," he told Clyde. "Not much difference."

"So why did you switch?" Clyde asked. "Why bother?"

"It's kind of complicated," Elliot replied as he picked up his case. "And I've got to get going. See you next week."

He'd told the truth. It was complicated. Very complicated. More so than he even wanted to contemplate.

CHAPTER 5

Very odd. Dr. Oakner was risking chemical burns to his hands, which were nearly priceless. Not like him at all.

OR nurse Hillary Beecham watched him carefully. He hovered over the surgical scrub sink, his hands raised to chest level. A thick foam of green surgical soap covered his flesh up to the elbow. A foam laden with alcohol targeted at the microbes that ranged over the surface of his skin. A foam that would turn on the skin itself if left on too long.

The doctor seemed lost in thought. He stood motionless. He stared straight ahead. His body stood straight and trim. He was fifty-six, and still athletic.

Perhaps he's immersed in the details of the operation, Beecham thought. It was a relatively new procedure. Still, she didn't want him to injure himself. She respected James Oakner, even in his difficult moments. Too bad about his bitch of a wife.

"Dr. Oakner?"

The doctor gazed benignly at his image in the mirror. A slight smile. Clear blue eyes.

"Dr. Oakner?"

The doctor blinked. He turned to Hillary while ducking his hands under the stream of rinse water. The offending foam slunk off down the drain.

"Yes?"

Hillary did a fast shuffle. "Are we going to use the same setting on the imaging as last time?"

"I don't see why not. You ready?"

"I'm ready."

He smiled at her. A smile that exuded the nearly irrational confidence common to many good surgeons. "Then let's go."

Oakner strode through the double doors into the operating room. Small and neat. No hacking here, no cutting. No clamping, no bleeding. All gone, and replaced by a winking, blinking matrix of instrumentation and displays.

The patient lay on his back, head clamped tight. The anesthesiologist scanned the parade of vital signs on a digital display. Hillary and the surgical assistant wheeled the last instrument tray into place.

Oakner put his gloved fingers on the patient's forehead, as if he could sense the little red bomb deep in the man's brain. An arterial aneurysm, a place where the wall of an artery had failed and blown a bubble. If the bubble popped, the blood would spurt forth and the surrounding neural tissue would starve. Big chunks of brain function would wink out. Maybe forever. At cocktail parties, people would speak quietly of what the patient was like "before the stroke."

Oakner turned to the anesthesiologist. "How we doing?"

"We're ready," the woman told him.

"Good." He turned to the instrument technician. "How's the signal?"

"We're looking good."

"Okay, let's get to work."

The procedure commenced. The small incision in the upper thigh. The insertion of a tiny tube, the catheter. The worming of the catheter up the arterial system. The arrival at the aneurysm site. Oakner worked patiently yet decisively.

Here he paused. "Let's have a little more magnification."

He studied the real-time image on the display. He assessed the curvature of the artery, the neck of the balloon, the shape of its cavity. He planned the nuances of his attack. He was very good. Quite possibly the best.

He turned to Hillary. "Coil please."

Hillary opened a sterilized container and extracted a thin, flexible wire. She carefully unwound it and presented the insertion end to Oakner. He held it up to a magnifier and examined a coil attached to it. Platinum. The width of a human hair.

"Okay, here we go."

Oakner worked the wire through the catheter up to the aneurysm. A thin serpent slithering through the arterial branches. Almost a ghost on the display.

He stopped at the neck of the bubble, where it pierced the arterial wall. He deftly manipulated the device that controlled the wire's motion. He poked the coil on through into the bubble, where it conformed to the bubble wall and took on the appearance of a tangled thread.

"Okay, there we are. Give me one milliamp."

The technician responded. A surge of electrical current shot down the stainless steel delivery wire. It dissolved the connection between the wire and the coil.

"Alright, let's do it again," Oakner commanded. It might take up to six coils to form the critical mass inside the bubble. Then a blood clot would form there. The clot would seal off the bubble from the artery. The problem would be solved. The patient's brain would be fortified. The seat of his soul preserved.

A new coil wire was prepped and snaked up the artery. Oakner proceeded confidently, precisely. The team sensed his attitude, his skill. They responded appropriately.

The second coil reached the neck of the bubble. Once again, Oakner paused. He carefully examined the display. "Let me have a little more magnification."

The technician obeyed. Oakner leaned slightly closer to the screen and stared intensely. Clear blue eyes hard at work.

A minute passed. A long minute. Oakner continued to stare.

Another minute passed. The team continued its respectful silence. Genius at work.

Then Hillary began to worry. Oakner was a statue. Just like in the scrub room.

"Is there a problem, Doctor?"

No response. Just embarrassed silence. Hillary exchanged glances with the anesthesiologist. Nobody talked. Nobody moved. Nobody wanted to break his concentration, if that's what it was.

Then Oakner slowly crumbled. He sank to a sitting position on the floor. One hand still held the control device. His blue eyes seemed lost in fog.

Hillary had the presence of mind to stoop down beside him and grab the control device. "Doctor, what's wrong?"

"Don't know," he said, very softly.

Then he went silent.

"Any change?" Hillary asked the head nurse of the Neural Intensive Care Unit.

"Not really."

"What do you think?"

"Looks like a stroke to me, but we're waiting on Dr. Fanning and the CT scans." The head nurse looked down the corridor. "We've got him right next door to the guy he was operating on. Never seen anything like it. Have you?"

"Not even close." They had been very lucky. Another neurosurgeon had been prepping in an adjacent OR. He intervened. He saved their asses.

"He's got a visitor, but you can pop in if you want," the head nurse offered.

"Who's visiting?"

A wry smile from the head nurse. "Wanna guess?"

"Don't need to."

Hillary worked on her attitude during the trip down the corridor. She owed Dr. Oakner at least that much. She managed a smile when she entered the room. She even addressed Christie Oakner in a civilized tone.

"Hi, Christie. I'm so sorry."

Christie sat bedside. All thirty-six years of her. All thirty-six toned, trimmed, tanned years. Hair tinted blonde and exquisitely feathered. Hermès handbag. Prada boots. Burberry jacket. Seven jeans. The perfect outfit for a family medical emergency.

"Thanks, Hillary. I know Jim would appreciate it."

She turned back to her husband. He rested with his upper body elevated. Blue eyes winked out. Mouth shifted into neutral. Hands folded peacefully on his flat stomach.

"He came here so often," Hillary started, "I never thought..."

Someone stepped in from behind her. A tall man, fashionably dressed like Christie. He ignored Hillary and went around to take Christie's hand.

"Christie." His voice dripped empathy. "I got here as soon as I heard. Have they told you anything yet?"

A small and tragic smile from Christie. "Not yet."

"It seems so incredible. I can't quite believe it." The man paused. He absently adjusted his perfectly knotted tie. "Well, he couldn't be in better hands. Pearson is the best for this kind of thing."

"I know," Christie replied and looked up at Hillary. "Oh." She gestured toward the man. "Hillary, this is Mike Hoffner."

She offered no further explanation. The implication was clear: *Get out before you bore us.*

Hillary considered prolonging the conversation just to irritate her. She declined. The fallen doctor put it in perspective. Life was short. She had better things to do. "I've got to go. It's still my shift. Let me know if there's anything I can do."

Like take a blowtorch to your Hermès.

"Thanks, I'll do that," Christie said.

Hillary left. Hoffner waited. He straightened one of his cuff links. Onyx with gold inlay. He leaned over the bed to get a better look at the comatose Oakner.

"You think he can hear us?" Christie asked.

"Doubt it." Hoffner moved his index finger in front of Oakner's eyes. They did not track the motion. "Doesn't look good." He turned to Christie. "But I'm not a medical doctor. So we'll have to wait and see." In fact, he was a Ph.D. Once a research doctor. Now a research administrator. Follow the power and you find the money.

"Do you think this has anything to do with what happened to him before?"

Hoffner smiled with academic confidence. "Highly unlikely. Just luck of the draw. Don't worry. You're covered. We have a deal."

Christie didn't answer. She gazed at her very distant husband. Was he still in there? She couldn't tell. No one could.

CHAPTER 6

Korvin reached the edge of the woods at a point over-looking the gleaming cluster of buildings that made up the Pearson campus. With each assignment, he liked to take in a visual representation of the problem at hand, like a chess player scanning the board, looking for opportunities. The place was larger than he expected. Dozens of structures and winding roadways snaked up and down the hill. A massive concentration of knowledge and wealth, and for what? So that people with decadent lives could prolong the inevitable. They came here with their brown lungs, their clogged arteries, their wasted muscles, and sought repair of tissues ravaged by their own indulgent behavior. The campus physicians would perform the appropriate procedures, deliver the proper admonishments and collect the established fees. The patients would return home and immediately revert to their pathetic, self-destructive behaviors. Doctors like the target, Oakner, profited mightily from this endless cycle.

Korvin considered several avenues of approach to the

problem of taking Oakner out. The steep roads allowed the possibility of severed brake lines. Korvin, of course, would be the first one at the crash site to finish what he started. An overdose of prescription drugs was also within reason. Doctors were notorious for closet drug problems.

A string of beeps from his satellite phone interrupted his deliberations. A voice asked him to recite a ten-digit sequence of numbers to verify his identity. A heavy dose of signal processing disguised the identity of the caller and gave the voice a mechanical, robotic quality. Korvin suspected the caller was Becker himself, but knew better than to ask. Whoever it was, they got right to the point.

"There's been a new development. We've just received word that your subject had some kind of seizure and is now in a comatose state."

"Where is he?" Korvin asked.

"He's in an intensive care unit on the campus."

Korvin immediately sorted through the problems of trying to exterminate someone in a place as heavily populated as an intensive care facility. It would be extremely difficult. "What do you want to do?" he asked the caller.

"We want you to refrain from any action until we get a better assessment of the situation. So just stay put for now."

"You realize that my contract will have to be honored under any circumstances."

"Yes, we do. We're going to wait for a prognosis, and then make a decision. There are certain complications, but they need not concern you. For now, just stand by."

"Very well. It's your money."

"Yes, it is. Goodbye now."

The signal terminated; Korvin slid the phone back into his pocket. It was crucial that the contract be honored. It represented an income stream large enough to let him permanently withdraw from the profession. He had already purchased property in a remote corner of eastern Europe where he could reside in a very elegant simplicity of the kind that required scrupulous forethought, careful design and costly construction. This job would provide the financial platform to bring it to fruition and carry it forward indefinitely.

He turned his back on the campus and walked into the woods, a place of clarity and purity.

PART 2

Sirius Rising

CHAPTER 7

The bastards got my opera. It took me forever to get it all on the iPod. Shit!"

The doctor stormed around in a tight little circle behind his new Lexus. Elliot peered in through the broken driver's-side window. Little gems of safety glass crunched beneath his shoes. More gems littered the driver's seat crafted of supple leather.

"I thought this facility was secure," the doctor raged. "I guess not, huh?"

"Yeah, I guess not," Elliot replied. The doctor occupied the upper reaches of the medical aristocracy here at Pearson. Chief pathologist at the hospital. He had certain expectations and they clearly were not being met. The physicians' parking garage was not vaccinated against petty crime.

Elliot flipped open his notebook. He already had the doctor's name, the car license and the insurance company. "Is there anything else missing?"

"Aren't you going to fingerprint?" the doctor demanded.

"We normally don't do that with these kinds of incidents," Elliot informed him.

"And why not?"

"Because it represents a considerable cost and hardly ever results in an arrest or conviction." Stock reply. Elliot had it down cold. "Is there anything else missing?" he repeated.

"All my *opera*," the doctor fumed. "Isn't that enough?"

"Yeah, I guess so." Elliot used his cell phone camera to record a couple of pictures of the damage.

"So, now what?"

"I'll write up a report and email it to you." Elliot handed his card to the doctor. "You can forward it to your insurance company."

The doctor scrutinized Elliot's card. "A detective? I didn't know we had anything like that up here."

"Only one," Elliot said wearily. "And that would be me." He put away his cell phone and his notebook.

"And what about my car?" the doctor asked.

"What about it?"

"What happens to it?"

Elliot fabricated a reply. Silently. He manufactured a special victims unit dedicated exclusively to ranking physicians and administrators. The unit would swoop down on the scene. The unit would ooze compassion. They would take the doctor's car away and repair it. They would drive him home in a limo. They would restore all his opera on a brand-new iPod.

"You drive it to an auto glass place," Elliot answered. "And they fix it for you."

The doctor didn't respond. He climbed into his violated vehicle and backed out. He took off with an angry little squeak of rubber.

"Thanks. Same to you," Elliot said to the retreating vehicle.

He looked at the empty parking space and glittering crumbs of safety glass as he took out his cell phone and called maintenance. An admin answered. The same admin as always. He made arrangements to clean it up. The same arrangements as always.

He walked the scene one last time. He always did this. Sometimes you caught something you missed.

This was one of those times.

A concrete curb sat at the far end of the parking space, about two feet from the wall. Elliot peeked over to the back side of the curb. Something shone at him. He leaned over and picked it up.

A flash drive. Also known as a travel drive, or USB drive. A little stick with a plug on one end for the computer connection. Several gigabytes' worth.

Elliot pulled the little plastic cap off the end of the drive and examined the connection. It seemed intact. The drive probably belonged to the doctor. He was so busy spouting about opera that he never took a real inventory of what might have been in the car. The thief probably tossed it after deciding it was worthless. He put the drive in the same pocket as his cell phone and left.

━━━━━━━━

Elliot wanted to take a nap. Report writing made him that way. The pathologist's operatic tragedy was no exception. He gazed out the window, looking for a distraction. The corner of the library loomed to the left, with the roof of the fitness center dead ahead, followed by the children's hospital. Even after a couple of years, he was still adjusting to the scale of the place. Two hundred thousand people came here for treatment every year, everything from splinter removal to brain surgery. A thousand more were here in medical school, with another twenty thousand in continuing education. Within the dozens of buildings up and down the slope, you could become a doctor, a dentist, a scientist or a nurse. You could be born, cured or die here. All the while, hundreds of labs probed the innermost secrets of various biological phenomena. A complex web of doctors, researchers and administrators formed the core of the place, with numerous political factions and pecking orders. The Pearson Institute of Health Sciences held sway over an economic engine that pumped several billion dollars into the local economy every year.

Behind him, Bobby Seifert returned with a load of booty from the vending machine. Cookies, a chocolate bar, Cheetos. Fuel for an afternoon of IT stuff in front of his flat-panel. Bobby was twenty-four and chubby. By thirty, he would be flat-out fat. A freckled balloon. He'd joined the Navy at eighteen. They'd given him an aptitude test and he'd blown them away. Two months later, he was working for the National Security Agency. He put in his time, then quit. He didn't like spying. He also didn't like corporate life. Pearson was a good alternative.

Bobby's return sent Elliot back into motion. He finished the email to the chief pathologist and attached the photo of the break-in. He hit Return and fired it out over the network.

Then he remembered the flash drive.

"Shit!"

"So what's with you?" Bobby asked.

"I just sent off an email on this Lexus thing, and I forgot something."

"That's because you're old."

"I'm thirty-six."

Bobby shrugged and munched an Oreo. "Like I said—old."

"Thanks, Bobby."

"Don't mention it."

Elliot smiled. He liked Bobby. He could have countered with something about Bobby's horrible diet, but he never did. Besides, Elliot himself was secretly addicted to peanut butter and jelly sandwiches. It took all his willpower to limit them to just Saturdays.

He took out the flash drive and considered his options. Easiest way out was to just phone the chief pathologist and ask him about it. He checked the directory and dialed on his desk phone. The admin on the other end gave him the standard runaround.

"Dr. Malvo's in a meeting right now. Would you like to leave a voice mail?"

Elliot aimed and fired. "This is Detective Elliot phoning about his Lexus. I need to speak with him absolutely as soon as possible."

"Oh." A pause. "Could you hold for just a minute, please?"

Malvo was on in thirty seconds. "Yes, Detective."

"Doctor, I did a final survey of the crime scene and found a flash drive where you were parked."

"A computer flash drive?"

"That's right. I wondered if it belonged to you."

"No. It does not."

"You're sure?"

"Yes, I'm sure. Is there anything else?"

"I don't think so. Thanks for your help."

"Not a problem. Goodbye."

The doctor hung up. Elliot leaned back. He held up

the flash drive. Nothing on it but a brand name. Only one way left to track down the owner.

Elliot plugged the flash drive into the USB port on the side of his computer and a drive icon popped up on his display. It was labeled H:BACKUP. He clicked it open. The drive directory held a single file. Some kind of graphic file.

Elliot clicked it open. It consumed the entire display. A medical image of some kind. A cross section of what appeared to be a brain. A group of data fields lined the bottom of the image. Maybe they would point to the owner of the image. They didn't. But they did point to the owner of the brain. It was spelled out in the PATIENT: field.

"Jesus!" Elliot exclaimed.

"What is it?" Bobby asked in mid-sip on his Mountain Dew.

"Check this out."

"It's a CT scan. So what?"

Elliot pointed to the bottom of the screen. "Check out the patient."

"Holy shit!" Bobby exclaimed. "It's Oakner!"

The Oakner incident was already legend around Pearson. Brilliant neurosurgeon collapses in the midst of a complex procedure. Felled by a stroke. The patient is saved, but James Oakner seems lost. Still comatose after almost a week. A tragic tumble down the Mount Olympus of medicine.

"Where'd you get this?" Bobby asked.

"I found it on a flash drive next to where the Lexus was parked."

"And where was that?"

"You really want to know?"

"Yes, I really want to know."

Elliot smiled and reached for his notebook. Bobby was

an obsessive collector of obscure information. It made him very good at what he did. "Parking Garage B, third level, space number 59. Feel better now?"

"A little bit. Was it part of the break-in with the Lexus?"

"No. I already checked that."

Bobby frowned in concentration. "Garage B, third level. That bugs me. Really bad."

He went back to his machine and took a swig of soda. Windows flashed on his display. "Well all right!" he announced. "Here it is."

"Here's what?"

"A theft report, two months ago. Stolen laptop. Garage B, third level, space 58—one space away from your Lexus guy."

Elliot came over and scrutinized the report on Bobby's display. "How come I don't remember this?"

Bobby leaned back. "You were gone for some kind of training. Roberts took the call and wrote the report."

"Does it say anything about a flash drive?"

"Nope. Just the laptop. Belonged to a Sam Lepert, the head IT guy over in radiology. Wow. Big gig."

"How's that?"

"Huge amounts of data. CT scans. MRI scans. X-rays. Zillions of patients. Very complex, very difficult to manage. No room for mistakes."

Elliot wrote down the name. "I best give Mr. Lepert a call and see if we've recovered some of his property."

"Sounds right to me. I'm going over to the cafeteria. You want anything?"

"Don't think so. Print that out for me, will you?"

Bobby set the printer in motion and left. Elliot turned back to his display. He opened the campus directory. Time to give Mr. Lepert a call. He dialed the number. A message told him that it was no longer in service. Elliot sighed. Pearson was forever churning. People moved. Phone numbers changed. The directory always lagged. He phoned the general number for the radiology department. "Hi, I'm trying to reach a Sam Lepert over there. Can you connect me?"

"I'm sorry, sir. He's no longer with the department."

"Do you know where he went? Is he still at Pearson?"

"I'm sorry, we're not supposed to give out forwarding information."

"This is Detective Elliot in Public Safety. This is a police matter."

"Oh."

"Do you know Mr. Lepert personally?"

"Not very well. He just left us."

"You know were I might contact him?"

"That's going to be kind of difficult."

"Why's that?"

"He took off on a big trip around the world. He's going to be gone for over a year."

"Sounds like fun. Thanks for your help."

Elliot hung up and leaned back. Dark clouds gathered outside, bringing the possibility of rain. He shouldn't have ridden his bike to work today. He had an old Cannondale, a mountain bike that had seen better times, which made it pretty much theft-proof. Still, it gave him a good workout pedaling up the hill in decent weather.

He leaned forward and copied the data from the flash drive onto his machine. He looked at the image of Dr. James Oakner's brain on his screen.

And the longer he looked, the more he wondered. What

exactly happened inside this man's head that brought him so low?

———

He slept the sleep of a saint, which he wasn't.

Christie Oakner sat bedside and studied the comatose face of her stricken husband. Eyes gently closed, as if angels had pulled down the lids. Lips slightly parted, murmuring as if in prayer. But she couldn't sustain the illusion. Instead, she sensed the great profusion of dead neurons, the absence of inner life.

She recalled this same face in the repose of sleep, but not here, not now.

It was in Mexico, and it seemed long ago, but in fact, it wasn't. The ocean light had slashed through a break in the curtains of their bedroom, crept across the tiled floor and played over his sleeping face. She'd been angry. She had rolled out of bed in disgust. He'd done it again. He'd been out drinking into the wee hours with Stennis down at the marina. It was turning into a nightly affair.

She knew the place. Thatched roof. Dark wooden floors. And the women who catered to the men who owned the big boats right across the promenade. They wore hip-hugging pants across perfect bottoms. Their breasts strained to escape their halter tops. They laughed and tittered and feigned fascination while they toyed with their drinks. They always deferred to the men. The men who tugged at their baseball caps to conceal heads going bald and gray. The men who strutted and crowed to their adoring audience. The men who pontificated endlessly about money, business and boats.

Her husband was regressing. The marriage was slipping into retrograde. She dressed and went down to the garage and backed out the Lexus. She turned toward town and looked down on the ocean, the marina, the beach, the hotels, the luxury liners.

She felt she was falling. Falling from a great height. Completely unaware that by the time the sun rose once more, she would hit bottom.

CHAPTER 8

The dog peered out through the wire grid that fronted the portable cage and inhaled the odors of transport. Gas, oil, rubber, plastic upholstery, stale coffee. It heard the hollow boom of a big city through the metal walls of the van. It could see through the windshield to a loading platform. A big security light shone in from somewhere outside and illuminated each scuff on the dashboard. It revealed the light cake of dust on the steering wheel hub and highlighted a small crack in the lower windshield. It played over some crumpled cellophane on the console, outlined the angle of the wiper blades, and highlighted the dirty arc of their sweep across the glass. The dog absorbed it all.

The dog flopped down. It rested its chin on the padding at the bottom of the cage. The trip had drained it. Twelve hours on the plane in a pressurized section of the baggage compartment. Vague memories of the lab, the compound, the exercises, the damp heat, the little apartment. Strong memories of Zainah's love. Then off the plane and into warm, dry air, drier than any the dog had ever known. Air heavy with jet fuel and grease and engine exhaust. Then a ride into a giant baggage complex to a place with other animals in other cages. A cat stared at it from the cage opposite. The dog was fascinated. The dog had never seen a cat.

Then into the night and onto another plane. When the ride ended, the belly of the jet sprang open on the wet tarmac. Cool air flooded in. Damp air. A combination the dog had never known. Then yet another van ride. Two people sat up front, a man and a woman. The dog smelled the difference. They spoke to each other in a babble the dog did not understand.

Now the dog could sniff their ghosts lingering in the seats. Bodies gone, smell still present. The dog cast its eyes down into the shadows of the cage. It found only sorrow in the darkness.

———

A chemical orgy raged inside Fritter's head. Neurotransmitters gone wild. Synapses awash with dopamine. All courtesy of fifty milligrams of methamphetamine, orally consumed.

Fritter couldn't contain himself. He had to share with Jojo. A verbal explosion ripped through the night and bounced off the back wall of the Biomedical Research Building. A buddy of questionable origin had told him about this place, a buddy who once worked as a custodian here. It seemed that all kinds of medical supplies wound up at this loading dock. Jojo promptly put a tweaker-fueled twist on this information, and the term "supplies" became synonymous with "drugs."

"This is right. This is so right, Jojo. This plan is so perfect. You find doctors, you find dope. You find dope, you get money. You spend money, you get high. It's a perfect circle, Jojo, and we're on for the ride. We can do this thing. We got the will, we've got the brains, we've got the tools, and we've got the balls. We've got it all. That's right, we've got it all. We're gonna make it happen. You and me, Jojo. We're gonna kick ass here. Know what I mean?"

Jojo nodded. Jojo couldn't talk. He was too high, too overjoyed. He simply fondled his bolt cutters and looked at the van parked behind the gate by the loading dock.

Fritter went biblical. "We will come out of the shadows and into the light. But the light will not shine upon us. We will labor under the shield of the shadow. It can be no other way."

"No fuckin' way," Jojo whispered. His eyes shone and his teeth rotted. Meth mouth. No need for dental hygiene. He was beyond that.

Fritter wallowed in the perfection of his plan. It would liberate him from his old lady and her rug rat of questionable origin. It would free him from a studio apartment stinking of dirty diapers. It would pull him out from under her welfare check.

"Okay, dude, this is it. Let's go."

They emerged from the shadow of shrub and advanced on the gate. They ignored the light, the security cameras: not part of the plan. Their bolt cutters bit a great hole into the chain-link gate's surface and they climbed through. They discovered a button that opened the gate from the inside. Their retreat was guaranteed. Brilliant.

They advanced on the van and tried the rear doors. Locked. They tried the front doors. Locked. They improvised. They devised a sophisticated method of entry. They smashed the driver's-side window and opened the handle.

Fritter scrambled in. Jojo peered over his shoulder. Fritter spotted the cage with the dog.

"Fuckin' brilliant! They put a dog in to guard the dope." Fritter reached for the cage handle. "Well, I'll tell you what, Fido, you're off duty as of right now." He flung the cage door open. The dog shrank backward.

Fritter beckoned the animal out. "C'mon, boy. Get the fuck outta there." The dog blinked, then obeyed. It cautiously extracted itself. It stretched its legs.

Fritter backed off to give the dog exit room. He feared a violent encounter with a hostile animal in a confined space. He silently applauded his caution. "Come on, now."

The dog seemed to get it. It scrambled up over the console between the seats. Fritter held the door open. "Here you go."

The dog hopped out. And Fritter hopped in. He wormed his way between the seats and stuck his head into the cage.

Jojo waited outside. He watched the dog. It had retreated a few feet and now sat on its haunches and stared back at him. A black Labrador retriever.

Fritter emerged from the van. "Somethin's wrong, man. Somethin's bad wrong. I'm not seein' what we came here for. This is really fucked. Someone really fucked us, man. *Shit!*"

Fritter's rage imploded. He grabbed his bolt cutters off the van's seat and hurled them at the dog. The dog came off its haunches and ducked the missile. The tool clattered and clanged over the pavement. Fritter punched the side of the van. He fractured his little finger. The dog took off and ran through the open gate.

Jojo had had enough. He dropped his bolt cutters and

sprinted for the gate. "The dog's got it right, man," he yelled over his shoulder. "We gotta get outta here."

"Wait!" Fritter commanded. But then he couldn't think of why, and took off after Jojo.

———————

The dog watched from concealment in the shrubs nearby. It saw the two men run out the gate and disappear between two buildings. Their frantic scent caught the breeze and quickly reached its nose. Then the people who operated the van came out of the building. They discovered the damage. They realized that the dog was gone. They panicked. The man ran back inside. The woman trotted over to the open gate and squinted out into the darkness. Then she ran toward the building. Two more men came out and peered into the van.

The dog stayed put. Soon, two vehicles arrived with red and blue flashing lights. Several men and one woman emerged. They talked with the people around the van. Someone pointed toward the open gate. Someone else came over and inspected the hole in it.

The dog stayed put. Eventually, the crowd around the van thinned. The patrol vehicles drove off. The rifled van drove off, too. The last people went back inside the building.

The dog emerged from concealment. Hunger gnawed at its belly. A hint of food crossed its nostrils. It quickly determined the bearing of the smell and headed in that direction.

A service road led the dog behind another large building. A big Dumpster sat on a loading dock. Plastic trash bags spilled over its top. Bags with garbage from the little deli within. The remnants of lunches consumed by doctors, receptionists, scientists, technicians, custodians.

The dog reached the foot of the Dumpster and looked up. The bags spilled over the lip and drooped down, each secured by a plastic tie of bright yellow. Too high. Beyond the reach of the dog's jaws. The dog backed off and carefully surveyed the situation. One of the yellow ties dangled down, forming a loop. The dog jumped up the Dumpster wall under the loop. Its front paws rested on the cold metal. It stretched its hind legs to the utmost. It craned its neck to the maximum. The loop remained a few inches beyond its jaws. It carefully examined the loop. It moved sideways along the surface until its right paw was over the loop. It suddenly twisted its entire body. The paw caught the loop. The dog came down. The bag came down.

The dog attacked the bulky bag and sank its paws into the yielding plastic. Its teeth ripped a big hole in its polyethylene wall. It promptly tore into the treasures within. Its belly quickly filled.

The approaching vehicle caught the dog by surprise. It jerked its head up from the bag and twisted toward the oncoming sound. Every lifter in the engine, every application of the brakes poured into its ears. It could see the sweep of the headlights gliding toward the loading dock. It spun and sought concealment on the far side of the Dumpster and hunkered down in shadow.

The dog heard a door latch click and the sole of a shoe hit the pavement. A human figure cast an elongated shadow across the dock. The shadow moved in the dog's direction. The dog looked to a little set of steps on the far side of the loading dock. It bolted.

"Hey, boy! It's okay."

The dog stopped to assess the situation. The human

figure was half lost in headlight glare from the vehicle. Now the human came slowly forward.

"It's okay, boy. Easy now."

The dog ran. Powerful legs thrust its mass through the night. It accelerated past the vehicle. It spotted grass, trees and shadow beyond the pavement.

Freedom.

CHAPTER 9

E lliot faced a bureaucratic phalanx. Three layers deep. Research Director, Director of Veterinary Services, Operations Supervisor. Their summons had come on his cell phone on the way to work. They had lost a dog. A highly valued dog. A major embarrassment. Hence the triple defense.

They all sat in a conference room on the top floor of the Science Building and watched the security video. Camera One showed two scruffy-looking men cut a big hole in the chain-link gate.

"How come it didn't set off an alarm?" Elliot asked.

"We're working on that." The Operations Supervisor seemed confident. Hopeful. They were taking action. They were looking into things.

Elliot watched one of the men in the video stab some buttons on a panel inside the gate. It swung open. Not good. The reception compound behind the Biomedical Research Building was supposed to be highly secure. It was a sensitive place. Animals of all types were transported to this location for distribution to the labs within. Not everyone found this morally acceptable. Organizations like PETA might target the place. Radical action might ensue.

"We might be able to get some prints off those buttons by the gate," Elliot commented. "These guys look like they're probably on file somewhere."

"That's going to be a little difficult at this point," the Director of Veterinary Services said. He gave his plastic coffee cup a nervous squeeze. His department was supposed to ensure that lab animals received humane treatment. Obviously, this didn't include letting them escape and be left to fend for themselves.

"How come?"

"Apparently our people went out to manually close the gate after the incident," the Operations Supervisor said.

"And they pushed the buttons?"

"Apparently they did."

Camera Two showed the same pair smashing the window of a transport van and the first one climbing in.

"So the transport crew left the vehicle unattended with the dog inside?"

"Yes, they came inside to get some coffee and start the paperwork," the Director of Veterinary Services responded. "They did follow protocol. They locked the van before they entered the building."

"That's very good," Elliot said. The bureaucratic trio shifted in their seats. His sarcasm was not appreciated.

Camera Two focused on one of the men backing out of the van. Then a dog hopped out. It hesitated, surveyed the scene, and walked out of camera range.

"It looks like a Labrador retriever," Elliot observed.

"That's correct. Female. About seventy-five pounds."

On camera, one of the sleazeballs backed out of the van and went into a rage. He pounded its side and threw a pair of bolt cutters into the dark.

"Didn't get what he wanted," Elliot said. "No dope, no money."

Camera Two showed the dog running through the open gate.

"It didn't look like it was wearing an ID tag or a collar."

The Director of Veterinary Services and the Operations Supervisor squirmed. They looked toward the Research Director for help. His name was Hoffner and he wore a very expensive suit. He tugged a bit on one of his cuff links before responding.

"It seems that there was some kind of mix-up during transport. This animal came from a facility overseas. They probably removed the ID for processing somewhere along the line and then just forgot to put it back on."

"What about the paperwork at this end? Do you have a photo?"

"Yes, we do have a have a photo," the Operations Supervisor said. "We'll email it to you right away."

"Is there anything else about the dog that might be helpful in locating it?" Elliot asked.

"I'm afraid not," Hoffner said. "It's just an ordinary Labrador retriever. Nothing special."

"Then why was it brought here from out of the country?" Elliot asked.

Hoffner didn't miss a beat. He was very good. "Lieutenant, if we had a couple of weeks, I'd explain the science behind what we're doing here, and why certain animals are part of certain processes. But that wouldn't get the dog back. And that's what we want here. We want that dog back. The two individuals don't count. All your efforts need to be focused on finding the animal."

"Well, I'll most certainly take that under consideration," Elliot said as he rose to leave. Hoffner scowled. He didn't like that. Elliot hadn't thought he would.

"You can contact me directly on this," Hoffner said. "Let me know what's happening."

"Right. See you all later."

Elliot chose to ignore Hoffner's blatant power play. For now, anyway. He already had some idea of Dr. Michael Hoffner's role in the hierarchy here at Pearson. Any time you took a job in a very large institution, you very quickly became familiar with two sources of power: your immediate boss, and those who occupied the highest levels of authority. Everyone in between fell into a kind of organizational haze. Hoffner was definitely perched at the highest level. Pearson took in about $1.5 billion per year from all sources combined, and nearly a half billion of this came from research grants in one form or another. All of it flowed through Hoffner before it got to the labs. The relationship between power and money was seldom so clearly defined.

So why would a guy in a playpen with $500 million be so intimately concerned about such a relatively minor matter? Hoffner had eight department heads reporting to him, including the Director of Veterinary Services, who should have been directly responsible in this case. Why had he blatantly bypassed his department head and told Elliot to report directly to him?

Elliot dismissed these questions as he left the building. Politics was one thing he would never understand. He suspected that no one else did either.

Elliot watched as Dr. Irene Walters plugged the flash drive into her big desktop machine with its high-res graphics. He was distracted by thoughts of the missing dog. Why did the damn dog have to pop up right now, of all times? For the first time, he had something interesting to look into with the Oakner CT scan, something to pull him away from the parade of laptops. And now the dog was going to eat up all his spare time. He'd have to check all the pounds, all the animal shelters. He'd have to wade through every homeless animal in the city. He couldn't even find Simon, his own cat, who'd failed to come home to his apartment one morning. He agonized over this because he'd let Simon out every night to romp with all the nocturnal beasties. It was somewhat irresponsible, but it was also Simon's most express desire. The big cat always stood by the door and yowled if he didn't get his way.

The image came up on Dr. Walters's display. Elliot liked her. He'd met her when he was looking into a drug theft by a rogue nurse. She looked both beautiful and drained by some distant tragedy. She was also a radiologist. She might be helpful with the Oakner image.

"Interesting," she said as she looked at the cross section of brain. After just a couple weeks on the job, Elliot had learned that doctors always said that when they didn't know what was going on.

"Oakner had a stroke, right?" Elliot asked.

"That's correct," Dr. Walters said. "But I don't think that's what we're looking at here."

"Then what *are* we looking at?"

"I'm not really sure." She pointed to the outer regions

of the image. "You have a lot of low density in the white matter in the frontal lobe."

"Which means what?"

"The frontal lobe is the outer layer of your brain toward the front of your skull. It's where the high-level stuff goes on. Like reasoning and personality." She pointed toward a fringe of pale gray on the outer edge. "This is the gray matter. It appears light here because the shading in the image is reversed." Her finger moved inward to a darker area. "This is the white matter. It holds the wiring that hooks the gray matter to the rest of the brain."

"And something's wrong with the white matter?"

"Definitely. It's probably from demyelination."

"Sounds serious."

"It is. All the wires in the white matter are normally insulated with multiple layers of this stuff called myelin. With demyelination, the insulation gets stripped off. All the neural signaling goes completely haywire."

"Can it be fixed?"

"I'm afraid not. Especially when it's very widespread, like here. Therapy's not going to help."

She opened a new window and traveled through a set of folders. "I'm going to bring up Dr. Oakner's image directory so we can see what his case looks like." She typed in a password. A new CT image appeared. It held a series of CT scans in thumbnail form.

"Each of these is a cross section of the brain from top to bottom." She clicked on one.

"Okay, this is more like it." She pointed to the upper portion of the image. "See the big dark cloud over the frontal lobe? This is the kind of thing you see with an ischemic stroke. Large areas deprived of blood supply. Much of the brain tissue is essentially dead." She closed the image and sighed. "Too bad. I never really liked Jim very much, but I wouldn't wish this on anybody. With this much damage, he's lucky he's even alive."

"You didn't like him? Can you tell me why?"

She shrugged. "Arrogant asshole surgeon with a hot babe trophy wife. What's not to like?"

Elliot couldn't help but smile. "So the image on the flash drive is a fraud of some kind, huh?"

"If it is, it's a very interesting one. Mind if I make a copy?"

"Not at all."

Dr. Walters copied the image off the flash drive onto her machine. "I'll do a little more with this when I get some time, okay?"

Back to the dog. The pesky dog. Elliot drove out of the campus proper and into the apartment zone. A place where students studied and copulated, and occasionally drank, and little else. The apartments butted up against the big forest that went on for hundreds of acres to the south. It seemed odd that this large tract of virgin woodland would exist right next to a mammoth medical campus in the middle of a major metropolitan area. But money, topography and politics all contributed to its survival. The land had originally been in private hands, but was transferred to public ownership as part of a complex tax strategy on the part of the original owners. Then local government discovered that the slope and drainage made it nearly impossible to convert into a conventional park site. The cost would have been astronomical. Instead, they installed a primitive trail system and designated it as an "urban forest."

Elliot parked the SUV at the end of the street and

climbed out. Instinctively, he patted his hip and checked for a sidearm. His years as a soldier and cop had grilled this routine into him. But cops at Pearson didn't wear holstered weapons. Campus crime didn't equate with street crime, and Elliot was still adjusting to this fact. He locked the vehicle and strode up to the trailhead. He smelled the dampness, all lush and green. A small breeze spilled down the slope. A fern leaf brushed the back of his hand.

This would be where the dog most likely went.

He hiked up the trail. Spring mud stuck to his shoes. After fifteen minutes he came to a fallen tree, an old fir. The forest was already eating it. Ivy sprouted from rotting bark. He used the fir as a landmark and aligned it with another tree that was still standing. They formed a line of sight. He left the trail and followed it.

He stepped gingerly over the green and yellow tangle beneath his feet. His route had to remain invisible. Such was the agreement with the King.

He first heard of the King during his second week on the job. Part of his charter was to manage the "vagrant problem." A large population of homeless people sought refuge here in the woods. Mostly males with drug and alcohol issues. The population swelled during decent weather, from mid-spring until early fall. And as it swelled, it eyed the campus. Bottom-feeders swarming over the daily discard. They demonstrated both cleverness and discretion in their approach, and seldom strayed onto the main sidewalks or entered the buildings. Instead, they followed obscure paths, or waited for cover of darkness. Then they preyed upon the multitude of Dumpsters. Food scraps. Serviceable clothing. Old lab hardware. Medical flotsam and jetsam. They took their booty back out into the woods, to camps carefully concealed in the forest. They ate. They fashioned primitive tools. They huddled under blankets. They drank and got loaded. They sometimes howled in the dark.

But a few failed to observe the established protocol. They wandered the sidewalks. They plunked down in lobbies. They passed out in parking garages. They yelled inappropriate things. They comprised "the vagrant problem."

Campus administration took a practical view of the problem. It couldn't be eliminated but it could be contained. Discussions were held. Policy memos were crafted. The memos instructed the Department of Public Safety to focus on chronic offenders, to seek them out, turn them over to the city. For prosecution and incarceration. In turn, the Chief wrote this mission into Lieutenant Detective Elliot Elliot's job description.

The Vagrant War. That's what the staff called it. And Elliot soon discovered a very unlikely ally in this conflict. When he questioned detained vagrants, some made mention of an extraordinary individual who lived among them. A man who resolved personal beefs, who dictated rules of behavior, who held nearly universal respect. It reminded Elliot of a person he had read about in an account of the Great Depression, a time of many vagrants: hobos, in the vernacular of the era. It seemed that one particular hobo had declared himself the Hobo King and actively publicized his ascendancy. This original king of the hobos might be gone, but the concept apparently lived on.

Elliot set about building a diplomatic bridge to the King. He let it be known that the King would have amnesty, that he would have immunity. The word seeped out through the forest. One vagrant at a time. After a while, word came back. A meeting was arranged. Both parties saw mutual advantage. Both knew the crazy element threatened the balance of things.

Now, Elliot climbed up over a small rise crowned by an ancient stump. Pallid mushrooms clung to its sides. He was only ten yards from the King's camp. He knew that from this old landmark. Still, the camp was almost invisible. He admired the King's skill in this matter.

Elliot continued forward. He knew that the King was already aware of his presence. Such a man would seldom be surprised.

The camp revealed itself. The King sat in an old lawn chair. Pink plastic and aluminum tubing. He was a big man and wore his age well. Maybe fifty, maybe much older. Broad of face and clean shaven, with graying hair pulled into a ponytail and green eyes brimming with amusement. He wore cargo pants, construction boots, and a fleece pullover. His huge hands held a paperback. He closed it as Elliot approached.

"Lieutenant Detective Elliot. Always a pleasure." The King gestured to a second lawn chair.

"Good to see you, Mr. King," Elliot said as he seated himself. He had no idea what the King's real name was. Nor would the King likely reveal it. Portions of the man's past were most certainly a matter of court record. Elliot simply called him Mr. King.

Elliot pointed to the closed paperback. "What are you reading these days?"

"Trash. I alternate. Substance followed by trash. I seek a balance."

"I guess we all seek a balance, don't we?"

The King shrugged. "Some more than others. Some not at all." He tossed the paperback into a box beside his chair. "You've come here all the way from the heart of the empire, and I doubt you did that to sample my literary leanings."

"And you would be correct. I'm here about a dog."

"A dog?"

"A female black Lab. About seventy-five pounds. Escaped from the lab during a botched robbery attempt."

The King grinned. "Escaped from the lab? Smart dog."

"It hasn't turned up anyplace on campus, so I thought I'd check up here with you."

The King turned thoughtful. "We do have a number of residents who have dogs, but I haven't seen any new ones lately."

"This just happened. If I were to guess, I'd say the dog is up here somewhere on its own, looking for its next meal. Sooner or later, it's going to want to cut a deal with one of your residents to get some food."

"And then what?"

"And then they're going to bring it by and show it off."

The King considered this possibility, and nodded. "It just might work that way."

Elliot rose from his chair. "If it does, I'd be very grateful to hear about it."

The King stood to show Elliot out of the camp. "And just maybe you will. Careful on your way out. I just vacuumed."

Elliot smiled. You couldn't help but like the guy. Great people skills. Probably a con man of some sort in his earlier years. "I'll be in touch."

The dog crouched in the brush overhead. She could not see the men below. But she could smell them. Two distinct odor signatures. One bearing the fragrances of soap and deodorant. The other full of dried sweat and dirty hair. And she could hear them. One deep and resonant. The other tending more toward the mid-range.

She identified the sweaty smell with the low voice, and the fragrant smell with the moderate voice, and was correct in this. How she did it was beyond human understanding, possibly forever.

None of which quelled the screaming in her belly for food.

CHAPTER 10

The neurologist spoke hopefully. He was a pleasant fellow with a sunny outlook, an old friend of her devastated husband. Christie Oakner paid polite attention to the bedside display of the CT scan as he talked the technical talk. Better to view the image than the vacant ruins of Dr. James Oakner.

"You can see here that it's clearly ischemic in nature. There was a blockage of blood supply."

Christie nodded. Had she really loved him? Or had she just talked herself into it?

"The blockage wasn't in the brain. We'd see that if it was."

Christie nodded. She already knew he wasn't coming back. She didn't need a complex medical explanation to tell her why.

"If you look at the pattern of the damage, you can see how it tracks along the anterior cerebral arteries."

Christie nodded. Should she be dressing like a widow? Jim wasn't dead, but he might as well be. Most people up here had already dismissed her as an opportunistic bitch, so in the end, it really didn't matter what she wore.

"If you look at the frontal lobes, you can see a loss of distinction between the gray and white matter. That's where the problem is."

Christie nodded. The Problem. What a nice way of putting it.

"We've done a lot of testing to track down the source of the occlusion, but nothing's been conclusive. That's not unusual. Sometimes it's never located."

Christie looked over at the neurologist. "He was in excellent health. He had a physical just a little while back."

The neurologist shrugged. "Sometimes it happens that way. In the end, nobody can really guarantee you anything."

Christie turned to her husband. "Obviously."

The doctor sensed sarcasm, which could lead to trouble. He turned off the display. "I wish I could give you some kind of positive prognosis, but I can't. It's highly unlikely he'll ever recover. Do you have any questions?"

"Yeah. What in the hell do I do now?"

"You have all kinds of options. There's counseling, there's support groups. My nurse can give you all the information." Oakner was toast. End of story.

Christie continued staring down at her husband. "Great."

"Call me anytime."

"Sure."

The doctor left. Christie put her palm on the back of her husband's hand. It felt cool. Very dry. Like night in the desert.

People didn't understand. She hadn't gotten a free ride with Jim. She had worked very hard at building their relationship. An enormous investment, with countless emotional and intellectual constructs. She'd worked hard to be a partner, to form an equitable division of labor within their marriage.

———

Elliot presented his card to the nurse at the entrance to the Neural Intensive Care Unit.

"Hi, I'm Detective Elliot from Public Safety. I'm here to see one of your patients. James Oakner."

The nurse scrutinized the card. She smiled in a naughty and knowing way. "You gonna give him a parking ticket?"

Elliot suppressed his amusement. "Actually, it's kind of complicated. We've been looking into some computer problems," he lied. "I need to check Dr. Oakner's ID bracelet."

"You mean like data theft?"

"Not really. You might say we're trying to plug the holes before the leaking starts."

"Oh."

Elliot hoped the nurse understood what he'd just said. He certainly didn't.

She pointed down the hall. "Last door on the left. His wife's in there with him right now."

"That's okay. I'll just be a minute."

He walked down the hall. In fact, he just wanted to see Dr. James Oakner in the flesh one time. Somehow, it seemed odd and inhumane to be investigating the documentation of his demise without paying a visit to what was left of him. He reached the room, went in, and saw the woman beside the bed where Oakner reclined.

He recognized her instantly.

"Christie."

"Elliot."

Time moves. Love stands still. He saw her as then, not now. And he could see it was the same for her.

"How are you?" he asked. Stupid question. He knew it instantly. "I'm sorry. I mean, how have you been?"

She managed a small and weary smile. "Where would you like me to start?"

He knew exactly where he wanted her to start.

———

Summer stars. A hot breeze off the desert. The big hull pushing upriver against the current. He, eighteen. She, the same. Just out of high school, dreams intact. Both working as crew on the big tour boat. A modern vessel carrying out-moded passengers.

She waited on tables in the main restaurant and scooped up miserly tips derived from fixed incomes. She moved with athletic grace. Her motion conformed perfectly to paths between tables. She seemed immune to the tackiness of the place. Her ambition moved far ahead of her current circumstance.

He worked as a DJ in the lounge, a newly minted profession at the time. He controlled the dual turntables. He slid the faders on the mixer. His hands danced over the dials and knobs. He played pop tunes, both new and old. He played Milli Vanilli. He played Sinatra. He covered it all. Management policy.

He watched her from his little stage. He took in the flow of her movement, the ease of her banter with the customers, the thick blonde hair, done up for work. Sometimes she would throw him a little glance. Blue eyes mating with his, then gone. He wanted her. He hoped it was reciprocal. He had no idea how to approach her.

She took care of it. She came to the stage and asked

him if he wanted anything to drink. She looked so good it made him dizzy. He mumbled a reply as he reeled about. She returned with a Coke and introduced herself. He did the same.

Work ended. A distant vacuum whined over a faded carpet. He asked her up to the top deck. To the wash of the water, the vigil of the stars. She said yes.

They stood alone at the railing, the ship slumbering beneath them. They shared the course of their lives to this juncture. Her mother worked in the hospital laundry up at Pearson. Her father drank. They were devastatingly poor. Her words crackled with anger. She had direction and momentum, the brains and the will. She would ascend somehow.

He listened and nodded and put it all aside. He drew her to him and kissed her tenderly. She melted into him. Love had its way with her. Dreams, ambition and purpose dissolved. Now there was only him.

The days passed. The ship sailed on. They built a great backlog of desire. There was no place to consummate it. Crew's quarters were cramped. Decks were dangerous.

The ship returned to port, to their home city. It was evening when they disembarked. The heat shoved clouds of blue and purple across the fading sky. They drove to her tiny studio apartment in his old VW. The air was stale inside, so they opened the windows. He wanted her very badly, but he knew to wait. The right moment would form of its own volition.

She disappeared into the bathroom. He would later learn that women often disappeared into bathrooms at times like these. He lay on an inflated air mattress. She would not be his first, but it didn't matter. He loved her.

He turned off the lamp and lay still in the heat. The

windows came alive with the glow of the city outside. A distant navigation light from an airliner crossed the soft lavender sky.

The first clap of thunder pushed through the open windows. A leaden thud coupled to a lazy rumble. It left an electric stillness in its wake. Then, the rain. Big drops plunging straight down. A few at first, then a torrent.

Cool air from the rain cut through the heat. Countless droplets pounded the pavement and rooftops.

The downpour masked her entrance. He wasn't aware of her until she walked slowly across his field of vision, toward one of the open windows. She never looked his way.

She wore a tank top, but was nude from the waist down. When she reached the window, she ducked beneath the raised sash and pushed herself out into the rain. She arched her back and raised her head toward the downpour. Her hair quickly wound itself into damp ringlets. She crossed her arms and rested her elbows on the sill and tucked one calf slightly behind the other.

He returned for an instant to the dawn of his sexual awakening. To a book of Salvador Dali paintings. To a work entitled *Young Virgin Auto-Sodomized by Her Own Chastity*. The power of image had instantly engorged him.

And now here she was, framed in wood and glass, in nearly the same pose. And here he was, once again hopelessly inflamed.

Still, he kept his distance. The storm sent little streams of water gliding down the slope of her hips. She straddled two worlds, the violence of the weather without and the hot stillness within.

The rain roared on.

He crossed the room and put his hands on her bottom. He gently stroked her along the curve of her hips and felt the goose bumps rise. She pushed her legs just a little further apart. She was ready. He entered.

Through the glass, he saw her head rear back, and a spray of droplets fly off her matted hair.

When he withdrew, he stepped to one side and helped her back through the window. Her face glistened from the rain. Her eyes glowed with the power of the storm. Her lips parted. He took her into his arms and kissed her ever so gently.

They walked silently back to the mattress. Both knew to keep silent. A spoken word would fracture the moment. She curled up against him while he gathered her in. They watched the rain, the spatters on the glass, the distant flashes.

A summer passed. Their lovemaking became more conventional. She gradually came into focus for him. Hard focus. Blue eyes always gazing into the distance, into the future.

She started to slip away in early fall; she was gone by the holidays. Hooked up with a new boyfriend. Some guy just out of the starting gate at an investment firm.

That winter, Elliot assessed his situation. A good mind. An empty wallet. He considered his options and joined the Army. Just in time for the Gulf, for the carbonized bodies.

He emailed her once from Kuwait. She responded. She had an internship at a hot high-tech PR firm. She was enrolled in college. She was launched. His heart sped a little when he received a reply. It meant that he still flickered inside her somewhere. They would always be bound by the heat, the boat, the summer storm.

He emailed her again, about a month later. He did it

amidst the smell of baking canvas coming off the roof of the tent. She never replied.

The next day, he drove up the highway into the charred tangle of vehicles. The Highway of Death, the media dubbed it. It severed any remaining connection he had to her.

Or so he thought.

———

Elliot sat across from Christie Oakner in the hospital cafeteria. He'd suggested that they come down here. It didn't seem right to be talking in front of her comatose husband.

"What do they say?" he asked. "Could he pull out of it?"

"Highly unlikely. That's what they say. That's doctor speak for never."

"I'm sorry."

"Thank you."

She seemed truly grateful. Was she?

"I didn't know you'd be here," Elliot explained. "I just came by to check his ID tag. It's part of an internal issue I'm working on."

"You work here at Pearson?"

"Yeah, I'm an investigator for the Department of Public Safety."

He braced himself. He waited for the condescension to spread across her face. It didn't happen.

"I hope everything's okay," she said. "I mean, I hope there's nothing wrong with his ID or his records. I've got plenty enough to worry about without having that thrown on the heap."

"It's just routine stuff." Elliot listened to himself lie. He didn't particularly like the sound of it. Especially with this particular woman at this particular time. Still, he had nothing definitive to tell her. Just a couple of medical images that didn't jibe with each other. So why tell her anything at all?

"Good," she said. "I've got a huge legal mess to deal with. I can't believe how complicated it's gotten. It feels like there's no way out."

"It always seems like that in the middle of a crisis," Elliot offered. "If there's anything I can do to help, just let me know."

"For old times' sake?"

Their eyes locked.

"I don't believe in old times," Elliot countered. "There's only now, and I'm here to help if I can."

"Thank you."

Elliot stood and gave her his card. "You can always get me at this number."

He turned to leave.

"Elliot?"

He turned back. "Yes?"

"What about his ID tag? Are you going to check it?"

"I'll come back later. You need your private time with him."

"You're right. I do."

"See you."

He drove along through a gentle spring rain. Why did it have to happen this way? You were supposed to run into your long-ago lover on a sun-drenched boulevard. Or a little café where you both took refuge from a cloudburst. You were supposed to have a glass of wine and roll around in warm memories. You were supposed to search for subtle signs of rebirth. You weren't supposed to find her in a hospital room with her comatose husband and her life put on permanent hold.

CHAPTER 11

The opossum dragged its full belly through the dense green bracken. It labored patiently up the slope to its shelter, a burrow scooped from the soft earth. During the cover of night, it had encountered extreme good fortune. A yard on the fringe of the forest had contained a feeder full of corn kernels for squirrels. Bits of kernel littered the ground below, where a rat was devouring the scraps. Partially distracted by its meal, the rodent failed to notice the approach of the opossum. A fatal mistake. The opossum was the size of a cat and armed with fifty sharp teeth. It sprang at the rat. The rat twisted to escape. Too late. The opossum severed its neck, nearly decapitating it. A short time later, most of the rat occupied the opossum's belly. The animal then turned to the bonus, the corn kernels, and ate them as well. A great and fortuitous feast.

But the opossum had miscalculated. Its full belly now slowed its progress up the slope. By now it should've been curled in the safety of its burrow. The cover of darkness was dissolving. First light settled softly over the woods.

The opossum began to panic. It now stood naked to predation. It sped its ascent and lost a degree of concealment in the process. The ivy rustled slightly. The ferns swayed a little in the morning stillness. Its new burst of labor exhaled a small cloud of pheromones into the air.

The dog sniffed the scent.

She identified a new smell, an urgent smell. Her head came up and her tail went straight out. Her nose moved in an arc to locate the source, the strongest scent. She found it on a little slope a short distance off. She saw the vegetation move in the dim light and took in the details. The tickle of one ivy leaf upon another. The flux in the arc of a fern branch. She read direction into the sum of the motions and she calculated the point of interception.

The dog launched. Her haunches shoved her forward into a full run. She bounded instinctively up the slope to the target.

The opossum heard the crash of brush. It felt the tremor of pounding feet shake the soil. Drenched with terror, it scurried ahead on feet small and pink, the color of a squirming newborn. Its sharp nose bored a hole into the underbrush as its fur bristled with fear. Concealment yielded to panicked flight.

The dog followed the ripple of motion. She vectored on the odor of dread. Her belly burned with the rage of prolonged hunger. She lunged at the point of encounter. Her jaws opened and her big canines spread in an awful curl. They punctured the opossum's neck, slicing through flesh and bone. She lifted the animal clear of the brush and shook it viciously. Its spinal cord ruptured and it went limp.

The dog deposited the lifeless animal on the ground. She reveled in this moment, the culmination of the killing bite. Exaltation muted her terrible hunger for a moment. Then it returned and she set about consuming her prey. Her paws held the body while her teeth ripped the hide and exposed the moist muscle tissue. Protein. Hers for the taking. Her teeth sank into it. She wolfed down one chunk after another. Her stomach begged for more. She fed on it as fast as she could.

She was stripping the last piece of meat off a femur when she noticed the coyote.

She stopped in mid-bite and raised her head. She cautiously appraised the newcomer. She equated its scent with the spray of urine on nearby vegetation. She had failed to read much of the information conveyed in the markings: the sexual signals, the presence of disease, the particulars of diet, the emotional state. She was new to the forest. Such things took time.

But now she sniffed a conflicted mixture of curiosity and hostility. The coyote loped forward a few steps on its long legs and stopped a few yards short of her. It stared at her with irises of pale gold. Its big ears pointed skyward. A hint of breeze rippled through its shaggy coat of grays and browns.

The dog held her ground. The kill was hers. She met the coyote's stare head-on. She stiffened her tail. Her ears pressed back slightly. She presented the coyote with a portrait of potential violence. She would not concede this patch of ground until the opossum was fully consumed.

The coyote remained still for the longest time. Its eyes remained locked on her, but the dog could see its ears relax slightly. She had won. She returned to the femur and stripped off the last full bite. As she chewed and gulped it, the coyote loped off.

She extracted the last minute scraps of meat with great

care. Her hunger receded, but did not vanish. She abandoned the entrails and the head, and buried the bones. She took several visual and olfactory fixes to mark the location of the remains. She would return later to suck the marrow.

She cut across the grain of the slopes in search of more food. The morning sun dappled the forest floor. The city hummed in the distance. Squirrels fussed and twittered at her approach. They bounded up tree trunks and skittered out to the limits of naked branches.

She came across a hiking trail. The ground here was moist and bore numerous shoe prints. Many overlapped and formed chaotic imprints. The compressed earth broadcast a carnival of city smells. Chewing gum, perfume, deodorant, marijuana, shoe polish, waterproofing, tobacco, spent matches.

She caught a hint of food in the air. It came from down the trail and she headed in that direction. She stopped after a hundred yards and cocked her ears. Something was coming up the path, maybe two things. Yes, two things. The labored breathing of human lungs working against the gravity of the grade. The panting of a dog, exhaling heat.

The rhythm of the human breath stayed steady. The panting of the dog accelerated. The animal had caught her scent and was bounding ahead.

"Felix, stay!" The voice was male, distant and weak. Beta, not alpha. No authority in the command.

She now heard the impact of the dog's feet on the soil of the trail. She inhaled traces of its mood. Happy, curious, excited. The scent filled her with anticipation. It had been a long time since she'd encountered another dog.

The new dog rounded the last curve in the trail and appeared before her. An animal larger than herself, a male.

A Siberian husky, although she could not know this. He bounded up to her. They circled and sniffed in the manner of dogs everywhere. They nuzzled each other. They hopped off the trail and trotted through a low patch of ivy, their flanks often touching. They playfully nipped at each other's snouts. It all came to her in the most atavistic way. It flooded her with a great contentment. They paused and stood panting in the ivy.

Then she spoke to the husky in the manner taught her by Zainah. A string of questions. *Do you live in these woods? Where do you find food? Are there other dogs here?*

She waited expectantly. The husky did not answer. He wagged his tail. His big pink tongue spilled out of a pleasant smile.

"Felix, come!"

The husky turned toward the voice. A man appeared on the trail above them. He wore rimless glasses and a crew cut.

"Hey, boy, who's your friend? Who's the new puppy?"

The husky hesitated, then walked back to the trail to join the hiker. He looked back at her wistfully.

The dog kept her distance. The hiker was male, like the attendants at the lab on the night shift. Or the men who took her from Zainah's apartment. Or the man who hurled the big metal object at her outside the van.

"Hey, pup, you out here by yourself?"

She tried to parse the stream of phonetics. She struggled to assemble the phonemes into meaningful groupings. She failed. She understood only that these sounds resembled those from after the big journey and not those from before. And this new mode of vocalization formed no symbols, held no meaning.

"Well, good luck. Come on, Felix." The hiker and the husky started on up the trail.

The dog sank into disappointment. She was not through playing. But then her belly spoke to her once more. Food took precedent over play. The most ancient of equations. She started down the trail, away from the hiker.

The first trace of sustenance crossed her nose just moments later. She lifted her snout to sample the air. The moisture in her nasal passages dissolved the incoming smells and deposited them on the internal surfaces. She sniffed repeatedly and built up a vast store of molecules that amplified the odors. They rippled through the nerve tissue and on to the brain.

She followed the smell down the trail. A big red squirrel chirped at her from above. She paid it no mind. She concentrated on bringing smell and topography into synchronization.

She stopped at a place where the bracken topped a small rise. She stared at the slope in a way few humans could manage. She saw only what was. All suppositions, theories, labels, meanings, classifications and associations melted away. She pierced the fog of knowledge. A pattern presented itself. In the way certain fern leaves were slightly twisted. In the way tiny twigs were fractured. In the way that the pollen dust coated some of the ivy leaves more than others. A path.

She followed the path over the rise and down to the camp. A green tarp stretched into a lean-to. Bedding and boxes inside. A couple of sagging lawn chairs. An ancient barbecue. A little table of wrought iron.

And the bag. A black plastic trash bag suspended two yards in the air. A bag full of food. All kept high and clear of the lower members of the forest's food chain.

The dog paused before entering the camp. She sniffed a human signature, male in origin. She looked and listened, but didn't detect the owner of the signature. She entered the camp and sat beneath the bag and looked up. Too high.

She backed off a few paces and sat once more. She looked at the knot that cinched the bag and the rope holding it out of reach. Her eyes tracked the course of rope as it moved up from the bag, over a limb and down to a tree trunk a short distance away. She moved to the base of the tree. The end of the rope wrapped around the trunk. A slip knot secured it. The end of the knot dangled loose. She jumped up, grabbed the knot and pulled. The entire assembly came undone. The bag fell to the ground.

She set upon it almost before it landed. The plastic yielded to her teeth. She tore into the food within—vegetables, bread, bacon—wolfing it down. Nature made no allowance for leisurely dining. Interruptions could occur at any time.

She almost missed the sound of someone stepping off the main trail onto the path. The snap of a small branch caught her ear. She bolted immediately. She lunged up and over the next rise past the camp and then slowed her pace to hide the sound of her escape. She had most of the food from the bag in her belly, and felt distinctly better.

—————

The King cautiously entered his camp. He'd heard the sound of something charging through the brush in the distance, but couldn't identify it. He looked at the slack rope, the ravaged bag, the scattered food scraps.

He scratched his head. The camp contained several items of far more value than the contents of the bag. But they remained untouched. So why go for the raw food?

Must have been an animal of some kind.

CHAPTER 12

The Gulfstream's engines poured out a distant drone as it sliced through the stratosphere, where all was thin and dry and deeply blue. Dr. Richard Stennis rested his drink on the heavy lacquer covering the Brazilian rosewood table. He looked out the window limned on its borders with a thin frost. A thunderhead below captured his attention. The convective forces within folded it and curdled it into a monstrous hemisphere. Not unlike the neocortex of a human brain, he decided. Bursts of interior lightning triggered great patches of illumination on its surface. It boiled and glowed. It thrust its violence to great altitudes, beyond the natural reach of men or birds.

Stennis gazed down upon the huge cloud from an Olympian viewpoint. They were six hours out of Tokyo and fifty thousand feet up. The hot fog of Kuala Lumpur was far behind him. He loved the play of the brutal high-altitude light over the cabin's interior. He loved the beautiful solitude. The attendant was hidden away in the aft compartment and the crew confined to the cockpit. Stennis understood completely why Becker owned such a plane, even if he rarely used it.

He also understood that he would soon have the option of owning such a plane himself. He wondered what his father would think of that. He visualized his father in the parking lot of a shabby convenience store, stubbled and gray. He imagined him opening the door of a dented old Buick and clutching a six-pack. He envisioned him looking up through the polluted haze to the pure blue roof of sky directly overhead.

Would his father's jaw go slack with awe? Would a tear of admiration streak down his cheek? No. His father would simply climb into the stinking car, open a beer and drive back to whatever dreary apartment complex he currently inhabited. His father had been a mathematician and his professional path was best described in mathematical terms. A negative slope. A line plunging down through the Cartesian plain to depths without limit. First, all bright with promise in graduate school. Then, when Stennis was a child, on a tenure track at a major university. Then, the trouble. The drinking, the brooding, the outbursts of rage.

His mother had taken the martyr's path and curled into bitter and righteous resignation. The university position evaporated. A high school teaching job later did the same. Tutorial work followed. His mother became a grocery clerk. Still, they maintained a social fiction. They lived in the same house in the same neighborhood full of professional people. The core was rotting, but the shell remained intact.

Stennis the confused child became Stennis the angry youth. He attended a high school full of university-bound peers, the offspring of the ballooning meritocracy. He, an heir to the opposite. He embraced the punk ethos of kinetic anger. He turned to the Sex Pistols, the Ramones, the Clash. His massive intelligence, always camouflaged, now slid entirely from view. He reached out as he fell but no one responded.

The bottom of his slide came his senior year in high school. In a doughnut shop deep in the suburban wasteland. A place of pinks, creams, Formica and despair. He sat in a booth, staring out at the night with two of his latest friends. Huffers, they were called. Sniffers of fumes created by glues, paints and solvents.

"Always use Ross," one of them advised, referring to a glue brand. "Testors will give you a headache."

The other gazed at a quarter, two dimes and a nickel on the tabletop. He furrowed his brow and looked up to Stennis. "How much money is this?" he asked.

Stennis didn't bother to tell him. Stennis got up and left. Forever.

He ambushed his educators with stellar SAT scores. He won a scholarship to a major university and he turned to the sciences. He would ride on his father's genetic legacy. Ambition, retribution, rage and resolve fueled his ascent. Personal integrity was a luxury of those already arrived. To Stennis, moral imperatives were flexible things.

He settled on the biological sciences. He intuitively understood that organic molecules would replace electrons as the technological currency of the new global economy. He received a doctorate. He won grants, substantial grants. He published. He attracted attention. Business opportunities presented themselves. He shrewdly held off, waiting for the perfect proposition.

Then came Becker. The man instantly understood Stennis better than he understood himself. That was part of his genius. He knew that the core of Dr. Richard Stennis craved respectability more than anything. He knew that Stennis needed some form of redemption to balance his ambition. Without it, he would become a dark prince, a permanent outcast.

And so it was that Becker manufactured a balanced equation for Stennis. One that reconciled social redemption and extraordinary personal gain. One that permitted ruthless pursuit of the common good. And now the funding, the company and the lab were fully functional. The fundamental research was done. The marketable technology nearly perfected. They stood on the brink of an extraordinary achievement.

Except for Oakner.

Stennis had seen the CT scans. It looked irreversible. Possibly fatal. But what if it wasn't? What if he came out of the coma? What if someone figured out what happened? Stennis knew that Oakner represented the wild card, the one that always appeared in any complex undertaking. Once again, he replayed the incident with Oakner on the boat. Once again, he concluded that there could be no other outcome.

The great thunderhead passed from view and Stennis shifted in his contoured seat. He needed to maintain maximum distance from the Oakner issue. Hoffner would have to handle it. After all, that was Hoffner's role in all this: expediter. He'd already taken some action, but a lot more might be needed. Becker would expect nothing less.

"Dr. Stennis?"

The attendant broke his rumination and handed him the phone. "You have a call from the U.S."

"Thank you." The display told him that it was Hoffner phoning from Pearson. "Hello?"

"Hi, Dick, it's Mike. Sorry to bother you, but we have another problem."

"And what's that?"

"We've lost the dog."

"What do you mean, 'we've lost the dog'?"

"Everything went fine from KL to here, but then somebody broke into the transport van when it got up here to Pearson. Looks like a petty burglary. But the dog escaped."

"Jesus!"

"I know. We're going to go out in full force to find it."

"We must have the dog, Mike," Stennis replied in a carefully measured tone. "We're dangerously exposed if we don't. You know that, don't you?"

"Of course I know that."

"Do I need to say anything more?"

"No. As soon as anything happens, I'll let you know."

"Good."

Stennis hung up. He looked back out the window. It was clouding up below.

————

The life was draining out of his face. Each visit, it became more evident. As if some demon stole into the room in the wee hours and rubbed a very soft eraser over his flesh. Christie Oakner shifted in her bedside seat and looked away. Her visits were now a matter of pure obligation. How could they be otherwise? There was no dialogue, no stimulus. Only silence and recollection.

She drifted back to that day, that day before the disaster. She had left him sleeping off his playtime with Stennis and driven down the hill to town. She had pulled into the private parking beneath a restaurant overlooking the marina. She climbed the twist of wooden stairs to the second story. The maître d' smiled and greeted her by name as she walked by the water-filled tub of live lobsters. They had a robotic quality about them that bothered her. They thrashed and squirmed to the dictates of the most primitive of algorithms.

She sat outside on the deck at a table overlooking the boats and the barren hills beyond. The image of the thrashing lobsters kept intruding as she drank a glass of chardonnay. She feared that they were all like the lobsters. Creatures both pitiful in their plight and brutish in their behavior. Doomed and flailing blindly out beyond the borders of salvation. At the every least, it seemed to describe the present state of her marriage.

She took a sip of wine and fondled the diamond-encrusted heart that hung from her neck on a chain of white gold. Jim had bought it for her when he started the company and they bought the place down here. It came from a store directly beneath where she now sat, one that catered to the Americans in their keeps atop the hill. It cost ten thousand dollars. She knew this because she saw an identical one beneath the glass one day as she idly perused the merchandise.

He'd never been her end game, and he knew it. She was still trending up sharply in her professional life when she met him. She was able to approach him at eye level, and it clearly touched him. At first, he gave her what was most precious to him—his time and his passion. The trinkets, the diamonds, and all the rest came later. Objects of barter in a relationship gone cool; not cold, but definitely cool.

She still wanted it to work. She craved success, she

hated failure. Was a failed marriage the equivalent of a business deal gone bad? Was that all there was to it with her? She searched within, and found no answers.

She finished her wine. A cloud obscured the sun, a thin smear of white against the brilliant blue so high above.

CHAPTER 13

Hello."

"Christie, it's Elliot. How are you doing?"

"Elliot. Oh. Hi. I'm doing okay, I guess."

"I just wanted to follow up with you."

"That's very nice of you. I appreciate it."

"I just wanted to make sure everything is okay."

"Everything's about as good as it's going to get for a while."

"I know it can't be easy."

"No, it's not."

"I don't like to bother you about this, but I'm still checking out the thing about your husband's ID. I need a little more information. Do you have any free time?"

"What did you have in mind?"

"I'd like to keep this thing moving, so the sooner the better. Can we meet later this afternoon?"

"That might work."

"Our offices here are pretty crummy, so why don't we go have coffee?"

"Where do you want to go?"

"Do you know where the Hillsider is? Right below the campus?"

"Yeah, that's fine."

"Is four okay?"

"Yeah, four's fine."

"Good, I'll see you there."

"Bye now."

"Thanks."

Elliot closed his cell phone. He began to decode the conversation, beginning at the top: She'd made an appreciative comment about his calling. That was good. She didn't have to.

She'd quickly found a window of time for them to meet. That was also good. She easily could have put him off.

In fact, she'd agreed to meet him this very same day. That was even better. She'd even consented to meet him in a social setting. Also good.

Finally, their meeting place was actually a bar, which was very good indeed.

Also very bad. All of it. Why was he speculating like this? He'd caught her at a vulnerable moment. She had a husband who looked like the living dead and would probably stay that way indefinitely. She was parked in some kind of limbo a lot closer to hell than heaven. He should back way off. True, he had a bogus medical image of Oakner that raised a number of questions, though he hadn't bothered to tell her about that, had he? But it was the only real pretext he had for seeing her. He would ride it as far as he could. And when it was fully exhausted and spent, he would face the truth of the matter.

"Bad news, Detective."

Elliot turned in his chair. Bobby Seifert stood there, soda can in one hand, corn curls in the other. "The Chief wants to see you. He said to go right on in."

Elliot sighed and pocketed his cell phone. "Did he say what it's about?"

Bobby shrugged. "The Chief never says what it's about."

Elliot tried not to smile as he stood. "And why is that, Bobby?"

"Because he doesn't know what it's about."

"A little more respect for authority figures might help your career."

"You're absolutely right, boss. I'll work on it while you go respect the Chief."

———

Carl Alphan. Director of Public Safety. The Chief. Resident of the only corner office in their building with a view. He hoisted his big frame up as Elliot entered, and gestured to the other occupant.

"Elliot, this is Mike Hoffner. Mike's senior research administrator here at Pearson. I believe you two have already met."

Hoffner didn't bother to rise. He sat at a little round conference table by the window. He didn't speak. Too far up the food chain for that. He merely nodded.

Elliot nodded back and sat down. Reciprocal arrogance. Too bad Bobby didn't get to see that. The Chief shot a quick glare at Elliot. The Chief never missed that kind of thing. He was ex-military: he'd spent most of his career shackled to various chains of command.

"Elliot, I read the report you filed on the dog and I guess it didn't give me a good picture of how serious all this really is. Apparently, this animal represents an extremely significant loss. Is that correct, Mr. Hoffner?"

Hoffner folded his hands dramatically. His right cuff slipped back just enough to reveal the gleam of a Patek Philippe watch. "Most of the laboratory animals we deal with are interchangeable with others of their species or particular genetic strains. Unfortunately, that's not the case with this one. It's targeted at a very specific application, and as such, not replaceable."

Elliot stifled his disgust with the pair. Hoffner was giving a blatant demonstration of institutional clout. And the Chief was passing the buck by suggesting that Elliot had been incompetent in his reporting.

"Move this up and make it your number one priority," the Chief told Elliot. "Cover the entire campus and all the adjacent wooded areas. Check in all the surrounding neighborhoods."

The Chief wore a tweed sport coat, wrinkled white shirt and plain tie. Next to Hoffner, he looked like a high school English teacher interacting with the CEO of a big investment firm. Clearly, Hoffner's visit was unexpected. Otherwise, the Chief would have tried to match him thread for thread. As for Elliot, he had on the same thing he wore every day: chinos, Skechers pull-on shoes, blue oxford shirt, and corduroy sport coat. In other words, the maximum casualness he could get away with. In addition, he had some short stubble growing between his sideburns and goatee, which no doubt irritated the Chief, though not enough for a reprimand.

"Coordinate with county animal control," the Chief continued. "And canvass all the animal shelter organizations in the metro area."

The Chief was presenting himself to Hoffner as a real

take-charge kind of guy. And at the same time, he was shifting all the accountability over to Elliot. Perfect.

"There's one other issue," Hoffner added. "All of this must be kept extremely low-key. No help from the media. We need to avoid press coverage at all cost."

"And why's that?" Elliot asked. He already knew, but he wanted to make Hoffner say it out loud.

"A lot of people have very different viewpoints on the use of laboratory animals," Hoffner replied. "We don't want to become entangled in public debate. You understand?"

"I understand."

"Good." Hoffner got to his feet. So did the Chief. "Gentlemen, I have another meeting. I expect I'll be hearing from you soon."

"We'll keep you continually updated," the Chief promised.

Hoffner left. The Chief turned to Elliot. "Everything else goes on the back burner. Someone reports a theft or something, you hand it off to the patrol staff. Got it?"

"Got it."

"I want daily reports. Something breaks, I want to know right away."

"Got it."

"I'll be the interface with Mr. Hoffner. You need something from him, you let me know."

"I'll do that."

Elliot sat in a booth at the Hillsider. Piped pseudo-jazz played in the background. Late afternoon light climbed over the treetops and bathed the room. He hadn't ordered yet. He would wait for Christie, who would be slightly late. She'd always been slightly late. He held a printout with a photo of the dog. Definitely a black Lab. That was part of the problem. A mutt would have many distinguishing characteristics. Easy to identify. All black Labs looked pretty much alike, unless you knew them well. He envisioned this dog's picture on the door of a family refrigerator, held in place by a little magnet covered by a plastic banana. He multiplied this vision by thousands of households. He didn't like the difficulties it presented.

"Hello, Elliot. Sorry I'm late."

He stood to greet her. "Don't worry about it. You've got a lot going on."

He had been wrapped in the thousand dogs and missed her entrance. She looked exquisite. She'd always looked exquisite.

"How's he doing today?"

She shrugged. "The same, only worse. If you know what I mean."

"I think I do. How long have you been married?"

"Five years." She rested her elbows on the table. A golden cascade of bangles spilled down her wrist and rippled against the cuff of her jacket.

"How did you meet him?"

"I was at a health care conference in Europe. Jim delivered the keynote. I was impressed. We met later that evening at a reception. The next year, I moved out here from New York and we got married."

"Your first?"

"Yeah, my first. What about you?"

"Never married. I came close a couple of times, but not lately."

"Just as well. As you can see, it's all pretty much a crapshoot. You just never know. You only pretend you do."

"So this whole thing was a surprise? His stroke, I mean."

"Totally. Jim had a complete physical just a couple of months ago. Routine, for insurance. No problems. There was absolutely nothing wrong with him."

Should he bring up the second CT scan? That was fully half of why he was sitting here, the professional half. He decided against it. He had to wait until he knew the whole story behind it. Right now, that film would just add more mud to a very murky situation.

"I know this isn't positive thinking, but what if he doesn't pull out of it? What happens to you then?"

A small laugh, bitter around the edges. "It depends on which attorney or accountant you ask. And how much they think they can bill you for the answer. Seriously, though, I'll be okay. There's health insurance, there's disability insurance, there's life insurance, there's this insurance, there's that insurance. It's all going to work out."

He sensed that that was not entirely true, but before he could probe any further, the waitress came to take their order. They both asked for wine. A Chablis for her, a Merlot for him. He raised his glass to her.

"To old times."

She silently raised her glass in return. It wasn't really a toast at all, and they both knew it. It was a portal into a very different emotional space.

"I've thought about you now and then," he ventured.

"Same here."

"Good thoughts?"

"Good thoughts." He took a sip of his wine and looked out the window. The hill had slipped into shadow. The foliage had turned a muted green. A hint of copper dusted the river and the city beyond. Lost light, lost youth. "We were young. What else can you say?"

"I really don't know, Elliot. Especially now."

He suddenly sensed that they were rudderless and drifting toward somewhere neither wanted to go. He switched to pleasantries. Politics at Pearson. Decorating her house. Her former career in PR. It got them through the wine and out the door.

He walked her to her car. The light was nearly gone and what was left painted her very softly.

"I know the circumstances are all wrong," he told her, "but it's really good to see you again."

"Thanks, Elliot." She slid into her car, a Lexus. The smell of new leather floated out into the evening.

And with that, she was gone.

For a while, anyway. They were now enmeshed on two fronts, one professional, the other emotional. Elliot turned toward his car. She knew a lot more than she was saying.

"Hey, you're fuckin' awesome!" the drunk told Tanya. "You sound just like Bonham. Maybe even better!"

"Thank you," Tanya responded with genuine modesty. Her short hair hung limp and damp from perspiration after pounding through forty-five minutes of Led Zeppelin.

The drunk tottered slightly, like a top in precession, searching for something else to say to a powerhouse lesbian drummer. He failed. "Well, see ya."

"Thanks for coming to hear us," Tanya said.

The drunk drifted off toward the bar. Elliot shifted in his chair next to Tanya and poured them both a glass of beer from a pitcher on the little table. They were playing in a funky hybrid joint, a fried chicken takeout place joined at the hip with a neighborhood bar. Elliot looked out the window into the parking lot. Full. Lots of beefy little pick-ups, some motorcycles and a few upscale sedans. A mostly male crowd.

"So what's new? You got a girlfriend?" Tanya asked.

"Nope. But I bet you do," Elliot countered.

They frequently went on like this. He was a straight cop and she was a gay laborer in a chocolate factory, but none of that seemed to matter. They liked each other.

"Nope, not right now," Tanya replied. She wore a sleeveless sweatshirt, which put her muscular arms on prominent display.

"So what happened to Delia?"

"She ran home to momma," Tanya answered as she drank half the glass of beer in a single gulp. "The little bitch," she added cheerfully.

"Sounds like it wasn't the best of relationships."

"I guess not. But what are you gonna do, huh?"

"Maybe you should get a pet," Elliot suggested. "They're supposed to give you unconditional love."

Tanya shrugged. "That's what they say. You got a pet?"

"Sort of. I'm looking for a dog."

"So how hard can it be to find a dog? Just go to a shelter or something and pick one."

"It's not quite that simple. This one's part of my job. It went missing up at the hospital."

"So what's a dog doing living at a hospital?"

"This one never made it that far. It escaped upon delivery. My boss is bent sideways about it."

Tanya managed a wry smile. "My boss is bent sideways about everything. All the time."

"Let me guess: Your boss is a woman."

"Kind of."

"Is she cute?" Elliot couldn't resist.

Tanya sighed. "Yeah, as a matter of fact, she is. But all she does is make chocolate and race bicycles."

"Sounds like a perfect match."

"Tell that to her three boyfriends."

"Maybe I could have them all arrested. What do you think?"

"Wouldn't work. I'd still be up against a dozen vats of chocolate and a ten-speed racing bike."

"Oh well. I couldn't pull it off anyway."

"Why not?" Tanya teased. "I thought you were some kind of big-cheese detective."

"I am."

"So what's the problem?"

"The dog. I'm dog poop until I find the dog."

CHAPTER 14

Becker ignored the traffic, the crowds, and the commerce outside the car. He worked in air-conditioned silence. He stared at his laptop behind multiple layers of Kevlar armor and bullet-proof glass. He read the displayed documents with astounding speed and comprehension. They were full of dense legalities. They described the process of putting a global empire on autopilot. His empire. He would retain ultimate control, but management functions would be carefully dispersed among boards, committees and key individuals. None would accumulate sufficient power to become a threat to the organization as a whole. All would dangle from threads of accountability. And if he died? A series of trusteeships would kick in. He had no heirs. He preferred not to dwell on their absence. It caused him a certain amount of pain.

He looked up as the car stopped in traffic. He stared at the twin doors on the back of the security vehicle ahead of them. A second vehicle followed directly behind. Both were full of highly trained men and sophisticated weaponry.

He closed his laptop and rubbed his eyes. This entire legal exercise, this massive transfer of executive power, would only be in effect for a year or two, at the most. It hardly seemed necessary.

His little caravan turned off Jalan Kinabalu and onto Jalan Petaling. The sky burned white and wet with the heat of central Kuala Lumpur's midafternoon. He looked out his window at an old Mercedes sedan. A 300-Series Turbo Diesel. It sagged under an aging skin of oxidation and rust.

He knew the model precisely. He visualized the wood trim on the dash, the symmetric flow of the grain. He felt the heft of the shift selector. He heard the flood of classical music from the stereo. Mozart and Mahler, most likely.

It was 1982 and he saw his father behind the wheel. The Teutonic profile, the high forehead, the receding hair, the ice blue eyes. The sure grip of his hands on the wheel. His father was German Swiss. He owned a bank. His mother was Lebanese Christian. She owned his heart.

His father taught him compound interest before he turned six, with stacks of coins on their boat on Lake Geneva. He understood perfectly. His father was pleased. His mother took him to Paris and introduced him to Monet. That, too, he understood perfectly. Those were the bright years.

Adolescence came on. His father now owned several banks. He no longer discussed finance with his son, despite the boy's formidable grasp of the subject. He seemed troubled, distant. The boy heard fragments of urgent conversation now and then. A few moments of a phone call, a hallway whisper to his mother. The business had grown to international proportion. Investments had been made in murky regions of the globe. Transactions of questionable character.

Still, they lived the life of the fortunate few. A new house of grand proportion in a fashionable section of Geneva. A big plane to complement the large boat. Vacations in New York, London and Hong Kong.

1982. His father went out on a lovely spring morning, climbed into the Mercedes and switched on the ignition. They later assured the boy that there had been no pain. His father had instantly become a scattered collection of smoldering flesh and bone.

A contingency plan went into effect. The boy knew nothing of the plan until it automatically engaged. He was the ultimate heir to his father's fortune, and his father had known this would put the boy in great peril. Moments after his father's funeral, he was whisked away from his grieving mother and transported to the United States. He was outfitted with a new identity. He was enrolled in a private school. His mother died of a broken heart in Beirut. He was unable to attend her funeral.

He earned an MBA at Stanford, pulled his father's holdings out of the trust and went to work. He caught the first wave of the global economy and rode its crest to immense fortune. He did it with almost complete anonymity, ensuring that the sins of the father would not return to visit the son. He mastered various forms of weaponry and formed a tight shell of security about him.

But not tight enough. It happened in Budapest. On a beautiful spring day, just like his father. But it was clumsy and heavy-handed. Three shots from a high-powered rifle as he was coming out of a hired car. All missed. The grouping of the rounds covered more than a meter, which indicated very poor marksmanship. He spent heavily with the police to keep the matter quiet. His own people investigated and quickly found the source of the problem, which was liquidated a few months later.

He had learned a vital lesson. Security must be pre-emptive instead of defensive. All this long before the World Trade Center was reduced to dust. He acted judiciously but swiftly whenever he deemed it necessary. There were no further incidents.

The old Mercedes fell from view. They reached the entrance to Chinatown. He waited for security, then climbed out and viewed the narrow street jammed with pedestrians. Old buildings with tile awnings rose to a height of two or three stories. A procession of metal poles lined each side and supported an arched framework of light blue canvas that spanned the street high overhead. Beneath it, a suspension of red paper lanterns zigzagged down the avenue. Shopkeepers stood by their wares in shorts and sandals, and haggled with passersby. Cooks shuffled pots and pans on propane-fired stoves. Signs beckoned in both English and Chinese. City dwellers mingled with tourists, who seemed numbed by the density of the place.

Becker gave terse instructions to the team. They were to give him some distance and form a loose perimeter. Eye contact only. They were to blend with the crowds. He waded into the throng of widely divergent ethnicity and started down the avenue.

His thoughts turned to the dog. It was incredible. They had already lost it once here, and now they'd lost it again in the U.S. The loss here at the facility was understandable. The woman had good credentials. She'd performed efficiently and reliably with the training and testing. There was no way to know that she'd try to sneak off with the dog in tow. Luckily, they'd contained the damage and retrieved the animal. But the loss at Pearson was sheer bad luck.

Becker emerged from his thoughts. The crowds milled around him. The merchants hustled. The restaurants hummed. The signs and banners blared.

He had no idea where he was.

He stifled a surge of panic. He methodically collected information. It was a city somewhere in Asia. The people, the architecture, the signage all told him that. He cast about for cues, for associative memories. He continued walking on his present course. If he had a destination up ahead, it might set him straight. He felt the presence of the cell phone in his shirt pocket and pulled it out. That did it. He was in Chinatown. He was here to make a private call.

He stepped under the awning of a little shop selling DVDs. The latest U.S. theatrical releases for about a dollar and fifty cents. He turned away from the street. He needed more than just the cover of street noise. Video or a trained observer could read his lips.

He dialed a number and listened. The signal from his phone traveled to a switching complex in his office, which sent it to a gateway and up to a network of satellites in Low Earth Orbit. They relayed it to a satellite over the western U.S., which beamed it down directly to the receiving phone. A male voice answered.

"Yes?"

"The verification code is 1532895456."

"Alright, you're verified."

"I assume you're in place by now."

"That's correct."

"We have a situation at your location. It's not what we originally intended, but it takes precedent. We believe that a dog may be loose in the area where you are currently located."

"A dog?"

"The animal has special value. That's all you need to know. I'm sending its picture."

Becker continued to speak while the image transmitted. "It's a breed called a Labrador retriever. It's female and weighs about thirty-five kilos. Do you have it now?"

"I have it. What's the course of action if I locate it?"

"You need to inform us immediately. Then we'll arrange a delivery procedure."

"Is there anything else?"

"No. Not now. As we told you originally, you're there on a contingency basis. We'll update you as the situation evolves."

"Goodbye then."

"Yes, goodbye."

Becker pocketed the phone. In truth, they could proceed without the dog, but the risk would be amplified considerably. And like all financial people, he was risk-averse at the core. He turned back to the street. He looked up and down the boiling river of people and trade. Which way was the car? He didn't know. This time, the panic advanced a little further before he tamped it down. Then he spotted one of his security people and made eye contact. He beckoned the man over.

"Let's head back."

The man nodded and started off. Becker followed.

Becker didn't like it. Becker never followed.

CHAPTER 15

The dog fought the urge to abandon her vigil. The hunger raged in her belly and screamed at her to take more immediate action. But she had weighed the alternatives and her current course continued to prevail. The woods had not produced sufficient sustenance. She had returned to the camp that yielded the suspended bag to her and failed to find more food. The bag and its rigging were gone. Two plastic ice chests rested in their place. She sniffed the traces of bacon and vegetables on their blue and white surfaces. She considered the latch assemblies and even captured one in the grip of her incisors, but it refused to yield.

Later in the day, she had managed to pounce on an injured Douglas squirrel, but the animal had been starving and yielded only minimal protein. Then she had come across the coyote again early this morning. Their roles were now reversed. The coyote had caught and killed a domestic cat. The dead animal was large and fat, the product of a rich diet and overindulgence. The coyote had torn the hide open and was ripping off a piece of meat when the dog approached. It looked up. Its ears went fully vertical. The white tufts on their borders bristled. Its blood-smeared snout curled into a snarl. Its tail extended straight out. Its ghostly eyes locked on her, the pupils dead and black with the promise of violence. She held steady on the coyote's stare. The most primitive of algorithms played through the depths of her brain. It considered her state of malnutrition, her size, the coyote's size, the potential power of each animal, the gain from a positive outcome, the loss from a negative one. She broke off the encounter and looked away. The coyote returned to its meal. She slunk off down the hill.

She had wandered along the slopes and picked up various scents, but all failed to yield food. A light drizzle fell. It coated the forest canopy with moisture, which accumulated on the surface of the leaves and consolidated into droplets that fell to the ground and onto the dog. She came to the far reaches of the forest, where it bordered the backyards of houses. She ranged along a series of fences and peered in. She saw patio furniture, wheelbarrows, barbecues, flowerpots, garden tools, birdbaths, squirrel feeders, coiled hoses, tricycles and trellises. Then she heard the roll of a sliding glass door and peered through the brush to investigate. A woman in sweatpants set a big bowl of dog food down on a patio protected from the drizzle by an overhang off the house. The woman returned to the house and shut the door behind her.

The dog's sight and smell locked on the bowl full of food. The food within overflowed the bowl's rim and formed a speckled ring on the concrete around it. The heap of wet food radiated through her olfactory system. She pressed her snout against the fence, a chain-link type woven into wire diamonds beyond the power of her teeth. She sniffed the ground and pawed at it. She started to dig where fence met earth. The hardened nails on her paws bit into the soil and propelled it backward between her hind legs.

She had scooped a ragged cavity nearly big enough to wriggle through when the sliding door opened again. Quickly, she backed off into the cover of the brush. A dog came through the door, a large dog bred of bad intention. A Rottweiler. It strode on massive shoulders and haunches to the bowl and wolfed down the food in a few enormous gulps. It then walked over to a pad set out for it and flopped down. Black ears drooped off the sides of its broad skull like wilted leaves. Its small almond eyes peered out at the world without a trace of pity.

The Rottweiler's ears lifted suddenly. It stared directly at her with its wide face of black and rust. It came to its feet and trotted across the yard toward her excavation. It issued a growl both deep and soft. Then an enormous burst of barking exploded through the morning drizzle.

The Rottweiler lunged into the hole beneath the fence. For a horrible moment, it seemed as though the huge beast would squirm through and be upon her. But the opening was too small. Still, it wedged its big head through and hurled one bark after another at her. Its lips curled, its gums glowed pink and its wicked teeth flashed white and mean.

Her ears smashed flat. Her tail arced down. But her fear was tempered by observation. The Rottweiler was not going to fit through. She was safe. Hungry and safe, a combination not favored by the natural laws.

The sliding glass door rumbled open once again.

"Jerome!"

The barking ceased. Only the animal's growl remained.

"You get in here right now!"

Growling, the Rottweiler gradually withdrew from the hole. It gave a great shake, sending loosened earth in a spray across the lawn. It turned and walked back toward the waiting woman at a pace both slow and defiant. It disappeared into the house. The woman stepped out, picked up the empty bowl, walked back into the house and rolled the glass door shut. A hiss, a little thud, then silence.

The dog came out from its cover and sniffed the loosened earth around the hole. She smelled the residue of unfettered rage from the bigger dog. But hunger instructed her to linger, to observe, to advance toward a workable solution. She reviewed the sequence of events. First, the empty yard. Then, the woman putting out the bowl. Then, the big dog eating and resting.

She focused on the bowl brimming with food, the bowl left exposed in momentary solitude. That was the key. She retreated from the hole and settled down where she could watch the house. The drizzle became a steady rain falling from a dank sky. It ran down her forehead and slid off her flanks. She remained very still to conserve her energy. She was burning more of it than she was consuming. Soon, she would grow weak. Soon, the spiral into starvation would start.

CHAPTER 16

The Chief slid his tray along the polished tubing. He halted in front of the dessert display and took out a piece of key lime pie. He turned to Elliot, who trailed him.

"You having dessert?"

"Not today." In fact, Elliot never had dessert at lunch. He also never ate in the hospital cafeteria. It was the road to dietary disaster. A place where cardiologists munched on buttered cinnamon rolls as if their arteries possessed some kind of professional immunity.

The Chief handed his charge card to the cashier. "This kind of reminds me of Baghdad. We had key lime pie every Friday."

He signed the charge slip and lifted his tray, which was laden with a cheeseburger, fries, soda and pie. "Only over there, you didn't worry about your weight, because a big gut was about the last thing that was going to kill you."

Elliot followed the Chief through the noontime din to a vacant table where they could sit across from each other.

Baghdad. How many times had he heard about Baghdad? About the Chief's previous incarnation as a lieutenant colonel in an Air Force security squadron? About blood and death under the blowing sand and blazing sun? In fact, the Chief had been an administrator at Baghdad International Airport. A place encircled with multiple rings of defense and about as dangerous as a church barbecue. However, Lieutenant Colonel Carl Alphan had been a clever and vicious combatant in the bureaucratic wars that raged within the military command structure. When he retired, he brought those attributes with him to Pearson, where he now maneuvered deftly within the system.

The Chief set down his tray and hoisted his big frame over the bench to sit. "We should do this more often, Elliot. I don't get enough time with you."

Elliot simply nodded and reached for his turkey sandwich. The Chief had asked him to lunch this morning. Never good. Now he was implying that this was quality time. Even worse.

The Chief chewed a couple of fries. "You know, I've always given a lot of slack to my senior staff. You take away people's initiative and you start to strangle their performance potential. So when it comes to folks like you, I let you pretty much run your own show. Everybody wins that way, wouldn't you say?"

"Yeah, I suppose so." Elliot took a sip of bottled water. He kept eye contact with the Chief. The more evasive he appeared, the harder the Chief would pounce.

"All I really ask is to be kept informed. That's all. Just give me the bare bones. You can chew on the meat. I just need the bare bones. That's how I keep the whole thing running straight and true."

The Chief tore into his cheeseburger. He chewed

longer than necessary. He let the tension build. He took a sip of Coke. He never took his eyes off Elliot.

"Like most people in my kind of position, I get information both from formal and informal channels. Then I put it all together and see what I've got." The Chief popped a single french fry into his mouth. "I heard indirectly that you have an investigation going into some kind of records fraud. But that couldn't be right, because you haven't submitted any documentation on anything like that—unless I've missed something. Have I missed something, Elliot?"

"I don't think so."

"Good. Maybe I'm not being entirely fair here. Maybe this is all about something that just started up. Maybe you haven't had time to write it up because you're so focused on this dog thing. Is that what's going on here?"

Elliot took another sip of water before replying. He'd been crafting his response since the first french fry slid down the Chief's gullet. "Something came up a little while back. A discrepancy in some medical records. Probably nothing to it. I've been watching it out of the corner of my eye, but there's really nothing to report at this point."

"Nor will there be, until this goddamn dog gets found," the Chief shot back. He was through with the long-range artillery. He was attacking full force. "Don't go sideways on me. We took a chance on you up here. So far, it's worked out. Let's keep it that way."

The Chance.

So that's how it was encrypted. Elliot hadn't known that. All the wheeling, the suffering, the dealing, the agony, the dickering, the pain, the subterfuge. All encoded into one neat little phrase.

The cafeteria dims. The drone of medical shop talk and

institutional gossip fades. The screaming of children fills the void. He's back in the dope house, the target residence. Just like dozens of times before.

Elliot lies flat on his back in the dark. The beams from the tactical lights slash through the rifle smoke. His whole side is numb. His ears ring painfully but through the sound he hears shouting. The house lights come on. Two of the team bend over him.

"Elliot! You okay, buddy?"

Elliot comes up to his elbows. "Yeah, I'm okay."

Lieutenant Sparks shouts from down the hall. "Call an ambulance! Get a goddamn ambulance!"

The pair watching Elliot look up, then start down the hall. The rest of the team follows. They want to see the shooter. Elliot wobbles to his feet and follows.

Down the hall, the children scream in dissonant harmony. Elliot passes their room and looks in. A boy and girl. Maybe six and eight. African American. Little shoulders hunched, hands covering their faces, wet with tears. Elliot flashes on the tricycle in the yard, all pink with plastic streamers.

He reaches the bedroom door and looks over the shoulders of the clustered team members. A black man lies faceup, blood pumping from his chest onto the shag carpet. He still holds a pistol, the one that put the round into Elliot's vest.

No gang. No Mexicans. No Colombians. Just a lone African American.

Elliot turns and shuffles down the hall and out of the house. Sirens wail. Police vehicles are converging from every direction. An ambulance shrieks through the pack. Uniformed men are running up the walkway.

"What have we got?" someone yells at him.

Elliot points his thumb back over his shoulder at the house. People rush past him. He crosses the street and walks up the sidewalk. His ears still scream at him. Scores of emergency lights lap at the wet street. He reaches the van and swings the door open. Stale air pours out, full of spent cigarettes. He climbs in and picks up Sparks's clipboard. The hinged clamp at the top holds down numerous sheets of paper. The very top one is a sheet torn from a pad. It has a note scrawled in ballpoint, an address, the dope house address. Elliot lifts the note and sorts through the official paperwork underneath. He finds the address of the target residence. Same street as the note, but the house number is different. 1057 instead of 1075.

Sparks screwed up. Sparks inverted the numbers. Sparks also inverted the entire rest of his life. They hit the wrong house.

Standard policy kicks in. The supervisors isolate the team members so they can't cover their asses. Internal Affairs arrives. So does the police union. They all ask many questions. They know by now they have a disaster on their hands. Elliot describes the entire chronology of the raid. His shoulder aches. He recounts everything, except for the note on the clipboard. When they're through, he goes back to the van. It's now sealed with official tape, but he can see in through the window. The clipboard still rests on the seat, right where he left it. The note on top with the scrambled address is gone.

A week passed. The episode dominated the media. Banner headlines. Lead stories on TV. National coverage. The man they shot was black, innocent, and the single parent of the terrified children. He worked as an assembler of wiring harnesses at an electronics firm. He was greatly loved and admired.

He was also deaf.

He survived the shooting and hovered near death for days. Then he began to recover. He told a ravenous clutch of media what happened. He had felt the concussion of his door being smashed in. He owned a pistol, a properly registered weapon. It was, after all, a bad neighborhood. He grabbed the weapon out of the drawer of a bedside table. He saw shadowy figures and flashlights. He fired. He defended himself and his children. He protected himself and his family against intruders so violent and bold that they beat his door down to gain entry.

The city's liability verged on limitless. The bureaucracy buckled and heaved. Factions formed. The current crisis became encumbered with old grudges and political agendas. Someone was going down, but who?

Elliot was on administrative leave when the attorney called, a lawyer who specialized in "police matters." A friend of the department, the lawyer said. Also a friend of the head of the police union, who had accompanied him on numerous fishing trips to Canada. The attorney took Elliot to lunch. They dined at the top of a tall building and were served by waiters in white jackets and bow ties of jet black. Elliot ordered the lobster bisque.

The attorney spoke of what a great tragedy had befallen Elliot and his fellow officers. He sympathized with Elliot and could only imagine the mental agony he must be going through. Then he moved on to the fallout, to the investigations. This was not the kind of incident that would dissolve of its own accord as it receded into the distance. The sooner the city sorted out the accountability in the police department, the better it would look. And right now, the investigative funnel was tapering down to Lieutenant Sparks. Sparks had led the operation, he had identified the target residence.

The attorney paused and gazed out the window at the sprawl of the city and the mountains beyond. He continued with a look of great sadness. Lieutenant Sparks had a wonderful record and was approaching retirement. A good cop on his way to a just reward. And now this.

A lot of people had agonized about the fate of Lieutenant Sparks, the attorney informed Elliot. They had searched mightily for a solution that would absolve this good and decent man and . . . Elliot cut him off in midsentence.

"I'm going down, right?"

The attorney affected a surprised look, but his eyes radiated relief. "Nobody's asking you to do anything," he told Elliot. "They just want you consider a certain course of action."

"Such as?"

"You need to think very carefully about the events in the van leading up to the raid," the attorney said. "It's quite possible that when Lieutenant Sparks asked you for the address of the house, you read it wrong off the paperwork on the clipboard. An honest but tragic mistake."

"And then?"

"It seems that there's an extremely attractive opening in the public safety department up at Pearson. A detective position. You'd be perfect for it. I don't see how you could miss. Neither does anyone else."

"And what if I don't want it?"

The attorney played with a silver saltshaker and then placed it back on the white starched tablecloth. "The investigation will drag on," he replied. "And from what I've heard, Sparks clearly remembers you telling him the wrong address. So do several other members of the team."

"I thought they couldn't communicate with each other about any of this."

The attorney's trimmed eyebrows furrowed into mock indignation. "Of course not," he said. Then he signaled the waiter for the bill.

———

The Chief took a stab at his key lime pie. He chewed and stared at the bright green wedge with its white cloud cover. He swallowed and grimaced. "Terrible. Not like Baghdad. We did it right over there." He looked at his watch. "Gotta go." He stood, then looked at Elliot. "You've got one job right now, and one job only. Don't screw it up."

Elliot watched the Chief plod away through the cafeteria. Briefly, he considered quitting, but stuffed it. He hadn't been here long enough. He had accepted the deal, and now he had to let it play out for a decent interval. Either that or work the order window at a fast-food joint. Noble poverty made for great reading but very ugly living. His cell phone snapped him out of it. His ring tone was a rap loop. Did somebody like Dr. Dre get a cut every time he got a call?

"Elliot here."

"Elliot, it's Christie."

"Hi. Are you okay?"

"Not really. Would you mind coming by?"

Which would mean shoving the dog aside for the afternoon and directly violating the Chief's unambiguous mandate. Which would put his whole economic future in jeopardy.

"Sure. Just give me directions."

CHAPTER 17

The dog rose and stretched. She shook the remnants of rain off her black coat. She looked over the top of the brush, through the chain-link fence and into the yard. The damp grass glowed with the light of late afternoon. The patio remained vacant, the sliding glass door shut. She would soon abandon her watch. She would take her failed enterprise back into the woods, into the dying light and struggle on against the bitter calculus of declining sustenance.

The sliding glass door opened. She crouched into concealment and watched with her ears perked and tail extended. The woman came out, set down a new bowl of food, then went back in. The dog moved immediately to the cavity she had excavated beneath the fence. She crouched down and squirmed on through. The fence's weave of cold wire scraped over her back. The wet earth slid beneath her belly. She headed straight for the bowl. She knew she had little time and substantial risk.

She just made it to the bowl when the barking

exploded from within the house. The Rottweiler flung itself against the sliding door. Its toenails clicked and scratched against the glass surface. It lunged and thrust each bark directly at her. Its lips were curled and its teeth set in a murderous array.

She wolfed down the food in great gulps, but had to pause to grind up the dry dog food that made up the bulk of her prize. All the while she watched the Rottweiler straining at the glass. Then the woman appeared out of the interior darkness and stared at her. A permanent scowl pushed the woman's mouth into a plunging crescent. Hard, mean little eyes remarkably like her dog's poked out from vacant hollows.

The dog wolfed the last bite as the woman reached to open the door. The dog pivoted and ran. She bolted for the fence, the avenue of escape. The door scraped open behind her on its aluminum track. The barking burst out and filled the yard with rage. Territory and food, both violated.

The dog reached her hole as the Rottweiler streaked across the yard to assault her. She plunged in. She squirmed frantically forward. She twisted her torso and pushed hard with her hind legs. She popped through and shoved herself up. The Rottweiler dove into the hole. Its teeth came down on the hock of her right rear leg, just above the paw. Pain stabbed through her. She pulled to escape, but the beast had her fast. He began to drag her backward into the hole. Her front paws gouged tracks in the soil that marked her retreat.

She had only one weapon left. Her free rear leg. She dug it into the ground and propelled a load of dirt back into the Rottweiler's eyes. It took the beast by surprise: it blinked for an instant and relaxed its bite. She pulled free and scrambled out of the hole.

She turned to face the Rottweiler. Its massive head protruded through the fence. Its powerful black body heaved and strained, but moved it no further. It barked savagely.

She turned and limped off into the woods with her full belly and a minor wound. She flopped down out of sight of the house and licked the wound clean. The pain receded.

The light began to fade. The city rumbled vaguely in the distance. She rolled onto her side to sleep. And dream.

The glass door opened. Zainah came out with the bowl of food and stroked her flank as she put it down. She ate and ate, but the bowl never emptied.

CHAPTER 18

Elliot drove through the dusty light of late afternoon along the ridgetop high above the valley. He kept trying to justify bringing a departmental vehicle on this trip, but it wasn't working. He gave up when he turned down the street leading to her address. It wound past one affluent monstrosity after another. Monuments to capital gains and surging equities. He pulled into her driveway and parked in the third slot.

He started up the curved walkway of contoured cement. A dense heat filled the air, a seasonal aberration. It felt thick as midsummer. He punched the doorbell and waited. The house was ashen stucco with tile roofing of terra-cotta. Two full floors comfortably snuggled into the contours of the hillside.

"Hi, Elliot. Come on in." She wore a plain white shirt, a simple gold chain and tight-fitting jeans with high heels. "Thanks for taking the time to do this."

"No problem," he lied. She led him through the ante-room and past a sunken living room of the kind never used.

They came into a big kitchen with industrial-strength appliances of beefy metal.

"Would you like something to drink?" she asked.

"Just a little water."

"Is that because you're still on duty?"

Elliot shrugged. "Something like that."

She smiled as if endowed with some special wisdom. She looked down at her watch, a slim band of precious metal. "Not anymore you're not. It's time for a glass of wine. Red or white?"

"Red."

She moved toward a cabinet of antique oak. "Red, of course. Guys always want red."

She poured their wine and steered them out onto a big deck off the kitchen. They sunk into padded chairs framed with tropical hardwood. They sipped in silence. The gush of distant traffic drifted up from the valley. The coastal range spilled a long shadow over the grid. Then she spoke. Her eyes never left the view.

"I don't want you to think I'm weak because I called you."

"I never thought that."

"Did you think it back then?"

"No, I didn't."

"You thought I was a slave to my ambition. I know you did."

"I might have thought that later, yes. But not at the time."

She turned to him. "And what do you think right now?"

He sipped before he answered. "I think you're a little overwhelmed by everything. But that won't last. You'll move forward. That's what you're all about, moving forward."

"That doesn't sound very nice."

"Sorry, I didn't mean it that way. You're strong, you're independent. You'll find a way to resolve it all."

"You really think so?"

"Yes, I do."

She stared down into her glass. All that remained was a little lens of golden liquid centered at the bottom. "I'm not so sure. Pearson's a very complicated place. You know that by now, don't you?"

"I knew it right from the start. The only difference is that now I'm living it."

"When I married Jim, I immediately got pegged as a trophy wife. I knew that's what would happen. I was prepared for it. Any social position I had was secondhand through him. So I worked really hard to redeem myself. I thought I could dig my way out."

"Did you?"

"I thought I did. The day that Jim collapsed, I got all kinds of support and sympathy. At least for a while. But not anymore."

"Why not?"

"Because people have now fulfilled their requisite social obligation. They've said all the right things. They've done all the right stuff. They're off the hook. Which leaves me with only my truest of friends."

"And which ones are those?"

"I don't know. They haven't told me." She laughed bitterly. "I expect they'll get in touch any time now."

"Could I be one of them?"

"You've always been one of them. You just didn't know it."

She suddenly looked away. She'd moved them somewhere they shouldn't be, and was rapidly retreating. She pointed to his wine. "Are you through? Let me take your glass."

A diversionary move, and slightly clumsy, even by Elliot's standards. He'd never seen her flustered. He handed her his glass and she hurried off to the kitchen.

He sat back in his chair and lost himself in the blaze of the setting sun. He dared not think. All the options, all the alternatives would overwhelm him. The air was absolutely still. It had drizzled earlier and the afternoon heat clung to the memory of it. The trees and shrubs on either side of the deck shut out the neighborhood beyond. They hung limp and green in the sudden warmth. He stared down at the rolling boil of life in the valley below, then shut his eyes.

Her returning footsteps brought him out of it. She passed him and stopped by the railing and looked down at the valley.

"It's getting late," she said. "Maybe we should talk again some other time." She turned to him. "Would that be okay?"

"That would be fine."

It wasn't fine at all, and they both knew it. They wanted to talk right now, and maybe move on to other things as well, but they couldn't.

On the way out, Elliot looked for something that would break the tension and resolve their parting. In the anteroom, he spotted a photo of a large house perched on an arid hillside.

"Is that your summer place?"

"That's our place, but it's more winter than summer."

"California?"

"It's on the southern tip of Baja in Mexico. Cabo San Lucas. It was nice. We had some interesting times there."

"You think it's all over?"

"You saw him. What do you think?"

Elliot saw the opening. He took it. "There's something I think you should know about his medical situation. There may be something wrong with his CT scans."

"How so?"

"I was working on this case involving a stolen laptop. I came across a CT scan with his name on it as the patient. It doesn't look like a stroke at all."

"How would you know that? Been going to night school in neurology?"

"I took it to a radiologist I know."

"Someone at Pearson?"

"Irene Walters. She said it definitely wasn't a stroke."

"Then what was it?"

"She's doesn't know. She's checking on it."

"How do you know it's his image and not somebody else's? In case you haven't heard, hospitals do screw up now and then."

"I don't know that. But I'd like to find out."

Christie closed her eyes for a moment and then she opened them. "Look, I really don't care. I see him every day. There's nothing left in there. I don't need a CT scan to tell me that. It doesn't matter what happened, because he's gone. I need to come to terms with it. I need to start over. The last thing I need is some excuse to go into denial. So do me a favor and forget about it."

"Sorry. I thought you should know."

"I already know way too much, believe me."

She opened the door and the warm evening spilled in. "I shouldn't see you again. Take care, Elliot."

"You, too," Elliot said.

Her words implied he had little say in the matter, and he knew that was true. They parted without touching.

He climbed into the SUV, backed out and started up the hill. A big BMW passed him going down, a brand-new sedan of smoky silver. He tracked it in his rearview mirror and watched as it pulled into Christie's driveway. He slowed to watch who got out, but then thought better of it. He was already far too enmeshed. He continued on up the hill and turned onto the main road.

———

"Who was that in the campus cop car?" Hoffner asked.

"An old friend," Christie replied. "From a long time ago."

"Just a social visit?"

Christie hesitated. "Not exactly."

"What do you mean?"

"He's an investigator. He stumbled onto a screwup in Jim's CT scans. He seems to think that some of them are phony."

"Oh yeah? How could he know that? Does he read CT scans in his spare time?"

"He took them to a radiologist."

"At Pearson?"

"A woman named Irene Walters. You know her?"

"No, I don't. But it doesn't matter. I sincerely doubt that there's any problem."

"Good. He's just trying to be helpful, that's all."

"Well, good for him. However, I do have a suggestion."

"What's that?"

"Next time he wants to talk, make sure you get your attorney involved."

"Isn't that going to look a little suspicious?"

"Maybe. But consider the consequences."

Christie did just that.

"I see your point."

The Main Duck pumped out a stupendous string of quacks just as Elliot arrived home. It resided in an artificial pond that ran down the middle of his apartment complex. The pond had quickly attracted a population of mallards that continuously cruised its length. Spring spawned little linear fleets of baby ducks that paddled these waters behind their mothers. The males retired to the banks and surveyed their reproductive handiwork. They seemed quite content, except for the Main Duck. He continually monitored the whole population, looking for trouble. He seemed to find it several times each day, and on each occasion his powerful quacking reverberated through the entire complex.

Elliot walked through the little square between his building and the next one. A woman in her early thirties approached from the opposite direction. An attractive woman. A woman with no wedding ring. She held a leash attached to a small dog, the kind that shivered even in warm weather. Elliot smiled and nodded as he walked by her. He didn't speak. That seldom seemed to work for him. Still, he couldn't help but speculate. It would be a great stroke of luck to encounter someone right now, someone who might pull him out of his spiral into Christie. At the very least, it would give him some interesting options.

"Hi, how are you?" the woman asked.

Unbelievable. It never happened this way. "I'm fine," Elliot responded. "What kind of dog is that?"

"It's a Chihuahua," the woman told him. "I live in 403."

Incredible. She was confident enough to tell him where she lived after only ten seconds of conversation. He had no idea how to respond. It didn't matter. She moved right ahead.

"The neighbors have been pretty good," she said. "I've gotten a little loud now and then. It's the panic attacks. Someone called the cops once, but we worked it all out."

"Are you feeling better?" Elliot asked cautiously.

"Yeah, a little. But I still have times when it happens all over again."

"What happens?"

She nodded at her dog, which was sniffing the flower bed. "He's a replacement for my last dog. It was a Chihuahua, too, but it was attacked by a pit bull and died. Sometimes it just happens all over again."

"Wow, that's terrible," Elliot said with genuine sympathy.

"It's okay," she said serenely. "I've come to understand what it was all about. That little dog was Jesus, and I'm Mary. That little dog died to save us all, and that makes me the mother of our salvation. I can live with that."

Elliot scanned her eyes as she talked, looking for some hint of dark humor. He found none.

"It's good that you've found a solution for yourself," he said. "Not everybody does."

"I know that," she said. "Goodbye now."

"Goodbye."

She gave a slight tug on the leash and the little dog followed her back toward the water feature.

The Main Duck quacked once more, sounding like an air horn blasting through a rubber sphincter. Elliot walked up the steps and into the solitude of his apartment. It was chilly inside. He always turned down the heat while he was gone. He took off his coat and went to the thermostat and brought it back up. He turned the corner into the little galley kitchen and immediately spotted the note. It was propped up against the faucet on the kitchen sink. Big capital letters off an inkjet printer of some kind:

DON'T FUCK UP. DO WHAT YOU'RE SUPPOSED TO AND FORGET ABOUT EVERYTHING ELSE. YOUR FUTURE DEPENDS ON IT.

He did a quick sort. The paper was undoubtedly some garden-variety stock. No watermark. Untraceable. Same for the font. He went back to the front door, opened it, and inspected the lock and the strike plate. Clean. He went back and read the note again. The wording was vague, yet the message was clear. It was an encapsulation of the Chief's admonishment: Drop the medical records thing, or else.

He took the note from behind the sink and sat down with it at his little dining table. He seriously doubted that it came from the Chief, who was far too cautious to directly implicate himself in something like this. But then again, the Chief might have made some secondhand comments to certain individuals downtown who would have all the necessary skills to make this type of delivery.

But why? Why raise the ante over Oakner's medical records to the level of extortion? Did the CT scan point to something much larger? Was he in way over his head without even knowing it?

That night, he dreamed badly. He wandered through the charred wreckage in the desert and came upon the van with the carbonized corpse. Its blackened arm crumbled to a fine powder, which fell upon two children huddled in the sand below. They screamed. The powder turned their skin several shades darker. They became the children in the dope house.

Then the quacking started, and the children stopped to listen.

Elliot awakened in the dark to the bellowing of the Main Duck. He knew the probable cause. Nocturnal predators were cruising the pond outside. Cats, raccoons, opossums. All had the same ambitions.

CHAPTER 19

The dog moved among the mottled shadows cast by the dense canopy overhead. Its leaves intercepted the sun's radiance and kept the ground cool and moist. She stopped and sniffed the air. It rose off a big field below, a field she couldn't yet see. It rode on the warm up-draft off grass heated by the afternoon sun and carried a massive collection of dog scent that told the story of hundreds of animals. She felt compelled to add her own story and continued on through the curled carpet of ivy. She picked up little bursts of barking. They resonated in mid-spectrum and rolled out in a relaxed cadence. Something inside her quickened.

She reached the bottom of the slope and looked across the field and the park. She remained in shadow while she collected her observations. The afternoon heat continued to cook the big expanse of newly mown grass. It threw wave after wave of olfactory impressions at her. A small dog trotted toward the middle of the field, a dog long in the ears and short in the legs. The dog was female and emitted brief barks of pleasure. A mid-size human, a male by smell, followed behind the animal. The breeze carried a whiff of leather and rubber from his shoes. A blue plastic rod hung from his hand. The bottom portion contained a scoop holding a tennis ball.

She looked beyond the pair and saw three other people. They sat on a bench and fetched food from a woven basket. A man, a woman, and a girl similar in size to the boy. They jabbered and laughed, and the meaning of it escaped her. No one here talked like Zainah did.

The boy raised his arm and swung the rod with the tennis ball. The little dog took off running. The ball left the scoop. It sailed through the warm spring air and its seams rotated lazily across the hemisphere facing the sun.

Primal forces assembled themselves within the dog. The imperatives of her breed bubbled to the surface. The ball became her world. She must have it. She must track its airborne trajectory, mark the place where it lands and then run it down. She must feel its fuzzy texture in the grip of her jaws.

She left the shadows' concealment and leapt into the light. She tracked the ballistic curve of the ball's travel and sped toward it. Her jaws parted. She concentrated intently on the point of impact.

The ball landed and bounced. The little dog sprang into the air and snagged it before it reached the ground.

The dog watched the clean intercept by the smaller animal. She slowed to a disappointed walk and circled as the other dog sprinted back to the boy. She noted how the dog stopped in front of him, dropped the ball, and sat.

The instant the boy picked up the ball, she understood the cycle. She formed a line of sight from the boy along the probable path of the ball. She began to trot toward the circle of probability where it would land. The little dog came to its feet, but waited for the ball's release. The boy swung the blue rod in a smooth stroke and launched the ball. The dog broke into a full run. She hurtled toward the ball's descent and was upon it on the first bounce after it landed. She caught it in her open jaws, but restrained her bite on its fuzzy skin. Her genes demanded it be done this way.

She circled back toward the boy and felt a great glow come across her. The smaller dog moved out of her path and sat in confusion. She reached the boy, dropped the ball, and sat.

"Hey, where'd you come from?"

"Can you share with Sadie?" He picked up the ball and pointed at the small animal, which was walking back toward them.

The boy's dialogue mystified her, but his actions spoke quite clearly. They formed symbols that presented a proposition. She acknowledged with a single nod of her head, just as Zainah had taught her.

The boy seemed delighted. "You got that, huh? Okay, let's see."

She moved to the side and sat again. He hurled the ball once more. She remained sitting and watched the little dog bound after it. It snagged the ball on the third bounce. The boy didn't even notice. He was staring at her.

"Wow. That was so cool. Who taught you how to wait like that?"

The little dog returned and dropped the ball. The boy spoke to it as he picked up the ball. "Okay, Sadie, this time you wait." He looked over to her, nodded and sent the ball winging through the air. She launched herself as he started his throw. The little dog did likewise.

"Sadie, stop!"

She knew the command was directed at the other dog, which ignored it and surged on. She broke into a full gallop and pulled far ahead. All the while, she computed the landing spot for the ball and adjusted accordingly. Her nose pointed directly along the curve of its descent. She caught it in midair before it landed, then circled back. She dropped the ball before the boy and sat.

"Okay, Sadie, you go now." He launched the ball and the little dog ran in happy pursuit. She and the boy watched the smaller creature chase down the ball and return. And so the cycle of fetching played out beneath the afternoon sun. In time, both dogs grew weary and rested on their haunches. The boy turned and walked toward his family on the bench. The little dog followed.

The dog hesitated a moment and watched the pair departing the field. She felt drawn to their pack. She rose and followed at a respectful distance. The boy sat down on the bench next to his sister, who passed him a paper bag containing food. The little dog rested at his feet. She sat down a few yards from the family and watched. The little dog's snout tracked every motion of the boy removing and eating the food.

The girl fished a piece of food from her bag and showed it to the little dog. "Sadie, you want a bite?" The animal hopped up and went to her. It sat facing her and brimmed with expectation. "What do you do, Sadie? What do you do?" The dog reared back on its haunches, raised its forelegs, tucked them in and curled its paws downward. "Good doggie!" The girl pitched the food chunk. The little dog sprang up and caught it and wolfed it down. "Want more?" The ritual played out once again.

The dog took in the detail from where she sat. She noted the chain of cause and effect. She dwelt on the net result. The paper bags swelled with food, and its scent bubbled out and spilt down like water from a fountain. It rolled to her over the grass and demanded action.

She got up and walked to the bench. The adult male smiled at her approach. "Pretty doggie!" She sat in front of him and waited for the presentation of the food chunk. "You want a little bite? Is that what you want?" She carefully emulated the smaller dog's behavior. She perked her ears and rose to full sitting height. He produced a chunk of food. She reared back onto her haunches. She raised her forelegs and depressed her paws. "Well, alright." He tossed it to her. She lunged just slightly and wolfed it down.

"She doesn't have a collar," the wife observed. "I can't believe someone would have a dog like that and not have a collar."

"Maybe she lost it," the daughter said. "Come here, girl."

The dog began to move in front of the daughter. The little dog intercepted her. They moved off a ways and played and sniffed. She retained the image of the daughter and her food bag. She would pursue it at a later moment.

A park attendant pulled his pickup alongside the garbage container located next to the family. He spotted the dog without a collar as he climbed out. He had been trained to do so. Park policy forbade unlicensed animals. He walked over to the family and pointed to the romping dogs.

"Those both your animals?"

"Nope," the father answered. "Just the little one."

"I'd be careful," the attendant warned. "I don't see a collar on the Lab. It might not have all its shots."

"I bet it does," the wife responded. "It's a beautiful dog. Somebody's been taking good care of it."

The attendant pulled absently on the bill of his cap. "Yeah, well, you gotta hope so. You folks have a nice day."

The attendant turned to empty the garbage into a trash bag. The family packed up to leave.

"Can we take her home with us?"

"No, sweetie. She belongs to somebody, and they're probably looking for her."

The attendant kept track of the dog while he emptied the other containers around the field. Nobody came to claim her. She slowly circled the field, sniffing as she went.

The dog watched the attendant's progress around the park. He emptied one container after another into trash bags and piled them into the bed of the pickup. He systematically eliminated any possibility of retrieving food. She left the field for the cover of the woods and headed back up the slope.

The attendant climbed into his truck. He turned the radio to a country station. The morning shift always left it on heavy metal, which he hated. He made a note to phone animal control about the dog.

CHAPTER 20

Richard Stennis pushed his chair over the wooden deck and into the shadow cast by the superstructure's overhang. He emptied a can of Sapporo into a tall glass and waited for the foam to settle. Japanese beer on a Norwegian boat in a Mexican port. The new global economic order had come to Cabo San Lucas.

From his position on the stern, he watched the tourists and vendors on the big walkway that bordered the marina. It was calm today, hot and dry and clear. The blue Pacific sprawled to the distant horizon. A sharp and cloudless crease delineated sea and sky. He imagined that it was probably raining up at Pearson. A cold, wet spring rain. The timing for his two-month sabbatical was perfect. The big work back at the lab was in a holding pattern until he completed his transaction with Becker, so they could afford to march on without him in the driver's seat for a while.

He sipped his beer and nudged his sandals on and off over his toes. All the while, he envisioned a tiny, dense network of pathways and the furious pace of travel over them.

They existed only in the abstract, but performed very real functions. Each represented the journey of certain molecules between the cells in a human embryo. Once the molecules arrived at their destination, they joined with others to form a great chorus of creation. A foot became a foot. An eye became an eye. Destiny became reality.

As he traveled the pathways, he scaled up and down the hierarchy from atoms to organisms. He did so with a grace and ease that few of his peers could match. It gave him extraordinary powers of perception and insight. The molecular networks were dauntingly complex. Most resided outside the realm of known science. He sometimes entertained the thought that they were indeed a miracle, a phenomenon beyond conceptual grasp. Then some small bit of revelation would present itself and he would press on.

A big motor yacht made its way through the marina and past his mooring. He reflexively compared it to his own boat. It lost. A 60-foot hull and twin diesels gave him a distinctly elevated worldview. Still, he had recently attended a party on a 105-foot boat at the other end of the marina. When he returned to his own vessel, he was struck by how cramped the stateroom appeared. Some would not notice, like the coeds he trolled for during spring break. But more discerning guests would immediately spot the difference.

Back to the molecular networks and their attendant signal channels. He suspected some sort of protocol, just as in a digital network. But protocols devised by humans were anthropocentric in nature. One thing told another thing that a message was coming. Another thing understood that it could now talk because some other thing was through talking. However, the protocol he had in mind would be a product of evolution and very opaque to human understanding.

He would have to excavate through millions of years of refinement to crack it.

He was further along on cracking the problem of the bigger boat. He had done a cost analysis that pumped in all the usual variables. A hundred-foot hull was within fiscal range. Maintenance and crew costs would scale up, but the curve was less than exponential. Financing was no problem. Becker would see to that. The bigger problem was human perception. People at Pearson knew about his current boat, but it could be explained away. An inherited windfall. Fortuitous investments. The indulgent economics of bachelorhood. The larger boat raised a whole new set of questions. Massive boats required massive money. Not the kind a scientist would accumulate through pure research. Questions might be asked. Official queries might arise.

Stennis took a more substantial sip of beer and settled back in the chair with its handcrafted cushions. He pondered the most ingenious synthesis of all, a strategy that would solve both biochemical and boat problems in a simultaneous and complementary manner.

It started with stem cells, the target of both blind outrage and exorbitant expectations. His early work had focused on intracellular metabolic pathways, but he soon saw the emerging opportunity and switched his focus. Stem cells were simple in concept and enormously complex in practice. About a week after fertilization, a human egg becomes a spherical mass of about one hundred and fifty cells. A blastocyst. The outer lining goes on to become the placenta and the inner cell mass goes on to become the baby. But not yet. These inner cells are still blanks, each identical to its neighbor. It will be another week or so before they start to organize themselves into the primitive germ layers that spawn into the grand collection of organs that comprise an individual human. At this point, the cells of this inner mass hold only potential, like the stem of a plant waiting to become fully realized as branches, leaves, shoots and blossoms. Hence the name, stem cells. If you breach the blastocyst, you can extract these cells and install them in a hospitable environment. You now have a culture that allows these cells to divide and multiply. Each retains the capacity to become virtually any part of the human assemblage. Each is termed pluripotent. Each represents the ultimate replacement part in the event of disease or injury. Need a new liver? Just coax a few stem cells down that path. In time, they deliver a new one. And so on.

But the coaxing turned out to be an enormous pitfall, both in the lab and inside humans. The required stimulus was subtle and extremely complex. It involved large numbers of genes and their resultant proteins. No one really knew how many. Erroneous stimulation also held the potential for all kinds of disasters. It might trigger faulty cues and take off in multiple directions, all wrong. The result would be a grisly thing called a teratoma, such as human teeth forming inside a liver instead of new liver tissue. Or they might go completely rogue and form a malignant tumor full of runaway cancer cells.

Still, it was widely thought that stem cells placed in the right tissue at the right time would act in a completely natural manner and quickly transform themselves into copies of their neighbors. But that still left the problem of rejection by the immune system. The surface of the injected stem cells would contain molecular shapes called antigens. The immune system would quickly determine that these particular antigens were alien, and destroy them.

The politics of stem cells rivaled the science in terms of difficulty. Most stem cells owed their origin to embryonic fetuses, the by-product of in vitro fertilization procedures. It started with eggs extracted and fertilized with sperm in the lab for transplantation back into the womb. As a hedge against failure, multiple eggs underwent this process. The unused ones were frozen for future attempts; some became the source of blastocysts for stem cells. And here the debate departed from science and entered the volatile realm of religion, philosophy and politics. Was emergent life being sacrificed in the name of technological progress? Or was a small collection of identical cells no more than just that? While a blastocyst gave no hint as to what it would become, some argued that its very potential made it human. It became a matter of interpretation, a subjective matter, an explosive matter. To compound the problem, the field was tainted by the Korean scandal. There, data was faked concerning the creation of cloned stem cells. Different governments and societies reacted in different ways. An entire spectrum of regulation evolved, from moderate to extreme. A great global migration of research and funding commenced.

Some time back, Stennis had conducted a thought experiment. First, he framed the problem. Regulation of stem cell research made moral sense. Even the vast majority of scientists agreed on that point. But regulation also restricted certain avenues, avenues that might yield extremely valuable data. It was all a matter of degree. Some procedures were simply out of the question. Others inhabited a gray area that was more a matter of personal conscience. Still, any legitimate research effort needed to adhere to the regulatory guidelines of its host country. It was the only way to obtain funding and participate in the mainstream scientific community, where results were published and data freely exchanged.

Or was it? What if there was a way to benefit from unregulated work that pushed at the edges of the gray area? The data might be extremely useful, even critical. And what if this data could then be incorporated into legitimate, mainstream research programs in a subtle manner that hid its origins? Potential dead ends could be avoided. Useful protocols refined. It might even win the race to develop therapeutic agents worth great fortunes.

For the sake of security, the link between the overt and covert operations would have to be very limited and circumspect. Perhaps restricted to only the project's principal investigator, who could guide the course of the research with the dual sources of knowledge. And of course, the money people. You always had to contend with the money people. But money people were very good at keeping secrets.

He took another sip of beer and felt the foam kiss his upper lip. Ironically, his entire line of thought might be well on its way to obsolescence, but not soon enough. The latest research demonstrated that perhaps you could avoid the morally contentious embryo issue all together. By adding some DNA to one of a person's skin cells, it seemed that you could turn it into a stem cell. If cells of this type proved viable, both the embryo problem and tissue rejection problem would be solved in a single stroke. But for now, the discovery itself was in an embryonic stage. It would be years—if ever—before it became a workable methodology.

And Stennis didn't have years. In fact, he might have only a few months.

Still, the day was warm, and the beer immersed him in a pleasant buzz. An almost perfect world.

Except, of course, for Oakner and the dog.

CHAPTER 21

"A re we through yet?" Bobby Seifert asked. He was only half joking.

"We'll be through when we find the dog," Elliot answered. They were both staring at their respective computer displays. Elliot drank coffee. Bobby munched on a cookie and gulped a soda of some sort.

"And what if we never find the dog?" Bobby asked.

"Then we'll never be through."

"Even if the Chief resigns or dies or something?"

"That's very wishful thinking, Bobby." Elliot sympathized. They had already waded through a dozen websites connected to lost dogs. Each website had to be searched and then contacted by phone. This meant the inevitable journey through an automated phone tree to reach a human being. All for nothing, so far. No female black Labs on tap anywhere.

Elliot's cell phone erupted in hip-hop. He perked up. They'd left numerous voice messages during the quest. Maybe this was the call, the one where they had precisely the dog he was looking for. "Lieutenant Elliot here."

"Elliot, it's Irene Walters over in radiology."

"Dr. Walters, how are you?"

"I'm fine. I'm calling about the CT scan of Jim Oakner, the one you gave me. I caught a lucky break and now I know what caused what we're seeing in the image. It's a little complicated to discuss on the phone. Could you come by for a few minutes?"

No, he couldn't. He was dedicated to the search for the dog. That was written in bureaucratic stone.

"I'll be right over."

——

Michael Hoffner stared at his reflection in his office window and used it to adjust the knot in his Charvet tie while he spoke on the satellite phone. "I recently had a conversation with Oakner's widow—"

"He's not dead yet," Becker interrupted. "You only wish he was."

"In any case," Hoffner continued, unruffled, "there's a complication with his medical records."

"I thought that was all put to bed."

"It was, but then someone discovered the original CT scan. Purely by accident."

"And who might this someone be?"

"That's the problem. He's an investigator for the Department of Public Safety up here. A guy named Elliot. He's a low-level campus cop trying to play detective. He showed the scan to someone in radiology."

"Elliot?"

"Yes, Elliot." Hoffner waited. Becker was obviously writing it down. "He's the only investigator we've got. Which means he's also the one in charge of finding the dog."

"He must be a very busy man, then. And who's the radiologist?"

"A Dr. Irene Walters. So far, we're okay. There's no way they're going to get to Lepert. He's fat and happy and completely out of reach. If the doctor comes up with anything, we may have to compensate her as well. But I highly doubt it. What happened is just too rare."

"I don't want you to take any action. None at all. You're not qualified for this kind of thing. You're an administrator, a dispenser of funding. We can't expose you to any further risk."

"I agree. But then how do we cover ourselves?"

"Don't worry. It will all be tracked independently. That's all you need to know."

"That's all I want to know."

"Very good. You're starting to get the idea."

CHAPTER 22

Elliot peered at the CT scan on Dr. Walters's computer display, not sure which image he was looking at. He was rapidly gaining respect for the discipline of radiology. "This is the one I found on the flash drive?"

"That's right," Irene Walters replied. "There's no way I would have pegged it. It was Dr. Takumura who spotted it."

"Who's that?"

"He's a radiologist from Japan. He was part of a group attending a seminar here at the department. He came into the conference room when I had your image up on the screen. He had a look, and knew immediately what it was."

"How could he do that?"

"He's part of a small group in Tokyo that has studied something called the interval form of carbon monoxide poisoning. It's extremely rare and not that well understood. Remember when we looked before and I pointed to this area here?" Her finger went to the frontal portion of the image. "We talked about the low density in the white matter, which meant that the brain's wiring in this area had been pretty much destroyed. It's a classic symptom in carbon monoxide cases. Dr. Takumura spotted the pattern right off the bat."

"Carbon monoxide poisoning? Isn't that what happens when people commit suicide in their cars?"

"Precisely. But these particular cases have a very strange and bizarre twist to them. What happens is this: An individual attempts suicide by piping exhaust into a car or some other enclosed space. But someone finds them in a comatose state and calls for emergency medical services. They're rushed to the hospital and put in a hyperbaric oxygen chamber, which floods their brain with oxygen, which counteracts the poisoning. In a few days, they recover completely and go home. Good as new. For most of them, that's the end of the story. But in a very few cases, things take a really nasty turn. After a week or a month or so of complete normalcy, they suddenly lapse back into a coma."

"Do they recover again?"

"Nope. This time, they're cooked. In fact, they were cooked all along, but there was no way to tell."

"You're sure about this?"

"Dr. Takumura said it wasn't definitive proof, but it very strongly pointed to the interval form of poisoning. He's looked at hundreds of images involving this malady, so I think it's a pretty safe bet. An MRI image would give us more information, but if this is really Oakner's image, it doesn't matter. The damage is irreversible."

"So Oakner may have tried to kill himself in his car a month or so before he actually collapsed in surgery?"

"That's what this image says."

"Somehow, I doubt that people around here would look very kindly upon something like that."

"Not in the least," Dr. Walters agreed. "You'd be ruined professionally. You'd never practice again. No one would license you. No one would insure you."

"For now, I think we need to stay in a holding pattern," Elliot said. "I don't even know if we're looking at the real image. Maybe he just had a stroke. Maybe this is all some kind of screwup."

Dr. Walters pointed to the poisoned brain on the screen. "On the other hand, if it isn't a screwup, you've got a ton of work ahead of you. A lot of people up here aren't going to want to hear about this. You know that, don't you?"

Elliot did know it. He knew it all too well.

Elliot left the radiology department and started down the hill to the human resources department. What if Oakner really did attempt suicide? Where did that leave Christie? Did she know about it? How could she not? Also, how could they hide it? There would be police reports, emergency room documentation, medical records. It couldn't be done. That meant the CT scan with the carbon monoxide poisoning must be bogus. But where did it come from? All trails led back to Samuel Lepert, the IT guy who had the discarded flash drive in the first place.

Elliot stepped up to the desk at HR and waited for the receptionist to get off the phone. She was a goth girl. Black hair, black lips, multiple piercings. Proof of diversity and tolerance in the campus HR organization. She looked up at him. "Can I help you?"

"Yes, I'm from Public Safety and I'd like to speak to Latisha Williams." He knew her from a petty theft case where they terminated a cafeteria worker a while back.

"I'm sorry, she's no longer with this department."

Her response was the standard script in cases where

the individual had been fired. Elliot wondered how you fired someone whose job was firing people. He also wondered what the goth girl did on Halloween. He gave her his card.

"I need to talk to whoever processes people when they leave from the IT group."

The goth girl seemed quite interested in his card. Was it some kinky police thing? Or was she just bored? "Is somebody in trouble?" she wanted to know.

"No. Nothing like that. It's just a routine follow-up thing."

Minutes later, he sat in the office of Joshua Harper, a mid-level HR manager. The man used a lot of hair gel. He scrutinized Elliot's card carefully. "Is this an official investigation?" he asked.

Damn. He would have to put it that way. "I suppose you could call it that," Elliot answered.

"Our privacy policy makes it quite clear that Mr. Lepert's records are available only through an official written request," Harper informed him. "I'm sure you understand. I mean, you wouldn't want someone casually going through your records, would you?"

"Absolutely not," Elliot replied. "And I don't need all that, anyway. Let me ask a couple of general questions. If they're out of bounds, just let me know. Did you conduct an exit interview with Mr. Lepert?"

"Yes, I did."

"Did he give any specific reason for leaving?"

"No, as a matter of fact, he didn't. I believe he simply wanted to pursue other opportunities."

"Were you aware that he had some very ambitious travel plans?"

"No."

"And that he was going to be gone for over a year?"

"No."

"Would his salary and vacation time allow for something like that? Probably not, right?"

Harper folded his hands in a very official manner. "Given the nature of the subject matter under question, I'm going to have to terminate this interview. If you want to obtain any further information, you will have to follow the policies and procedures in our official guidelines."

"Of course," Elliot conceded.

The photo on the wall. There it was again. It punched big holes in his walk back to his office from HR. It wouldn't stay away. It kept rudely pushing back into the center of his attention. The big house by the sea in Cabo San Lucas. The winter refuge of the good doctor and his wife. Every few steps, it intruded a bit more and Elliot knew precisely why. The photograph provided a plausible explanation of the CT scan with the poisoned brain. It created a way for Dr. James Oakner to attempt suicide and avoid a trail of records of the kind you would find in the U.S. Which meant that Christie might be deceiving him.

So, now what? He could confront her about it. They could sit out on the deck and have a nice glass of wine and he could ask her point-blank, *Did your husband try to kill himself? And now that I said that, might you still have a thing for me?*

Not yet. He needed more information. He opened his cell phone and dialed a number in the police department downtown.

"Central Precinct."

"Yes, Lieutenant Sparks, please."

A pause, a ring, and a classic monotone cop answer. "Sparks here."

"It's Elliot."

It took Sparks a beat to recover. Elliot liked that. "Elliot. How you doing?"

"I need a favor. An easy one."

"Okay. What can I do for you?"

"I need a foreign travel rundown on two individuals. A James and Christie Oakner. Spelled just like it sounds."

"Currently in the U.S.?"

"Right here in the city. I just need coverage of the last couple of months."

"It'll take a little time, but I'll make sure you get it. How you like your job up there?" Sparks was pretending to be friendly.

"It's okay."

"Well . . . I'm glad to hear it. Anything else I can do?"

"Not right now." Elliot left it open-ended. Sparks would not be happy about that. Too bad. "I'll be waiting to hear from you," Elliot said.

"Okay then, talk to you later."

Elliot pocketed the cell phone and continued walking up the hill. He knew exactly what Sparks would do. He would talk to the feds, to the Department of Immigration. He would feed them the names. They would then scan the names against their database, which would then run through every exit and entry into the country for the past two months. If James and Christie Oakner had gone to Cabo San Lucas, it would show up.

And if they had, the logic was simple. There was a possible window of one month between Oakner's ultimate collapse and any suicide attempt through carbon monoxide poisoning. If Oakner was in Cabo San Lucas during this time, the suicide scenario became a strong contender.

Of course, there was a much simpler way to find out about a visit to Mexico. He could simply ask Christie. He could work it casually into a conversation. It wouldn't sound suspicious at all. Just a casual reference to the house in the photo.

But he wasn't going to do that. He was going to go the long way around with Sparks and the feds. Why? Because she might lie, and he didn't want to hear it. Maybe later, but not right now.

His cell phone rang. It pumped out two full measures of hip-hop before he got it out of his pocket. "Elliot here."

"Bobby here. Just got a call from animal control over at County. You might have your first big break with that missing mutt."

PART 3

You'd Better
Not Go Alone

CHAPTER 23

It was about this same time of day." The park attendant pointed to the bench as Elliot listened. "They were sitting right here. They gave the black dog a few bites of food. It didn't have a collar and they said it wasn't theirs. It backed off when I came around, then it left."

"Which way did it go?" Elliot asked.

The attendant pointed to the south, toward the slope and the woods. "It went up there. That's the last I saw of it."

Elliot handed the man his card. "If you think of anything else, or if you see it again, let me know right away, okay?"

The man read Elliot's card. "You're a detective, huh?"

"That's right."

"How come they got somebody like you out lookin' for a dog?"

"Let's just say it's a very special dog."

The attendant shrugged. "Must be."

Elliot watched the attendant drive off in his pickup full of trash bags. He looked over to the wooded slope, which led up to the campus. He felt a surge of relief. The dog was still in the proximity of the campus. It hadn't ranged out into the city or the suburbs. That was going to simplify his search greatly.

He got out his phone to call the Chief, and got the Chief's assistant. "Hi, it's Elliot. Is the Chief in?"

"Hi, Elliot, he's in a meeting. You want his voice mail?"

Not really, thought Elliot. As soon as the Chief gets the news, he'll want the dog on a platter by sundown. Not a reasonable expectation. "Okay, put me through."

He left the Chief a brief message and scanned the field one last time. Empty. He climbed into his vehicle and drove off.

───────

The dog sat in shadow and watched the second man drive off. A slight breeze brought her his smell signature. She got up and walked cautiously along the periphery of the field, past all the freshly emptied trash cans. She passed the far edge of the field and walked down a path through a stand of trees. The promise of food drifted through the air from this direction. She had been this way once before and now retraced her route. She got her bearing from the big track to her right, a compressed oval. A lone runner pounded along it.

She reached the park's edge and stood on a sidewalk bordering a wide street. A big wooden pole sprouted from the cement next to her. Its top bristled with slender wires, and its wood smelled dry and long dead. Vertical fissures covered its surface. Pieces of rectangular paper occupied its curvature. A metal box clung to its circumference several yards up.

She looked across the street and down the middle of two parallel white stripes. On the far side of the street, a similar pole pushed up. Its metal box flashed a symbolic human. She watched the icon carefully, mindful of what happened last time she was here. A car sped by as a reminder. These big machines of metal, rubber and glass had no fear. They would confront you directly, they would bear down on you, they would kill you if you didn't avoid them. But they did heed the little icon in the box. When it assumed a particular shape, the cars came to a halt, and remained docile until the icon changed once more.

The dog could now distinguish between the icons, and waited for the correct one to appear in the box. A big vehicle came to a halt just outside the white stripe. She crossed in front of it. It stank of burnt oil, leaking fuel and spent exhaust. She reached the far side and continued a short distance down the sidewalk. She had arrived at the potential food source.

A chain-link fence and an open gate stood next to the sidewalk. Both had a metal weave in a diamond pattern, like that in the Rottweiler's backyard. But these also had vertical wooden slats pushed through them to obscure the view beyond. She passed through the gate and entered the little alley inside. It spanned just a few yards, with a cement retaining wall on the side that wrapped around the rear. The back of a restaurant and its two attendant Dumpsters made up the other side. She stopped before one of the big metal containers and sniffed the remnants of the lunch trade. A big black lid topped the Dumpster and held its contents prisoner.

A gray metal door lurked on the peripheral edge of her vision, open just a crack. She recalled it from her last visit. A man had come through the door, a small man with slender arms. He had beckoned her forward, toward the great river of food scent coming from inside the building. But she had backed away and run out the gate.

Now she moved to the second Dumpster. Once again, a black lid sealed its contents. She sat and pondered it. She sensed motion in the door crack to her left, but the door itself remained mostly shut. She continued her contemplative vigil. She had inferred a presence behind the door, but knew she had a safe route of retreat.

The owner of the restaurant peeked out through the sliver of open door. Sure enough, the dog was back today and eyeing the garbage. It appeared to be an animal of some quality. Its situation reminded him of someone in formal wear waiting in line for a free meal at a charitable institution. The other day he had tried to entice it inside, but failed. Was it pride or caution? He wasn't sure. But in any case, he now had a much more workable plan. Once he'd pulled it off, he would give the dog to animal control so they could find it a decent home.

He gently closed the door and hurried through the restaurant and out the front door. He trotted to the corner of the building and turned onto the sidewalk. Here he slowed his pace. He crept up on the open gate and peeked through. Good. The dog was still there. He swiftly stepped forward and swung the gate shut. Its framing of galvanized pipe slid into the metal fork latch on the fence post with a loud *ping*.

The dog started at the noise. She twisted and saw the man staring at her through the wire mesh.

"Got you," the man said, and left.

She cautiously approached the gate and tested it. The latch held it firmly shut and was beyond the reach of her nose. She retreated into the alley and walked to the rear, where the cement retaining wall loomed to impossible heights. She was trapped.

CHAPTER 24

Christie reached out and felt the top of his hand, so cool and dry. The hospital room's fluorescent light rendered it ghostly pale. His fingers rested in perfect stillness on the bedding. Even now, they were long and graceful. The archetypal fingers of the skilled surgeon.

She withdrew her hand. The gold hoops on her wrist rearranged themselves in a delicate jangle. It triggered a recollection of how the sun had caught her jewelry that day in Cabo, the day before the disaster. She had pecked at her lunch in the restaurant above the marina. The sun had danced over the dangling surfaces of crafted gold. She had rotated their marriage in her mind and looked at it from many angles. None presented a simple solution. She'd paid for her meal, walked down the stairs and started back toward her car.

But she didn't want to go home. She wasn't ready to face him. So she turned and walked down the promenade that bordered the marina. Frigate birds circled high overhead. Boats bobbed gently at their moorings. She came upon an old Indian woman sitting on the curb next to a display of merchandise set upon a white dishtowel. Seals and tortoises carved from hardwood. Small winged dragons brightly painted and detailed. Tiny wooden turtles in greens, pinks and blues. Beaded necklaces with pendants of polished stone.

Christie picked up a necklace and examined it. The old woman smiled at her from under a hat of sun-bleached straw. A necklace strung from wooden beads rested on her blouse of shiny purple. Deep lines of age creased her brown face. Still, her eyes held the spark of purpose.

Christie wondered about the trajectory of this woman's life, the men, the children, the struggles, the failures, the resolutions. It made her retrace her own. Her mother had worked in the hospital laundry at Pearson. No one there knew this. It was Christie's secret, her shame, her triumph, her revenge. The daughter of a common laborer elevated to the top of the institution's professional aristocracy. But first, the little jobs, and the pursuit of the requisite education. Then, the struggle amidst the cubicles. The fight to be considered "strategic" instead of "tactical." Followed by the private office with its condensation of power and a clear view of the struggle on the street far below. A series of relationships with men of continually escalating substance. And then Jim. Brilliant, prosperous, renowned. An acceptable exit point for her.

At least, so it had seemed.

CHAPTER 25

Korvin heard the intruders long before they arrived. Two of them, by the sound of it. Distant murmurs threaded through the trees. They made no effort to conceal their movement. They probably thought none was necessary. They most likely viewed themselves the ultimate keepers of predatory power in this place.

He sat atop a stool fashioned from an empty can of industrial solvent. Its base sank into the mat of decaying leaves that made up the floor of his campsite. A wedge of camouflaged tarpaulin gave him shelter, and a fire pit of ringed stones provided heat for cooking. He adjusted his position on the stool and picked up a slender length of branch to whittle with his utility knife. The knife would serve the same purpose as the diversionary item in a magic trick. It would draw attention to the wrong place and the wrong action.

He whittled and listened. The distant conversation died. They intended to surprise him, to immediately put him on the defensive and keep him there. He welcomed their intrusion. They would participate in a scenario of his own design.

"Hi there, friend."

He looked up from his carving and feigned surprise. The two men wore winter jackets turned dull and greasy with grime. Unruly bushes of dirty hair burst from beneath their woolen caps. Blue carpenter's overalls spilled down to heavy construction boots. The one with the blue cap spoke first, identifying him as the alpha member of the pair. His mouth was nearly lost in his thick beard. His eyes glowed bright and cruel above his porcine nose.

"I'm afraid someone's made a big mistake," he said. "This here's our camp. Always has been."

"I'm sorry. I didn't know," Korvin responded. His voice modulated with fear and alarm. The second man with the red cap smiled at this. He twinkled with amusement. He and his companion stood about three meters away from Korvin, an ideal distance. The one with the blue cap let his eyes survey the campsite.

"That's okay. Looks like you kept it real nice for us. We were gone for a while, you see. We were guests of the state. We didn't like that very much. But now we're happy just to be home, if you know what I mean."

"Yes. That must have been difficult." Korvin folded up his utility knife as a gesture of reconciliation. "I'll just need a little time to pack my things."

"Well, ya know, I'd like to accommodate you," the blue cap said. "But we're on a schedule here, and I'm afraid there's no time for that."

"But what am I going to do?" Korvin pleaded. "I'll have nothing and no place to stay."

"You should've thought of that before you plunked

down here," the blue cap said. "I'm normally a pretty patient man, but I'm starting to run a little short here."

Korvin injected a small pause, then delivered the pivotal remark. "I'm sorry, but I can't just get up and go. I can't do that."

A challenge. A deliberately weak one, but a challenge nevertheless. The red cap lifted his jacket and removed a hunting knife from a scabbard on his belt. His alpha partner did likewise.

The pair began to separate, to encircle Korvin. It was playing out precisely as he knew it would. The great weakness of most such men was their predictability. They would move to encircle him, to where his vision could no longer embrace them both. Then they would make their move.

Korvin faced the blue cap, came off the stool, and went down to one knee, as if to be knighted. He dropped his folded knife and merged his hands together in supplication. "Please don't hurt me. I'm begging you."

The blue cap's eyes burned fiercely. They left the knife Korvin had dropped and came up to meet Korvin's eyes. He would feast on Korvin's fear and let it fuel the moment of murder.

Korvin unclasped his hands and dropped his left one to the ground for balance. His right hand went into the leaf cover and grasped the spear. He lifted it out of the leaves in a smooth arc until it reached the height of his head, then rotated his wrist so the pointed tip aimed at the blue cap's torso. He reared his throwing arm back for leverage and thrust the spear at a savage velocity.

The blue cap would never understand the nature of the weapon hurtling at him. He wouldn't know that the shaft was carefully fashioned from downed oak, a dense wood supplying the necessary mass. He wouldn't appreciate the subtle shaping that gave it the proper balance and heft. He wouldn't comprehend the design of the point, fashioned from a lawn mower blade, filed to a fine edge and carefully wound into the shaft with bailing wire.

The strength of Korvin's arm endowed the spear with sufficient energy to pierce the blue cap's torso, skewer his body, and embed the point in the tree trunk behind him. The blue cap's mouth sprang wide open, a pink cavity in a brown forest of dirty beard. His eyes nearly burst from their sockets.

Korvin wasted no motion. His right hand dipped down and removed a knife tucked in his boot as he came up to a standing position and pivoted to face the red cap. The man had already stopped his advance and gone limp. His jaw sagged in horror and his eyes pleaded. He held out his hand with the knife and dropped it in a gesture of surrender. Korvin found this contemptible.

The red cap backed up, then turned and ran blindly into the brush. Korvin followed at a measured pace. The red cap blundered down the slope, stumbled, crashed and rolled. Korvin simply followed the sound. The red cap scrambled up and continued his aimless flight. Korvin calmly tracked the cascade of snapping twigs, breaking branches, and the hiss of ferns raking over the waterproofed jacket. The man went down with a loud thud.

Korvin came upon him all sprawled and filthy. His arms were raised and his hands extended in a final and futile gesture of self-defense. He was speechless with terror.

"I think you forgot your knife," Korvin said, and then set to work.

Korvin stirred the cocoa mix into the bubbling boil of water in the small pot over the fire in his camp. Both came from the backpacks of the intruders. He had found them in a predictable place below his campsite. The pair had undoubtedly shed them to gain freedom of motion during their assault on his position. A sensible precaution, though all their subsequent actions were profoundly stupid.

He poured the cocoa into his cup and let it cool. Steam drifted off the surface.

He used this interval to consider different methods of disposing of the bodies. It was imperative that they not be discovered. He hadn't counted on these woods being this densely populated. Even if word of this incident didn't reach the outside world, it would reverberate through the woods and compromise his presence.

A gurgle interrupted his train of thought. A highly constrained gurgle full of liquid and death. He looked up to where the blue cap was pinned to the tree by the spear. The weapon had missed the heart and the major arterial trunk running down the center of the torso. It pierced the intestines, sheared off the top of a kidney and exited just to the right of the spine. Well within the margin of error for a weapon of this type, but not sufficient to cause instant expiration. Internal hemorrhaging would eventually do the job. But until then, the blue cap listed to his left and stared at the quiet forest light through eyes polished to a high gloss of agony.

The satellite phone rang. Korvin put down his cocoa and answered. The robotic voice came on, most likely Becker. Only the blue cap witnessed their conversation. He had the synchronous grace to die at the same moment Becker hung up with new instructions.

Korvin picked up his cocoa and blew on it. A tiny squall spread across its surface, then calmed. He raised it to his lips and sipped cautiously. He didn't want to risk a burn. That would hurt.

CHAPTER 26

The dog sniffed her way along edges of the enclosed space that held her prisoner. A few weeds sprouted from a seam where the cement retaining wall and alley met. A rusting canister and discarded fencing rested along the back wall. No exit. She worked along the opposite side, the back wall of the restaurant. She peered into the grid of a heat pump's condensing unit. Traces of copper and coolant wafted out and into her nose. She approached a rogue weed that had thrust through the crack between the wall and the walkway. It put out a dry perfume, but yielded no sustenance. She reached the door that led into the restaurant's kitchen and ran her nose along the aluminum threshold. A vinyl gasket seal yielded traces of food scent, but nothing more. She arrived back at the Dumpster and the gate at the front. The Dumpster was a metal fortress of forest green and unassailable to her. The fencing and gate along the front presented the last possibility. She hopped up and inspected the fork latch on the gate. She understood the mechanism but inferred no solution from it. She hopped down and retreated toward the back of the enclosure and flopped down on the far side of the condensing unit. Her only option was to conserve energy until a solution presented itself.

The warm afternoon cooled toward a mild evening. Traffic sounds swelled as the rush hour commenced outside. The dog remained prone and still.

Then the clank of the fork latch reverberated off the cement walls. The dog's head came up. She craned forward so she could see around the condensing unit. A male human had entered the enclosure. A man short and wide, dirty and gray. A pink nose of broken capillaries capped his great beard of soiled white. One of his eyes wandered slightly. He occupied multiple layers of clothing topped by an ancient ski jacket blotched with stains. Fingerless woolen gloves of olive drab covered his hands. A filthy ski cap crowned his head of matted hair.

He shut the gate behind him and cautiously peered through the slats. His movements were stiff and arthritic. He moved immediately to the Dumpster and opened the black lid of plastic composite. The smell of food blossomed out. He rested one elbow on the Dumpster lid while he sorted through its contents. He fished out a plastic trash bag and gingerly squatted down before it. His stiff fingers fumbled with the twist tie as he opened the top. He extracted a white takeout container and pried it open. The scent of pork fried rice erupted from within. He removed a plastic fork from his jacket pocket and started devouring his meal.

The dog could bear it no longer. Hunger trumped caution. She rose to her feet, walked slowly to within a few paces of the man, then stopped. At first, he ignored her as he shoveled the rice through his beard and into his gullet. Then he turned his head to her as he continued to eat.

"Well, hi there, pup. What you doin' here? You live here? Somebody got you all penned up?"

The dog focused on the food, but also assessed the tone of the man's voice. It carried no threat.

The man could see that the dog's eyes were trained on the contents of the container. He smiled and held it up. "You hungry? Well, hell yeah you are. Hang on." He reached into the trash bag and pulled out a second container. "How about a little treat?" He opened the container and tore off the flaps. More pork fried rice. "Here ya go."

He stepped forward, set the container down halfway between them, then backed off. The dog hesitated. "Oh yeah? Never saw a Lab that didn't like to eat its ass off." He squinted at the dog. "You're kinda spooky. Somebody done a bad thing to you? Well, not me. That's for sure."

She moved to the container and wolfed down a single mouthful, then backed off to gauge the man's reaction. He twinkled and smiled. "Go ahead, girl. My name's Hank. I'm not gonna hurt you."

He rummaged in the trash bag and pulled out another container. "Excuse my manners, but I'm gonna go right ahead and get my belly full." He dug into the container and excavated a forkful of chop suey.

The dog looked at the man, then at the opened container before her. She understood. They would not compete. She moved to the container and devoured its contents. Hank laughed.

"Well, son of a bitch. How 'bout that. You want a little more?"

She leapt over the language barrier and interpreted the

tone of his delivery, his expression, the attitude of his body. She nodded, pitching her nose up and down twice.

Hank's eyes and mouth opened wide. "I'll be goddamned go to hell. Did you just say yes?"

She nodded once more.

"Son of a bitch!"

Hank recovered enough to get her another carton, tear off the flaps and present it to her. "Well then, here ya go."

Hank and the dog settled into their improvised protocol and jointly consumed the remaining containers in the bag. The shadows in the enclosure crept eastward. The breeze vanished.

Hank went back into the Dumpster and extracted a second bag. He opened it, peeked at the contents and tied it closed. He turned to the dog. "This one here's for the road." He slung it over his shoulder, moved to the gate and lifted the fork latch. He hesitated and looked back at the dog. "They got you locked up here, don't they? Well, that just don't seem right. I been locked up a few times myself, so I know the feelin'." He stared at the dog, thoughtfully kneading his beard. "Tell you what, I'm lettin' you outta here. You wanna come with me, that's fine. You wanna go your own way, that's fine, too."

Hank opened the gate and looked cautiously up and down the sidewalk. He turned to the dog. "Looks okay. Let's go, girl."

He stepped out and headed down the sidewalk to the crosswalk. There he stopped and looked back.

The dog stood outside the gate. She watched the man looking back at her with his bag of food. She pondered their shared meal, and judged him to be a good risk, possibly even a companion, like Zainah.

Hank smiled as the dog came to his side and sat. They

waited in silence for the crosswalk light to change. He reached down and gave the top of her head a single pat.

No more was necessary.

_____

The second time it happened, the dog absorbed the full meaning of the ritual. Hank raised his hand and stopped on the trail. He hunched and listened intently to the forest. The dog required no such intensity of effort. Her hearing covered twice the frequency of his. It could reach into the natural babble of the woods and isolate even the smallest of noises. She knew he heard snatches of conversation from two people coming down the trail from above.

"C'mon," he said to her, and headed off into the brush. His gait was stiff and bowlegged as they moved up and over a small rise, then stopped. He sat down with labored breath. "You never know who's comin', girl. Might be somebody nice. Might not. Best not to take a chance. You wanna treat? I bet you do." He opened the plastic trash bag and peered in and smiled. "Aha. You're a lucky doggie." He extracted a bone and held it out to her. She took it in her teeth and sat down to gnaw on it. Her teeth and gums reveled in its texture. She sank into a moment of great contentment.

She had cut through to the marrow by the time the hikers passed them on the nearby trail. A male and female. She couldn't understand their words, but if she had, she would've heard about how their relationship was changing, and how the male was not adapting. She precisely pinpointed the voices' origin as they moved down the hill. Then she returned to the rewarding crunch of tooth against bone.

"Let's get movin'," Hank commanded. He slowly unfolded and rose to his feet. "We got a ways more to go and it's gonna get dark pretty soon."

She stood with the bone in her mouth and raised her head until she looked directly into his eyes. She froze in that position and he looked down in puzzlement. "So what you tellin' me?" She nodded once with the bone. "You want me to take the bone?" She nodded again. "Well, okay." He reached out and grasped the bone as she relaxed her grip. "But then, what are you gonna do?"

She walked up over the rise and back to the trail. He followed and watched as she headed up the path without him. "You all through with me? Is that the deal? Well, you be careful. That's all I gotta say. You be careful."

Hank labored alone up the hill. His joints and muscles protested with each step. His breathing rasped. It masked the distant sounds of twittering squirrels and squabbling birds, all caught in the hormonal swirl of spring. He considered abandoning his booty from the restaurant, but thought better of it. He didn't want to make another trip. His legs could no longer afford it. Too bad about the dog. He liked the dog.

He came to a crook in the trail. When he rounded it, he encountered the dog coming down from the slope above. Her unexpected return warmed him. "So, you decided to come on home, huh?"

The dog sat on its haunches and stared at him. She raised a paw to the height of her shoulder and extended it upward.

"That a stop sign? You tellin' me to stop?"

She repeated the gesture, then moved off the trail and waded into the ivy. She stopped and looked back at him.

Hank chuckled. "This better be good, girl. My legs don't want no more side trips right now."

She moved further into the brush. The old man reluctantly followed. She stopped when they were concealed and plopped down. Hank did the same. "What you tryin' to tell me? You wanna another doggie treat? Is that it?"

Her head jerked in the direction of the trail and her ears perked. Hank twisted to look in the same direction. Then he heard the approaching voices. Two men.

"I'm gonna kick his ass. That's what I'm gonna do."

"Damn fuckin' right. You should do that."

"I don't put up with that kind of shit, you know what I mean?"

"Yeah, I know."

The conversation died. All that remained was the thump of their boots on the packed earth of the trail. Soon, that also died. Hank turned to the dog.

"You knew, didn't ya, girl? You came back to tell me. I'll be goddamned go to hell." He dug into the trash bag. "You wanna treat for that? Hell, I'd give you a whole number three combination dinner if I had one." He came up with some sweet and sour pork. She gobbled it down.

Hank closed up the bag. "Sorry. We can't stay here. Gotta get movin'."

They returned to the trail and assumed their new routine. The dog moved on ahead and Hank labored slowly up the path. The hillside slid into shadow. The woods became cool and dark green and blue. The breeze died. The birds sang the dirge of the approaching dusk.

Hank stopped, wheezing. He wanted to sink down, to take the weight off his joints, but instead he leaned slightly forward with the bag slung over his shoulder. His left hand rested on his knee. He stared at his feet, at his scuffed boots and rawhide laces.

"That's quite a trick your dog does."

Hank twisted to the voice.

"You teach her that?"

The stranger sent a pulse of fear through him. The man had appeared from nowhere.

"Not my dog," Hank responded. "Didn't teach her nothin'."

"That so?" Korvin said. He looked over Hank's shoulder and up the trail. "Let's ask her about that."

The dog smelled the trouble long before she had the pair in sight. An aromatic cloud of fear. A frantic dance of adrenaline and perspiration pouring off the old man. But another scent alarmed her even more. She remembered it creeping under the door of the room in the tiny apartment and recalled that it was a prelude to the men in coveralls, to the loss of Zainah, to the scent of recent violence as they stuffed her in the cage.

Hank and the man both stared at her as she stopped and turned around a few paces up the trail from them. The man both frightened and fascinated her. He was pure alpha. Her canine genes pulled strongly in his direction. The three of them formed a de facto pack of sorts, and the newcomer was the undisputed leader.

"Call the dog to you," Korvin commanded. He considered getting out the satellite phone and verifying the dog's image, but he didn't need to. This was the right animal. A medium-sized female black Lab.

"I would if I could, but she ain't mine, and she won't mind me," Hank protested.

"I think you better try anyway," Korvin suggested. "I think it would be the very best thing for you." He reached into his jacket pocket for a length of nylon rope, an improvised leash he'd devised in anticipation of this moment.

Hank turned reluctantly to the dog and held out his grimy hand. "Come on, girl. I need your help right now."

Korvin moved to where the old man blocked the dog's view of him. He uncoiled the rope and shifted its knot to form a large loop.

The Lab moved toward Hank's outstretched hand, but traveled an angle that would reveal the man behind him. "C'mon now," Hank commanded. The dog processed his voice. She heard the conflicted timbre, the hesitant delivery.

The dog put Hank aside, and focused on the ominous presence behind him. The coiled rope came into view just as the man put it into motion. He moved with amazing speed for a human. The rope opened into a loop that turned and twisted through the air. She rotated sharply and launched herself toward the brush. The loop bounced off her neck and collapsed onto the ground.

"Stop!"

She struggled with the terrible power in his voice, but kept moving.

Hank looked over to Korvin, who calmly coiled the rope and returned it to his jacket. "I told ya, she ain't my dog," he declared.

Korvin smiled savagely. "We'll see about that," he said, moving closer. "But for now, I think you should forget all about this. What do you think?"

Before Hank could answer, Korvin delivered a head butt that caught the old man in the middle of the forehead. Hank collapsed to a sitting position on the trail. He floundered inside a red ball of pain.

"So," Korvin said, "what do you think?"

"Never saw you," Hank mumbled.

"Very good," Korvin replied. "Have a good evening."

He started up the trail with a powerful stride. His pace was brisk and his mood foul. The dog had defeated his attempt at capture. And now his presence here was compromised. He could have killed the old man, but he had already killed two other people. Too risky. Then he considered the upside. The dog would undoubtedly link back up with the old man, and he already knew the area where the old man was encamped. At this point, it was simply a matter of timing.

The dog peered down the slope from its position in the brush. The old man struggled to his feet. He shouldered the trash bag and began to stagger up the trail. She wanted to join him. But she knew she had to wait. The alpha male was simply too dangerous. She'd failed to detect his presence, and might fail again. She turned and headed off into the waning light.

CHAPTER 27

The King brewed some tea on a small burner fueled by a butane bottle and listened thoughtfully while Elliot updated him. The flames of blue and orange dabbed away at the bottom of an old teakettle.

"The park attendant was pretty sure about it," Elliot said. "The dog was definitely a female Lab and about the right size. The last time he saw it, it was heading into the woods and back up the hill in this direction."

The King put a teabag into a chipped mug and poured in the heated water. "You're sure you don't want a cup?"

"No thanks," Elliot replied. "I'm fine. And I'll be a lot better once I find this dog."

"Dogs don't stay loose or abandoned around here," the King said. "At least not for long. We've got a lot of very responsible pet owners. They have a real affinity for strays. Most of the humans up here are loose or abandoned themselves, so they have a strong feel for animals caught in the same situation."

"Makes sense," Elliot agreed.

"It also makes your search a little tougher. First of all, no one around here is going to call animal control when they see a stray. They have neither the phone nor the inclination. Second, one of them that doesn't have a pet will probably take the dog in. And once that happens, they aren't going to do anything that might cause them to lose it."

"Swell."

"But let's not give up so easily," the King suggested. "If the dog surfaces, maybe we can broker a deal of some kind with the new owner. Maybe we find him another pet. Maybe we guarantee that the dog is going to a good home, and not to the pound. Something like that."

"I can't guarantee that'll happen. I wish I could, but I can't. This dog won first prize at the county science fair and I'm not sure what that means."

The King smiled and sipped his tea. "That's why we like you up here, Detective Elliot Elliot. You have integrity. Let's just wait and see how this plays out, okay?"

"Okay for now," Elliot said. "But not forever."

The King pulled gently on the string attached to his teabag. "Nothing's forever, Lieutenant. You might want to keep that in mind."

"I'll do that," Elliot promised. "Mind if I ask you a personal question?"

"Probably not. Ask me and see."

"Most everybody up here makes their living by foraging down in the city or combing the campus. That's how they eat. But you don't seem to do that. You're always around and taking care of business."

"You want to know how I get enough to eat?"

"Precisely."

"Let me ask you this: Does the mayor or the governor

need a second job to buy groceries? Of course not. And where does the money come from to feed them?"

"Taxes."

"Same here. People appreciate what I give them, so they bring me stuff. And as long as they continue to value my services, they will continue to bring me stuff. When they don't, I'm out. It's the democratic process in action."

Elliot smiled at the thought. "Did you ever think you'd wind up in public service?"

"Did you ever think you'd wind up as a detective in a humongous hospital?"

Elliot shrugged. "Can't say as I did."

"Same here." The King stared down into his mug, frowning. "It's not always an easy job."

"You've got other problems besides loose pups?"

"Something's wrong up here. People seem edgy and weird." He peered up the hill through the trees. "There's something bad out there, but I haven't figured it out yet."

"Can I help?"

"I wish you could, but it's a different world."

Elliot knew exactly what he meant.

On his way back to the office, Elliot considered the King's comment about trouble and fear spreading through the woods. He imagined himself as a homeless person sitting in a little camp out there in the dark of night. Alone. No walls, no doors, no locks, no cops to call. The margin between safety and disaster would be very slim. All the time. It wouldn't take much to arouse your paranoia.

He'd put the thought aside by the time he reached his cubicle. He was nearly settled in to check his email when Bobby came back from the vending machine clutching a bag of corn curls in his freckled fingers. He saw Elliot stare at the bag with disapproval.

"Hey, lighten up," he suggested. "This stuff is all low sugar. That's my new thing, low sugar."

"That's great, but it's also high fat."

"One thing at a time," Bobby said as he sat down and tore into the corn curls. "You have to deal with these kinds of issues incrementally. Oh, and speaking of issues, the Chief's looking for you again."

"What did he say?"

Bobby swallowed a mouth full of corn curls before replying. "I don't remember. All I remember is his color."

"His color?"

"Yeah. You know how he's always that pinkish color? Well, now it's more of a hot pink. Something closer to red."

Elliot headed down the hall to the Chief's office. It was better than sitting in his cubicle and speculating wildly. The Chief's door was open. He peeked in and saw that Bobby was right. The Chief had gone several new shades toward red.

"Where've you been?" the Chief demanded.

"Working on the dog," Elliot replied. This time, it was entirely true.

"Come in." The Chief gestured with his raw slab of a hand. "Sit down."

Elliot slid into the chair facing the Chief's desk.

"You know who the vice president of human resources reports to?"

"The president?"

"Very good, Elliot. Very good. The president. And you know what that means?"

"I'm not sure."

"It means you want to maintain a pleasant and productive relationship with this person. It means you don't want to piss them off."

"Sounds reasonable." Elliot had a bad feeling about where this was all going, but he tried to maintain an optimistic outlook.

"I got a call today from this very same vice president. She was a somewhat less than happy person. It seems that someone from this department attempted to invade the privacy of a former employee. A bunch of crap about world travel plans and salaries. She wanted to know if it was an *official* investigation. And you know what, Elliot?" The Chief's face contorted into an extremely ugly smile full of carnivorous teeth. "I had to tell her I didn't know. I had to tell her that I'd get back to her. I had to look like I don't have any idea what the fuck's going on around here."

"I think I can help you with that," Elliot suggested. He kept his cool. Any hint of fear would drive the Chief to unspeakable heights of wrath.

"Well then, why don't you give it a go?" The Chief settled back in his chair, his internal magma chamber throbbing.

"Let me back up a little," Elliot said. "A few days ago, I was investigating a car break-in. Routine stuff. I found a flash drive on the ground near the scene. It had a CT scan on it. The patient was Dr. James Oakner. Our very own Dr. Oakner, who is currently comatose and will probably stay that way. I took it to one of our radiologists, who was suspicious when she studied it. She checked his records, and sure enough, the image I found wasn't the same as the one on file. It looked like a completely different disease. One of the images is bogus. No one's sure which. I checked on the IT manager responsible for CT scans. Turns out that he'd just quit and sailed off into the sunset. Literally. So, at the very least, there may be a big screwup in data management, and at the worst, there's some kind of fraud. I went over to HR to see if I could get a little background on him. Looks like I might have overstepped a little bit."

The Chief struggled for composure. "Some people are very skilled at digging their own graves, Elliot. But you, my friend, are excavating yourself an entire mausoleum. First, you flake out on the dog search. And now, you devote yourself to running down clerical errors in the radiology department. Unbelievable. Simply unbelievable."

"Nobody knows if it's really an error," Elliot pointed out. He deliberately omitted the possibility of carbon monoxide poisoning and suicide. The Chief was very close to the brink.

"Can you count to four?" the Chief asked Elliot. He formed the words exclusively with his lips and teeth. His jaw was close to seizure.

"I think so," Elliot said.

"*One.* You have acted in direct violation of my specific orders about the dog. *Two.* You have violated HR policy in the extreme. *Three.* You don't have any fucking idea what's on those images. *Four.* If word leaked out about a mix-up in medical records, it would trigger a PR nightmare. And you know what would happen then?"

"I don't think I do," Elliot admitted.

"I would get a call from the VP of public affairs. And you know who *she* reports to?"

"The president?"

The Chief leaned back in his chair with a savage smile. "Very good, Elliot. Very good. You're starting to comprehend the chain of cause and effect around here. And you know who's at the very end of that chain?"

"I'm pretty sure that's me," Elliot admitted.

"Right again," the Chief said. "So let me reduce this conversation to one very simple concept. I owed some people downtown some favors, and that's why you're here. But I'm pretty much paid up in full. Do I need to elaborate any further?"

"I think I get the general idea," Elliot said. It wasn't true. The Chief was in permanent hock to downtown. A couple of years back, he'd been pulled over in a routine traffic stop. Stinking drunk. Sleazy babe in the passenger seat. Not the mother of his three children, who all played on suburban soccer teams. The city cops fixed it on the spot. And then they added it to their private ledger. Elliot held this card in reserve. He would only play it as a last resort. Still, it provided him with a certain level of comfort during this kind of encounter.

"When I was talking with the VP of HR, I asked what an appropriate action might be in a case like yours," the Chief said. "I was told to write a memo of corrective action and submit it to you. That's step one. Do you want to know how to avoid step two?"

"By all means."

"It's so beautifully simple, Elliot. Just find the fucking dog. That's all. Just find that fucking dog."

The Main Duck let loose just as Elliot opened the sliding glass door to his little deck. He smiled and tossed a chicken breast on the barbecue. He found something very amusing about the duck's belligerence; he suspected that everyone wanted to act like the duck from time to time. To step outside the strictures of the social contract and bellow and roar. He took a sip of his wine and closed the lid on the barbecue just as his cell phone rang with a message alert. He punched through the menus and brought the text up. It was from Sparks.

> **Your party of 2 went
> to Cabo San Lucas 8 weeks
> ago. Stayed 2 weeks &
> then returned.**

He closed the phone and put it in his shirt pocket. He assembled the factoids. The CT scan on the flash drive showed a possible suicide attempt from carbon monoxide poisoning. If so, the attempt would have occurred within the month before Oakner's final collapse. Christie and Oakner were in Mexico during this time. In Mexico, it might be possible to make it go away.

Every new bit of data pointed in the same direction. Toward a botched suicide and a consequent cover-up. Which meant that Christie knew about it. Which, in turn, meant that she could be stringing him along. Not a pleasant thought.

Still, everything he had was circumstantial. If he confronted her, he ran a huge risk. He might be wrong; he might alienate her for nothing.

He simply couldn't do it. Not right now. He needed to be absolutely sure. And there was only one way to do that. He would have to go to Cabo San Lucas. On his own dime and his own time.

He took another sip of wine.

The Main Duck let loose once more.

CHAPTER 28

Would he forgive her? Would he raise his comatose hand and extend his index finger in absolution? Would he achieve sainthood in his neural twilight?

Christie put her purse down beneath her bedside chair. He seemed more absent than ever. She wondered what he would think of Elliot. He probably wouldn't understand what she and Elliot shared. His arrogance would carry the day. If his wife was going to have an affair, it should be with someone of the same social stratum.

But in truth, there was no triangle. The doctor's vertex had disappeared, along with the destruction of his mind. The triangle had collapsed into a single line, with her and Elliot at its poles.

She let the room fall away and retreated to that day down in Cabo San Lucas, the day before the day of reckoning. She had purchased a necklace from an old Indian woman and continued on down the promenade. She had come upon a second woman sitting curbside, a younger woman with two children. The woman held up a tray of woven and shellacked fiber. It held small packages of gum. The woman said something softly in Spanish in a tone suggesting urgency and desperation. Christie picked out a half dozen packages and paid the woman fifty pesos. The woman accepted the money with no sign of gratitude. Her desperation had evaporated. The marketing portion of the transaction was over. It was, after all, purely an act of transient commerce. The woman sold almost exclusively to tourists she would never see again. Investments in "customer relationships" were a waste of energy.

Christie was not offended. She understood. She acknowledged the pragmatism of someone operating at the subsistence level. There had been times when she wasn't that far above it herself. She looked away from the woman to the children. They were beautiful. A boy and a girl, maybe three and four. She smiled at them, and they looked at each other and giggled. She shouldn't have done it. The longing and the aching were suddenly there in full force, beyond the pull of reason. She wanted to hug them and hold them. She wanted to take them home. She wanted to tuck them in between immaculately laundered sheets. She wanted to read stories to them until they drifted off into the flawless sleep of the truly innocent.

She thought of her own babies, the optional babies she had never even conceived. Their ghosts came to her sometimes. They excavated a cavity inside her heart, a sad void of almost unbearable proportion. But she always endured, and moved on. Their time would come, she rationalized. The right partner and the right circumstance would make it happen. It was not her selfishness that stood in the way. It was the inexorable thrust of the world about her.

Their time did come, of course. And their time passed. She lost all her babies. In a way she never expected.

CHAPTER 29

Hank sat in a sling of rotting canvas atop the old portable stool. He stroked his gray cascade of whiskers. His camp resembled Hank himself. A ring of trash encircled the periphery. Piles of discarded clothing lay open to the elements. Small mud puddles abounded. His lean-to sagged in the middle.

He regarded the dog, who sat opposite him. She stared at him with a very inquisitive look. He wondered if she sensed the coming proposition.

The dog looked at Hank and built a composite of all the smells that he broadcast. A far more rich and interesting mixture than that of most humans. She was growing hungry again, and knew that he held the key to solving that problem. She wondered how he would go about it.

Hank pulled an old leather collar out of his coat. A dog license dangled from it, stamped in stained metal. He undid the collar's buckle and draped it over his fingers.

Hank cleared his throat. "Okay now, I know you're a really smart dog. So I'm gonna tell ya this just like I would anybody else." He held the collar out toward her. "This here's called a dog collar, and I know you ain't got one, so you're probably not gonna like it. Hell, I know I wouldn't, but here's the deal. See this?" He pointed to the license. "It's called a dog license. I got it from a buddy whose dog up and died on him. Anyway, if you don't have one, people figure it out real fast. You wind up attractin' attention. Next thing you know, you're in the pound. Next thing after that, you're dead."

Hank paused. "You with me so far? Good." He reached into the trash bag at his feet and pulled out some pieces of sweet and sour pork. "Now I know we gotta make a deal to make this work, so here's a little down payment." He placed the meat scraps on the ground in front of him and motioned to the dog. "Come and get it."

The dog was perplexed by the flow of babble and the sudden display of generosity. They had regularly scheduled eating times, and this was not one of them. But she was also very hungry. She got up and went to the old man and gulped down the food.

Hank moved the collar into place as the dog ate. He waited until she'd finished to make his move. "Now all you gotta do is just hold still, just for a minute." He wrapped the open collar over the dog's neck and reached around to loop it under her throat.

The dog felt the collar encircle her neck. She sensed all that it meant, jerked away, and went back to her place opposite the old man and lay down. She looked at him warily.

Hank held the empty collar. "I don't think you quite get it, girl. You're gonna be a lot better off with this thing on than with it off." He pondered the problem for a moment, then grinned. "Tell you what we're gonna do..."

He placed the collar on the ground and formed it into

a circle. He reached in the bag and pulled out a few meat scraps. He placed them in the circle's center. "Okay, let's try this one more time."

The dog observed the food inside the looped collar. She equated a possible connection between the two. But then she factored in the vast emptiness in her belly. She got up and moved to eat the food.

Hank squatted down as the dog moved forward. He gently lifted the collar over her head as she gulped down the scraps. "All right now," he said softly.

The dog immediately felt the encirclement of leather. She pulled away and returned to her place opposite the old man.

"Well, goddamn it," Hank exclaimed. "I don't think you quite get the deal." He rose to his feet and sat on his stool. He sighed and bowed his head in concentration, and then suddenly looked up at the dog. "Let me put it this way," he said to her.

He squatted down with the collar. He formed it into an open-ended circle and put a few scraps of meat in the center. "All yours," he said. "Come and get it."

The dog grasped the rhythm of the game. She knew she could eat and escape the collar faster than the old man could get it on. She got up and started toward the food. She was halfway there when he reached into the circle, grabbed the scraps and ate them. She stopped and puzzled over this new behavior. It didn't fit the pattern.

"You wanna eat," Hank told her, "you wear the collar."

He put some more scraps in. The dog moved forward. He grabbed the food out of the encircled collar and ate. They repeated the cycle maybe a half dozen times. Then he stopped. "You think about that for a bit," he told her.

The dog lay down and looked at the old man and the

collar and the bag with the food. She considered the basic dimensions of the problem. Her need to eat. Her trust in the old man. The confinement of the collar. She carefully weighed the alternatives.

Hank watched the dog slowly come to her feet and walk gingerly to the collar, then look at him. "Well, all right!" he exclaimed. "I do believe we got ourselves a deal."

He put a generous portion of meat in the collar to reinforce the bargain. He wrapped the collar around the dog's neck just as she finished, and buckled it into place. "Good girl," he said.

The dog was not so sure. The feel of the collar disturbed her. But not as much as going without eating.

Hank slipped around to the side of the dog, out of the range of her vision. He petted her softly on the head, reached into his coat pocket, and produced a dog leash made of braided nylon. His calloused thumb retracted the bolt on the coupler and he attached it to a metal ring on the collar. He tested the new assembly with a gentle tug on the leash.

"Now I know this wasn't part of the deal, but it's gotta be this way," Hank apologized. He pointed down the hill, toward the city. "They got leash laws down there, and we could get busted if they see us without one. So you best get used to it, okay, girl?"

The dog walked to the limit of the leash and felt its restraint. Very distasteful. She twisted about to try to get the collar off her neck. Nothing worked.

Hank held the leash fast against her struggle. "Hey, let's calm down now. It's all gonna be okay. Here, let me show you." He reached in the bag and emptied all the remaining pork scraps on the ground. The dog ceased her struggles and moved immediately to eat the food. He reached behind him and grabbed a length of nylon rope, which he tied to the leash while the dog was occupied. He paid out the rope and tied the other end to a small tree near the lean-to. The dog finished the food. She looked up at him.

"I gotta go pee," he told the dog. "You don't wanna be peeing where you camp. I'm goin' down the hill aways. You can get used to your rig while I'm gone. Don't worry. I won't be long."

The dog watched the old man shuffle out of the camp. She tried to follow and quickly reached the end of the tether. She twisted in the collar until she faced the taut rope at the end of the leash. It stretched in a straight line back to the tree. A small wave of motion traversed its length, an artifact of her twisting. She tested the strength of the connection. She pushed backward with all four legs. The collar dug into her neck. The rope held firm. She moved forward to relieve the pressure and plopped down.

Hank looked at the steam rising off the damp circle of urine as he zipped up. He turned and started his stiff journey back up the slope. He didn't want the dog to be alone with the leash for any longer than necessary.

He had labored only a few steps when he felt a giant ball explode in the center of his chest. It threw off a bolt of pain that traveled down his left arm. He sank to his knees and the world spun. He pitched facedown into the bracken. A fallen oak leaf, crisp and yellow, tickled his cheek.

He was no longer there to feel it. His body lay still amidst the ferns.

CHAPTER 30

Stennis floated peacefully facedown in the Sea of Cortez. A big school of surgeonfish swam through the oval boundary of his snorkeling mask. Their yellow tails fanned the blue water and propelled them forward at a leisurely pace. Stennis wondered if they were on a mission of some kind. Maybe they had a steering committee that defined the direction and duration of their journey. He had difficulty imagining any kind of life without a mission.

He let the fish pass from view, then started the brief swim back to his boat nestled in the little cove. A flock of frigate birds skimmed the water's surface and led the way. For a moment, he imagined that he could swim past all the current difficulties. The relentless pressure from Becker. The comatose Oakner. The missing dog. He would glide through warm and gentle water with strokes both powerful and effortless. He would eventually reach the open ocean. A place free of constraint. A liquid plane of infinite possibility.

The notion lifted his spirits and let him move several conceptual steps ahead. It took him deep into the human brain, the seat of the soul. An extremely powerful yet infinitely vulnerable place. The right blow to the skull, the right virus, the right errant protein, the right occlusion could quickly damage it beyond repair. Its dazzling complexity put it far beyond hope of reconstruction. All the king's horses shuffled back to their stables. All the king's men milled about aimlessly.

But what if the brain itself could become the surgeon? What if the brain itself could make the necessary repairs? It had seemed an outrageous proposition until recently, but stem cells changed everything. It was beginning to look like the brain could use them as raw material to fix itself. Theory dictated that the brain could direct them, specialize them, and finally integrate them into the right neural neighborhoods. Experiments delivered tantalizing steps toward confirmation. The embryonic stem cells of mice were coaxed into making neural progenitor cells, which ultimately produce neurons themselves. The progenitor cells succeeded in repairing severed spinal cords. Previously paralyzed mice were made to walk. An achievement of near biblical proportions.

But the gap between theory and practice in humans proved immense. One major barrier was the automated response of the immune system. Because of the blood-brain barrier, the immune system was less diligent in the brain than in other places, but not entirely dormant. It would identify the incoming stem cells as foreign invaders and destroy them. One solution was to create so-called therapeutic stem cells, a form of cloning. Each would bear the genetic imprint of the donor and thus be ignored by the immune system. But cloning at this level of sophistication was still an elusive pursuit. The fraudulent episode in Korea made this all too clear. And also, a human brain held no margin for error.

Even if stem cells survived the onslaught of the immune system, what would they actually do? Would they roam through the neural tissue and work wonders? Or would they launch a catastrophe right at the seat of human reason and consciousness? Any trial with a human being represented an incredible gamble. The only cases that made ethical sense were particularly devastating brain diseases, where no other therapy was remotely possible. To date, only a few extremely cautious attempts had been made.

The harsh reality of economics presented even further complications. Therapies for very rare brain diseases served very small markets, and thus generated very small returns. The big payoffs would be reserved for stem cell treatments that addressed very common neural afflictions, like Parkinson's disease. But in these cases, stem cells would compete with many other therapies that had demonstrated at least limited success. In turn, this meant that human trials would have to wait until stem cell technology matured substantially and the ratio of risk versus reward was tilted in favor of success.

A giant manta ray glided below Stennis. He stopped swimming and peered down at it. Long, graceful waves rippled through the beast's great wings. They gave the illusion of effortless propulsion. Its gill vents opened and closed in a hypnotic rhythm as it pitched downward and vanished into the blue murk. A single remora clung to its back. Stennis continued on toward his boat. Life was full of remoras, merely along for the ride on vehicles of greater power and size. Becker understood that implicitly.

Becker also saw the way out of the stem cell conundrum. He saw through the debates, the controversies, the maneuvering, the technical barriers. He knew that the archetypal evil scientist was largely a myth. He also knew that the ambitious scientist was very much a reality, the scientist who would not step over absolute moral boundaries, but would range along their borders, looking for competitive advantages. He would approach such an individual with propositions wrapped in very clever packaging that offered the best of all possible worlds. Fame, money, professional respect, humanitarian redemption. The complexity of stem cell research offered unlimited possibilities. Certain strategies and procedures would be controversial if later exposed, but not completely outrageous. More important, they would win the race. And in science, as in geopolitics, history was written by the winners.

Stennis reached the swim platform on the back of his boat and hoisted himself aboard. The trickiest part would be the human trial. But Becker had already solved that problem in a way that was acceptable to everyone.

Stennis heard a quiet rush of water and turned toward the sea. The giant manta had just breeched the surface. Its great wings embraced the air of the world above. It soared to a breathtaking height, and then pitched forward. Bright little water beads shed off its wings and caught the brilliance of the noonday sun. It rotated completely in the air, and then dived below. A very clean dive, a dive that left barely a ripple.

Still, the remora hung on.

CHAPTER 31

Korvin stood on the slope in the dark of the woods and looked down on the house. A fence of failing wood stood between him and the backyard. Two of its pickets were missing. The gap exposed the lawn within, telling him that there probably wasn't any animal with jurisdiction here.

The night held no moon and smelled of dampness. Korvin shrugged off the chill and concentrated on the task at hand. Becker had been in contact earlier in the day. He had described specific goals, but had not elaborated on tactics. Korvin preferred it this way. He felt that he delivered maximum value when left to improvise. No plan of any complexity unfolded completely as specified. His very best moments had come when he had to rethink an operation in real time and come up with a novel solution.

This case was slightly different, however. He looked across the backyard at the split-level home. Two floors faced the rear, the lower one darkened. The top floor was lit with life. A sensible life. He could see into the living room through the dining room window. A middle-aged man in a bulky sweater watched television. Twin images of its screen danced on his glasses. The big sweater meant that the heat was set low. Energy was being conserved. Dollars saved. Very sensible. Korvin couldn't see the garage, but he could visualize the fuel-efficient vehicles within. Both with low mileage, but purchased used. A wise mode of acquisition.

A woman in a sweater and loose slacks passed through the frame of the kitchen window. Short brown hair. Quick to dry, easy to maintain. She was probably on her way to the den, with the broadband connection. She would log on to the site that managed their retirement and college funds and check the current balances. All adequately funded. Of course.

Korvin knew that these people pursued comfortable lives in a purgatory of mediocrity. He knew that they both repressed this fact, that it surfaced only occasionally and was immediately tamped down. If he were another kind of person, he would feel compassion, but the concept of compassion was lost on him. Instead, he felt only contempt. Perhaps he should inject a big exclamation mark into their lives.

The man rose with a slight effort and turned off the TV. He carried a bit of belly. He left the framing of the window and the living room went dark. A red pinprick of light from an electronic device was all that remained. Possibly a burglar alarm. No matter. Korvin mentally tracked the man's journey through the house. The dousing of the kitchen light. The stop in the bathroom. Right on time, the bedroom light came on. Its radiance crept into the night through louvered blinds.

To pass the time, Korvin checked his watch and estimated the couple's bedtime. He waited another ten minutes, then checked for the large screwdriver in his jacket pocket. He made his way silently down the slope to the gap in the fence. Some shrill little dog a few houses down picked up his scent and barked frantically. He waited until the barking stopped to step through the gap and into the yard.

He crossed the lawn, neatly clipped and trimmed. He would leave no trace from indented blades of grass. His motion activated a sensor and a security light came on. A bluff, like most such lights. He ignored it. He came up to a garden shed. An inexpensive, sensible solution to sheltering and securing all those tools acquired at home improvement centers. A padlock hung from a hasp on the door.

The security light gave up its automated vigilance and winked off. He reached into his pocket and extracted the screwdriver. He poked the blade through the hasp, grasped the tool by both ends and twisted. The hasp immediately ripped out of the plastic siding with a brief snapping noise. He looked up at the bedroom window. It remained dark.

He opened the door and closed it behind him. He pulled out a small flashlight. Its beam played over the tools and quickly located the two items he required. He picked up a large pair of garden shears, and then ran several meters of garden hose off the spool where it was neatly wound. He severed a section out of the middle of the hose with the shears and carefully rewound the balance with the nozzle dangling just as before. No one would notice the loss until summer. He replaced the shears. He wound the severed hose section around his shoulder.

Just then, a sliver of illumination sliced through the crack in the shed door. He froze. A door opened outside.

He could hear its weather stripping scrape over the surface of the cement walkway.

"Hello?" The voice was cautious, sensible and stupid. As if an intruder might actually answer him, as if the whole thing might be some kind of silly mistake. A kid prank or something.

Korvin tested the sharpness of the garden shears and then took up his position. The shed's door opened outward, which meant the man would be fully exposed to him. He would then use the shears to sever both the larynx and the carotid arteries, destroying the man's capacity to scream as well as killing him.

After a brief interval, however, the door closed and the light went off. Korvin opened the shed door slightly and peered out. Nothing. He stepped out and headed across the lawn. It was an overcast moonless night. Too dark to spot him from inside the house. He quickly reached the gap in the fence, the one piece of errata in the household scheme of sensibility.

He stepped through and was gone.

━━━━━━━

Clyde exhaled a cloud of pot smoke and passed the last of the joint to Ian. Elliot was always amazed that Clyde could remember all the Jimmy Page guitar parts after getting loaded. But then again, Clyde was a software engineer, and to him, the songs were algorithms. Once installed in memory, they always followed the same path of execution.

"You were a little loose on 'Whole Lotta Love,'" he commented to Elliot.

Over time, Elliot had learned to give Clyde a little slack in such matters. The man was not long on social skills. "Yeah, maybe so," Elliot responded.

They were standing on the bar's little outdoor patio that was closed after dark. The breeze lifted Clyde's ample fringe of gray hair up toward his bald pate.

"We need to tighten that tune up," Clyde went on. "It definitely needs work."

Ian exhaled and stubbed out the remainder of the joint. Elliot never partook. He just had a couple of extra beers to make up the difference.

"Yeah, it needs a little work," agreed Ian. He had blond curly hair every bit the equal of Robert Plant's, and was nearly as skinny. "But so does 'Fool in the Rain.'"

Clyde's eyes darted over to Ian. "Fool in the Rain" was Clyde's musical nemesis. It was an odd sort of shuffle with a staggered phrasing that somehow eluded him. He even had software that would slow it down to a crawl, so he could pick it apart at the atomic level. Didn't work. As soon as he tried to play it at normal speed, it simply fell apart.

Elliot stifled a smile. Clyde was now neutralized. Ian, so very politically astute for his young age, now changed the subject.

"So how's things between you and the docs up on the hill?" he asked Elliot.

"Not good."

"How so?"

"It seems that I've performed with complete and utter disregard for those who oversee my actions."

Ian shrugged. "So what are you gonna do? Are you going to repent and reform, or something like that?"

"Nope. My next move's very subtle and clever," Elliot replied.

"Oh yeah? Like what?"

"I'm going on vacation."

CHAPTER 32

The plane hit the runway hard and took a nasty bounce before settling down and braking. The woman behind Elliot let out a spontaneous yelp of fear. Every hard landing inevitably produced a yelper or two. Elliot tried to ignore her, with no success. The trip had not been pleasant. The plane was packed. Elliot had expended the last of his meager stock of air miles to grab an aisle seat near the back. He was constantly jostled by people lined up to use the restroom at the rear.

They came to a halt and he grabbed his solitary suitcase from the overhead. The aft cabin door opened and the heat and light of the Baja Peninsula poured in. It felt good. Maybe even worth his one day of earned vacation time. It was a Saturday, so he had the weekend plus Monday to find what he could in Cabo San Lucas and get back.

He walked across the tarmac toward the terminal and saw several big private jets parked to the side. He visualized Christie stepping out of one and adjusting her three-hundred-dollar sunglasses to acclimatize herself. The Oakners probably didn't own their own plane, but a charter or time-share was definitely within their range.

He cleared customs and took a van to Cabo San Lucas. He shared the ride with three median couples of median age. They exchanged pleasantries about kids in college, previous vacations, golf, and mortgages. He was silent. They seemed very distant to him. Their conversation never touched on the like of carbonized corpses.

The hotel was more than he could really afford, all swaying palms and turquoise pools and baking tourists. But he had no choice. It was still high season and he had to take what he could get, just like the plane. The trip had drained him physically and he sat slightly stunned on the little balcony off his room on the third story. Two stories below, disco music thundered out of speakers mounted by the pool. They drove the bobbing and prancing of swimmers arranged in a drunken circle for water aerobics. He had no plan, no grand strategy to get what he needed. He toyed with the idea of renting a car, but put it aside. He would only get lost and waste time. Besides, he spoke almost no Spanish.

The sun tipped toward evening and the balance of the day was clearly useless. He decided that getting a beer and some food was the most appropriate course of action, so he went down to the pool area and met two divorcées from Calgary, of all places. One wore a cowboy hat of straw and packed a few extra pounds in a graceful sort of way. She had accommodating eyes of liquid brown. Her companion was raw and combative. Elliot knew she would quickly sabotage any attempt to split the pair. He excused himself and wrote the whole episode off to his generic curse.

He continued past the pool and toward an open-air restaurant that overlooked the beach, where the Pacific shook hands with the Sea of Cortez. A ragtag flotilla of vessels bobbed in the blue waters. Behemoth luxury liners, fishing boats, glass-bottom boats, monstrous pleasure craft, Jet Skis. Legions of sunbathers gazed out at them from little white tents in the coarse sand. He ordered a chicken salad and a Corona and stared at the chain of parched hills to the west that rose into the cloudless sky. Frigate birds rode the thermals overhead and traced lazy arcs through the mild breeze. Their tails were split and their wings, which spanned over six feet, appeared almost reptilian in form. Elliot looked down the beach at the swarm of people and commerce, then back up at the birds. He knew that they had patrolled these skies for eons, when the hills were silent and empty and the surf beat upon a shore devoid of humans. He also knew that they would someday do the same again. He finished his meal, returned to his room, and instantly fell asleep.

███████████

He hit upon a plan over coffee the next morning. He could rent a taxi for a reasonable rate for a couple of hours to scout the town in search of the truth behind the Oakner incident, if indeed there was a truth. He stood at the curb as a taxi, a dented Econoline van of deep blue, pulled up. The door slid open and he met the driver, Jesús. The man was small and dark, with quick eyes. His English was limited, but he swiftly grasped the concept behind the mission. Elliot showed him a copy of the picture on the wall at Christie's depicting the Oakners' home down here. It had turned up on a popular photo-sharing site known to Bobby Seifert, who did a little maneuvering that got him into the private section housing Oakner's posted pictures.

"Do you know where we might find this house?"

"Pelegras," Jesús responded.

"Pelegras? What's that?"

"Private. Only residents."

"You mean like a gated community?"

"*Sí.* A gated community. Big houses. American houses."

"Can you get us in?"

Jesús deliberated for a moment. "Maybe. I will try." Elliot got the impression that the challenge of it was more important to him than the money.

They drove through the central town by the marina, where the hot stink of exhaust lingered in the windless air. They continued on and climbed modestly in elevation until they turned down an empty street under an arch announcing their arrival at Pelegras. A security checkpoint stood at the far end, with a guardhouse and a wooden barrier arm painted with red and white stripes. Jesús rolled down his window to the guard, who held a clipboard, the universal icon separating supervisors from laborers. A brief conversation ensued in Spanish. Then the barrier rose and they drove on through.

"Well done," Elliot said. "What did you tell him?"

"I cannot say," Jesús replied.

Of course not, Elliot thought. I shouldn't have asked.

They climbed up a winding cobblestone street whose bumpy surface discouraged speeding and sent a crude little hum through the van. They came around a sharp curve and the true measure of the place suddenly played out before them. House after house of massive proportion clung to the contours of the parched hillside. Most adhered to traditional stucco-and-tile exteriors, but this basic theme diverged into a stunning array of individual designs. The homes seemed to increase in size along with their elevation.

The ones atop the ridges were truly palatial in dimension. Elliot pointed to one of the topmost.

"How much do you think that cost?"

"Fifty million dollars," Jesús replied without hesitation, as if its value was common knowledge.

Elliot pointed to the Oakner photo. "So how high up will this one be?"

"About halfway," Jesús said.

He was right. After several forks and turns, the house suddenly appeared before them, three stories of white stucco. Gracefully rounded decks on each floor, adorned with spiky desert shrubbery. Dark green against brilliant white. Elliot instantly realized that the doctor's house up north was simply a cheap cover for this, the real thing. A heavy gate of iron mesh next to the garage was open to reveal steps of polished stone and a terraced garden leading up to the floors above. A gardener was working on the second terrace. A man of almost pure Indian extraction, he was pruning a long shrub that tumbled over the edge of the terrace wall like a breaking wave.

Elliot pointed the gardener out to Jesús. "Let's see if we can talk to him."

They left the van and walked to the open gate. The gardener looked down at them suspiciously, but Jesús quickly disarmed him.

"Buenos días," Jesús said, and that ended Elliot's comprehension of the dialogue that followed. His ear told him that it warmed considerably as it went along. Jesús turned to him at its completion.

"I told him you are an American friend of the owner here and that you stopped by to see the beauty of this house."

And quite a bit more. Elliot visualized the CT scans

and their telltale signs of carbon monoxide poisoning. Something happened here, goddamn it. He wouldn't let it go.

"Tell him I was sorry to hear about the doctor's accident," Elliot ventured. "Then ask him if he was here when it happened."

Jesús translated. A brief conversation followed.

"He says he wasn't here, but the housekeeper was. It was a terrible thing. They all feared the doctor would die."

Boom, there it was. After a lot of money and miles, he had it. All he had to do was carefully reel it in.

"Does he know the housekeeper?"

Jesús translated once more, then turned to Elliot. "The housekeeper is his niece."

"Is she working today?"

More translation. "No. She is at his sister's house."

Elliot raced to compose a pitch that would let him talk to the niece without scaring off the gardener. It turned out to be unnecessary.

The gardener spoke at some length. "He is through for the day," Jesús explained, "and he will have to walk all the way down the hill to the bus. He wants to know if we will take him home. He lives near his sister. We can talk to his niece and then drop him off. She will tell us what happened here."

Elliot promptly agreed. He stood by the van while the gardener locked up. Far below, two luxury liners lay at anchor in the blue water. Their cargo of charge cards was safely ashore and threading its way through the shops and restaurants that lined the beach and the marina.

The taxi traversed streets laden with dust, past adobe buildings open to the heat and fumes of unfettered combustion engines. Artifacts of commerce sat out in the raw dirt that fronted these structures. Stacks of grease-laden fuel pumps. Open crates of produce. Spools of rusting cable. Everywhere the scamper of children on slender little legs. Everywhere the meandering of lean dogs. The gardener sat in back and aimed an occasional burst of amiable Spanish at Jesús. Elliot remained silent and immersed himself in this journey from the second to the third world.

The taxi turned off the pavement. It moved down a road composed of dusty sand lined with wicked fingers of scrub. They turned again and the scrub ended. A ragged line of small shacks ran along either side of the road, naked before the sun and sky. The gardener spoke up and Jesús pulled to the side and they all stepped out into the withering light.

"This is where his sister lives," said Jesús. He pointed to a space roughly ten yards square surrounded by a barbed wire fence. In the center stood a hut covered with corrugated metal turned the color of dark chocolate by rust and weather. The patchwork of metal sheets lay open at one corner to expose gray construction brick beneath. They walked through a gate improvised from a discarded shipping pallet and past a clothesline strung from the hut to the fence. Three children appeared at the doorless entrance. Two women came up behind them. The older of the pair put a protective hand on the shoulder of one of the children, a small boy. He stared gravely at Elliot, but showed no fear.

The gardener talked with the women, with an occasional gesture toward Elliot. The dry wind blew a plastic bag through the dirt and it caught on the bottom row of barbed wire, where it fluttered and flapped in protest. Finally, the family conference ended, and Jesús turned to Elliot.

"We can talk out here," he said. Behind him, the older woman brought out two old folding lawn chairs and set them up on the shaded side of the hut. She and the gardener disappeared into the interior. "The niece is named Bonita," Jesús said.

Elliot and Bonita sat in the chairs while Jesús perched upon a big stone and faced them. The solemn little boy came up and stood close to Elliot. The boy stared at him in silence. Elliot wondered if some kind of expectation lurked behind those deep brown eyes, but wasn't sure what it might be.

Jesús interrupted the face-off. "The señorita wants to know why you came so far to speak to her."

"Tell her I am a good friend of the doctor's family and that I am very concerned about his health."

Jesús translated. Bonita seemed to relax slightly. Her jet-black hair was pulled into a circular knot in back. Her dark eyes seemed fixed in a slight yet permanent squint.

"Tell her that I am trying to understand what happened here so I can help the doctor stay well."

Jesús translated to Bonita, who nodded gravely and began to speak. Elliot occasionally interrupted with a question, but for the most part, he just listened.

There was a great deal to listen to.

That morning, Bonita had arrived by bus and made the long walk up the hill, as she did every week. When she got to the house, she prepared to unlock the gate at the foot of the steps. Suddenly, the garage door opened and a great fog of auto exhaust billowed out. She saw Señora Oakner leaning into the doctor's car and sobbing. He was unconscious behind the wheel. Señora Oakner yelled at her to call an ambulance, which she did. She returned and helped Señora Oakner roll the car out into the open air. The doctor remained slumped behind the wheel with his eyes shut and his mouth open. His breath smelled strongly of alcohol. The ambulance arrived and the attendants pulled the doctor from the car and loaded him into the back. Señora Oakner hopped in and they roared off in a blaze of sirens and lights. Bonita wasn't sure what to do, so she stayed and did her housework, then locked up and left.

"Did she have any idea where the doctor was the night before they found him?" Elliot asked.

Bonita replied that she did not know for certain. But she had heard from others that he was at the boat of "some other doctor" in the marina. When she came to clean the next week after the incident, the doctor was home, and he looked just fine. Neither he nor his wife ever spoke of that terrible morning again. It was as if it had never happened.

Elliot slowly digested Bonita's revelations on the ride back to the center of town. He became trapped in a ping-pong between what Christie had said and the reality of what had happened down here. She had clearly tried to keep him in the dark. She had obviously known that Oakner had suffered a medical disaster well in advance of his collapse at Pearson. Also, she had tried to steer him away from pursuing the puzzle of the two CT scans. Was she covering an attempted suicide? Or something even worse? He could try to track down the hospital that treated the stricken doctor, but decided against it. He didn't have enough time. That left "the other doctor" and his boat.

He had Jésus stop near the center of town, and paid him a bonus for his help. He started down the long promenade that sat on a bed of riprap above the boat docks. A steady stream of tourists strolled its surface. Tiki bars with thatched roofs did a brisk business. Indian women sold tiny creatures made of wood. Pitchmen offered fishing excursions. Halfway down, Elliot realized that his quest was impossible. Literally hundreds of boats floated at their moorings, all behind gated gangways with security guards.

He retreated to one of the bars and drank a beer, slowly surveying the marina from his elevated vantage point. It bristled with masts carrying all manner of electronics and rigging. He stayed until dark and drank too much beer. He looked out at the sprinkle of marine light shining from tinted windows, portholes and masts. He tried to picture the two doctors out there in a boat of vulgar proportions. He tried to imagine what they might have discussed, but he couldn't.

Then he tried to imagine why he ever let himself get emotionally involved with Christie again. Once more, he failed.

CHAPTER 33

The stairwell. A vertical canyon of monotony and concrete. Korvin moved up quickly through its confines. It ran the full height of the parking garage, a privileged place reserved for senior staff. The stairwell's smooth walls and ordered geometry seemed odd and unnatural after his time in the woods. His last visit here had given him the same impression. On that trip, he wore a hat and sunglasses and a stolen rain jacket. A primitive disguise, but adequate for the limited resolution of the security cameras. It gave him the cover he needed to survey the vehicle's position and the camera placements.

He reached the level he wanted and entered. The parking garage was shoved back into the contours of the hillside, like everything else on the campus. Natural light quickly fell off in its recesses, replaced by cold fluorescent illumination. The cameras were stationary, but their coverage was well planned. He would have to be careful to adhere to his preplanned path of travel. The parked vehicles reflected the highly favored position of the health care industry in the new global economic scheme. The sedans and SUVS were all luxury models and seldom more than a few years old. The medical aristocracy obviously traveled in great comfort and shiny opulence. At this hour, many of the stalls were empty, but enough remained occupied to give him adequate cover.

He checked his watch. The target would be arriving soon, a creature of habit who worked long hours. He made his way along the wall, under the view of the camera. He came to the far corner, crouched, and surveyed the small space between the bumpers of the vehicles and the wall that opposed them. Just enough room. He patiently worked his way down the row until he arrived at the target's vehicle. On his last visit, he had carefully observed the target's mode of entry to the SUV, which was key to the operation's success.

He stared at the front license plate while he waited. Four Phillips screws of black anodized metal held it in place. The embossed stamp of the identifying letters and numbers elevated them above the metal and formed narrow plateaus of enameled inscription. Small chips exposed the underlying metal here and there along their ridges. The current tags were slightly askew and exposed hints of months and years gone past.

The elevator arrived with a big mechanical clunk and the doors slid open. A single pair of footsteps set forth. Their cadence and impact matched those of the target. Korvin crouched low and looked out from beneath the undercarriage. He could clearly see the feet moving his way. The shoes matched those from his previous observation, so he moved swiftly to the passenger side and rolled underneath the vehicle.

Dr. Irene Walters reached into her purse and pulled

out her car key. She decided not to stop at the store for fresh groceries. Instead, she'd pull something out of the freezer and shove it in the microwave. At one time, she'd loved to cook, but since her husband died, she had neither the energy nor the inclination. She pressed the upper button on the car key, sending a prescribed set of pulses to her vehicle that popped the lock open on the driver's door. A second press on the button opened the remaining locks, including the rear hatch, where she always put her bulky briefcase. It always went in back so she wouldn't have to lift it across the high console dividing the front seat.

Korvin waited until both her feet lifted into the vehicle and the driver's door closed. Then he spun out from under the vehicle, crouching low by the passenger door. The starter motor turned and the engine came to life. He grabbed the handle, opened the door and slid inside.

Walters could hardly believe that the man was there. He came in so quickly and naturally, as if he rode home with her every night. Then the fear hit.

"What are you doing? Get out!"

The man smiled as if made of stiff rubber. He held her steady with his gaze. "I understand you're a doctor."

"Get out! Now!"

His knife seemed to come out of nowhere. "I've had some medical training myself, but it's really not my thing. Let's see if we can keep it that way."

No more fight. Time for flight. Walter grabbed for her door handle and pulled it.

Korvin's hand shot out. He grabbed her earlobe with his thumb and forefinger. He pulled hard.

She gasped at the sudden pain. Her head instinctively moved to relieve it. She let go of the door handle and then the knife blade was at her throat.

"We're going about this all wrong," the man said. "Let's start all over again. It's so simple. All you have to do is drive."

"And what if I don't?" she asked. Her voice trembled. She couldn't help it.

"I have this blade at your neck," the man explained. "But I'm giving you a false impression and I apologize for that. It's not where I'd start cutting. We both know that there are many other places to cut and leave you wishing you were dead even though you aren't."

She grasped the wheel with both hands to steady herself. "What do you want?" she asked.

The man let go of her ear and removed the knife from her throat. Still, he held it where he could be upon her in an instant. "I want to give you a chance to save yourself. And the way to do that is to drive out of here just like you always do."

———

"Slow down and turn left up here," Korvin instructed.

Walters peered along the beam of the headlights into the night. She saw the dirt road leading into the woods. This would be her last chance. Right here. Step on the gas, wrench the wheel. Put the car into a roll and hope she survived and this monster didn't.

Then she felt the knife blade press its chill against her upper lip. The cutting edge sat against the base of her nose. She understood. A single slash delivered with sufficient force would sever her nose from her face. She sagged in despair as she turned down the dirt road. Brush licked the doors and fenders. Branches caught the headlights and stood naked against the darkness beyond.

Korvin removed the knife from her nose. "Stop right here."

She brought the vehicle to a halt.

"Well done," Korvin said. "You know, we all live our lives with the illusion that we're actually in control, but it's times like these that make us realize that that's simply not true. We were never in control, we merely had good fortune. And when fortune begins to fade, we cling as hard as we can to any control we have left. And now, for you, there is one last element of control that you possess."

"What do you mean?" Walters asked.

"You can choose how you will die," Korvin said. "I offer two possibilities. First, I sever your abdomen and pull your entrails halfway out. Second, you inhale a gas that makes you slowly lose consciousness and finally expire. I know which one I would choose, but then again, I'm not you. You don't have to speak. If you choose the gas, simply nod."

Walters closed her eyes and nodded.

"Excellent choice," Korvin said as he reached over and removed the key from the ignition. "I want you to stay right where you are. If you don't, I will exercise the other option. See? Even now, you have choices and decisions."

He opened the door and examined the ground. It was dry and wouldn't leave any shoe prints. He reached down into the brush beside the door and grasped a coiled section of garden hose and a short length of soft cotton rope. He turned and looked at the target. She sat staring straight ahead. He climbed back in with the rope and bound her wrists securely to the steering wheel. Next, he put the key back in the ignition and pressed the button to open the passenger side window. A motor in the door issued a tiny whine and the glass came down slightly, just enough to accommodate the hose. Then he got back out and threaded the hose through the open crack and closed the door.

He brought the balance of the hose to the rear of the

vehicle and put it down next to the exhaust pipe, then moved on to the driver's door and opened it. The target remained motionless. He had seen this before. For all intents and purposes, she was already dead. He suspected that there was something deep in the victims' psyches that triggered this kind of behavior, but he didn't care to speculate. Better to simply exploit the phenomenon. "Don't worry, this won't hurt," he told her. He extended the remaining length of rope down around her ankles. With the target secure, he reached across and put the key in the ignition and started the engine. He pulled the rope taut so her bound feet couldn't reach the gas pedal and closed the door on the end of it.

All the prep work was complete. He walked to the rear and inserted the hose into the exhaust.

Soon, Irene Walters would be with her husband. He had died two years ago, suddenly and tragically. He came down with the sniffles on a lazy Sunday morning as they traded sections of the *New York Times* and munched on cinnamon rolls from a beautiful little bakery down the street. By morning, he was burning and coughing and wheezing. By Thursday, he was dead. Viral pneumonia. It killed him, devastated her, and terminated what had been a good marriage. In the time since, he had never moved far from the center of her heart. Friends had told her it was time to move on, and she had nodded politely and kept on dying inside. Now the process would be complete.

Korvin moved back down the road a short distance and turned to survey his handiwork. The dome light still burned and illuminated the interior. The tinted windows filtered the light so that little detail was visible. Then the light went out in deference to some digital timing device deep in the vehicle's electronic bowels. It did a slow fade that mimicked what was happening inside the car.

Korvin walked leisurely up to the main road. He could make out the tops of several campus buildings over the tree line in the distance. A crane sat on the roof of one with a brilliant red light at its peak. The campus itself was an organism of sorts, alive and constantly growing.

He heard the hum of tires and walked back down the road and out of sight. When he arrived at the vehicle, he opened the door and the dome light came back to life. He turned off the engine. The target's body sagged in its seat belt, with the head slumped so that the hair hid the face. He pressed his index finger to her neck. There was still a pulse, just as he anticipated. He removed all the rope and coiled it into his pocket. He had one more task, and it had to be done quickly.

He massaged the target's wrists and ankles, where the rope had indented the flesh into a concave pink. The skin still felt warm and pliable beneath his fingers. He worked patiently, but deliberately. When the target finally expired, it would be like the release of the shutter in a camera, leaving a snapshot of the physical state at the moment of death. Without his current attention, the rope traces would remain and the skin would no longer rebound.

For just an instant, he visualized how this scene would look if viewed from nearby. The utter darkness of the woods. The feeble glow of the dome light. He on one knee beside the open door, applying a gentle and loving touch to a woman lost in sleep.

When he finished, he checked his work with a small flashlight. The skin appeared clear. He turned the engine back on and shut the door one last time.

CHAPTER 34

The Petronas Towers shoved their way ninety stories into the warm tropical haze. The eighty-fourth story was ostensibly reserved for maintenance functions, and not listed anywhere in the building's official directory. All of it belonged to Becker. Today he was running hard on an exercise machine of great technical complexity. He pounded out eight-minute miles as his lungs sucked in massively filtered air, cooled to room temperature. It rendered him free of the particulates and hydrocarbons that threw a poison blanket over the lower regions of the city. His feet pounded the conveyor belt with a rhythmic ferocity while his gaze traveled out the window and over the urban sprawl. Clusters of new construction formed islands of cement that erupted out of the green vegetation.

The endorphins collected within him and formed wings that propelled him back to the marina in Geneva so many years ago. She wore an American baseball cap. Her long hair flowed from the cap's ridiculous confines and tossed about her in a most glorious and insolent way. No other girl could have pulled it off. She was the daughter of the marina manager, working there for the summer. He loved to watch the torsion in her legs as she secured lines and carted buckets. So strong and deliberate. She held him in no particular regard, despite his family's station. There were many boats, many families, many boys. He spoke to her only in passing. And every time he did, he felt the longing expand within him.

He was alone on the boat the night it happened, a warm night full of promise. His parents were off to some social obligation. He leaned on the deck railing and watched her approach, then asked if she would check if the mooring was secure. A silly request, but the best he could do at seventeen. She hopped aboard in a single, fluid motion, removed her cap, and shook her hair free. A tiny silver cross hung from her tanned lobe, caught by the remaining sunlight. He fixated upon it. To look straight into her eyes would have been overwhelming. But then he did, anyway. And her eyes told him it was the right choice. They never even discussed securing the mooring.

They were belowdeck and entwined in each other when his parents came home. Time had escaped them. The layout of the boat offered no discreet exit, so she had to emerge and depart in full view of his parents. They pasted on pinched little smiles and tight nods as she passed. He followed her up to the deck, desperately groping for ways to salvage the situation. None came to him. Without a word, she hopped down onto the dock, waved once and was gone.

His father wisely disqualified himself from the aftermath. In the muted light of the salon, his mother launched into a cruel and rambling discourse. Its outer layer was about responsibility and maturity; its inner core and

essence was about people of one stratum of society interacting with people from another. She downed three glasses
of wine as she spoke.

Becker stepped off the exercise machine and stretched
his legs. He was now running every other day without fail.
From a factual standpoint, exercise would not help, but
from an emotional standpoint, it created a feeling of control.
Depression and resignation were companions he could not
afford.

The buzzer sounded on the security console. The
video displayed one of his assistants waiting outside. He
stabbed a button that let the man in.

"Yes?"

"You have a call waiting. It's from the U.S. A Mr.
Hoffner."

"Hoffner? Give me the background." He nearly always
made the assistants go through this ritual. Sometimes he
knew what they were talking about. Others, not.

"Mr. Hoffner is the senior research administrator at
the Pearson Medical Institute in the United States. He
holds a graduate degree in biochemistry and a master's in
business administration. He oversees funds supplied by a
grant from the Xanos Foundation, which you control directly. He periodically contacts you about matters relating
to the progress of research which is supported by funds
from the grant."

"Very good. Maintain sixty-four-bit encryption for the
duration of this call."

"Thank you, sir."

He picked up the receiver. "Mr. Hoffner, you're keeping some very odd hours. It must be the middle of the
night there."

"Are you aware of what's happening here?"

"I'm afraid you're going to have to be a little more specific."

"A radiologist was found dead in her car. A suicide. It just happens to be the same radiologist that we talked about some time back."

"And what did I tell you then?"

"You said that the whole problem would be handled independently. Jesus, man! I don't want to even think that there's a connection."

"And why would you think that?"

"I don't like to tell you this, but this whole thing is starting to unravel. If anyone looks close enough, they're going to find that Oakner got gassed in his car, just like this woman."

"We both know that Dr. Oakner's misfortune was an accident, brought on by none other than the good doctor himself. There was no suicide involved, yet alone hostile intent. Any connection to this radiologist person and whatever happened to her is purely coincidental. I think the best course of action for you, Mr. Hoffner, is to relax. Your paranoia is manufacturing a situation that simply does not exist."

"We both know *exactly* what happened to Oakner, and that it was a stupid, drunken accident. That's not the problem. The problem is everything that happened before and after that. And now there's this Elliot poking around the edges."

"Who?"

"Elliot. Remember? The investigator. The campus cop. He's an old pal of Oakner's widow. We have some exposure here."

Becker did not remember. His memory was littered with random holes such as this. He did remember the gene, however. It nestled in chromosome number one, and went about its awful business. It came from the Volga River Valley. A good German gene, undoubtedly contributed by his father.

"One moment," he told Hoffner. He went to the computer and typed the name "Elliot" into a database search. His recent note immediately popped up and he rapidly scanned through it. But not as rapidly as he once did. Or was that his imagination?

"I think we should monitor the situation with Mr. Elliot, but we can't press too hard," Becker said. "We're in a double bind here. He might be on the brink of something with Oakner, but he's also been charged with finding the dog, right?"

"That's about it."

"Let's do some creative problem solving here. Is there some reason why Elliot's the only one that could run the search for the dog?"

"Not really. I think the department has a couple of other senior people that could take it over."

"Good. Because then we could focus on defusing his queries about Oakner."

"And how would we do that?"

"I don't know, but I'm sure we can come up with something. Something oblique. Something roundabout." Becker added these qualifications to pacify Hoffner. The man was already paranoid enough about the dead radiologist.

"So where do we go from here?"

"Very simple. You continue on as though none of this ever happened. Keep in mind, Mr. Hoffner, that none of these events relates directly to you. In the end, you have simply been a conduit for the flow of funds. And that's the way we want to keep it."

"I couldn't agree more."

"Good. I'll be in touch."

Becker disconnected and looked back out the window. He would have to have his operative at Pearson deal with Elliot, but very carefully, in some way that couldn't be backtracked.

His vision reached beyond the haze and back to the boat, to Geneva, to the girl. Marna was her name, yes, Marna. He could still see the little cross dangling, the sun setting, her long hair. He could remember all of it, in glorious detail. Fragments of other women were left, but only broken pieces. He regretted that more than anything else. The closer they were to the present, the more invisible they became. He knew there must be some ghosts out there, entirely missing. What had he shared with them? What had he lost? Would it ever be recovered? He was determined to find out.

CHAPTER 35

E lliot immersed himself completely in the images on his laptop. The din of the customs area in the LA airport seemed very distant. He would look up occasionally and see the line shrink as people rechecked their bags for the flight north. If he scrutinized the images closely enough, the upset in his stomach seemed to recede slightly. Irene Walters was dead, an apparent suicide. Bobby had reached him on his cell when the plane landed, and had given him the news. It had sickened him and had immediately created a chain of cause and effect in his stricken mind, from his first contact with her to records fraud to murder. Now he was fighting intuition by applying reason. Maybe it really was suicide. Maybe the best way to verify that was to eliminate the alternatives.

He started with the security camera system in the parking garage. The cameras were all digital and sent a compressed data stream to a central database where the images were preserved for several days until erased to make room for new data. Bobby had executed a series of deft maneuvers and isolated the cameras on the floor where Walters parked. He then went to a second database and pulled the information on her car and parking privileges, including the parking space number. From there, it was simple enough to locate her car on one of the cameras. All the video was time-stamped, so they could focus on the window when she left that night. Bobby then sent Elliot the video from this window, and he retrieved it in Los Angeles over a wireless connection in the airport.

Elliot set the video to start once again. The frame was empty, except for the row of cars. Then Irene walked into view and image quality suddenly improved. Bobby had explained that the camera had a motion detector: it went to a higher resolution when someone or something moved in the frame. She already had her key button out and pointed it toward her vehicle. The taillights flashed in response. She opened the hatchback and put in her bulky briefcase.

Elliot paused the sequence here. If the signal from the key opened the hatchback, it probably opened all the other doors as well. An intruder would now have multiple points of entry.

He restarted the sequence. Irene closed the hatchback. She came around to the driver's side and disappeared from view. He watched the time code spin at the bottom of the screen. Nine seconds elapsed. A puff of exhaust issued from the tailpipe. She had started the car. Then nothing. The vehicle remained motionless. He watched the time code spin. Sixty-nine seconds elapsed before she started to back out. What was she doing?

He slowed the video to a crawl to watch her vehicle back out of the parking space, all the while focusing intently on the driver's-side window. He could make out her arms and her hands on the wheel and part of her shoulder, but the angle of the view obscured everything else in the front seat. Worse, the windows were all tinted. The vehicle backed toward the camera, then stopped while she shifted into drive. He paused the video. He could see directly through the large back window. Two sets of headrests blocked the view to the front. Then he saw it—part of her profile emerged from behind the driver's headrest. Nose, mouth, chin, hair.

He captured a freeze-frame of the paused image. He isolated the area around the headrest and magnified it. Sure enough. She was turning. She was turning to face someone in the passenger seat. He was sure of it.

Or was he?

CHAPTER 36

The dog patrolled desperately along the circumference inscribed by her tether. It covered most of the old man's camp, but not all. She had identified a number of potential food sources that lay outside her reach. A discarded soup can. A plastic package of frozen vegetables, now thawed and wasting. A packet of miniature donuts buried under discarded clothing. She stopped and lapped brown water from a small mud puddle. The puddles were drying, and soon her supply of water would run out.

She moved back into the camp's center and her tether went slack. She turned to examine it yet again. The nylon rope defied the vigorous chewing she had applied to it. Her molars had ground on its hard, flexible fibers with little effect. Same problem with the leash of thick nylon. And no combination of twisting, turning and pulling would free its grip on her neck.

Several days had passed since the old man left. Her belly could count every hour since she had last eaten any amount of real substance. She moved to an old hand mirror perched atop a wad of clothing and gazed upon her image. She looked into her own eyes, so full of iris and nearly devoid of white. They seemed mournful to her, and she knew they reflected her suffering. Her ears folded over themselves and hung limp, like the leaves of a malnourished plant. She turned from the mirror.

She walked under the shelter of the sagging lean-to and flopped down to rest upon a sleeping bag that she had dragged into the range of her tether. She had analyzed her situation and extrapolated it forward in time. She knew that she would soon die here. A combination of dehydration and starvation would inexorably drain the life from her. Her dreams were already troubled.

She caught a scent on the breeze. The coyote. She came to her feet and moved out along the tether in the direction of the smell. It grew stronger. The beast was moving this way, up the slope. She quickly surveyed her confinement, looking for the proper defensive position. She didn't want the coyote to perceive her predicament and take advantage. She grabbed the tether in her teeth and moved back to the lean-to. After positioning it behind her, she descended once more onto the sleeping bag.

The coyote's head poked up over the bracken just outside the camp. Its ghostly eyes met those of the dog and held steady on her. Its ears came to full height. It ducked down again abruptly and the dog could hear it move through the brush along the clearing's edge. It was investigating the urine markings she laid down when she first arrived, before the tether. They defined the periphery of her territory here, and were produced when she was still in a vigorous state. The signature would cause the coyote to proceed cautiously.

The coyote emerged from the brush and boldly regarded her once again. It had moved well within the circle of scent markings. Its bushy tail was elevated in a gesture of defiance. It began to sniff around and quickly discovered the soup can that lay outside her tether. It gave her a cautionary glance, and then ran its tongue along the can's innards.

Both her food and her territory were slipping away from her. She fought the urge to respond and remained prone on the sleeping bag. Surprise was her only advantage. Her eyes traced an imaginary line along the limit of the tether and placed the coyote's position in relation to it.

The coyote came upon the torn bag with the frozen food now gone to rot. It gave the bag a perfunctory sniff and moved on. It moved ever closer to the imaginary line.

The dog remained still on the sleeping bag. Inside her, a very dark and desperate deliberation began to boil. It welled up from the most extreme evolutionary depths, the place of marauding reptiles. The coyote itself was the last food source left to her. As she struggled with this thought, all the normal checks and balances of her species began to dissolve. The stark imperatives of hunger and starvation were all that remained.

The coyote spotted a mutilated milk carton within the imaginary circle. The dog had long ago ripped it open and licked it clean, but the coyote still detected some remnant of its original content. Before moving to it, the beast once again locked eyes with the dog. This time, she looked away in deference to its dominance. Or so it seemed.

The coyote turned its attention back to the carton and moved toward it with a confident strut. The dog pulled into a tight crouch of tensed muscle. She narrowed her focus to the thick bush of fur covering the coyote's throat.

"So what do we have here?"

The dog and coyote both jerked their heads toward

the speaker. The dog recognized him instantly. The man on the trail. The man who tried to capture her. The man who appeared from nowhere. And now he'd done it again. He stood at the edge of the camp, a hellish apparition. The coyote gave him a single glance and skittered off into the brush. The man came forward and squatted down to appraise her.

"So, we meet again," Korvin said. "It would seem that you've got yourself into a difficult situation." The dog averted her eyes from his gaze. He radiated the strongest alpha presence she had ever experienced. She remained absolutely still.

Korvin rose and methodically rummaged through the camp. He pocketed a flashlight and a pair of pliers. From a mildewed canvas bag, he took a spool of tough cord, the kind chalked by carpenters to mark lines on wood. In the rear of the lean-to, he came upon three wooden dowels. He picked one up and examined it. Its round shaft was slightly thicker than a pencil, and about a meter in length. Then he noticed a slash of red amidst a heap of clothing. He pulled the pile apart and unearthed a cellophane packet of small donuts. Nine remained, and he picked one out and ate it. For just a moment, he savored its essence of fat and sugar as he chewed. But only for a moment. Addiction and indulgence eroded diligence and opened holes of vulnerability.

After depositing the donut package and the dowels on the ground, he returned to the dog. The animal continued to avoid eye contact as he squatted down and appraised it.

"So why do they want you so badly?" he asked the dog. "Why are you such a big prize?" He looked at the dog's flank. The ribs rose into shallow ridges of malnutrition against the black fur. "Let's see if we can find out."

He took the donut packet and turned away from her. She could smell the rich aroma when he tore it all the way open. She came to her feet. She couldn't help it.

Korvin placed five of the donuts in a row about a meter away, and the remaining three right at his feet. He stood and moved to one side, exposing the treats to the dog, and watched carefully. For just an instant, the dog hesitated. Then it leapt right past the row of three and devoured the five in the outer row. Finally, it returned and ate the last three donuts.

"Aha." Korvin smiled. The beast could count. Any normal dog would have torn right into the closest food and then moved to the more remote. This animal did not. It knew which group yielded the most volume, and went there first. "You just told me a great deal about yourself."

Korvin squatted down by the dog once more. The animal's chin hugged the ground and its wilted ears rested on the sleeping bag's dirty surface. The eyes appeared mournful and stared out into the woods.

"Can you understand me?" Korvin asked in English. "Do you know what I'm saying?" He watched the dog intently and detected no reaction. He stood. "Either you're the master of the bluff, or you just don't get it. Give me some time. We'll figure out which is true."

He secured the dog's leash to the base of a bush, reached in his pocket and took out the satellite phone. Things were going very well, indeed. It was 3 a.m. in Kuala Lumpur, but Becker would want to be immediately informed. He placed a call, went through the necessary protocols, and the banker came on the line. "You're calling at an odd hour," he commented.

"I've secured the dog. I thought you'd want to know immediately."

"The dog?"

"Yes, the dog." Becker's reaction seemed quite odd, given the circumstances. Korvin heard the sound of typing on a keyboard, and then Becker came back on.

━━━━━━━

In Kuala Lumpur, Becker fought off the fog of sleep as he scanned a flood of text on his computer screen. He also struggled with another fog, a more profound one, a fog that grew thicker all the time. The dog, here it was. The animal that Hoffner and Stennis needed. The one that escaped. Korvin had been assigned to retrieve it. It would then be handed off to Hoffner at Pearson. It was all here in his notes.

"You're sure you have the right animal?" he asked Korvin.

"Positive. It's a very unusual animal, but you already know that."

"You need not concern yourself with the specifics. That's not what you're being paid for."

"Very well then. How do you want it delivered?"

"I want you to give it to a certain individual at Pearson. I'm going to contact him as soon as we're through here and make necessary arrangements. Then I'll call you back with the details." He typed a stream of notes as he talked. Nowadays, it seemed to be the only way to guarantee continuity.

"Alright, I'll stand by for your call," Korvin said.

"Good. I'll talk to you later."

Becker kept typing as he hung up. He wanted to capture as much detail as possible about the upcoming transfer of the animal. He generated a memo that described the specifics of the handoff. He didn't want the two men to meet face-to-face. He needed to keep maximum distance between them in case something went wrong. Korvin was expendable in a crisis, but Hoffner was not. He was critical of the project's success.

Becker wrote a note describing the upcoming handoff. First, the dog would be securely tethered in a secluded area by Korvin, who would then leave the scene. Ten minutes later, Hoffner would arrive and take the dog away. Hoffner would later explain to the Pearson staff that he found the dog by happenstance, as the animal rummaged for food in a Dumpster behind the hospital kitchen.

When he stopped typing, he reread the scenario to ensure its accuracy. Just as he finished, a call came in on another line. London. The markets had just opened. Big setbacks on several key holdings. What should the trading strategy be?

Ten minutes later, the issue was resolved. He turned back to the notes about Korvin and Hoffner and the dog. He had no recall of his actual conversation with Korvin. He never knew which memories would stay and which would go. That was the way of it. Only the notes were left.

He read them through once more. Good news. The dog had been found by Korvin, and then given to Hoffner in a handoff that kept the two at arm's length. Perfect. The problem was solved, and he could get some rest. He encrypted his writing, shut down the machine and went back to bed.

Korvin kept the phone out and waited for Becker to call back with the delivery details. The day warmed, insects buzzed, crows squawked, squirrels scampered. No call. He considered calling back, but decided against it as he looked down at the wary animal. "What can I tell you? Mr. Money moves in mysterious ways. In the meantime, I think you might be of some use to me."

He started up the slope with the dog in tow. The animal matched his pace perfectly, keeping a small amount of slack in the leash.

The dog watched the man's feet move with grace and agility through the brush as they walked up the hill. They were a pack now, and he was the leader. The leash was hardly necessary.

CHAPTER 37

Elliot checked the clock in the conference room as Sparks walked in and sat down. Three p.m. No wonder Sparks's beard looked so bad. Its follicles were out in full force. His whiskers were pushing toward their next encounter with the razor's edge, and they all intended to live life to the fullest before that happened.

"Elliot. You get some coffee? You know where it is."

"No, I'm fine." Elliot knew precisely where the coffee was in this corner of the city police department. He had consumed untold gallons during his tenure here. He noticed that Sparks had brought a file folder with him. A folder thick with the tragedy that had once been Dr. Irene Walters.

"You like being in Homicide?" Elliot asked.

"At this point, Elliot, I like being anywhere they put me. I'm almost outta here, as you well know, so it doesn't really make a lot of difference." Sparks looked at the folder he was holding. "So, why are you so interested in this? I mean, it's a doc for sure. But it didn't happen on the campus. So what's the big deal?"

"We don't get a lot of doctors up at Pearson who drive out of the campus alone and turn up dead a few hours later," Elliot said. "Just curious, that's all."

Sparks opened the folder and started thumbing pages. "I hope this isn't too disappointing, but it looks like a classic suicide. Turns out that her husband died a while back. Quite suddenly. Some kind of infection. Her friends say she never got over it. She was on antidepressants. I guess they didn't work too well, did they?"

"What's the coroner say?"

"Death by asphyxiation due to carbon monoxide poisoning. No signs of a struggle, if that's what you're looking for."

"I don't know what I'm looking for. Mind if I see the crime scene shots?"

"Video or still?"

"Still will do fine."

"Be my guest," Sparks said. He opened the folder and slid a series of photos across to Elliot.

Elliot skipped rapidly through the shots of Irene slumped in the front seat. They bothered him and told him nothing. He stopped and examined a picture that showed the passenger side of the SUV. A length of garden hose hung down from where the window held it against the top of the door frame. A subsequent shot showed how it was inserted into the exhaust pipe.

"This hose," Elliot said. "Somebody cut it to the correct length."

"Well, yeah," Sparks replied in a flippant tone. "I think a medical doctor would probably be really good at cutting things, don't you?"

"Do you know where it came from? Did it come from her house or her garage?"

"Now I know this is probably going to amaze you, Elliot, but we thought of that. And the answer is: No, it didn't. We don't know where it came from."

"Are you going to find out?"

Sparks rubbed the thick stubble on his chin. "Come on, Elliot, you know how it works. We have a preponderance of evidence that points to a suicide. We have one inconclusive piece of evidence that points nowhere. So what are we supposed to do? It's not worth the time and cost to follow up on it. End of story."

"What about when she left work? Did you look at the video from the parking garage?"

"And wouldn't you know it? We did that, too." Sparks was sliding into full-bore sarcasm. "She walked to her car, got in, drove off. All by her lonesome."

"I looked at that same video and saw it a little differently," Elliot countered. "She got in her car, and more than a minute went by before she backed out."

"Elliot," Sparks implored, "go out on the street and watch people getting into their cars. Start making a catalogue of all the things they do before they drive off. It'll keep you busy for the rest of your life."

Elliot took a folded printout from his pocket. He opened it and slid it across the table to Sparks. "This is from the video when she backed up to drive out. It's a zoom on the back window. Look at the driver's side on the front. You can see the edge of her face. She's looking toward someone in the passenger's seat."

Sparks scrutinized the image in silence. He pushed it aside and stared blankly at the table. Finally, he looked up. "Same problem, Elliot. She could've been looking at approximately ten million different things—if she was looking at anything at all. Doesn't work." He leaned across the table. "Look," he said intently, "I owe you. I know that. But there's really nothing here. I'm sorry. Just hang on and do your job up there. Sooner or later, something will happen where you can make your mark, okay?"

"Maybe so," Elliot replied. For an instant, he was tempted to pile the whole thing on Sparks. The CT scans, the records fraud, the Oakner suicide attempt. Then he caught himself. The minute Sparks smelled a real case, he was in and Elliot was out. Elliot would lose control not only of the Walters murder, but of everything else. He got to his feet. "You ever see any of the guys from the old team?"

"Never."

"Me neither," said Elliot as he headed for the door. "See you around." His point was unmistakable. It wasn't over. Sparks still owed him.

CHAPTER 38

Elliot listened to the Main Duck rage at the setting sun. Then he turned to his laptop and went on-line. A window opened that presented him with eligible women, at least in principle, in proximity to his zip code. He scanned the thumbnail pictures and wondered why he was doing this at all. It seemed kind of futile, but maybe he wasn't giving it a chance, maybe he was sliding back into the pre-digital dark ages. Besides, it was a different medium and it might produce a different outcome. No flaming boyfriends. No Jesus Chihuahuas. He had signed up a couple of weeks ago and created a profile, a blurb about being a law enforcement professional interested in jazz and blah blah blah. He avoided any mention of carbonized corpses and screaming children in dope houses.

He scanned the listings and picked a presentable-looking woman about his age. "Nicole." He went through her profile. She liked the usual laundry list: hiking, skiing, walks on the beach, pop music, travel and "getting to know new people." She was divorced with no children. He had to wonder just who it was hiding behind all this. She was currently online, so he clicked to open a chat dialogue:

Hi Nicole. My name's Elliot. Can you chat for a while?

Hi Elliot. Yes I can. What kind of person are you?

I'm not exactly an average guy. Is that okay with you?

It might be. What do you do?

I'm in law enforcement. I'm a detective. I work in public safety at Pearson.

Wow. That sounds really interesting. I know a little about that kind of stuff.

You do?

Yeah. The cops were here a couple weeks ago. I got to talk to them quite a bit.

What did you talk about?

My former husband drove his Jeep through my living room window.

What happened then?

He wanted to stay for dinner. I think he was a little stoned.

Sounds like it. So you called the cops?

No. The neighbors did that.

What did you do?

I started fixing dinner.

Even after he drove his car into your house?

I know this sounds funny, but it was his way of telling me he still cares. I liked that.

Nicole, I wish I could agree, but I can't. I wish you the very best.

You probably think I'm a little weird, don't you?

Not really. You're pretty much the same as everybody else. Goodbye now.

Goodbye, Elliot.

Elliot closed the laptop. He sipped on his wine and watched the chicken grill out on the deck. Sooner or later, he was going to have to learn to fix something else for his dinner. So now he knew. His current trend with women applied to the entire Internet. Maybe Buddy was right. Buddy thought it was metaphysical. Buddy was his mom's longtime live-in boyfriend. He looked like Waylon Jennings. He repaired diesel engines. He played pedal steel guitar. He was very devoted to Elliot's mom. Elliot liked him. Buddy said Elliot's problem was kind of like a curse, but not quite. A real curse only happens when you've done something bad to bring it on. Elliot had done no such thing. Or so he hoped. Maybe there was some kind of guilt by association because of the dope house incident. In any case, that episode had pretty much ended his love life. The police counselor told him that this was often the case, a symptom of post-traumatic stress. This didn't make Elliot feel any better about it.

Elliot pawed at the chicken and picked at the instant rice. He really wasn't hungry. Irene Walters kept coming back. He wouldn't rest until he found out what really happened. He was almost certain that it was bad, very bad. He also knew in his heart what he had to do to start setting it straight. He dumped the remnants of chicken and rice down the disposal and started the dishwasher.

The Main Duck signaled sunset with a single blast as Elliot locked up and walked to his car.

CHAPTER 39

Korvin's camp touched very lightly upon the forest. It seemed to grow naturally out of the earth and become an extension of it. A section of downed tree trunk served as a sitting place from which he could survey his domain. The dog lay near the circle of stones that enclosed the embers of the fire. A very primal tableau. Korvin admired the purity of it. He preferred to deal with the essence of things, the distillations that stripped away the annoying complexities imposed by humanity at large.

One of those complexities was cradled in his hand. The satellite phone output a small beep as it finished the download from Malaysia from Becker. He scanned the contents, including a picture of the target. Only this time, the term "target" didn't apply. This time, the individual would be the subject of a more subtle manipulation. This time, Korvin would get to apply creativity and ingenuity to his work. He pulled up the picture of Lieutenant Detective Elliot Elliot again. The man's face radiated both intelligence and conviction, a dangerous combination. Korvin welcomed the challenge. The greater the opponent, the greater the victory. It had always been this way, and would never change. He was certain of that.

He ran through the other data on Elliot. Military and police records, credit information and so on. The whole concept of privacy was a comfort food to keep the general population complacent. Every system had a back door, intentionally or not. And a door meant a set of keys. You didn't break down the door if you wanted in. You simply bought a set of duplicate keys. And one way or another, the keys were always for sale. Such was the human condition. And Becker was a master at exploiting it.

He looked over at the dog, which lay by the fire. Why had Becker shifted his attention to Elliot, and off the dog? Who knew? And given his level of compensation for this assignment, who cared?

The dog's chin rested on the warm earth heated by the nearby flames. Her belly was reasonably content. The man fed her on a spartan but regular basis. This time, she made no attempt at escape. The magnetic power of a pack leader constrained her at least as much as the tether. Her eyes shifted to him. He stared at a small black box in his hand, a box he sometimes talked to. She wondered if the box talked back to him. She suspected it did, but had no proof. Simply another mystery in an infinitely mysterious world.

Korvin smiled as he looked at the text scrolling on the phone display. It was a police report Elliot had filed a while back at the Department of Public Safety at Pearson. It detailed a contact with a person up here in the woods called the King. It seemed this person functioned as an authority figure who represented the general vagrant population. It also seemed that Elliot was cultivating a relationship with this person to help control the presence of troublesome individuals on campus property.

Korvin put the phone away and fetched a knife from the lean-to. He would practice while he considered the King. The knife's design dictated stabbing and cutting, not throwing, but he had adapted his throwing technique to accommodate its weight and balance. He held it by the handle, swung it up in a broad circle, brought it back down, and released it. It hurtled toward a nearby tree trunk, sliced through the bark, and buried its blade in the wood. He fetched it, and repeated the cycle over and over. The rhythm of it propelled his thinking. He already knew where he could find the King. He had recently come upon a campsite that differed from the others, and he'd observed it from a distance. Most encampments up here reflected the character of their inhabitants. They were loosely assembled and quickly abandoned. But not this one. This one had a sense of permanence about it. Now he knew why. It was serving as a seat of government, and the large man with the ponytail who lived there must be the governor of sorts. The King.

———

The dog watched the man throw the knife repeatedly at the tree. She immersed herself in the mechanics and details of the motion. The grip on the handle, the disposition of the elbow, the arc of the windup, the moment of release. She became mesmerized by the precision he achieved with each throw.

———

Korvin stopped throwing and looked at the dog. The beast seemed resigned to its fate. It was remarkably intelligent. What were they going to do with it? He could only speculate, and he wasn't a man given to speculation. He turned his thinking back to the matter with Elliot. His mandate was clear. He was to remove Elliot from his current post without committing any violence upon him.

He already had some ideas.

CHAPTER 40

A black-tie event. Of course. Elliot should have known. The dedication of the new wing of the children's hospital. The Chief hadn't been invited and he'd fumed over the perceived snub. No cops, only docs. Elliot walked in sans tie with chinos and a tweed sport coat. He kept to the far periphery of the big reception area and watched the campus glitterati mingle. A piano trio accompanied their collective buzz. He took a position to the side of catering, where he wouldn't be conspicuous.

There she was, in a beaded evening dress of dark plum. Hair all done up and swept back. He knew she couldn't stay away, even with a brain-dead spouse parked just a few blocks down the hill. He traced her path through the crowd and watched it weave a tale of trouble. Without Oakner in tow, she had been cut from the herd. People were clustered into little conversational galaxies, bound together by professional gravity. She wandered from one group to the next and looked for an opportunity to insert herself. None came. She searched frantically for some way out of the intergalactic void. She wandered over and got some wine. She looked at a model of the new wing. She collected some finger food. She was out.

He intercepted her as she wandered toward the catering table. The instant she saw him, she did a quick scan of the room to see if anyone was watching her with the man in the tweed sport coat. They weren't.

"Elliot. What are you doing here?"

"Business."

"What kind of business?"

"You."

"What do you mean?"

"Remember the radiologist I told you about? Irene Walters?"

"I saw the thing in the paper about her. It's very sad."

"Yes, it is. I missed the article. I was gone on vacation. Want to know where I went?"

"Where?"

"Cabo San Lucas."

Her lips parted ever so slightly. It was the only giveaway. "Very nice. Did you get some sun?"

"I got a lot more than that."

"You did?"

"I got to have a nice long chat with your housekeeper down there."

She did another lightning scan of the room. Only this time it was frantic. "And what did she tell you?"

"She told me this incredible story. About the doc unconscious in his car. About the exhaust fumes. About the trip to the hospital. And so on. No need to bore you with the details. You already know them."

She grabbed his wrist. Her hand was cold and moist. "Elliot, you don't understand."

"You know, you're right about that. There's a lot of things I don't understand. But there's one thing that I do understand. If anybody here at Pearson knew the doc went into a coma from carbon monoxide poisoning, his license would have been toast. Which means both of you would have been totally screwed. But now he's completely zonked and it's only you who's totally screwed. How am I doing here? Maybe I've got it all wrong. That would be nice. So why don't you help me? Why don't you explain to me why I've got it all wrong?"

Her grip tightened on his wrist. "Please. Please don't do anything before I can talk to you."

"And when might that be, your ladyship?"

"Just let me get through this and get home. I'll be there in a couple of hours. I'll call you."

"I got a better idea. You be home in exactly two hours, and I'll be there, too."

She released her grip on him. "Okay. Alright. I'll see you then. I've got to go now."

He watched her stride off into the crowd. She turned once before she disappeared into the black-tie galaxies to see if he was watching.

He wasn't. He was already out the door.

CHAPTER 41

Elliot and Christie sat in her living room, the show-place that no one ever really sat in. The party dress was long gone. She wore sweats of plain cotton. A red rubber band bunched her hair into a crude ponytail. Her legs were drawn up to one side where she sat on the couch. Her arms were folded protectively over her chest. Elliot sat facing her from four yards away across an antique Chinese rug. The lights from the valley struggled to make it through the drizzle in the window behind him.

"Do I need a lawyer? I've been told I probably do."

"Who told you that?"

"An interested party."

"You can tell the interested party to fuck off for the time being. I'm going to be straight with you. If and when you need a lawyer, I'll let you know. Right now, it's just you and me."

She smiled bitterly. "Like old times?"

"I wish," Elliot said. "I really do. But I'm afraid not."

"So, what do you want?"

"I want to know exactly what happened down there. Both on the morning you found him and the night before."

"The night before," she echoed. She looked at the carpet and her eyes turned inward. She drew her legs closer and clutched her chest tighter. "We were at home. We were going to have dinner, and instead we had a fight. He was very angry. He was about as angry as I've ever seen him."

"What were you fighting about?"

"I'm not going to tell you that. It has nothing to do with what happened. That's all you need to know. Now, do I need a lawyer?"

"No. You don't. So what happened after the fight?"

"He left. He'd cooled down some by then. He drove over to see Dick Stennis on his boat in the marina. I was exhausted from the fighting and went to bed. I was too tired to wait up for him. He and Stennis went very late sometimes, over at the bars by the docks. There were probably women involved. I didn't want to know."

"Stennis? Who's that?"

"He's the principal investigator on a large research project up at Pearson. Jim thought he was absolutely brilliant. They had a business deal going."

"What kind of business deal?"

"They were partners in a company called Stemix. I don't know all the details. You can probably find it all on the web. It never made any money, but Jim didn't seem to care. He said that sooner or later, it would make us extremely wealthy."

"So, this Stennis is basically a scientist, right?"

"Right."

"Isn't it a bit unusual for scientists to have boats in harbors in Mexico? I thought they just kind of lived from one grant to the next."

"I don't know. He had this grant that seemed to go on

forever. Jim used to joke about Stennis and his perpetual-funding machine. Also, people said he had family money."

"So, you went to bed and didn't see the doctor until the next morning?"

"I woke up early because I went to bed so early. I thought Jim would be home and in bed with me, but he wasn't. At first, I thought he'd just spent the night on the boat, but then I began to worry and couldn't get back to sleep. I went out to the garage to see if his car was there, and that's when I found him."

"Unconscious?"

"And drunk. He smelled like a brewery. The garage door was down and the engine was running. I freaked out. I ran and opened the door, then went back to make sure he was still alive. That's when Bonita showed up.

"She called an ambulance. He was too heavy to lift. All we could do was back the car out into the fresh air. The ambulance took him to the hospital and they put him in a thing called a hyperbaric oxygen chamber."

"They got that kind of stuff down there?"

She snorted. "Of course they do. They've got a whole bunch of rich gringos to pay for it. At first, it didn't do any-thing, and I was completely freaked. I called Dick Stennis. He was the only one I had for support. On the phone, he advised me not to tell anyone what had happened because it could really hurt Jim's career. By the time Dick got there, Jim was already snapping out of it. By the next day, he was fine, just like nothing ever happened, and he came home."

"Did he remember what happened?"

"Part of it. He did go to Dick's boat, and then later he went to one of the bars by the docks. He remembered he had quite a few drinks and then drove home and into the garage, but nothing else." She shook her head. "It was all so stupid. He got drunk and nearly died in a dumb blunder. He was really paranoid after that. He said we could never mention it to anyone or he would lose his license."

A moment of silence set in. They both stared at the pattern in the carpet.

"Lawyer or not, why are you willing to tell me all this?" Elliot asked.

"Because it's not my fault," she said. "None of it is. I want you to know that. Because of what you've found out, you now have it in your power to more or less destroy me. Is that what you want?"

"No. That's not what I want. I want to find out what really happened to Irene Walters. Anyway, I don't quite understand your total destruction theory. I mean, your husband won't practice again under any circumstances, so losing his license is pretty much a nonissue at this point."

"Wrong. It's all about the insurance. Jim has a big disability policy. Most doctors do. It's what I'll live off of. If he dies, there's also life insurance that kicks in. But he might stay like this for years, and as long as he does, all I get are the disability payments. Which leaves me with a very big problem: If he was practicing under false pretenses, the policy is null and void. The minute they find what happened down there, I'm completely screwed."

"So what about real estate? You've got this house, plus the one down in Cabo. Couldn't you cash in on some of it?"

"I'm afraid not. Our accountant has hit me with a whole bundle of little surprises. It turns out that Jim was a far better doctor than money manager. We're leveraged to the hilt. It's a big house of cards, and I'm the one left holding the deck."

She shifted in her chair and absently tugged her ponytail. "So now you know. What are you going to do?"

"I'm going to ask you one final question, and if you're straight with me, I'm not going to do anything at all."

"Then ask."

"Do you know anything about the cover-up with the CT scans?"

She tensed and squirmed in her chair. "I didn't have anything to do with it."

"That's not what I asked. I asked if you knew anything about it."

She breathed deeply, then sighed. "There's a third party involved in all this, and I'm not going to identify him. He's like me, he's been pretty much sitting in the bleachers and watching, but not playing."

"Are you sleeping with him?" Elliot got the question out before he could stop himself. He didn't want to know, but he had to know.

"The answer is no, and it's also none of your fucking business. It has nothing to do with what's happened. And don't tell me that you'll be the judge of that."

"I'm not judging anything. Like I said before, all I want is to find out what happened to Irene Walters."

"Did it ever occur to you that she just committed suicide? Why are you trying to make it so complicated? Besides, the person I mentioned has way too much to lose to be involved in any kind of criminal action. Give it a rest, Elliot. You'll feel much better in the morning."

"Somehow I don't think so. Don't bother getting up—I'll show myself out."

———

The rain had stopped by the time Elliot pulled into his apartment complex. The ducks were silent and the air damp. He reviewed his conversation with Christie as he walked to his unit. He could have pushed harder and gotten a little more, but he might have alienated her permanently. He simply couldn't do it. Some small part of him still held out hope for them as lovers, stupid as that might be. He wasn't happy about being this way, but he was realistic enough not to deny it. And anyway, he probably had enough information to ferret out the so-called "third party."

The only thing that gnawed at him was Oakner in Cabo. Based on what Christie and the maid said, it seemed highly likely that the doctor drove into the garage, clicked its door shut, and passed out before he could leave the vehicle. So much for that. The big question was: Why did he get so stinking drunk in the first place? It didn't fit his usual pattern of behavior or his character. Something must have really upset him, something between him and Stennis while they were on the boat. But what? Whatever set Oakner off was the blasting cap for everything that followed.

Elliot entered his unit and turned on the kitchen light. His cell phone sat in the middle of the dining room table. Damn. He'd completely forgotten it when he took off. Suddenly, it buzzed and did a little dance across the bare wood as the vibrator kicked in. A message alert. He picked the phone up and punched the message up onto the display. It was from Bobby Seifert.

> **A guy phoned 4 you.**
> **Said he was the king.**
> **Wants to see you in the**
> **morning about the dog.**

CHAPTER 42

The King was reading a book when Elliot appeared. He looked up, creased the page corner to save his place, and smiled.

"Lieutenant Detective Elliot. Always a pleasure." He gestured to a small stump near the fire. "Have a seat. How about some coffee?"

"Thanks, I think I will," said Elliot. He watched the King pour the steaming liquid into an old mug. "What are you reading?"

The King handed him the mug and held up the book. *"Moby Dick.* I'm off the trash and back on the hard stuff."

"All I remember is Ahab and the White Whale," admitted Elliot.

"That's a good start." The King put the book down. "So what's up? Or are you just on a little morning hike before work?"

"I got your call yesterday. About the dog."

"My call? What call?"

"You left a message you wanted to see me, right?"

·"Wrong. I've been right where you see me for the last twenty-four hours."

"We may have a problem," Elliot said.

––––––––

"So you see," the woman said, "I'm Mary and that little dog was Jesus, and he died to save us all."

"Well, of course," Korvin said. "It makes perfect sense."

"It's very nice to talk to you," the woman said. "I don't always connect with people."

"I know the feeling," Korvin said. "Sometimes it's hard."

"Are you from around here? I haven't seen you before."

"No, we're just out on a walk."

"How long have you had your dog?" She pointed at the dog on its leash, a black Lab that looked at her very inquisitively. It was almost like the dog wanted to tell her something. She was sensitized to that kind of thing.

"Since she was a puppy," Korvin said. "She's a big part of our family."

·The dog looked at the little Chihuahua on the end of the woman's leash. It gave off scented waves of agitation. It didn't own this space and had no markings here, but it clearly resented the dog's presence. Its big ears stood at attention. Its bulbous eyes remained locked on her. It seemed absurd that so small a beast would present so large a challenge. The little animal didn't understand the consequences of a physical conflict with a much larger dog. It was unable to ponder the future.

"I got my dog as a puppy, too," the woman said. "Right after the pit bull killed my last one."

"Yes, you told me that," Korvin said. "I'm sorry, I must be going. My wife's expecting us back."

"Your wife? Oh. Well, it was nice talking to you. Have a nice day."

"I'm sure I will."

She tugged on the Chihuahua's leash and walked off toward a rock-lined pond in the center of the apartment complex. A cluster of mallards paddled over its becalmed surface.

Korvin headed in a different direction, toward the next cluster of units, the one listed in his downloaded files on Elliot. The dog was serving him well. A man walking a dog was assumed to be domesticated, not unlike the dog at the end of the man's leash. Only the man was bound by a much larger leash, invisible yet extremely powerful. Very few would regard him as a rogue male, a potential marauder.

He soon reached a little square bordered by two clusters of apartments. Empty and quiet. Blinds closed. He climbed the stairs to Elliot's unit on the second floor, with the dog pacing him step for step. Along the way, he donned a pair of disposable latex gloves. He reached the landing and brought a lock pick and tension wrench out of his pocket. He deftly inserted the pick and pushed the wrench into place. He felt the wrench rotate slightly as he pushed each internal pin to the shear line. He quickly reached the last pin and the lock rotated freely. He was in.

He opened the door and scanned right and left. To the right, a living room with a sliding door to a little deck. Love seat, easy chair, flat-screen TV, bookcases. Not likely locations. Possibly the kitchen, but the best bet was to his left, the bedroom. A man living alone had little reason to cleverly conceal a weapon. And Korvin knew with certainty that there was a weapon. The Becker data package included the digitized registration documents. He closed the front door and headed for the bedroom. He let the dog loose in the confines of the apartment.

The dog went immediately to the kitchen, the food source. She sniffed the small space between the double doors under the kitchen sink. Her nose deciphered a wealth of edible items in the plastic garbage container within. Chicken scraps, fried rice, carrot tops, coffee grounds, tomato trimmings. She tried to nudge one of the doors open, but couldn't quite get the required leverage.

Korvin went immediately to the dresser in the bedroom. Three photos sat atop it in their cheap stands. Korvin paused to take measure. One showed the subject dressed in combat gear with companions, and a Bradley fighting vehicle in the background. Another displayed him in tactical police dress next to a van. The last showed him with two older people, possibly parents. The woman appeared pleasant and happy, the bearded man came off rugged and self-assured. A strange instrument sat in the foreground, an elongated rectangle with many strings on a stand with pedals. Korvin opened the second drawer down and immediately located the weapon behind some roughly folded undershirts.

The dog drifted into the bathroom and smelled the signature of a single human. She knew it was only one individual from the composition of the odors. She also knew that there had been certain traces of this same signature in the woods. She was thirsty. The man was lax about providing water. She went to the toilet bowl. The water within reflected the overhead light onto the white porcelain. She looked at its glasslike surface, dipped her head in, and lapped the water with her long tongue.

Korvin briefly examined the weapon. A standard-issue 9mm Glock. A classic cop gun. He released the clip. A couple of hollow-point rounds pushed against the top. He slid the breach open and checked the chamber. Empty. He replaced the clip and slid the weapon into his coat pocket. He looked at the family picture one more time.

"You should be very proud of your son," he told the picture. And then he took the dog and left.

CHAPTER 43

So where you been?" Bobby Seifert asked when Elliot came in.

"The woods," Elliot said as he took off his sport coat. "How would you like an all-expenses-paid trip to Baskin-Robbins?"

Bobby looked up from his computer display in mock indignation. "How could you say such a thing? I'll go to HR. I'll get an attorney."

"Yeah, you could do all that. Only trouble is, they won't match my offer."

"What do you need?"

"First, I need your utter silence. This is unofficial."

"Which means it's not dog-related. Correct?"

Elliot pulled up a chair next to Bobby's display. "Remember the phone message about the dog and the guy called the King?"

"Of course I do. How often do we get calls up here about dogs and kings?"

"Did you log the number?"

"I did."

"How long would it take you to track down where it came from?"

"You mean in the real world?"

"Yes, Bobby, there is such a place. It exists right alongside cyberspace. Think of it as *The Matrix* in reverse."

"Give me three minutes?"

"That quick?"

Bobby smiled impishly. "I have friends in telecommunications."

"Do it."

Three minutes and thirteen seconds later, he had the answer. "It's a pay phone. A medieval device. Right here on campus. On the corner between the eye clinic and the old administration building."

"Well done," Elliot said. "Now I need you to set me up so I can search the database with the security cam data. From my machine."

"Nothing to it," Bobby said as they walked to Elliot's computer. "Even a law enforcement official can do it. I also see the method in your madness."

Cursors danced and windows blossomed and died as Bobby did the setup. "There you go."

Elliot dove in. He scanned a map of all the camera locations on the campus. Hundreds. Only one interested him. He clicked on the little camera icon for that location and crossed his fingers. He wasn't sure if it covered the pay phone, but it was definitely worth finding out.

"What time did that call come in?" he asked Bobby.

"Late. About seven-thirty. It was dark out."

"What were you doing here that late?"

"My own stuff. Where else are you going to get on the web at these speeds?"

A window opened on Elliot's screen. He was staring at a real-time picture from the camera. And there was the pay phone in the far left corner, maybe fifty feet away. He filled in a series of data fields that described the time window he wanted. He hit Enter. A video player opened and showed the location as it appeared at 7:02 the previous evening. Good. The phone stood out in a pool of light. He hit play and watched. Cars came and went on the street in the background. Pedestrians strolled by on the sidewalk in the foreground. He hit fast-forward. Cars sped. Pedestrians sprinted.

And then a man approached the phone. Elliot stopped, reversed and watched him enter the frame. Lean. Athletic and spare in his movement. Dressed in a water-proof jacket, jeans and boots. Wool cap over what looked like a buzz cut. The man stopped and scanned all around him. Elliot immediately understood. The man was looking for the camera, but somehow he missed it. He stepped up to the pay phone, picked up the receiver and dialed. The video provided just enough resolution for Elliot to see his lips move in a brief conversation. He hung up and quickly walked away.

The surveillance database allowed Elliot to make a copy of the video containing the incident. He brought the file over onto his machine, and repeated the process he used with the Irene Walters video. He pulled a freeze-frame of the man and magnified it. The man's face appeared bland and agreeable, and strangely featureless. The distance of the face from the camera and the limits of the video resolution amplified the effect.

Why did he call? What did it have to do with the dog?

Elliot didn't know the answers. He only knew that they were not good.

━━━

The dog lay by the fire pit, well within the confines of its tether. She mulled over the odd journey she had taken with the alpha man. They had walked out of the woods and through the city for a very long time. Then the Chihuahua, the woman, the empty apartment. Finally, they had returned and eaten. She could still feel the warmth from the coals of the cooking fire. After the meal, the man had secured her and left. He was still gone. She understood that she was at a critical point. If she didn't attempt to escape the tether while the alpha man was gone, there might not be another chance for a very long time. The man fed and led her, but he gave no love because he had no love within him. She knew this because she had searched with both her eyes and nose and found none. Life with him would be bleak.

She got up and carefully assessed her situation. The leash and rope formed a bond impervious to cutting or chewing. She walked within its limits and searched for a solution. A sharp stone. A jagged piece of metal. But she found none. She went to the far end of the tether and looked back at the taut line it formed. And here she saw the answer.

━━━

"Bobby, how would you like to earn a bonus prize?"

"Such as?"

"The rest of the day off for that trip to Baskin-Robbins."

"So what do I have to do?"

"I need you to search the campus web for references to a company called Stemix."

Bobby put his mouse into gear. His fingers danced on the keyboard. "And then?"

"Depends on what we find." Elliot watched as a list of references to Stemix appeared in Bobby's browser. The first was a press release. Something about manipulating specific genes in stem cells.

"I'm scrolling to the bottom," Bobby told him. "They always put the techno stuff first and the biz stuff at the end." He frowned. "Stemix. Doesn't say much. And there's no link to a website. Unusual. Even the most rinky-dink companies have some kind of web presence."

"What about the top part? Does it say who's running the project?"

Bobby scrolled back up. "It's a Ph.D. named Richard Stennis. That sound familiar?"

Elliot didn't answer. It was time to start being very careful. From his time as a city cop, he knew that a lot of courtroom time revolved around who knew what and when.

He pushed his chair back and stood up. "Keep digging, Bobby. Go deep. Come back with much more."

Bobby dug deep and was back in nineteen minutes.

"Ever heard of the Xanos Foundation?" he asked.

"Can't say that I have."

"It's the funding source for the research stuff that Stemix is doing. Outside of that, there's not much. These guys don't seem to be into publicizing their work."

The Xanos Foundation. Elliot hadn't heard of it, but it opened a path of inquiry. He knew how the research game was played on campus. Everybody did. It was the sine qua non of economic survival up here. It started with a group of scientists forming a private company to pursue a promising technology. The scientists then sought financial support for their work through grants from private foundations and government sources. Once they locked in the money, they used the campus lab space and infrastructure to support their work. Part of the grant funding went to support these "indirect costs," which became the university's cut of the action. But the ultimate economic issue was: Who got what if the technology was eventually commercialized and made a lot of money? A series of very specific provisions were put in place to split the proceeds among the parties involved.

So here was Stemix at Pearson operating on money supplied by Xanos. During the research phase, the flow of this money started with the foundation, went through Pearson and on down to Stemix. Along the way, Pearson would rake in the indirect costs, then the balance of the money went to Stemix for actual research operations.

So who kept track of all this money flow? Who was the overseer? Who made sure it was all well spent? Elliot already knew the answer. It was the Director of Research. Michael Hoffner.

"Bobby, go to the state records, and see if Stemix is incorporated here."

It took Bobby four minutes. "Here you go. Stemix. Privately held by three principals. Richard Stennis, James Oakner, and some outfit called Evergreen Ventures. Probably a venture capital group putting money into the thing."

"One more shot," Elliot said. "Check and see if Evergreen Ventures is also registered here in the state."

Bobby typed and searched. The answer popped up almost immediately. "Here you go. An LLC with a single owner. Michael Hoffner." He paused. "Hey, isn't that guy the Director of Research up here?"

"Indeed he is," answered Elliot.

Bobby was always very quick, but it took him a moment to put this together. He grinned at Elliot. "Now I know why you're the boss. You're a goddamn genius."

"We'll want to make sure that gets in my performance review, Bobby. Tell me exactly why you think I'm a genius."

"This Hoffner administers the money going to Stemix from this Xanos Foundation. I mean, that's what Directors of Research do, right?"

"Right."

"But Hoffner's also a silent partner in Stemix, which means he's part of the company he's feeding grant money to."

"Right."

"That doesn't sound too ethical."

"No, it doesn't."

The dog kept the tether very taut and walked along its circumference until it stretched over the fire pit. Then she moved a few steps toward the middle of the camp to relax the tension. The nylon rope drooped down, coming to rest on top of the coals. Soon the nylon began to boil and sizzle and smoke. The acrid fumes offended her nose, but she waited patiently. The section of rope touching the coals became a bubbling mass. When she judged the damage to the line was maximized, she gave a sharp jerk. The rope parted at the burn point, coiled through the air and landed at her feet. She was free.

She chose a path of escape that would present maximum difficulty to a human pursuer. She traveled uphill and cut across several of the creek drainages carved into the hillside. After a time, she stopped when she heard a sudden sound, a brutal sound she had never before experienced.

Nearby, the crows rose up and beat their black wings and cawed in a most hideous manner.

CHAPTER 44

I t wasn't hard to find the crime scene. Elliot simply followed the string of cops, firemen and emergency medical people up the trail. He wished Sparks or someone downtown had at least had the decency to inform him, but they hadn't. Instead, they immediately staked their claim and left the Pearson Department of Public Safety completely out of the loop. Technically, of course, they had every right to do so. The woods weren't part of the campus; the woods were part of the city proper. Elliot didn't even know what was going on until midafternoon, when one of their campus security patrol guys saw the squad cars and emergency vehicles suddenly converging at the trail head.

Each step up the trail made him a little queasier. Each fork confirmed where he was going.

The King was dead. Long live the King.

Yellow crime scene tape came into view. It threw a rude yellow slash across the quiet green vegetation. He showed his badge to the patrolman posted at the trail's edge and climbed over the little rise to the King's camp. The body lay in plain view, sprawled faceup. All the usual crime scene personnel milled about. Sampling, photographing, videotaping, measuring. All under the supervision of Lieutenant Detective Sparks of the city Homicide Division.

"What took you so long?" Sparks asked Elliot.

Elliot didn't answer. He looked into the King's dead eyes. He had lost a friend. He had never really had a father, but the world had been kind enough to provide a few reasonable substitutes. The King was one of them.

Sparks picked up the vibe. "You know him?" he asked.

"Yeah, I knew him," Elliot answered. "Everybody up here knew him."

"How's that?"

"He was the leader of the pack. He was the King."

"So that means there were a whole lot of people that might have had a beef with him. Right?"

"No. That's not what it means at all. It means he did a lot of good things for a lot of people who never got a break and never will."

"Funny you should put it like that," Sparks said. He pointed to a solemn pair of vagrants, an older man and woman. They stood in stricken silence on the periphery of the scene. Tears streamed down the woman's cheeks. "They said just about the same thing."

"Were they the ones who called it in?" Elliot asked.

"Yeah, they flagged down a patrol car. Didn't have enough change to make a phone call."

"Did they see anyone on the trail?"

"No. Doesn't matter. It looks like we've got the murder weapon. All we need is verification through the ballistics."

"You mean someone left it right here at the crime scene? Come on, how dumb can you be?"

"You've been a cop long enough to know," Sparks said. "It wasn't a cheap-ass gun, either. It was a Glock."

A Glock. Elliot stiffened. It couldn't be. Why was he even thinking such a thing?

"Is it still here?" he asked.

"It just went downtown. The serial number's intact, so we can run the registration, for whatever that's worth. Probably registered to some gangbanger who's been in the pen for the last five years. I'm betting we get lucky with fingerprints. If someone was dumb enough to toss it, they probably didn't wear gloves when they used it."

"You could be right," Elliot said. "Do me a favor, okay? Keep me in the loop on this thing."

"The outer loop," Sparks responded. "The *outer* loop. Understand?"

"Understood."

Elliot started up the stairs to his apartment. Alternate steps produced alternate images within him. First, the dead King, with a bullet hole placed in almost perfect symmetry in the center of his forehead. Second, the blurred video face at the pay phone, leaving a message about the King and the dog. In a very few moments, he would know if they were connected.

He unlocked the door and scrutinized the deadbolt assembly. The bolt showed no signs of manipulation. The brass strike plate bore no scratches. He entered, leaving the door open, and went directly to the chest of drawers in the bedroom, second drawer down. He shoved his hand into the pile of undershirts and begged for the pistol to be there. Nothing. He took the drawer out and dumped it on the bed. He tore through the jumbled mound of white cotton. Nothing. Maybe it was the wrong drawer. Yes, the wrong drawer. He pulled out the third drawer and repeated the process. Nothing. The fourth drawer. Nothing. Same for the fifth drawer.

He sat down on a little bench at the foot of the bed and tried to think it through. He'd been set up. So what was his next move? He shut his eyes. He breathed deeply. He waited for the solution to present itself. It didn't.

He rose and went to the open door. The Main Duck blasted out three quacks as he shut the door and went to the stairs.

Sparks stood at the bottom of the steps. He dug his hands in his jacket pockets and looked up at Elliot in silence. Elliot stopped and stared down at him.

"It's gone," Elliot said.

"It sure is," Sparks said. "And you want to know where it is right now?"

"Where?"

"It's in a plastic evidence bag. In the glove compartment of my car. Somehow the chain of evidence got screwed up. Happens all the time."

"So where do we go from here?"

Sparks shrugged. "People know. But they're all in the inside. That's the good news. The bad news is that someone on the inside will probably let your boss know."

"Do you want me to tell you what's happening here?" Elliot asked. "Do you want to know what's really going on?"

"There's only one thing I needed to know, Elliot, and now I know it."

"What's that?"

"We're even." Sparks turned and left.

Elliot understood. Whatever leverage he had over Sparks from the dope house incident was now gone. In return, Sparks was letting him walk on the problem with the King and the murder weapon. The books were balanced.

———

Elliot looked at the pile of the clothes on the bed. He picked up one of the drawers and peered into its naked interior. He couldn't deal with the mess right now. Whoever killed the King probably did it shortly after he'd left the campsite. The autopsy would undoubtedly bear that out. Which put him at the scene in the time frame of the murder. All he had to back up his position was a cryptic phone message and some blurry video. The Irene Walters incident had already taught him what blurry video buys you.

His bladder interrupted his train of thought. He walked to the bathroom and started to unzip in front of the bowl. He looked down at the oval of white porcelain. A sprinkle of hairs covered the front of the rim. Not his hair. Not curly and pubic. Short, straight and black.

Dog hair.

CHAPTER 45

C hristie sat down bedside and set her purse on the
floor. It was his birthday, his fifty-seventh. She'd
considered bringing a card, or a little cupcake with a
candle. But it all seemed too maudlin. Instead, she brought
only herself, which required more and more effort with
each visit.

She glanced at him only briefly this time, and then
gazed out the window. It faced the upward slope of the hillside. Big houses crowned the ridge above. She knew the in-
teriors of many. Parties for this, lunches for that, cocktails
for everything else.

She recalled many journeys up many hillsides, both
topographical and metaphorical. All over the world. But
one in particular leapt out at her. From that day in Mexico,
the one that launched this whole awful business.

She had left the marina wearing the necklace from the
old woman and carrying the candies from the woman with
the children, the beautiful children. They stayed with her
as she drove out of the clutter of town and back to the en-

trance to their gated community. The guard with his clipboard nodded at her in recognition. He wrote something down in an officious manner, then nodded to a second man in a nearby booth. The barrier of red and white came up and she drove on through.

She felt the distant mutter of the cobblestones through the tires as she started up the hill. Jim would be awake and ready to fight. They would open by presenting their demands. She wanted him to stop his regressive behavior. He wanted her to have a baby. His defense was always the same. Socializing and business were inextricably intertwined. Sure, they had a few drinks, but they also sorted through a lot of issues. Her defense on the baby issue was more oblique, and she knew it. She couldn't plead money problems, or lack of time in a busy schedule. She'd speak of feelings, of personal choice, of spiritual explorations, of paths less traveled. He would have none of it. For him, it was brutally simple. He was on the far side of middle age. It was his last chance to leave his biological imprint upon the world. If she really loved him, she would have his child. She would respond with everything but the truth, which she kept in a tightly secured vault deep within her.

She pulled up to their home and pressed the button to open the garage door. He would be waiting, he would be surly. Sooner or later, he would push her past the point of discretion, and she would blurt out the truth in a moment of blind retaliation. It would be ugly, very ugly.

And when it did happen, later that day, it was indeed very ugly. And of course, the fallout was horrific. She could still smell the toxic cloud of trapped exhaust. She could still see him slumped over the steering wheel.

But now, sitting here with his empty shell at Pearson, it all seemed very distant. He would never father her children.

Nobody would. The irony was obvious. At this time, when she most needed a family, she had no family at all. Her mother had died years ago. She had no siblings. If it weren't for Elliot, she would stand utterly alone.

Her gaze shifted from the window to his limp form in the bed. He had changed after the catastrophe in the garage. He had become more reserved, more pensive, less combative. She suspected she had mortally wounded him with what she said that day down in Mexico.

And now she had to wonder if she hadn't also mortally wounded herself.

CHAPTER 46

K orvin sat in his camp in the muted light of late afternoon. A Douglas squirrel chattered from its perch high above. An anonymous rodent snaked through the nearby ivy. Korvin noticed none of it. He stared at the melted end of the rope that once held the dog. He surveyed the camp. The animal had used the remnants of the fire to sever her bond and escape. He had seriously underestimated her. She had demonstrated a remarkable degree of intelligence. Her scientific value to Becker and company was now fairly obvious, even if he didn't know the technical details. No wonder Becker was paying so generously for this project. And now he had no choice but to contact the man and update him on what had happened. He activated the satellite phone and made the secured connection. He'd start with the good news. As soon as Becker answered, he took the initiative:

"The detective Elliot has been completely compromised. He should no longer be a problem to you."

"Very good," Becker answered. "Hang on a minute."

Korvin heard typing in the background. Then Becker came back on. "There's still the dog to take care of. I haven't gotten any verification from Pearson about the delivery. Was there a problem?"

"You were going to call me back and tell me where to drop it off. I never heard from you." A long silence followed. "Are you still on the line?" Korvin finally asked.

"Yes, I'm here," Becker said. "So where's the dog right now?"

"I don't know. It escaped."

"What do you mean, 'it escaped'?"

"Just that. I'll have to recapture it."

"I didn't retain you to make mistakes, Mr. Korvin, especially this kind of mistake."

"The first mistake was yours, Mr. Becker. You failed to let me know what I was really dealing with. I should've been informed about the animal's intelligence."

"I'm not interested in your opinion. I'm interested in results. I don't pay for failure. Unless you get the animal back, the terms of your contract are null and void. You can keep the advance to cover services rendered to date, and forget about the rest unless you bring me that dog, and soon."

The call went dead. Korvin stroked the melted rope with his thumb. He must move immediately to track down the dog, while it was still in the forest. If it drifted out into the city, the situation became infinitely more complex. He did a swift inventory of the items in his camp, looking for a solution. His eye came upon a coil of metal wire. He'd found it at a construction site by Pearson. Now it would earn its keep, just as every item in his camp eventually did. He took a pair of pliers and twisted one end of it into a small loop, and set out into the woods.

The dog trailed the severed yellow rope as she climbed the slopes. It kept getting underfoot and made travel difficult, but she had no choice but to keep moving. The man, the alpha man, the cruel man, would undoubtedly be hunting her. He would find her and he would do it quickly. She didn't understand the origin of his powers, but she feared them greatly. Her only chance to stay free was to find a way out of the woods and into the city, which had proved to be full of danger and uncertainty. Still, she had no other option.

However, the neighborhood perched on the slopes above might present a solution. She had already caught its collective scent even though it remained hidden behind the canopy of conifers and deciduous trees. Lawn feed, baked chicken, children at play, minivan exhaust, perfume, exotic plants, spent heating oil. She could visualize the character of the place, with its tidy yards and patios and play structures and lawn furniture.

The distant squawking of crows floated up the slope. She turned her ears to it and listened intently. Something had set them off.

Korvin referred to his mental map of the trail system as he bounded up the slope at a near run. He could project with some certainty what the animal would do. She had enough experience by now to know that life on the street downtown or at the Pearson campus would have a bad ending. Still, she had to leave the woods to escape him. This left the neighborhoods above the forest as the most likely choice. An ordinary dog would simply wander into the street and head down the sidewalk until someone noticed and detained it. But not this animal. She would conceive some course of action that would guarantee her safety from him. It was imperative that he capture her before this happened. He headed up the trail toward a point of interception.

The dog proceeded cautiously up the trail, with its switchbacks that climbed the hillside in long, lazy undulations. She stopped periodically to sniff the dank air, rich with organic rot and rebirth. She caught no scent of the man, but found no reassurance in this. He was very clever at masking his presence, in ways she couldn't begin to understand. She needed to reach the relative safety of the neighborhoods above before he found her.

Korvin stood at the elbow of a switchback and spotted the dog stopped on the trail below as she sniffed the air. Perfect. He waited until she started up again, and then started straight down through the brush off the trail. It took all his skill to suppress the noise of his descent. In a short time, he reached the elbow below her. There he took out the metal wire and cinched it into a loop. He found a young alder, and snapped it so it bent over the trail, partially obscuring the path in either direction.

The dog froze at the snapping noise. She turned in the direction of the sound, which came from somewhere down the slope. She rounded the elbow of the switchback and looked up ahead. She saw nothing except trees and brush.

Her vision verged on monochromatic vision and presented no subtleties. She moved cautiously forward.

━━━━━━

Korvin retraced his path through the brush until he reached his point of departure on the elbow above. He parted the leaves at the edge of the trail, and looked down the path. There she was, moving up toward him.

━━━━━━

The dog suddenly caught a trace of the alpha man's scent, a trace so minute it nearly dissolved into the background of forest smells. She stopped cold, and peered ahead. Nothing. She started up again and quickened her pace, with a small dose of panic instilled in her step. She had only moved a few yards when the man stepped out onto the trail in front of her. At that same moment, the breeze shifted, and the full force of his scent slammed into her. And with it, her sense of independence evaporated. She was back in the pack.

━━━━━━

Korvin locked his stare onto the animal as she froze and looked away to avoid his gaze. He realized this entire exercise might be simpler than he'd thought. He kept his eyes fixed on her and moved slowly forward.

"Stay. Don't move."

━━━━━━

The phonemes, the syllables, the words meant nothing to the dog, but their force and shape meant everything. His alpha presence was rapidly leaching away any traces of her personal volition.

───────

"I'm going to take the rope now. I want you to stay still while I take the rope."

───────

His hand was out and reaching for the rope when something burst in the very center of her, something very powerful and ineffable. She turned and sprinted down the trail.

"Stop!"

───────

She heard his command. She felt the pounding of his footsteps as he pursued her. None of it mattered. She swiftly put substantial distance between them, and bent around to look only when she reached the elbow. He was far up the path, walking at a vigorous pace, but not running. She slowed to a trot and continued to descend. A fallen alder partially blocked the path ahead. Her myopic vision obscured the details of foliage, and she pushed on through.

It was then that she felt the metallic loop of the snare glide over her ears, down her neck, and pull tight about her.

───────

The dog had quit struggling by the time Korvin caught up to her. She was panting heavily and had pulled the snare taut.

"Alright now. I'm going to hold the rope and remove that. We're taking you back where you belong."

Korvin took the length of yellow nylon leash and wound it once around his right hand. With his left hand, he loosened the snare. He slid it off.

In the brief instant when metal loop cleared her head, the dog realized she had an opening, possibly the last one ever. She darted out and nipped the man's left hand in the fleshy pad below his thumb.

Korvin instinctively leapt backward, away from the attack. As he did so, he relaxed his grip on the leash. The dog gave a mighty yank, and the leash slid abrasively over his flesh and snaked into the air.

The dog sprinted up the trail. The thorns on an overhanging blackberry vine tore into her left ear, ripping out fur and flesh along the outer edge. She barely noticed. She flew on and rounded the next elbow. And another. And another.

She didn't stop until she reached a place where the trail emptied onto a street in the upper reaches of the hills. It resembled the exit from a tunnel, with a circle of brilliant light framed by a ragged border of leaves and brush in silhouette. She ducked off into the concealment of the brush and plopped down in complete exhaustion. Her left ear stung and she was panting profusely. But she was once again free, and that was all that really mattered.

PART 4

The Hunt

Elliot stared at the image on his computer screen of the man using the pay phone just a few hundred yards from where he now sat in his office. Bobby sat across the way, engrossed in techno-esoterica.

Elliot struggled to collect what he knew. A company called Stemix. Owned in part by a comatose surgeon. A cover-up of the surgeon's monoxide poisoning. A foundation called Xanos feeding money to Stemix. A corrupt director managing the cash flow in league with a rogue research scientist. A missing dog that obviously had immense value to Stemix. And now, two people dead, with Elliot essentially blackmailed by the downtown cops. So how did the man at the pay phone fit? He'd clearly set Elliot up, and probably murdered both Irene Walters and the King. But why? What was driving this whole thing?

"Elliot."

He looked up and saw the Chief standing in the door. And not his usual, bellicose self. He seemed quite relaxed, hands in his pockets, hip leaning against the doorjamb. A very bad sign.

"How you doing?" The Chief asked it in an almost paternal manner.

"Fine," Elliot lied. "I'm doing fine."

"Could I get you to come down to my office for a second?"

"Sure."

"Great."

Bobby looked up at Elliot as he walked to the door. Bobby knew it was bad, very bad.

Elliot walked down the hallway behind the Chief, who strolled along at a leisurely pace, hands still in his pockets. Elliot had never seen the Chief put his hands in his pockets. They reached the Chief's office, where he gestured at the seat in front of his desk.

"Go ahead, have a seat. Want some coffee or something?"

"No thanks."

The Chief settled back in his chair. "Elliot, I know you and I have had our differences, but that's all been purely professional. In the end, we're both decent guys just trying to do our jobs, right?"

"Yeah, I guess."

"Good. Because that kind of mutual respect is important. And it'll help you put things in perspective as we move on here."

"What things?"

The Chief leaned forward, elbows on his desk. A sad smile curved his lips. "I think it's time for you to resign."

"Resign? What for?" *He knows,* Elliot thought. *He already knows.*

"Well," the Chief said pensively, "there's a whole cluster of circumstances involved. We could sort through them, but I just don't see any point in opening a bunch of old wounds. Do you?"

"Maybe I do. I'm the one that's bleeding here, not you."

"I had lunch downtown today, Elliot. With some old friends."

"And what did you talk about?"

The Chief shrugged. "I can't really say. It's privileged information."

"Might there be some connection to my proposed resignation?"

The Chief maintained his miraculous composure. "Elliot, everybody up here and down there is rooting for you. We all want you to find yourself. We're prepared to give you some glowing references to help you along."

"Let me guess: If I don't resign, I don't get the references. I'm just another guy who got canned from his job."

The Chief repeated his philosophical shrug. "We certainly have cause. You were already written up. But it doesn't have to end that way. It's all up to you. You're the one in charge here."

Elliot was tempted to comment on the irony of that statement, but held his tongue. He was out. That simple. At least he could keep his references intact. "So, how long have I got?"

"All I need is a quick letter. Just a few sentences. You could get it done this afternoon. I'm going to throw in an extra month's severance to get you going. You can be out of here and on vacation by tomorrow. You need to relax for a while, Elliot. It'll be good for you."

"I'm sure it will."

The IT geek was coming out the office door with Elliot's laptop as he returned from the Chief's office. "That wouldn't be my computer, would it?"

"Not anymore," the geek said smugly, and pushed on by.

Elliot entered and looked at Bobby. "How am I supposed to write a letter of resignation without a computer?"

Bobby pointed to Elliot's denuded desk. Only a single sheet of paper and a pen remained. "They got this down, boss. They do it all the time. So what happened?"

"You want the short story or the long story?"

"Short story now, long story later," Bobby said.

Elliot moved to clear his personal stuff out of his desk and talked while he worked. "We uncovered a can of worms. All that stuff about Xanos and Evergreen Ventures and Hoffner. Plus the dog and the dead people. So they came to the source, and the source was me."

"So why don't you get a smart lawyer, or talk to a nosy reporter? Why don't you fight back?"

"That's the long story," Elliot answered.

Bobby reached in a drawer and pulled several high-density disks. "Well then, here's the first couple of chapters." He handed them to Elliot.

"What's this?"

"I knew they were coming, so I went and got the best of Elliot Elliot off your hard drive. And I somehow erased the original data in the process. Real clumsy of me."

"Real clumsy. Thanks. I'm not through with this thing."

"Then neither am I," Bobby said. "Keep in touch."

"I appreciate that." Elliot looked at Bobby's desk, searching for a little levity. "So where's your afternoon snack?"

"Seems like I've lost my appetite."

"Me, too."

The Main Duck split the morning wide open with a colossal series of quacks. Elliot quacked back. A reasonably good imitation. Elliot was drunk. Elliot had imbibed the better part of a bottle of cheap cabernet sauvignon. He had no job, no gun, no love interest, no future. He had, however, acquired some powerful enemies. He was also not safe here. Whoever stole his gun not only knew where he lived, but also knew he was at least temporarily unarmed. Still, the day was warm and the sun was out. He would ride through it suspended in a soft alcoholic fog. And then he would contact Christie. After all this time, it came back down to Christie. He let out one more counterfeit quack, but the Main Duck was not impressed and failed to respond.

CHAPTER 48

The dog felt the morning sun on her back as she strolled down the street of a neighborhood above the forest. Earlier encounters with such neighborhoods had demonstrated a particular pattern of occupation. Houses with children typically had resident pets, which would be potential rivals if she attempted to intrude. Houses with no children also had pets, smaller animals, often of an anxious and tremulous nature. Once again, not a good choice. However, a few houses appeared to have children and no pets. She could approach such a household and make contact with the children first, who seemed to be more open to the overtures of animals. The children would then present her case to the parents, and would do so in a far more convincing manner than she could.

The six-foot rope of severed nylon dragged along the pavement behind her. It was a day called Saturday, although the dog didn't know this. People were out tending their yards, which were emerging from winter chill and sprouting new life. Children ran about or rode small vehicles powered by pedals and a pumping motion of their legs. The dog was lost in the wonder of it all, and had to concentrate to find the correct house at the end of the block. She had originally determined its location from the back side facing the woods, and now everything was reversed and she had no landmarks to give her a bearing. The color of the house was of no help. Her vision pulled strongly toward shades of gray and feeble hints of blue and yellow. Fortunately, the front yard had been recently treated with a lawn fertilizer that gave off a distinctive scent, a beacon that guided her toward it.

Along the way, her severed leash and her path down the center of the street attracted attention. A boy sprinted out a driveway and attempted to grasp the rope and restrain her. She recognized his intent and skittered away, the rope bouncing and snaking behind her. The boy laughed and fell and rolled when he missed his grab.

"Hey, doggie, come on back!"

She moved toward the curb to avoid a big SUV making its way to a soccer game. She came upon a man mowing his lawn with a power mower that emitted an incessant throb. He stopped the mower and walked toward her. "Hey, pup! Where'd you come from?" She quickly sprinted out of range down the center of the street.

She came upon the house. The sun cooked the fertilizer embedded in the lawn and produced an unmistakable odor. She faced a three-car garage and walked around the side of it, to where a gate opened to the backyard. She passed through the gate, flopped down on the grass and waited.

Soon the dog heard the purr of an engine, which was quickly smothered by the grinding of the motor and gears of a garage door opener. She rose and moved cautiously through the gate and into the driveway. A minivan occupied the cave produced by the open door. Its brake lights winked out and the front doors opened like two mechanical ears. A woman stepped out of the driver's side, and a girl of about twelve out of the other side. The girl spotted the dog immediately.

"Mom, look!"

The mother looked, and looked less than pleased. The girl ran over and bent down near the dog. "It's okay, puppy. It's okay now." She held out her hand.

The words flew by the dog, but the emotional tone was unmistakable to her. Sweetness and compassion. She moved forward and gave the girl's hand a lick.

"Looks like she got loose from someplace," the mother said. "Probably down the street somewhere."

The girl reached out fearlessly and stroked the dog's head. The dog had memories of another female doing this same thing, but those memories were beginning to slip away. "We have to keep her until we find out who owns her," the girl proclaimed.

"We don't *have* to do anything," the mother countered. "We'll wait until your dad gets home from golf, and then we'll see."

"What if she's hungry?" the girl asked.

"You go over to the Simpsons' and see if you can borrow a little dog food. Be sure and offer to pay. They won't take it, but you be sure and offer it."

"Can she come in the house?"

"You bring her in the back way, and she can't come upstairs. You got that?"

"Got it." The girl draped her arm over the dog's neck

and gave the dog a hug. "We'll take great care of you, girl, don't you worry."

"It's someone else's pet, honey. You can't get too attached, okay?"

"Okay."

"You want to see, girl? You want to see?"

The girl pointed to the display on the computer in the recreation room. She had taken the dog's picture with a digital camera and composed a poster entitled LOST DOG. Underneath the dog's photo, a caption read *Found on Saturday morning on Ash Street. Phone 310-555-0987 for more information.*

She hit the print command. A printer launched into its electromechanical ritual that would produce copies of the poster.

The dog looked at the display. She saw a wild flickering. Her vision couldn't fuse the image into a steady picture. The computer refreshed the image sixty times per second. The dog couldn't see a solid image below eighty times per second.

The girl took a copy of the poster from the printer tray and presented it to the dog. "See this? I'm going to go put them up everywhere so your owner can find you."

The dog looked at the poster. It seemed very odd to see herself compressed into two dimensions.

The girl started up the stairs with posters in hand, and then turned. "Really, I don't want them to find you. I want you to live here. But I want you to be happy—and I know you'll be happy when you see them."

The girl shut the door at the top of the stairs. The dog

stretched out on the carpet. Her belly was full and she had bathed in the girl's unabashed affection. She dozed.

She was awakened by a male voice coming down the stairs. "So let's take a look."

The father appeared, followed by the mother. "Boy, I don't know," he said. "Did you check it for fleas before you let it on the carpet? And what's this?"

He reached out and lifted the dog's ear where the branch had torn at her during her escape from the alpha man. "Looks like some kind of open wound or infection." He turned to the mother. "It's gotta go. I'll take it out to the pound tomorrow."

"But she just put up a bunch of posters," the woman protested.

"I know. If somebody phones this evening, they're in luck. Otherwise, we tell 'em we took it to the pound."

CHAPTER 49

Becker gazed out the window of his office in the Petronas Towers and rested his fingertips on the cool surface of the glass. He was feeling a strange kind of peace, a dissolution of conflict. In truth, it was the dissolution of his mind as he lost the details of the affliction that was grinding him down. He had forgotten much, but he still remembered the first incident. It happened in Rome, when he was negotiating a complex deal involving oil futures. He'd flown in from Malaysia in his Gulfstream and had immersed himself in the details of the proposed transaction the entire trip. He deplaned with several members of his team and was whisked to the hotel by secure transport. He paid little attention to the hotel, a beautiful and venerable establishment on the Via Veneto, as he checked in. Instead, he remained focused on the task at hand, a transaction that would net him large sums over a protracted period of time and fuel the cash flow of several other ventures he had in mind.

The negotiations took place in a sleek corporate setting

in the central business district and lasted twelve hours. He was very weary when he left, and decided to walk the streets to unwind before returning to the hotel. It was a balmy spring evening and he walked for nearly an hour before hailing a taxi. He exchanged pleasantries with the driver, who asked him where he was staying.

And he could not remember.

He reached into his pocket and extracted his card key, but it had no information printed on it. He didn't want to look like a fool, so he gave the driver the name of another hotel. While they drove, he got on his cell phone and phoned his personal assistant in Malaysia. He made up a story about a mix-up in reservations to get the name of the real hotel.

When he finally arrived there, he felt a sick panic. He didn't remember the lobby. He didn't remember checking in. Only when he reached his room did his surroundings become familiar. He poured a drink and then another, and rationalized. He was overworked, he was mentally exhausted, he was disoriented from traveling. A perfect storm of reasons. Together, they conspired to make him forget. He had a third drink, slept ten hours, and awoke feeling fine.

It took about a dozen other such incidents to drive him to a neurologist. And for the first time, the word "Alzheimer's" was mentioned. It seemed inconceivable. He was in his forties and in perfect health. But it turned out that a phenomenon called early-onset Alzheimer's disease accounted for about five percent of all cases. Most victims were in their fifties, but very occasionally the disease reached down and claimed someone in their forties. More bad news followed. DNA tests revealed he had a genetic predisposition to this form of the disease, a fault on chromosome 1 called presenilin-2. Because he was so young, any realistic prognosis was difficult. Early-onset Alzheimer's tended to progress much more rapidly than the conventional form of the disease, and his case might just be the earliest ever. The best guess was that it might follow a curve of acceleration, which meant his current symptoms could very quickly become considerably worse.

He did what he could. Daily doses of Aricept. Vitamin B_9. Antioxidants. All done in almost total secrecy. Only a handful of people in the world knew about his condition. Any leak would have devastating consequences. He erected barriers of deception. Few had personal access to him. Those who did were dealt with in carefully scripted scenarios. Increasingly, he relied on his system of notes to plug the holes in his memory.

All the while, he sought a cure. At any price. Which eventually led him to Dr. Richard Stennis. It seemed, in theory, that stem cell technology held real promise to cure Alzheimer's. But a workable therapy was years off. Or was it? What if there were ways to streamline the research process? What if there was virtually unlimited funding? Thus Stemix and the Xanos Foundation were born. And now they were on the verge of delivering the unthinkable. A nonsurgical, nonpharmaceutical cure for a fatal brain disease. It would make Becker whole again. It would make Stennis and company fantastically wealthy. And incidentally, it would relegate Alzheimer's to the same museum of past pathologies that included polio, smallpox and many others. Worldwide, millions of people would be spared an excruciatingly devastating demise.

But time was running out. Becker was entering into a paradoxical stage of his affliction. Hour by hour, the details of his disease and its potential cure were beginning to slip away from him. Soon, he would come completely un-moored and drift through an endless ocean of dementia. Unless the therapy was administered now, it would be too late. He would be killed by a phantom monster far beyond the bounds of his present cognition.

Sometimes, he felt the monster nudge against him, feeling him out for the final assault. He fought a growing suspicion that a palace revolt had been mounted against him, that he was being held prisoner here in the building by hostile agents of an indeterminate nature. Only a por-tion of him believed that this was a symptom of his disease; the rest accepted it as an absolute truth. Soon, the paranoid zealots within him would triumph.

He walked away from the window and sat quietly be-hind his desk. At least, he assumed it was his desk.

CHAPTER 50

Elliot stood over the grave with Buddy, his mom's significant other. Creases in the ground marked where the turf had been freshly replaced after the burial. A small headstone identified the occupant as one Douglas McFarland. To Elliot, he would always be the King.

"He was a good man," Elliot said to Buddy. "Thanks for coming out. He deserved more than just me."

"No problem," Buddy replied. "Well, so much for him. Now what about you? You gonna take some time off? Maybe look for another job? Your mom wants to know. She's worried."

"You can tell her that I'm worried that she's worried."

Buddy smiled and chuckled. A thousand lines shifted position on his weathered face. "Why don't you come on over and tell her yourself?"

"I will, but not just yet. I'd rather wait until I've got things figured out."

Buddy chuckled again as he started toward the car. "Well, I'll tell ya, as soon as you got everything figured out, let me know right away. I've been tryin' to figure everything out for about sixty years, and so far, I'm not havin' a lot of luck."

Elliot walked with him. "Sometimes it seems like there's just not a lot of luck to be had."

"Sometimes. But not all the time. Best I can do is tell you about Joaquin Jones."

"Who's that?"

"One of the greatest pedal steel players ever. Worked out of Bakersfield in the fifties. Never recorded. I was real lucky—when I was a kid, I got to hear him a couple times. Used some fake ID to get into this joint out on the highway where he was playing. He blew me away. Played a Fender double-neck with the standard tuning, nothing fancy. He could make you cry and then turn right around and make you laugh. Even the guys playing pool stopped and listened when he played a solo.

"He was a huge man, and half Indian to boot. Must've weighed three hundred pounds, and had a ponytail—way back before that was a cool thing to do. He looked like a master craftsman sitting at his workbench when he played. It was the Indian side of him that kept him from recording. He said that once his sound was stolen and captured on records, he would never get it back. That cost him a lot of money, but I don't think he cared much about that. He worked part-time as a welder at a place that made utility trailers.

"He didn't drink much, but he did have a thing for the ladies. And once they heard him play, they forgot all about the three hundred pounds and the ponytail. And that's what got him into trouble, at least the way they told it back then."

"So what happened?"

"It's one of the most goddamned amazing things I've ever heard. He was playing at this honky-tonk joint downtown on a hot summer night, and they took a break before the last set. He went out to the parking lot to have a smoke. The lot was half empty because it was a weeknight. This guy named Sammy White followed him out, and it seems Sammy was pissed because Joaquin had a thing for Sammy's wife. So Sammy pulls out a pistol, a big old Smith & Wesson revolver, and says, 'You been fuckin' with my wife, Joaquin. So now I'm gonna fuck with you. It's time you quit playin' and did a little dancin'.' He fires a shot into the ground near Joaquin's feet. And then another. Just like in the old cowboy movies.

"Joaquin doesn't even flinch. He casually puts out his smoke. He says to Sammy, 'If you'd spent a little more time dancin' with your wife instead of fightin' with her, you wouldn't be havin' these kinds of problems. So I'll tell you what I'm gonna do, I'm gonna show you how to dance with her, and then everything's gonna be just fine. We're gonna do a slow waltz is what we're gonna do.'

"Joaquin puts out his arms like he's holding a woman and starts to twirl. Here's this three-hundred-pound half-breed waltzing across the gravel like he's as light as a feather. Sammy's confused, but he's still pissed. He fires off another shot near Joaquin's feet. Joaquin keeps right on dancing and says, 'You're a little off the beat, Sammy. Make sure you keep the time right.'

"Sammy keeps right on shooting. He puts three more rounds in the ground near Joaquin, who never breaks the rhythm with his feet. Sammy's gun is empty, and he sits down on the gravel, and just starts weeping. Joaquin walks over and puts a hand on his shoulder and says, 'Sammy, come on back inside, and let me buy you a drink.'"

"Wow," Elliot exclaimed. "You think all that really happened?"

"Heard about it from someone who was there, so it's probably pretty close to the truth."

"So what am I supposed to take away from all this?"

Buddy opened the car door. Then he paused before getting in. "When you're in a really difficult situation, you need to get real loose and feel the rhythm of what's going on. If you can do that, it will show you the way out."

"And just how do I find the rhythm?"

"That's the hard part. You can't. You have to let the rhythm find you."

Buddy got in and shut his door. Elliot watched him leave. Then he turned back toward the cemetery for one last look at the King's grave.

He couldn't pick it out.

CHAPTER 51

The dog sat erect on the soft carpet in the girl's bedroom. She watched the girl stare at a laptop computer display, with its frantic flicker, and wondered why anyone would subject themselves to such a thing. At last, the girl turned away from the screen and smiled at her.

"You get to sleep in here tonight. Did you know that?"

The dog heard the rush of syllables, the tumble of vowels and consonants. She struggled to organize them into something coherent and failed.

The girl got down on her knees in front of the dog. "I'm done with all my school stuff, so we can play now. What do you want to play?"

The dog watched the detailed motion of the girl's teeth, lips and tongue as they formed the unintelligible stream of sounds. She wondered how to respond.

"I know what we can play." The girl scrambled to her feet and took a box of cards from a drawer. She knelt once more. "You're going to like this. It's really fun."

The girl took a deck of cards from the box and shuffled

them. The dog was fascinated by the warped blur and snap-ping sound of the shuffle. The girl dealt out a matrix of twelve cards. Each card had one of three symbols: an oval, a diamond or a rectangle. Each also had its symbol repeated one, two or three times. Finally, each card had its symbol filled solid, shaded or empty.

"You have to find three cards where everything is the same, or completely different," the girl instructed the dog. "Watch this." The girl took three cards out of the matrix and put them in a row. "See."

The dog looked at the row. The first card was a single empty oval; the next, two shaded diamonds; the last, three solid ovals.

"Or you could do this." The girl reached into the ma-trix and pulled out three more cards. The first card had two empty ovals; the next, two shaded ovals; the last, two solid ovals. "All the shapes are the same and so are the numbers, and all the shading is different. Do you get it now?"

The girl picked up the cards and shuffled the deck once more. "I'll go first." She dealt out a new matrix and examined it carefully. "Look at this." She reached in and created a row of three cards. All contained a single dia-mond, each with a different shading. "Okay, now it's your turn. You can do it like this." She picked up the dog's right paw and placed it on a card. The dog let her paw rest on the card for a moment and then pulled it back. "Alright, I'm going to help you." The girl pulled three more cards from the matrix. "See?"

The dog watched intently. The game was beyond words, the game was beyond culture, the game was com-pletely symbolic. The exercise it demanded was purely log-ical.

The dog understood.

"Okay, my turn again." The girl dealt a new matrix and pulled out two correct combinations. "You ready?" She dealt once again, and looked expectantly at the dog, who stared at the cards, but did not act. The girl touched the dog's right paw. "Remember how to do it?"

The dog hesitated, then placed her paw on two solid rectangles.

"That one? Okay." The girl removed the card from the matrix.

The dog placed her paw on a single solid rectangle.

"Good job!" The girl removed the card.

The dog moved its paw to three solid rectangles.

"Yea! You did it! Yea!" She laid the cards in a row and stroked the dog's neck. "Good girl! My turn now."

They played several more cycles of the game. The dog continued to recognize the proper combinations. The girl was delighted and impressed, but not overwhelmed. At ten years of age, she had not yet slipped entirely out of the domain of magic. Then her mother entered with a blanket under her arm.

"Bedtime, dear," the mother announced. "Put the game away."

"Did anyone call?" the girl asked anxiously.

"Nobody called."

"So now what happens?"

The mom managed a faint smile. "I don't know. We'll talk about it tomorrow."

The girl saw the sadness in the smile, but put it aside. "She knows how to play. She's really smart. Want to watch?"

"Not now. It's getting late. You pick up while I make the bed for your new friend."

The girl returned the cards to their box, and the mother folded the blanket into a pad for the dog. The dog smelled the ocean in the blanket. Fresh kelp, desiccated fish, sea foam. She didn't know their origins, but she could smell the life of the world in them. The dog settled onto the folded blanket.

"Look!" the girl said. "She knew it was her bed. She went right to it."

The mother didn't respond. She started out the door. "Good night, dear."

The mother left. The girl ran over and gave the dog a tight hug. "They're not going to let me keep you. Do you know that?"

The dog felt the trail of mysterious words travel far above her. She settled down into the warmth of the room, the soft cushion of the blanket and the smells of summer at the beach. She sank into a pleasant lull, and stayed there.

CHAPTER 52

We need to talk."

"Are you sure?"

"Yes, I'm sure."

Christie reluctantly stepped aside to let Elliot enter. She followed him down to the showcase living room.

"I'd offer you something to drink, but I don't think we have anything."

"I didn't expect you would."

"So what exactly do you want to talk about? I thought we took care of all that last time."

"Did you know that I'm out at Pearson?"

"No. But I'm not surprised, given the way you tend to handle things."

"How well do you know Michael Hoffner?"

"He was a partner in Stemix with Jim. I see him occasionally at social things."

"I've done a little research on Stemix and Mr. Hoffner. Seems he's engaged in some very questionable financial transactions."

"And you think I helped him?"

"No. But I do think he used some of his funny money to alter your husband's medical records in a way that was highly advantageous to you."

"And why do you think he'd do such a thing?"

"I'm going to need some help with that. That's why I'm here—among other things."

Christie leaned back in her chair and laughed sourly. "And if I don't help, I can kiss my insurance goodbye, right? I believe that's the way you so eloquently put it on your last visit."

"I don't want it to come to that. I really don't. Let's assume for a minute that Mr. Hoffner did it, but didn't tell you until afterwards."

"Keep going."

"Why would he do something that risky? Why would he care about your insurance problems?"

"Let's assume that he wanted me beholden to him. Let's assume it's because he wanted to buy the stock back."

"Stemix?"

"Stemix. We own a big chunk of the company. Or rather, I do. When you're permanently comatose, money doesn't matter much."

"How much do you know about the science behind the company?"

"Just about zip. It's not my thing."

"Hoffner's putting a lot of time and energy into looking for a lab animal that escaped recently up at Pearson. Could there be a connection?"

"What kind of animal?"

"A dog."

"Oh my God. *The dog.*"

"You know about it?"

Christie stared at the carpet. "After we returned from the mess in Cabo, Jim told me that they did some very weird thing with a dog as part of their research. He wouldn't say exactly what. But it was bad enough that it could've ruined the whole project if it leaked out."

"So your husband has something on them, and they have something on him, and it all canceled out."

"Jim didn't want anything more to do with the company, but he refused to sell his shares. He said that if they tried to blackmail him and reveal what happened down in Cabo, he would go public about the dog."

"And now, with the doctor out of the picture, they think they can deal with you directly?"

She shrugged.

"Well, here's what you're dealing with: Two people have been murdered and I'm no longer in the law enforcement business because of the dog." Elliot stood to leave. "I wish you the very best of luck, Christie."

Christie looked up. Tears filled her eyes. "Don't go. Please don't go."

He didn't stay, but before he left, he gathered her in and felt her clinging to him ever so tightly. It felt good. It lasted much longer than it should have.

CHAPTER 53

Becker picked up the paperweight, a steel cone plated with gold. He looked underneath it and then placed it in a paper bag. He picked up an onyx bookend carved in the Haida tradition, and did the same. He repeated the process for the opposite bookend and then for the books themselves. He cycled through every object on the desktop until it was completely clear. Then he took out the center drawer and dumped its contents onto the desk's polished granite surface. He sorted through every object and placed each in a separate bag. He did the same with the other drawers.

Still, he could not find the card, the memory card, the card that held the decryption algorithm to his notes. He looked out across the office at a little forest of paper bags that littered the floor. He needed to sort the contents of each bag once again. What choice did he have? Without the card, he would drift through an uncharted wilderness, devoid of bearing. Until now, he had remained confident that the card's location would survive in his memory.

He used it every day and felt that this frequency of use somehow guaranteed it a permanent imprint. But then, when he needed it earlier today, he had come to the sickening realization that he had no idea where it was. He couldn't even remember if he carried it on his person or hid it somewhere.

He noticed the door to the small closet, a place where he kept a spare suit and a few extra shirts. What was in there? His perforated mind gave him not even a hint, not even the slenderest of threads. He came around the desk, wove through the paper bags and opened the closet. A single suit hung on its hanger, one of distinctive weave and texture. He stabbed his hand into one of the coat's pockets and felt something. He came out with the card and stared at it. How had it wound up here? When had he worn the suit? All gone. Not just now, but forever.

He wove his way back through the bags to his computer and inserted the card into its peripheral slot. The machine instantly executed the algorithm, and his notes sprang up. He slumped in relief. From now on, he would simply leave the card inserted. It compromised his security, but security was no longer the main issue. He had to preserve his mental integrity any way he could. He looked out across the paper bags and realized that, for the first time in many years, he would have to clean up his own mess. He couldn't afford to have anyone see his office in this state. Undoubtedly, there were already rumors about his condition; something like this would most certainly exacerbate the matter.

He stared out the window and past the city. Rain clouds billowed up on the green horizon. He retreated into a decimated past, and stumbled across a pleasant episode that still remained intact. He was in San Francisco, at a restaurant at the top of a tall building. He sat with a woman at a table by a window overlooking the lights of the Bay Bridge. She sipped her wine and regarded him with a look of pleasant amusement. He regaled her with tales of international finance, making it sound like something out of a Hollywood action film. She was enormously attractive, and seemed almost out of reach, a woman with infinite options, with himself reduced to commodity status. He must have her, and he loved the passion she enkindled within him.

But what was the name of the woman? The building? The restaurant? Would they ever return? Stennis had explained to him that even if they restored all his cognitive function, much might be lost. He would have to build anew. He didn't mind that. He was an adventurer, and adventurers seldom dwell on the past.

Becker rose from his computer and began the task of emptying all the bags and returning their contents to their appointed places.

CHAPTER 54

Korvin sat in his camp in bitter silence, obsessed by the loss of the dog. He had never suffered this kind of professional reversal. The animal's cunning he'd expected; it was the violence of the bite that took him completely by surprise. Once again, the beast had outmaneuvered him. A smoldering anger now played in an endless loop within him, and prevented him from forming a realistic recovery plan. He needed a distraction, something to sever the loop, so he could move forward.

He reached into the rear confines of the lean-to and extracted a curled strip of oak. He had begun working this wood upon his arrival in the forest, a hobby of sorts to pass the time in a productive manner. When pulled back into a taut arc, the wood formed a bow, one constructed in the classic manner of the Mongols. It had been the most formidable weapon of its time. A good archer with a strong pull could put up to 150 pounds of force into a shot, and Korvin was an excellent archer. The arrow could accurately strike a target a quarter of a mile away.

Korvin examined the bow's laminated surface. When the weapon was drawn back, its belly faced toward the archer and compressed under the distortion. At the same time, the back of the bow stretched and expanded. The energy stored in these distortions accelerated the arrow when the string was released. Like other hunting cultures, the Mongols realized that certain materials added to the snap of the bow upon the release of the string. They discovered that sinew was ideally suited to the task. In animals, sinew forms a tough and fibrous connection between bone and muscle, and transmits the force of motion. On the back of a bow, its molecules fight violently to restore this tissue to a neutral state after being stretched. Large animals provide a good source of sinew for weapons applications, but Korvin had none. He had spotted deer here on numerous occasions, but had no way to bring them down. Fortunately, he had an alternative. He'd had the foresight to extract a generous amount of sinew from the legs and haunches of the two vagrants he had killed a little while back. He dried it and glued it to the back of the bow and let it harden into place. It provided an animistic advantage as well as a physical one. The violence he had committed upon the two men would now be loosed with each arrow.

The grip in the center consisted of a multilayer winding of cord glued to the wood. The string was simple. A rawhide boot lace. The arrows he fashioned from the dowels he'd collected from the old man's camp. Their fletching came from the black feathers of dead crows. Their tips originated from various materials, from table knives filed to deadly points, from a piece of bone off the man with the blue cap.

Korvin sat down with the bow and the string. He placed his feet near the center of the belly of the bow and drew back the ends. He felt its power and flex as he attached the string to the bow nocks at either end. He placed it on a log and fetched the arrows from a plastic trash bag that protected them from moisture. There were only three. He had carefully shaved their cylindrical surfaces to compensate for any curvature that might impact their trajectory in flight. He picked the bow back up and tested the draw. For a brief moment, he savored the thought of hunting down the dog and putting an arrow all the way through her, piercing her heart and lungs. He could almost hear her shriek as her legs buckled under her, see the arrow sticking out her flanks on both sides.

But the thought was not practical, and his disciplined adherence to his craft ensured that he would not act upon it. However, it did break the loop of obsession within him and reset his thinking. It was time to move on and get the job done.

CHAPTER 55

E lliot drank his coffee and watched Christie out on the deck doing her morning stretching exercises. He hadn't been sure that she would be up this early, but indeed she was, and had listened carefully to what he proposed. He took another sip of coffee and listened to the rude whine of the vacuum operated by the housekeeper. She was of Asian descent and absorbed in her work and barely noticed him. When she finished, she powered the machine down, packed it up, pulled out a cell phone, and launched into a cheerful conversation in a language that was utterly lost on him.

Christie came back in, and Elliot poured her coffee. "So we're agreed about Hoffner?" he asked her.

"I don't like it, but I don't have a better idea. I think he's just going to clam up. He's a very cautious person."

"He's also a person who's only one step ahead of a whole shitload of trouble. That may make him more reasonable. Once he hears what we know about the dog and the bogus medical records, he's not going to have a lot of choice."

"But what real leverage do we have? You're an unemployed cop and I'm the has-been trophy wife."

"Don't call yourself that. You don't deserve it."

"Maybe not, but Hoffner's one of the most powerful people in a multibillion-dollar medical empire."

"That he is, but I also suspect he's in a really nasty bind. The dog is obviously incredibly valuable, and he hasn't been able to track it down. It's been missing for over a week. He's already committed fraud to try to keep this whole thing under wraps. Maybe a lot worse than fraud."

"He wouldn't hurt anyone," Christie insisted. "Mike's not that kind of person. Besides, look at who he is at Pearson. He has too much to lose."

"You're probably right, but I think he's probably put himself in proximity to some very bad people."

"That freaks me out. I don't want to think about that."

"Then don't. All you need to do is set up a meeting for the three of us to talk. We've all got our own problems: we may be able to help each other."

The squirrel nestled snuggly in its hollow high in a fir tree. It sat on a bed of cedar bark and moss and methodically peeled a scale off a pinecone. It plucked the resident seed out with clawed digits that gave a high degree of articulation, almost like the fingers of primates. It held the seed in place, nibbled it into a delicious mash and swallowed. All the while, it maintained a constant vigilance with its accutely tuned sense of hearing. It was able to instantly discriminate between the benign sounds of forest life and those representing a potential threat.

It finished eating the seed and began to peel another scale off the pinecone, but stopped and looked up toward the hole connecting the hollow to the forest below. Something didn't sound right. It took in the entire sonic signature and subtracted the murmur of the breeze, the rustling of leaves, the chirp of birds and a host of other sounds. It was left with an ominous collection of noises, distinct in their content and pattern. The snapping of small stalks, the tearing of plant roots, the impact of considerable weight upon the ground.

It clambered up and looked out the hole. Its eyes saw only in monochrome, but with extraordinary resolution. They immediately picked up the motion of a large animal about fifty feet away on the ground.

The squirrel now had enough information to act in its role as sentry against potential predators. From the safety of its hollow, it began to telegraph a very loud string of pulses that merged a chirp and a chatter into an urgent plea for caution. Another squirrel picked up its frantic chant. In this way, the alarm spread, like a wave radiating through the woods.

———————

He should have known better. It was a long shot, and he'd lost.

Elliot picked up the segment of bright yellow crime scene tape and stared at it. It was all that was left of the King's camp, except for the bare frame of branches that once supported the lean-to. He could guess with a high degree of certainty what had happened. The vagrant community had patiently waited for the authorities to stumble on down the trail. Then they had returned and, crime scene or not, stripped the place clean.

He had hoped to find some minute shred of evidence, something that would point him toward the King's killer. But the wonderful efficiency of those roaming the deepest strata of the world had denied him that. Nothing up here went to waste. Everything was recycled. In this regard, they were years ahead of the community at large. He smiled at the lone piece of yellow tape, and wondered what use they would make of all the rest of it.

He climbed over the little rise that hid the campsite and looked back down the trail toward Pearson. Overhead, a squirrel pelted him with a stream of angry jabber. He turned and started up the trail deeper into the woods.

Korvin idly flexed the string on his bow as he pondered how to locate and extract the dog from the neighborhood up above. The last time he hunted with a bow was in Afghanistan, under contract with Pakistan's Directorate of Interservices Intelligence. A small department within this bureaucracy, called Joint Intelligence Miscellaneous, had hired him to take out a clan leader hostile to certain elements of the Taliban.

The clan occupied a village on a barren, mountainous outcrop. The location of any gunfire would quickly be placed, and the terrain offered nowhere to hide from retribution. A bow and arrow solved the problem. The bureaucrats had offered to supply him with a commercial hunting bow, but he refused and instead resorted to a Mongolian bow. He glassed the village for several days, waiting for the right opportunity. He needed to catch the clan leader alone.

On the second day, he saw the man come down a steep trail alone, and took out his bow. A distance of about one hundred and seventy-five meters separated him from the target. He placed the arrow nock in the string and drew it back, storing a great backlog of elastic potential energy. He aligned the arrow with the target and elevated it to follow a precise arc dictated by the pull of gravity and air drag. He let the string go. All the energy stored in the bow was instantly transferred into the explosive surge of the arrow. It sped along its prescribed arc at nearly two hundred miles per hour and reached its target in just under two seconds. Just enough time for Korvin to savor the beauty and grace of its trajectory. It pierced the man's chest with such impact that it knocked him over onto his back. Through the binoculars, Korvin watched as his feet twitched and he made one desperate attempt to grasp the arrow and extract it. Then he lay still. The arrow sprouted from his chest like a slender tree, with the fletching as sparse and clipped foliage.

Now, in the woods, Korvin set the bow aside, and listened to a tsunami of squirrel chatter swirl through the forest canopy above him. He had become perfectly attuned to the ebb and flow of forest noise and knew the cause of the outburst. Someone was coming up the trail from below.

He had no choice but to routinely investigate the activity on the trail. His camp was expertly concealed from the trail's path as it zigzagged up the slope, but his location could still be uncovered through a variety of techniques, including infrared scanning devices. Since disposing of the King, he had to consider the possibility that law enforcement officials would choose to search up here in spite of the damning evidence against Elliot. It was a remote probability, but he knew numerous associates who had come to horrifying ends by excluding such elements of chance.

He picked up a compact telescope of considerable power, one of the basic items he'd brought with him into the country. He rested the scope in the crook of the limb of a downed oak branch and pressed up to the eyepiece and watched. Anyone coming up the trail would pass through his line of sight several times before they came anywhere even close. A puffy ball of dandelion seed floated through the field, followed by a meandering dragonfly. Nothing else moved. Overhead, the waves of squirrel chatter glided through the canopy.

Then he saw a man staring absently at the ground as he ascended the grade. Elliot. It was Elliot. Korvin knew immediately from the images transmitted to him from Malaysia. What was he doing here? It seemed incredible that he had located the campsite. At best, he knew that someone had stolen his gun and killed the vagrant, but that was all. How could he have determined that the perpetrator was actually encamped in these woods?

The man he identified as Elliot moved out of the scope's view. Korvin removed the instrument from the crook and walked hastily back toward his campsite. He would have to take preemptive action. By now, Elliot could have procured another firearm, which would make him a legitimate threat in a confrontation. He must be brought down at a distance as he hiked up the trail.

Korvin picked up the bow and sat with it pressed against the soles of his shoes. He felt it consume a great surge of energy as he pulled it back and attached the string. He would place Elliot's corpse in the King's camp. It would appear as though the forest's vagrant community had exacted their revenge. The use of a primitive weapon would be consistent with the character of the place. Of course, he would be forced out of the woods and into the city, which presented its own set of problems as he searched for the dog. But at this point, it was far riskier to let Elliot close in on him.

He shouldered the bow, plucked an arrow from a makeshift quiver and examined the needle-sharp barb wound onto its tip. He was ready.

CHAPTER 56

The dog stared out the back window of the minivan and felt a great awe. She had never been transported in a vehicle with windows that permitted a clear view outside. They were speeding along a great concrete river of vehicles of all shapes and sizes. Right now, they passed by a stubby one that towed two giant boxes mounted on many sets of wheels. Directly out the back window, a hooded creature covered with a black hide hunched down on a two-wheeled machine sprouting chrome pipes. Another vehicle shot past with an open box in the rear containing a dog, a fat animal with its fur whipped to a frenzy by a mysterious wind. Was this the standard method of transport for dogs? Was the driver obeying instructions issued by the dog? And where did the violent wind come from?

The minivan left the great river and traveled down a small tributary. The dog looked over the back seat toward the front. The man from the house gripped a slender wheel and moved it slightly. The van slowed and the dog braced her body against the deceleration as they came to a stop, and then turned. They traveled along a road next to tall metal towers with what appeared to be thick ropes strung between them. The ropes sagged greatly under their own weight. The dog couldn't imagine a rope this heavy. They passed by an enormous building topped by cement tubes that spewed white smoke into the sky. Was there a big fire inside? Would the structure soon burn to the ground?

They turned again and drove down a short road and stopped in the parking lot of a low-slung building. The dog immediately spotted several other dogs on the far side of a chain-link fence. All wore collars and leashes and walked in weary resignation behind human handlers. The building sprawled behind them, with dozens of openings set uniformly along its length. A gate of galvanized metal covered each. As the dog watched, one of the gates rose and a small dog walked out. It seemed intimidated by the open air.

The rear gate of the minivan sprang open and the man immediately grabbed the yellow rope, which was still attached to the dog's collar.

"Okay, let's hop down here and get this done."

The man tugged on the rope and the dog jumped down onto the ground and was hit by the collective scent of the place. Fear, anxiety and agitation boiled in the morning air. A turbulent stream of muffled barking came from within.

The man led the dog toward the entrance. She resisted his pace, but he pulled her forward. They passed through a glass door and down a short hallway. The noise seemed nearly overwhelming to her after the calm of the woods. Yelps, yips, barks, growls, whines, howls. They flooded the hallway and saturated the air.

They stopped at a place where a woman sat behind a

window. She looked down at the dog and smiled, and then up at the man.

"Hi. I've got a lost dog here. No ID. My wife found it wandering in the neighborhood." The man held up the rope. "It looks like it got loose from someplace."

The woman asked the man for some information. They exchanged words in a rhythmic babble that defied the dog's comprehension, so her attention shifted to the window that framed the woman. She had never seen a window that was indoors. What purpose would such a thing serve?

Another woman dressed in coveralls came down the hall and squatted down beside her. She stroked her head affectionately and removed the nylon rope. She spoke softly and kindly as she replaced the rope with a leather leash. The dog turned to check on the man.

He had already left.

CHAPTER 57

The squirrel perked its ears to the anxious chatter created by its peers. Its hearing soared to pitches far beyond that of humans, and it processed these sounds into intricate patterns. They revealed two nodes of agitation, one on the slopes above, and the other moving up the trail from below. The squirrel calibrated its present position in three dimensions, including its height above the ground in an aging oak tree. It perched on a limb that forked and drooped toward a nearby alder. Its present location offered relative safety from ground-based predators, but left it several trees away from the hollow where it lived. It elected to stay put and relay the chatter for the time being.

━━━━━

Elliot's labored breath reminded him that he was not getting enough exercise on a regular basis. The occasional bike rides to work weren't making much of a difference. The trail's moderate grade shouldn't have taxed him much at all, but he could feel the exertion in his lungs, his legs, his pulse. He considered turning back, but continued on, driven by a combination of defiance and guilt. Splotches of sunlight leaked through the canopy and warmed the ferns, which put off an exotic perfume. He longed to be lost in the moment, but the gravity of his situation kept intruding. Hoffner and the dog. It all came down to Hoffner and the dog. He kept envisioning the dog hairs in his apartment. The man at the pay phone who stole his gun also seemed to have possession of the dog. Had the animal been handed off to Hoffner? Had Hoffner made a deal with the devil? Would he come clean when Elliot and Christie confronted him? Who knew?

———

Korvin took the bow off his shoulder and leaned it against the trunk of a small tree next to the quiver. He placed the scope in the crook of the branch and trained it on the line of sight down the slope. He brought his eye up to the eyepiece and adjusted the focus. By now, he had fully objectified Elliot the cop into Elliot the target. As the target walked up the trail, it would follow a pattern that took it in and out of the field of view several times. Then he saw a hint of motion in the far right of the circular field. An instant later, the target crossed the field, body bent slightly forward in exertion against the grade. Korvin removed the scope from the branch and picked up the bow. He carefully placed the nock of the arrow into the string and turned to face along the line of sight. He had already timed the transit. He knew precisely when and where the target would present itself again.

———

The squirrel deftly analyzed the acoustic array of chatter as it shifted through time. The source of agitation from upslope remained stationary. The source from below was moving closer. The squirrel processed its options. It could remain in place or move to a location closer to its hollow. It rapidly sorted through an intricate spatial map it retained of all the potential routes along the interwoven branches between the trees. An acceptable route presented itself, and the squirrel skittered down the oak limb and onto one of its secondary branches. The little animal continued on to where the oak branch tapered to a point too slender to bear its weight. It focused all its senses on the impending jump to a branch on the alder.

Korvin already had the bow in place when he spotted the target making its transit along the line of sight. At this distance, the target was small but easily discernible against the sylvan backdrop. He drew the string back and made a rapid calculation before launching the arrow. He accounted for the drop in elevation, the drag on the arrow, and the tug of gravity. That done, he released the string. He heard a nasty hiss as the arrow accelerated to a lethal speed along its intended trajectory.

The squirrel propelled itself into the air approximately one second after the arrow left the bow. It spotted a hint of motion out of its right eye, but too late. It had committed itself to the jump. It sailed along its premeditated path and met the arrow halfway through its airborne journey. The squirrel nearly cleared the missile, but its hind legs grazed the shaft and the fletching, inflicting a severe scratch, but no other damage. It clambered onto an alder branch, and made a terrified dash along its route home.

The arrow had to travel another fifty meters to strike the target, and the deflection caused by the squirrel significantly altered its path. The fleeting compression of one of the three pieces of fletching sent it veering right.

Elliot heard the arrow's impact before he saw it. He traced the blunt, sucking sound to a tree trunk about two yards up the trail and level with his chest. The shaft oscillated in a violent shiver from the force of the collision with the bark and wood. He froze in a moment of confusion and disbelief, and then instinctively ducked down.

Korvin was angry. The launch had been flawless, the trajectory perfectly executed, yet the shot missed the target. He had seen just the faintest flicker of motion as the arrow neared its target. Something had deflected it. He must break camp and leave the woods immediately. He shouldered the bow, grabbed the scope and quiver and headed back to his campsite to begin his exit.

Elliot sprinted down the trail at a speed just below the threshold of panic. Twice he stumbled and fell and crashed into the brush. He reached the trailhead filthy and soaked in sweat. He had no idea how much time had passed as he sat and gasped for breath. All he could think about was the horrible tremor of the arrow buried so deeply in the tree. He'd been prey. He'd been hunted.

CHAPTER 58

The dog followed the woman into a room of harsh fluorescence and beige masonry. A man pointed a digital camera at her, and she winced and blinked at its sudden flash. The man turned to a computer and typed something into the keyboard. A printer whirred and crackled and spit out a tag, which the man mounted on plastic backing. The woman took it and put in the pocket of her coveralls.

"Aren't you going to tag her?" the man asked. His eyes sagged under the weight of the perpetual bureaucratic ritual: You photographed the dog. You tagged the dog. You took the dog to the Intake Kennel. You put the dog's picture on the website. You waited three days. If no one claimed the dog, you tested it for temperament problems. If it passed, you took it down the hall to the Adoption Kennel. If it failed, you gave it an injection of a powerful barbiturate. End of story.

"I ran out of straps," the woman responded. "I'll get some on the way out." She was a volunteer, and new to such things.

"She's got a cut on her ear," the man observed. "Better have the vet tech take a look at her."

"I think they're all busy."

"They're always busy. Do it anyway."

"Okay. Come on, girl."

The woman led the dog back out the door and down the hall. A door opened at the end of the hall, and the chaos of the Adoption Kennel flooded out and into the dog's ears and nose. Fifty dogs formed a primal chorus as they competed for the attention of prospective owners. The dog recoiled from it. She did not feel part of the madding crowd. She slowed her pace and put tension on the leash. The woman slowed to accommodate her, and spoke kindly and softly.

"It's okay, girl. We're not going there."

They passed through a swinging glass door into more fluorescence and masonry. A low-slung table sat at the center of the room. White shelves and cabinets lined the walls. A woman in a white lab coat turned to them from a small desk.

The dog noticed none of it. The dog's attention went to the beast in one of the cages at the room's rear. It jumped to its feet and snarled at her presence. Its lip curled up to reveal a predacious row of teeth in its huge, blunt snout. The sinew in its shoulders rippled beneath fur. A bright red border defined the missing half of its right ear.

"Whose dog is that?" the woman asked.

"We'll never know," the vet said. "It was probably bred to fight and lost too many times and was abandoned."

The dog smelled the hate and the murder pouring out of the beast. She stopped cold. The vet tech petted her. "It's okay, sweetheart. He can't get out. Let's hop up and take a look at you." She helped the dog up onto the table and gently lifted her wounded ear. The dog felt pain and flinched but did not yelp. "This should heal just fine," the vet tech observed. "I'm going to bandage it and that ought to do it. Where's her tag?"

The woman pulled the tag from her pocket. "I didn't have a strap for it."

"Put it over on the desk," the vet tech ordered. "I've got some around here somewhere."

"You want me to wait?"

"No, I'll call someone when I'm done."

The woman left and the vet tech went to a cabinet and came back with some tape. The dog stayed focused on the snarling beast. She didn't trust the cage. The vet tech gently dabbed some disinfectant on the nick in her ear and folded an adhesive-backed bandage over the wound.

"There you go," she told the dog. "Now let's get you tagged."

She rummaged through a drawer and located a small strap designed to attach the tag to a collar. She spotted the tag itself amongst the litter on the desktop and returned to the dog, where she attached it.

"Now we've got you pegged," she said, and returned to the desk and picked up the phone. "Would you send somebody down to exam? I've got one ready for Intake."

The dog understood none of it. She continued to look in the direction of the furious beast, but avoided eye contact. She didn't know that there were two tags on the desk, and that the vet tech had grabbed the wrong one.

She now wore the tag of the beast.

CHAPTER 59

Elliot stepped from the shower and absently reached for a towel. He failed to notice the monogrammed "O" in the corner, for Oakner. He also failed to notice that the dirt and sweat from his tumble through the woods were gone. He was consumed by the arrow, the vibrating arrow buried so deeply in the tree. If it had struck his chest, it would've gone nearly all the way through. It would've punctured a lung, or blown out a heart chamber, or severed his spinal cord. It seemed far more horrifying than a gunshot wound. And every time he put the arrow aside, emotional conflict took its place. He had run, he had fled, he had cowered. Still, he knew it was the right thing to do. He had no other option. If he'd stayed and played cat and mouse, he would probably be dead.

Christie poked her head in the door. "He just called on his cell. He'll be here in a few minutes."

"Hoffner?"

"Yes, Hoffner. Are you going to be okay?"

"Yeah, I'll be okay."

"Are you going to tell me what happened?"

She appeared suitably worried. Maybe even truly concerned about him. All she knew was that he came here a mess and headed straight for the shower. "Not right now. Later."

"I'm going to make some coffee."

"Put a shot of bourbon or something in mine."

"Okay."

She left and he went into the bedroom. He had no clothes here, and would have to put on some of Oakner's. He didn't like that. Then the irony struck him. He was lusting after the man's wife, but squeamish about wearing his clothes. What was that all about?

"Uh-oh." Christie was looking out a window toward the driveway when he got to the front of the house. He came to her side and saw the problem. Hoffner's BMW was pulling in, but it was followed by a second car, a late-model Lexus.

"You got a gun in the house?" he asked her.

"Bedside drawer."

Hoffner emerged from his car and pressed the remote lock on his key as soon as the door shut. A careful man. A moment later, the driver of the Lexus got out. Elliot had seen him before at the courthouse during his downtown cop days. A lawyer. Another careful man. Both wore tailored suits and ties of subtle yet rich patterning. Their shiny shoes shouted back at the overcast sky.

"He's brought a goddamn lawyer with him."

"So what do we do now?" Christie asked.

Elliot shrugged. "We play it by ear."

The doorbell rang. Christie answered. Elliot positioned himself in the showcase living room and watched her greet the pair.

"Christie, how are you?" Hoffner spoke as if they were all at a cocktail party. "This is Hal Farlow. Given the nature of this meeting, it seemed appropriate to bring legal counsel." Farlow smiled, and nodded politely.

"This way," Christie said in a very neutral tone. For her, the party was long over.

"Elliot." Hoffner gave Elliot a curt nod as he sat down next to his attorney. He didn't bother to introduce him. Elliot watched as Christie followed behind the pair. She would deliver a silent message by where she chose to sit. Would she pick a neutral spot, or sit on the couch with him? She came to the couch. He felt a little surge of elation, but tucked it away for future consumption.

"I understand you want to talk. So go ahead. Talk," Hoffner said.

Elliot leaned back and relaxed. "I hardly know where to begin. So let's build a timeline. That's probably easiest. You partner up with Drs. Oakner and Stennis in a company called Stemix. But for some strange reason, you shield your participation with a front company called Evergreen Ventures. Maybe it's because you're the one in charge of funneling grant money to the company from something called the Xanos Foundation. I'm not an expert on the ethics and legality of this kind of arrangement, but it smells funny. Know what I mean?"

"I don't think that—" Farlow the attorney began.

Elliot held up a hand and cut him off. "Hold on, Counselor. We've only just begun. So then you run into a few little problems. You use a dog as part of your research, a very special dog. Dr. Oakner's not happy about it. He gets drunk and damn near asphyxiates himself down in Cabo San Lucas. It turns out he's a time bomb that goes off a month or so later. So you decide to cover it up. You pay some IT guy to fake Oakner's radiology records. Sounds an awful lot like fraud to me."

"Mr. Elliot, you're hardly in a position to make that kind of call," Farlow said smugly.

Elliot leaned forward. "You're absolutely right, Mr. Farlow. It's the kind of thing that should be determined in a court of law. But let's move on. A radiologist gets real lucky and figures out what happened with the records switch. And guess what? She conveniently commits suicide a very short time later. Coincidence? You tell me."

Farlow glanced over at Hoffner with a look of alarm. Hoffner hadn't told him about Irene Walters, Elliot was sure. He quickly bore on before they had a chance to recover.

"And then you go and lose the damn dog! You just can't get a break, Mr. Hoffner, can you?"

Elliot leaned back again. The room went silent.

Farlow stood. "Would you excuse us for a moment?"

Elliot nodded. The pair got up and walked out of sight into the dining area. Urgent murmuring could be heard. Christie's hand reached over and covered Elliot's for a moment and then withdrew. The two men returned and sat. Hoffner remained expressionless. Farlow plucked a minute thread off the lapel of his suit and then looked up.

"You presented your case, Mr. Elliot. Now allow me to present ours. Let's start with Mrs. Oakner, since that's a relatively simple matter. It would seem that she fully understood that she was participating in a conspiracy to suppress information that would have cost her husband his medical license. She knew he was temporarily rendered comatose in Mexico by carbon monoxide poisoning and yet returned to perform surgery on innocent people. Fraud? Well, like you said, that would be up to the courts.

"Now, let's move on to you, Mr. Elliot. It seems that a vagrant was recently murdered in the forest area adjacent to Pearson. Now, in and of itself, that's not unusual. Life is tough at the bottom of the heap. However, there's an interesting twist. As a member of the justice system, I have certain contacts in law enforcement, and I hear facts and I hear rumors. Sometimes it's hard to tell which is which. Like right now there's this story floating around that the gun used in the murder belonged to you. It's also said you knew the victim personally."

"It's also said that I was never even considered as a suspect," Elliot responded.

Farlow held up both hands. "I never said any such thing."

"Fine, fine," Elliot said. "So let's see if I can put all this in a usable perspective. We all have issues that we don't want to grind through the legal system, correct?"

Farlow nodded. "Go on."

"Well, add this into the mix: whoever killed the vagrant, as you call him, probably has possession of the dog."

"You're sure about that?" Hoffner asked. His composure evaporated.

"When my gun was stolen, I found short black dog hair in my apartment. Like you'd find on a black Lab."

"Jesus," Hoffner muttered.

Elliot reached in his pocket and unfolded a piece of paper. "Better yet, I've got a video frame of him." He handed it to Hoffner. "Recognize him?"

Hoffner stared at the image of the figure at the pay phone. "Never seen him."

"And you know what?" Elliot said. "I believe you. I think you might have fudged some records, but I think everything else is something that's spun completely out of control."

"All right then, Mr. Elliot," Farlow interposed before Hoffner could speak, "let's see if we can establish some quid pro quo. Let's start with Mrs. Oakner." He turned to Christie. "What would you like to get out of all this?"

Christie didn't hesitate. "I want it all to go away. All of it."

"And what do you want, Mr. Elliot?" Farlow asked.

"I want information. I want to sit down privately with your client. I want him to tell me every damn thing he knows."

"And how might you benefit from that?"

"I want to find out who killed my friend and set me up. It's probably the same person who killed Dr. Walters. It's all connected."

"And since we're operating outside the legal system, what do you intend to do once you find this person?"

"I haven't decided. And when I do, I don't think you'll want to know."

Farlow paused and reflected. "You're right. And finally, then, what's in it for my client?"

"He gets the dog."

Farlow and Hoffner looked at each other. "Everything else stays private?" Farlow asked.

Elliot nodded. Farlow thought for another moment and then stood. Hoffner followed his lead.

"We'll be in touch shortly," Farlow said.

"The shorter the better," Elliot said.

CHAPTER 60

Korvin was driving a cheap rental sedan of the compact variety. He hated the mechanical feel of it, the compromised engineering. He disliked the stink of the air freshener. He loathed the checkered pattern of the shabby upholstery. Most of all, he feared the security risk it represented. He'd rented the vehicle with a fake driver's license and a credit card backed by an offshore bank. Now he ran the risk of getting pulled over for some silly infraction in a traffic system that was not completely familiar to him. He had to assume that the license would stand up under a computer search of the state data base, but he didn't know that for a fact. Earlier in the day, he'd used the same documentation to buy clothes at a discount store and rent a modest motel room on the fringe of the city's industrial area. He wondered how long he might last in such a state of compromise. The shabbiness and sleaziness of the place was grinding away at the sharp edge he so carefully cultivated through denial and discipline. Once this job was complete, the problem would dissolve. He would live splendidly in semi-isolation and sample the pleasures of civilization in carefully measured doses.

He saw the poster just as he prepared to make the turn. He pulled over to the curb, and made his habitual check out the rear and side mirrors before getting out. It was the dog. He was sure of it. Three green thumbtacks held the poster to a telephone pole. The fourth was missing, and the unsecured corner oscillated in the breeze. The poster sat low on the pole, as if a child had put it up, which was probably the case. Sure enough, the smudged image on the poster was the dog's. He tore the poster off the pole and took it back to the car, where he examined the photo. It wore the same collar it had in the woods, with the nylon rope still dangling from it. A scabbed nick of some kind was visible on the beast's ear. Most important, there was a phone number.

He slipped the car into drive, turned around and headed back toward a small commercial cluster he had passed on the way up. Becker would want to know immediately, and would then supply the name of the local contact who would take delivery of the dog. As soon as the delivery was verified, Korvin would be redeemed in terms of the deal, and the funds transfer would be expedited.

He reached the commercial cluster and pulled into an oil-stained parking space in front of a convenience store. He got out and looked at the Starbucks across the street as he went to the pay phone on the sidewalk in front of the store. The parking spaces in front of the Starbucks lacked such oil stains. Odd.

He referred to the poster and dialed the number. After several rings, a voice message came on saying that no one was home right now. He hung up before the cue to leave a message. Time was now the critical factor. He would arrange the delivery connection first and contact the house with the dog later.

He returned to the car and got on the satellite phone to Malaysia.

———

Becker looked out his office window and watched the morning creep in like a warm fog over the city. As time passed, the view seemed to grow more remote, his vantage more elevated, the detail below more abstract.

"Mr. Becker?"

"Yes."

"You have a call on the secure satellite line."

"From whom?"

The assistant gave a code number. Becker had no idea what it meant. "Alright, put it through."

"Do you want it encrypted?"

"Yes, of course." What did that mean? Was there some kind of code?

Becker brought his notes up on his computer while waiting for the call. He now needed more than just the notes. His cognitive powers were ebbing. He failed to see the logic behind spreadsheets he had created just a short time ago.

The notes came up. He typed in the code number. It was an operative in the U.S. Someone named Victor Korvin. He did a cross-reference. Korvin was currently involved in an attempt to recover a dog. The animal was involved in some kind of research project for a company called Stemix. What was that? What were they doing with the dog?

"I've located the dog." The voice on the phone spoke

in English. Becker couldn't place the accent. Becker could no longer place much of anything.

"Very good," Becker said, a vague response that would buy him a little time.

"I need the delivery instructions."

"Yes, you do." Becker frantically scanned the notes. There it was. A list of contingencies.

"You are to contact a Michael Hoffner, who works at the Pearson Institute of Health Sciences. He'll arrange the details and verify the transfer."

"And that will trigger the transfer of funds, correct?"

"Yes, I imagine so." Becker knew it was a mistake as soon as he said it. In the past, he'd never had these kinds of lapses in judgment.

"Imagine? What do you mean, 'imagine'? We have an agreement. A very specific agreement. If I recover the dog, I receive the full amount."

"Yes, of course you do, and the agreement will be honored."

"Alright then. I don't see any need for further contact. Do you?"

"No, I don't."

The call terminated. Becker looked back out the window. They had told him that his particular case was extraordinarily rare, that the disease might unfold in a novel and very unpredictable manner, that it might accelerate as it progressed.

But what disease were they talking about?

CHAPTER 61

Korvin felt the drizzle sprinkle his shaved head as he walked across the motel parking lot toward the adjoining gas station. He passed an older van, the kind with a ladder on the back door ascending to the roof. Promotional decals from tourist locations lined its rear windows. Most were chipped and ragged. A woman of considerable girth opened the passenger door, put her leg down, and gingerly felt for solid ground to support her descent. He ignored her and revisited his phone conversation with Becker. Something was wrong. He could still hear the voice saying, "Yes, I imagine so." Becker had never been vague or evasive about money matters or contractual arrangements. Was it a slip of the tongue? Or was he trying to somehow cheat on the deal?

He reached a pay phone near the corner of the gas station and pulled out his copy of the poster for the lost dog. He dialed the number. A woman picked it up after the third ring.

"Hello?"

"Yes, hi. I'm phoning about the dog you found. I just saw the poster. Thank God. We were really getting worried about her. Is she okay?"

"Yes, but she's not here now. My husband took her to the pound."

"He did? How long ago?"

"Yesterday afternoon. We didn't get any calls, so we thought it was the best thing to do."

"Yes, of course, I understand. I'll give them a call. Thanks for your help."

"No problem. My daughter will be glad to hear she has a home again."

"Thank you. Goodbye now."

Korvin slammed the receiver into its cradle. His eyes shot down to the yellow pages, which dangled from a short chain. He scooped them up and thumbed furiously. The dog pound. What would they officially call it here? It took him ten long minutes to track it down. He dialed the number and wrestled his way through the message system, which promised him "the next available representative."

His fingers drummed the booth's stainless steel counter as he waited. How long would they keep the dog before exterminating her? What did he have to do to claim her? Would he need some proof of ownership?

Minutes passed. Korvin drummed the counter and watched the highway rigs rumble past. More minutes. No "next available representative."

Korvin grabbed the receiver's coiled metal cable half-way down its length, and swung it at the booth's window as hard as he could. The tempered glass flexed and rebounded, but the receiver's plastic shell cracked along its spine. He dropped it and quickly looked around. No one had noticed. He was starting to lose his professional composure built through years of discipline and denial. Very bad. He needed to bring this assignment to closure as quickly as possible.

He tore out the yellow page with the address of the pound and headed toward the gas station to purchase a map.

———

Elliot sorted his bills into a neat array on the bare tabletop. They offered a depressing reminder that his expenses would continue unimpeded even though his income would soon cease. From outside, the Main Duck weighed in with a quack that sounded suspiciously like a jeer. Elliot was totaling the monthly damage when his cell phone rang. It was Bobby Seifert.

"I've found the dog."

"What?"

"I've found the dog. It's at the pound."

"You're sure?"

"I'm looking at it right now online. Female black Lab, about seventy-five pounds. Right?"

"Right. How long has it been there?"

"Since yesterday. They just posted its picture this morning in their lost doggie gallery. I'm sending you a copy as we speak."

"How long will they hang on to it?"

"Pretty much indefinitely. They hold it for three days to see if it's claimed. If not, they put it up for adoption."

"I'm on my way. Thanks, Bobby."

"Not a problem. Let me know what happens, okay?"

"Absolutely. How are you doing? How's things with the Chief?"

"I'm doing fine. And things with the Chief will clear up about the same time there's peace in the Middle East."

"Sounds about right. Stay in touch, okay?"

"Most certainly. Email comin' at ya."

"Got it. Talk to you later."

Elliot fought bewilderment as he hung up and opened the photo attached to the email. How did the dog wind up at the pound? The man at the pay phone had used the dog to set him up, and then brought it here to the apartment when he stole the gun. He must know its value. Why would he let it loose? Or maybe he didn't. Maybe it got away somehow. No way to tell.

He opened the picture and stared at the dog. He needed to be certain, so he inserted one of the disks Bobby gave him, and brought up the official picture of the escaped animal. He sized them equally and placed them side by side.

They were identical. He grabbed his car keys and headed for the door.

The dog sprawled low on the floor of painted cement and listened. Again, she heard the clank of a gate opening down the row. The voices of the two attendants drifted above the piped-in music.

"How come we're doing a bunch of them at once?"

"They have to be done by a licensed anesthetist. He only comes once a week, so they save them up."

"Well, maybe it's better that way. I'd sure hate to be doing this every day."

The gate clanked shut, and the two attendants walked into view. They led a muzzled pit bull.

"How many more we gotta do after this one?"

"Just one."

CHAPTER 62

Becker stared down through the still heat of morning at the streets and buildings below. The city was holding its breath, and as the day progressed, it would exhale an oppressive flood of heat and vapor.

But what was the city called? Becker walked back to his desk and sat down before his computer. There were notes on here somewhere. They would tell him the city's name; they would tell him his mother's name; they would recount his professional exploits; they would reveal his plans for the future. But first things first. There were certain procedures that produced the notes, certain technological rituals that had to be observed. He idly dragged the cursor arrow over the folder icons and opened one at random. Was this the way in? Was it the first of the prescribed steps? A long list of folders appeared. He opened one. Another long list appeared. Folders within folders. He must start over, but how do you back out and begin again? Incredibly difficult. Bad software design.

He pushed back from the computer and sought

comfort in that which he still knew. *Electra.* The name of a boat, a beautiful white vessel on the waters of Lake Geneva. He could still visualize the shape of the hull, and follow the flow of the grain in the oaken decking. He had been on that boat, he was sure of it.

He pushed away from the computer and soaked in the silence, both within and without.

CHAPTER 63

Was your dog licensed?"

Elliot stood before the reception window. He knew this would come up. "No, she wasn't. We've only had her for a couple of weeks. She lived with my sister out in the country, but she got divorced and moved into an apartment, so we took the dog."

The woman in the reception window seemed sympathetic. "She probably ran away trying to find your sister," she suggested.

"I hadn't thought about that, but you're probably right," Elliot said.

"It happens a lot," the woman said. "Go down the hall and take a left and go to the end. That's the entrance to the Intake Kennel. I'll let the attendant know you're coming. She'll take you in, then you can just verify that it's your dog."

"Thanks."

The dog lapped water from the bowl on her cell floor. It tasted slightly odd, but she needed to slake her thirst. She came up to a sitting position, but felt slightly giddy. She struggled to solve the mystery of the muzzled dogs. Once they were taken away, these dogs didn't seem to return. They couldn't possibly eat in those strange devices that covered their mouths, so what was happening to them?

The two attendants appeared and walked straight toward her cell. One carried a leash; the other, one of the little baskets with the straps. A thing of bad intent, she decided.

They opened the gate, and she considered bursting by them into the main corridor, but her legs dictated otherwise.

———

Elliot walked with an attendant down the main corridor of the Intake Kennel. The dogs all eyed him warily, still in shock from their recent incarceration. An instrumental version of "The Summer Wind" floated out of the speakers overhead and bathed the animals in mediocrity.

They arrived at the dog's designated cell number. Empty. Nothing but a plastic bowl. Elliot turned to the attendant. "So what's this mean?"

The attendant shrugged. "Don't know. Some kind of mix-up."

Elliot fought to contain himself. "Let's start with a basic concept: The dog's around here somewhere. You posted her picture on the web, which means she's gone through your system, so let's be optimistic, okay? It's simply a matter of tracking her down."

"We'll have to go out to the front and check the

records," the attendant said, as if this might be an almost insurmountable barrier.

"Well then, I guess we will." Elliot turned and headed down the corridor, followed by the attendant.

They came to an intersection and Elliot looked to his right. Two attendants were walking a dog in their direction. A muzzle obscured its breed and identity. They pushed on through the double doors and started back down the hall toward the main office.

———————

The dog walked on legs gone slightly to rubber. She followed the tug of the leash through the double doors and into the hall. A door opened momentarily up ahead and the smell of death floated quietly down the corridor. An unmistakable scent, the one created when an animal's spirit left its flesh. A smell genetically imprinted in the most primal depths of her memory.

Through a light mental fog, she assembled the pieces of her present circumstance. The muzzle, the one-way journey of her confined neighbors, the terminal smell. They were going to kill her. She was following the pull of the leash to the place where she would be put to death.

She was not prepared to die. She would not follow. She folded her legs and lay down.

The attendant felt a pull on the leash. He turned to see the dog settle onto the linoleum floor. "C'mon, girl. Let's get up," he commanded. "C'mon."

The word "girl" caught Elliot's ear. He turned to see an attendant tugging at a leash attached to a dog on the floor. The same dog he'd glanced at a few moments before. A black dog. A dog of medium size. And now, it seemed, a female dog.

"Where are you taking that dog?" he asked.

"It's scheduled for euthanasia."

"Maybe not."

Elliot walked back to the stalled animal. He held up his hand. "Hold it. I think you've got my dog."

"You sure about that?" the attendant with the leash said.

"Let's take the muzzle off and see," Elliot said.

"That's not a good idea. This is a dangerous animal."

"I'll take my chances." Rather than wait for permission, he knelt down and gave the dog a pat. "How you doing, girl?" He undid the muzzle strap.

"We can't take responsibility," one of the attendants warned.

"Then don't." Elliot pulled off the muzzle and smiled. He'd found the dog.

"So now you're official," Elliot said to the dog as they pulled out of the pound's parking lot. He had just sprung for a license and vaccinations to bring her in line with local regulations. Elliot glanced back at her. The dog was sitting up in the back seat and looking out the window. She seemed intensely curious. "And just what makes you so special, huh, lady?" The dog regarded him momentarily, then turned back toward the window and the grand spectacle unfolding before her.

CHAPTER 64

Korvin carefully composed himself as he walked down the hall in the dog pound to the reception window. He must restrain himself even though the flow of events had taken a decidedly negative turn. He smiled as he approached the woman stationed at the window.

"Hello, I'm here to claim my dog. I apologize for letting it get loose. I didn't think she could do it."

"Happens all the time," the woman said with a sympathetic smile. "Does she have a license?"

"No, I'm afraid not. We intended to get one, but we put it off. I guess we waited a little too long. Is there some way I can just look and see if she's here?"

"Did someone find her and bring her in?"

"Yes, that's exactly what happened. I checked with them."

"If you'll wait a minute, I'll have someone take you back to the Intake Kennel."

"Thank you."

"What kind of dog is it?"

"It's a black female Labrador retriever."

"Uh-oh." The woman frowned.

"Is something wrong?"

"We just had a big mix-up with a dog like that. It was almost euthanized. But then the owner came and got it."

Korvin held himself steady. "But I'm the owner."

"Uh-oh," the woman repeated. She turned to her computer and brought up a photo. There was the dog, complete with the nick on its ear. "Is this her?"

"Yes, that's it."

The woman eyed him nervously. A vein near his temple had begun to throb. "I'm afraid she's already been claimed," she said. "Just a little while ago."

"But how could that happen? It's my dog."

"She didn't have any ID. She wasn't registered to an owner. So we just have to trust people about ownership."

Korvin fought to relax his jaw muscles so he could speak in a normal tone. Local governments the world over were the same. It would be useless to protest their policies and procedures. "This is all a big mistake. I'll need to contact whoever took my dog, and explain. I'm sure they'll understand."

"I'm sorry, sir. Our policies just won't allow that. The first party to claim an unregistered animal gets ownership. We're not in the business of mediation."

Korvin spun and headed toward the exit. From deep within him, great bubbles of rage rose toward the surface and threatened to explode all over the hallway. He had been fucked. He should have known it. Becker was very weird on the phone. And now Becker had the dog. He must have set it up through this Hoffner. And with the dog secured, he'd claim that the deal for its retrieval was null and void. Becker had played it perfectly, but then again, that's why he had billions of dollars. Without the dog for collateral, Korvin had no bargaining power. And a physical attack on the man was unthinkable. Becker was better protected than most heads of state. Blackmailing him was also out of the question. Korvin was illegally installed in a country where he had already killed four people.

Korvin flung the door open and burst out into the fading afternoon. If the contract wasn't honored, he was ruined. He had heavily leveraged himself to buy the property in eastern Europe, all with the expectation of the fat proceeds from this job. Without it, he would be reduced to a very finite existence.

They were seriously underestimating him.

"You have a call from the satellite, sir."

Becker hesitated and struggled to comprehend. Why would a satellite phone him? What would it want from a human being? There was only one way to find out. "Put it through, please."

"Shall we encrypt?"

"No, don't bother." Becker eyed his assistant suspiciously. He was feeling a growing paranoia about palace revolts, and now it sounded like they wanted to put him in a crypt. He would play along for now, but must keep his guard up. He lifted the phone to his ear. "Hello?"

"You tried to fuck me. Nobody does that. Not even you."

"Who is this?"

"You went behind my back and got the dog back yourself. And now I suppose you think you don't have to pay up."

"Pay for what?"

"That's exactly what I thought you'd say. But just

remember, you're there and I'm here and so is the dog, and so is your good friend Mr. Hoffner. We're not done yet, Mr. Becker. Not by a long shot."

The line went silent. Becker felt a terrible chill. No enemy is worse than the one that cannot be known or explained.

"How are you feeling, Mr. Becker?"

Becker looked up as a middle-aged man in slacks and a sport coat entered his office. He presented the polished smile of a practiced professional.

"Who are you? How did you get in here?"

A look of sad concern came over the man. "I'm Dr. Morgan. I'm a neurologist. I've been treating you for some time. I operate a clinic in Geneva. You used to live there, right?"

Becker ignored the question. "Why are you here?"

The man produced a video disk. "You and I both knew it would eventually come to this." He crossed the room and inserted the disk in a player. "And here's how we prepared."

Becker watched. He and the doctor appeared on the screen. The background was this very same office. Together, they told the story. It seemed Becker had the earliest case of Alzheimer's on record and that it was progressing with unprecedented rapidity. Arrangements had been made for an extremely experimental treatment at some point in the future. Research on the treatment was a work in progress by a group led by a Dr. Richard Stennis. It also seemed that Becker had agreed to trust Dr. Morgan's judgment about managing his care.

The video ended. Becker had trouble tracking the details, but grasped the general flow. "What do we do now?" he asked wearily.

He could no longer fight. He could no longer defend himself. He could only trust.

━━━━━

Dr. Richard Stennis shut the heavy glass doors from the stateroom to the rear deck. The noise from the harbor slipped away into the background. He nervously paced with the phone at his ear and listened.

"Farlow seems to think the deal will work," Hoffner told him. "Elliot will keep his end because he risks a real legal mess if he doesn't. And Christie just wants it all to be over."

"And all we have to do is spread out every piece of our dirty laundry so this Elliot can pick through it?"

"Look," Hoffner said. "Neither one of us had any idea that anything like this would ever happen. We just took a slight twist with the research. It might have been questionable, but it wasn't criminal. Elliot needs to understand that. He needs to realize that there's a lot of distance between us and what it looks like Becker has done."

"And we get the dog?"

"Yes. We get the dog."

"When?"

"I don't think Elliot knows that. It depends on when he finds this monster that Becker let loose."

Stennis paced the full length of the room in silence.

"Richard? You still there?"

"Yes. There's a complication. I just got a call from Morgan in Malaysia. The disease seems to be accelerating. If we don't act very soon, no amount of therapy is going to pull him back. Morgan has put the contingency plan into effect. They're preparing to transport him to Geneva."

"So we need the dog now?"

"Absolutely. We're flying almost blind. No clinical trials. No nothing. And without the data from the dog, we're flying completely blind. It's just way too risky."

"I'm afraid you're right," Hoffner agreed. "And after everything that's happened up here, I'm getting a very bad feeling about all this. If Becker doesn't survive the procedure, we may lose a lot more than just our careers."

"Probably best not to dwell on that right now," Stennis suggested. "Morgan's going to do a complete set of imaging on Becker as soon he gets to Geneva. Then we'll know how bad it really is."

In fact, they both knew very well how bad it was. Very bad, indeed.

CHAPTER 65

Elliot halted the car in the parking lot of the elementary school and turned to the dog in the back seat. "Too much heaviness lately. Time for a break."

The dog eyed him in a very noncommittal way, and then turned to view the grass playing field visible out the window. Elliot had a vague feeling that animal was reserving judgment about him. Was that possible? He was far from an expert on canine behavior. He hadn't had a dog since he was a little kid and they had a mutt named Mitzi, who chased one too many cars and came to an untimely end.

Elliot grabbed the bag on the seat beside him that held a tennis ball of fluorescent green and a blue plastic launcher. He'd stopped at a store to buy a bag of dry dog food and noticed these two items in the pet supply section. After all the dog had been through, she deserved a little fun. And so, come to think of it, did he.

He stepped out into the school parking lot and opened the rear door for the dog, making sure he had a grip on the leash before letting her out. The last thing he needed was the dog back on the run. He'd chosen this particular field because it was entirely fenced, with a single gate for egress.

The dog hopped down and followed him through the gate, which he carefully closed behind them. He removed her leash. She didn't bolt. She looked up at him expectantly: *Now what?* He opened the bag and removed the ball and the launcher. At the sight of the ball, the animal leaped straight up, becoming briefly airborne. She landed panting heavily, eyes ablaze.

"Aha. So you know the name of the game, huh?" Elliot threw the bag in a trash can next to the gate. He placed the ball in the launcher and heaved it out into the field. The dog sped after the ball at a truly impressive pace. She intercepted it in midair as it took a bounce, and immediately circled back toward him. Was this instinctual? Or had somebody taught her? Elliot had no idea.

She dropped the ball directly at his feet and looked up at him. And for just an instant, it seemed like he was dealing with something that might be much closer to a peer than a pet. He shrugged it off. It was too absurd to even consider. He promptly forgot about it.

He picked up the ball and launched it once more. The dog streaked through the warm afternoon and fetched it. They repeated the cycle over and over. Finally, on the last throw, the dog returned with the ball and flopped down a few feet away, clearly spent. Elliot went over, crouched down, and petted her gently on the head. "You've definitely got the moves."

He went over to where he'd left the leash, picked it up, and walked back toward the dog. As he approached she looked over, and her eyes went immediately to the leash.

She shoved herself to a standing position and turned to face him head-on, slowly backing off.

"Uh-oh. Are we going to have a problem here?"

The dog spun and bolted. Elliot's heart nearly stopped. Could she vault the fence? He didn't want to find out. But she stopped about ten yards away and faced him in a wary crouch.

He held out the leash. "We just need to put this on to get you in the car. Then it can come off, okay?" He started forward. The dog backed off, spun, and sprinted another few yards before stopping again.

"So now what?" Elliot realized that there was no way he could get close enough to attach the leash. The dog was too fast. He turned toward the gate and parking lot beyond, and saw a solution. Since the leash seemed to be the problem, they'd work around it. He could bring the car right up to the gate, open the car door, and let the dog jump in. He would be standing by with an extended hand to grab her collar if she tried to bolt.

"All you have to do right now is stay put, okay?"

He gathered up the ball, the launcher and the leash, and walked to the gate. As he opened it, he turned and saw that she had followed him. Still, she kept a safe distance between them and remained about ten yards out into the field.

He opened the gate, walked through and closed it behind him. He looked back and saw that the dog remained in the same place. He walked to the car, opened one of the rear doors and tossed the leash and play gear inside.

He was just closing the door when he heard the two kids at the gate.

One of them, a boy about ten, was already off his bike and sliding the gate wide open.

"Hey!" Elliot shouted.

Too late. The dog charged forward, sprinted through the open space, and into the parking lot.

"Oh my God!" Elliot felt a sickening shock push its way through him.

But instead of veering off and setting a course of escape, she came directly toward him, slowed, and stopped about ten feet away.

Now what? He'd just have to play it by ear. He squatted and beckoned her forward. "It's alright. No leash." He held his hands wide. "See."

She sat on her haunches and cocked her head slightly as she observed him. But she didn't move any closer. It was his move.

At that moment, the truth of the matter presented itself to him, fully formed, before he had a chance to question it or pick it apart: The dog knew that he was still in possession of the leash, that it was waiting inside the car to once again restrain her.

He stood up, opened the door, took out the leash and held it up to her. "Okay, here goes." He flung the leash as far away as he could. The dog's head rotated toward where it landed, and then back to him. He stood beside the open door and gestured to the interior of the car. "Have we got a deal?"

The dog stood, trotted forward, and jumped into the back seat.

Elliot nearly collapsed in relief.

━━━━━━━━

Elliot found a place for the big sack of dry dog food in the utility closet around the corner from Christie's industrial-strength gas range with its black knobs the size of baseballs.

She was off to a pet store to buy a dog bed, undoubtedly a very nice dog bed. One look at the animal and she had been instantly smitten.

He shut the closet door and went to the sink, where he could look out the window. The dog lounged comfortably on the wooden planking of the deck. She rested on her side with legs extended and crossed. The dog dish behind her was licked completely clean. Her voracious appetite amazed him. In all, she seemed in good health, except for the small bandage on her ear. Not bad, considering that she'd been on her own in a strange city for the better part of two weeks. When things were a little more secure, they could take her to a vet for follow-up. But right now, security was everything. He didn't dare take her to his apartment, because the man at the pay phone would undoubtedly check there if he was searching for her.

So what made her so valuable? Why was she so vigorously pursued by so many people in both high and low places? Weren't lab animals usually commodity items? What made her so different? He kept coming back to the incident of the open gate in the parking lot by the playfield. It was the only hint that he had. It seemed very much like she'd consciously cut a deal with him about the leash. But that had to be his overactive imagination at work. As a cop, he'd learned that intuitive speculations seldom held up in court.

He went to the refrigerator and opened its massive door of brushed stainless steel. The intrusive shriek of a vacuum charged in from the living room as he opened a bottle of water. He shut the refrigerator as the vacuum wound down, and crossed the floor to the deck entrance. Outside, the dog turned her head toward him and rose to her feet. He opened the door and she immediately strolled in.

He squatted down in front of her and looked her square in the face.

"So what's the deal with you, huh?"

She cocked her head as she looked back at him, and he had the strong sense that she was searching for some different frame of reference, some novel angle of approach to him. But how could he be sure?

At that moment, the dog spun around without warning and faced away from him. The housekeeper had packed up the vacuum and was coming through the dining room, chatting happily on her cell phone. The dog galloped over and followed her as she walked. The dog looked up at her expectantly and started panting.

Elliot watched in amazement. This woman must be radiating something extraordinary that the dog was receiving and he was missing. The housekeeper finished her call and looked at the dog with a friendly smile. She reached down and gave it an affectionate pat. "Nice doggie," she said.

The dog immediately stopped panting. Elliot would have sworn that animal looked disappointed somehow. What had changed its attitude? What had the woman done? He replayed the scene: the dog spinning around, the woman on the phone, the dog's excitement, the dog's apparent disappointment.

He came to a conclusion so bizarre that he nearly dismissed it. Only one thing had changed during the dog's shift in attitude.

"Excuse me," he said to the housekeeper. "I've seen you here before, but I don't know your name."

"It's Aisah," the woman replied.

"What nationality is that?"

"It's Malaysian. I grew up in Kuala Lumpur."

"Aisah, I'd like to ask you to do something for me. Would you mind saying a few things to the dog in Malay?"

Aisah bent down. She smiled at the dog, which looked up at her expectantly.

"Hi, suka tak rumah baru ni?"

The dog immediately opened its mouth, unfurled its pink tongue, and started panting. It did a little jump to signal its excitement.

"Apa yang seronok sangat ni?"

The dog's panting grew even more pronounced, to the point where it seemed uncontrolled and erratic.

"Can you tell me what you said?" Elliot asked the woman.

"First I said, 'Hi there. Do you like your new home?' Then I said, 'What are you so excited about?'"

"Would you mind staying for a while?" Elliot asked. "I'd like you to spend a little time with the dog. We'll pay for the overtime."

Aisah shrugged. "Sure. Why not? What do you want me to do?"

Elliot knew the answer instantly. No thought required. It all came down to a single query.

"I want you to speak to the dog again. In Malay."

"And what do you want me to tell it?"

"I want you to say 'Nod your head if you understand the words I'm saying.'"

The woman gave him an incredulous smile. "You're kidding?"

"No, I'm not. Let's try it."

Aisah looked down at the dog, who continued to look up at her expectantly.

"Angguk kepala kalau kamu paham apa yang saya cakapkan ni."

The dog hesitated only an instant. Her head dipped emphatically in affirmation and came back up, eyes lit with elation.

"Son of a bitch!" the woman exclaimed.

CHAPTER 66

Michael Hoffner, Pearson's Director of Research, came out of the upscale grocery store, the land of arugula and certified organics. He walked through the dusk into a parking lot full of luxury vehicles not unlike his own. He clutched a bag that housed a container full of olives purchased at the olive bar inside, which offered over a dozen varieties in nuanced shades and stuffings and tastes. These particular olives were grown in the Abyssinian tradition and imported from Africa by air freight and sold at prices to match their particular mode of transport and origin, and were the perfect complement to gin and vermouth in a well-mixed martini. And tonight, he planned to lose himself in the liquefied splendor of several such martinis.

He pressed the transmitter button on his key and watched his car reply with a flash of its amber parking lights. A monstrous SUV was parked beside him, and he made his way into the space between. He was reaching for the door when he heard the voice. It made him jump involuntarily.

"I want my money. And I want it now."

Hoffner turned and was consumed by horror. The man's face was flat and dead, just like his voice. The eyes were lost in black cavities of terrible depth. His muscular frame filled most of the gap between the vehicles.

"You've never met anybody like me, have you?" the man asked.

"No. No, I haven't." Hoffner fought back a stutter while he struggled to comprehend what was happening. The man looked vaguely like the video frame Elliot had shown him, but he couldn't be sure.

"You're very lucky, then. And if you want to stay that way, you'll pay up right now. You people fucked me on the dog, and now I'm going to fuck you unless you release the funds."

The dog. Hoffner launched on a frantic sprint of reasoning. *This monster must work for Becker and be hunting for the damn dog. Did he find it? Did Becker try to cheat him somehow? He must be the object of Elliot's search. He might hurt me, or kill me. He is clearly the product of violence in the extreme. My only hope is to stall him until I can talk to Becker and understand what's going on.*

"I don't know the details of your arrangement," Hoffner offered. "I'm sure this can all be worked out, but I need to make some calls. I need a little time. You have to understand—"

Korvin reached out with his index finger and touched Hoffner lightly on the cheek. Hoffner flinched and blinked. He stepped back.

"Because of your trade, you have a detailed knowledge of suffering," Korvin said. "The same is true for me." He turned and started away.

"How will I find you?" Hoffner asked.

Korvin stopped and looked back. "You won't have to." He pulled something from his pocket, and a dull screech filled the space between the vehicles as he walked off.

Hoffner waited for what seemed a discreet interval and then walked out into the open. The man was gone. He slumped and sighed and started back toward his car.

And that's when he saw the gash, the ragged rip that penetrated the wax, the paint, the primer and scored the underlying metal, all the way from the taillight to the front bumper.

lliot looked at the dog and tried to imagine her predicament. This animal had somehow acquired spectacular cognitive powers while in her native country, and then was suddenly uprooted and sent here. She was familiar with the fundamentals of human speech, but couldn't comprehend even a single word of English. Did she understand the idea of a foreign language? If not, it would seem like all humans spoke in a meaningless and mysterious babble. It seemed as good a place to start as any. He turned to the housekeeper.

"Tell her to nod once to say yes, and twice to say no."

Aisah, the housekeeper, spoke to her. The dog nodded once, apparently to communicate that she understood. *Yes.*

"Ask her if she can understand anyone else here, besides you."

The housekeeper translated.

No.

"Ask here if she knows that there are different ways to speak in different places in the world."

No.

"Did she have a teacher?"

Yes.

"A woman?"

Yes.

"Does she know why she was brought here from her home?"

No.

The door to the garage opened, and Christie came in. She carried a large sleeping pad and a shopping bag. Her attention went straight to the dog. "Hey, girl. Look what we got for you."

She opened the bag and spilled out several chewing toys and other canine diversions. The dog looked at them quizzically and gave one a brief sniff. She returned her attention to the housekeeper.

"Uh-oh, not a big hit," Christie said. She sounded disappointed.

"I think you may have gotten infant toys for someone who's in the fifth grade," Elliot told her. "Watch this." He turned to the housekeeper. "Ask her if she has ever had toys like these."

Aisah translated. The dog nodded once. *Yes.*

"Now ask her if she still plays with toys like these."

No.

"Two nods means no," Elliot explained to Christie.

"I don't believe it," Christie said. "She's just doing that at random. How do you know she's not?"

Elliot considered this. Christie had a legitimate point. "Don't think so," he said, and turned back to the housekeeper. "Tell her to nod once for each person she sees here in the room."

Aisah translated. The dog nodded three times.

"That's fantastic," Christie said softly. "It's just too fantastic."

"Fantastic is right, like fantastically valuable," Elliot observed. "Aisah, you can't tell anyone about this. Absolutely no one. If you do, you'll put yourself in considerable danger. I'm going to show you why."

He pulled the printout of the man at the pay phone out of his pocket, and put it down in front of the dog. "Ask her if she knows this man."

Aisah translated. The dog nodded. *Yes.*

"Did he capture you in the woods?"

Yes.

"Do you know his name?"

No.

"Did you escape from him?"

Yes.

"Does he know where to find you?"

No.

"Do you think he will figure out how to find you?"

Yes.

"Does he have weapons?"

Yes.

Aisah turned to Elliot in alarm. "What's happening? What does this mean?"

"I'm sorry that you're involved," Elliot apologized. "I can only tell you this: The more information we can get from her, the safer we'll be. All of us. And we need your help to do it. Will you do it?"

"I think I better go now," Aisah said shakily. "This is all too strange..."

"You'll keep this to yourself?"

Aisah nodded vigorously. "Oh yes."

"I'd like you to ask her one more thing before you go."

Elliot turned to Christie. "Have you noticed that she sounds funny when she's panting?"

"You're right," Christie said. "When most dogs pant, there's a kind of rhythm to it. When she does it, it sounds like she's stuttering part of the time."

"Ask her if she's trying to talk with us, to speak words with us," Elliot told Aisah.

The housekeeper translated, and the dog replied.

Yes.

CHAPTER 68

Michael Hoffner's house adhered to a hillside over-looking the city's downtown. Its three floors contained over five thousand square feet of living space. In marketing terminology, descriptors such as "enhanced" and "premium" and "sophisticated" would be used to describe the lifestyle within its well-insulated walls. None of these applied to Hoffner's disposition as he guided his lacerated BMW into one of the three stalls in the garage. The damaged side faced the far wall, so no one would see it for now. Tomorrow, he would take the "small" SUV in the next stall over, while his wife continued to use the "big" SUV. She was out tonight at a fund-raiser of some kind, and his two daughters were in Cancún on spring break from Stanford. He wasn't comfortable with the pair being down there, but now it seemed extremely insignificant.

He clicked the garage door shut and walked into the house on the middle floor, ignoring the console for the elaborate security system, with its sensors, cameras, detectors and alarms. It was all worthless when arrayed against someone like the monster in the parking lot.

He wandered into the kitchen and poured himself a glass of whiskey, a small-batch premium bourbon. He consumed it in just a few swallows, and went downstairs to his den, where he picked up the satellite phone and went into the home theater room. He punched the big flat-panel screen to life with the sound muted. A basketball game came on in high definition, but the content wasn't important. He wanted to be swaddled in color and motion, and oblivious to the rest of the world. He sighed. It wasn't going to work.

He picked up the satellite phone and dialed Kuala Lumpur. As he waited for the connection, he tried to anticipate his dialogue with Becker. He couldn't. Stennis had said Becker was failing rapidly. Hopefully, the man still had enough wits to clear up this mess. It was absolutely bewildering what was going on. It made no sense to think that Becker had recovered the dog and failed to notify him. And why would he try to cheat this horrible monster from the parking lot? Money meant little to Becker, and even less under his present circumstances. Hoffner still shuddered every time he recalled the encounter with the flat face and sunken eyes. The instant he'd seen them, he knew the worst-case scenario was true beyond any doubt. Irene Walters had been killed as part of the cover-up. The very same cover-up he had instigated by buying off the IT manager in radiology. Did that make him an accessory to murder? He just wanted it all to go away.

"Hello." The voice at the other end of the satellite connection spoke fluent English, but was not the same one that usually answered.

"This is Dr. Hoffner calling from the U.S."

"I'll need a code."

Hoffner rattled off an alphanumeric code to the man and waited. Somebody missed a three-pointer on the big screen in front of him.

"This particular code can only be accessed by Mr. Becker himself."

"I already know that," Hoffner said impatiently. "Just go ahead and put me through. Tell him it's a matter of extreme urgency."

"Mr. Becker is not available at this time."

"If you'll look at the code again, you'll see that I have access to him on a 24/7 basis."

"That provision is no longer in force."

"I see. So is there some kind of contingency for a situation like this?"

"Not that I know of."

"Well then, nice talking to you," Hoffner said acidly as he disconnected. He was too late, and he knew it. And now he was going to take the hit. But not alone.

He put down the satellite phone and got out his cell phone. He stabbed in a number.

"Hello?"

"You've got to get up here," Hoffner told Stennis. "Now. This thing is spinning totally out of control."

"What do you mean?"

"I just got cornered by the creep that Becker put up here. He thinks Becker screwed him out of his money somehow. Something to do with the dog. If he doesn't get paid, he's coming after us. I tried to get Becker and he's gone. Maybe like permanently gone."

"They just took him to Geneva. Morgan said it doesn't look good at all."

"Well, it looks even worse here. You better get the next plane back."

"Okay. I'll let you know when I get in. What are you going to do in the meantime?"

The answer came to Hoffner as soon as Stennis finished asking the question.

"I'll tell you when you get here."

CHAPTER 69

I need to call upon your professional past," Elliot told Bobby Seifert.

They sat in Bobby's cubicle in front of his computer. From there, Elliot's old desk could be seen, all bleak and barren and lit with a rose-colored streak of halogen light from the streetlamp outside.

"You mean when I was James Bond?" Bobby had slimmed down in the waist, but had the same spark of mirth in his eye.

"No. Before that. When you were a mere computer geek at the NSA."

Bobby held up his hands. "Don't know anything about that."

"Of course not," Elliot said. "Nor would I ask you anything about that experience." He produced a flash drive and inserted it into Bobby's computer. "This is an audio recording of a dog panting."

"Just a random old dog?"

Elliot nodded. "Just a random old dog. Nothing special. Go ahead and give it a play."

Bobby clicked on play and listened, then smiled. "That has to be the weirdest random old dog on the entire planet. Its mom didn't even teach it how to pant right."

"Keep on listening. Tell me what you hear."

Bobby leaned toward the computer's speakers and listened intently for a full minute. When he looked up, his smile was gone. "There's something going on there. Can you give me a clue?"

"I'd rather not."

"Okay, be that way," he muttered as he opened a new program. "Let's try this. We're going to keep the pitch the same, but slow the delivery."

The result sounded strange and alien to Elliot. You could now clearly hear the intervals in the panting. Bobby hunched over and closed his eyes in concentration. He nodded in silent affirmation.

"Okay, enough of the theatrics," Elliot said. "What's going on?"

"It's one of the oldest tricks in the book," Bobby said. "It's Morse code."

"As in S.O.S. and telegrams?"

"You got it. Old dog, old trick."

"Jesus!" Elliot exclaimed.

"Wrong exclamatory. Some members of certain religious persuasions might be a little less than happy about this. What we have here might be considered your basic abomination." He paused. "I'm not quite believing it myself. Know what I mean?"

"Me neither," Elliot conceded. "But for now I suggest we behave like good law enforcement professionals and pursue the facts, regardless of what we believe."

Bobby straightened up. "Okay then, let's go back and pick some of this apart. There are a couple of reasons I know it's Morse code. Listen closely." He replayed a segment of the slowed-down panting. "The panting is broken up into little bursts of sound. There are two distinct sounds and one of them is about four times longer than the other. That's how the dits and dahs in Morse code work. Short clusters of them make up letters and numbers. Like the dit-dit-dit for 'S' in S.O.S. When you're done spelling out a word, you pause for slightly longer at the end of it."

He grabbed a pencil and pad. "So let's go back and see what's coming over the doggie wire. I'll do it by hand right now, but it'll be pretty simple to write a little program that does it automatically."

He played the stream of panting, scribbling on the pad as he did so. When he finished, he shoved the pad over to Elliot. "Here you go. Whatever it is, it ain't English. It might be nothing more than doggie talk, which would make all this go down a lot easier."

"Doggie talk," Elliot repeated as he stared at the words on the pad. "You're probably right." He didn't want to reveal any more than he had to, even to Bobby. "How long will it take you to write the conversion program?"

"A few hours. I'll do it tonight. Just tell me one thing."

"What's that?"

"Tell me you made all this up. Tell me it's a very slick trick of some kind."

"I wish I could, but I can't. What's happening here may be the biggest scientific discovery of the last couple of millenniums."

Elliot was just crossing to the far side of the hills toward Christie's house when his cell phone rang. "Hello?"

"It's Mike Hoffner. I need to talk with you right away."

"Did you check with your attorney about this?"

"That can wait. I need to talk to you right now. To-night."

"Where are you?"

"I'm down at the Harbor View. I can meet you in the bar."

"Can you give a sneak preview of what we're going to talk about?"

"There's no time, believe me. Please."

"Please?"

"Please."

Impressive, Elliot thought. A humble Mr. Hoffner. "Okay. I'll be there in about half an hour."

"Thank you."

Elliot pocketed his phone and took a right on one of the winding roads down to the city center. He considered the tone of the conversation. Almost contrite. Sincerely grateful. Terminally frightened.

A very ominous combination.

CHAPTER 70

A piano trio played a credible version of "Blue in Green" in the background. Only the room's oak paneling listened. The Harbor View was a grand old hotel now restored to its former elegance, with prices to match. Hoffner wore chinos and an open oxford shirt. The equivalent of a combat uniform, given his usual elegant attire.

"Thanks," he said when Elliot reached him. "Let's get a table."

They sat down beneath a sconce that put out a gentle yellow light. Elliot slid his valet parking ticket across to Hoffner. "I'm sure you don't mind," he said. "I didn't want to waste time looking for parking."

"No, no. No problem," Hoffner said nervously. "I'll take care of it. We're checked in here. Do you want something to drink?"

"Maybe later. You're checked in here?"

"Yeah, my wife and I. I told her it was a surprise, a little mini vacation."

"And what is it really?"

Hoffner inhaled deeply, struggling to compose himself. "Remember the photo you showed me? Of the guy at the phone booth? I think I ran into him today."

"Where?"

"In a parking lot at a grocery store. He just appeared out of nowhere. Jesus, it was awful."

"I'm sure it was," Elliot agreed. "What did he have to say for himself?"

"He said he'd been screwed on a deal to find the dog. He wanted money. I told him I didn't know anything about his deal. He didn't believe me. He's going to come after me."

"Let's see if I can get this straight," Elliot said. "First of all, you're hiding out here because you're afraid to be at home. Second, you can't go to the police about this because of all the other complications. Third, you need someone with law enforcement experience to provide you with security. Fourth, you haven't met anyone like him at cocktail parties in the higher elevations of the hills. Fifth, that's why we're talking."

"All true," Hoffner conceded. "Plus, he seems to be the person you're looking for."

"Could be. Does this mean you're ready to have a productive dialogue without the presence of your attorney?"

"Yes, that's what it means. Dick Stennis is flying in from Cabo San Lucas. I'd like him to join us."

"That would be your partner in Stemix, correct?"

Hoffner nodded. "I guess you could say we're all in this together. It's better that you hear it all at once. He'll get here later tonight. We can meet tomorrow, whenever you want."

"Okay then, here's the deal. You guys have to tell all,

and I mean *all*. Otherwise, this guy's going to figure out how to get one step ahead of me. And now that you've met him up close and personal, I think you know what that means."

"Yes," Hoffner said weakly. "I think I do." Half the life had drained from his face.

Elliot stood to go. "You'll be okay for the time being. Just stay here. Don't go anywhere else. Let me have your cell number and I'll be in touch tomorrow."

"I forgot my cell at the house," Hoffner said. "Call me right here. Will that work?"

"That'll work," Elliot said. "Sleep tight."

───────

Elliot smiled as he peeked into the master bedroom. The dog dozed peacefully on the new sleeping pad, which occupied the carpeted space near the window. Christie was sound asleep in bed, but her handiwork was self-evident. Half a dozen dog toys surrounded the sleeping pad. The mother in her was out in full force.

He continued down the hall to where he was bunked. So near, so far.

CHAPTER 71

Korvin paused to scan the console that was charged with the security of Michael Hoffner's home. The digital master clock reported that it was 2:13 a.m. and all was well. Korvin was quite familiar with this particular system, and equally well acquainted with numerous techniques to circumvent it. He gained an undetected entry in less than four minutes.

He ignored the view of the city below, climbed to the top floor and checked the bedrooms. The house was vacant. Hoffner and family had apparently abandoned it in favor of a safe haven somewhere. Korvin was nearly certain the man was still here in the city. A person of his station was shackled to a complex web of meetings and appointments. He couldn't spontaneously leave town without some plausible explanation. It would take time to engineer such a thing.

He descended to the bottom floor and located the office. The walls were lined with diplomas, accolades and the usual self-congratulatory array of framed photos. The computer was secured with a password, and the surface of the desk was devoid of notes or other scraps that might reveal his whereabouts.

The home theater didn't seem likely to yield anything useful, either. Just some fat leather chairs facing a big screen and bank of consumer electronics. But then he saw it, on one of the little tables between the chairs. A cell phone. He cracked open its clamshell case and pulled up the list of entered numbers and the names assigned to them. Items like "office," "assistant," "lab," and "voice mail" appeared. The phone was almost certainly Hoffner's. The fool had fled in a panic and left it behind.

Next, he scanned the list of recently dialed numbers. The number at the top was by far the most interesting. The call was to a name programmed in as "Oakner." He pocketed the phone and considered the source of the name. His original target upon his arrival here had been a Dr. James Oakner. Could they be one and the same? It seemed highly likely. Hoffner and Oakner were both big players in the Pearson universe. Their connection could rapidly be verified online.

But why had Hoffner called Oakner's number? After all, the doctor was lying comatose up at Pearson. Was there somebody else there that Hoffner had an interest in?

It was definitely worth following up on.

CHAPTER 72

Bobby Seifert knelt on one knee and gave the dog a friendly pat on the head. Her black fur glistened in the morning sun that flooded the kitchen. "Hey, girl, pleased to meet you. Did you know that you're the doggie of the century? Can I be your agent?"

The dog gave Bobby an affectionate lick on the hand.

"I'll take that as a yes," Bobby said. "We'll have the lawyers work out the details later." He looked up at Christie. "So, where do you want to do it?"

"Right here on the kitchen table will do just fine."

"I want to go over this one more time for good measure," he told Elliot and Christie as he fired up the laptop computer he'd brought along. "You never saw this machine, you never saw any of the software we're going to use. As a matter of fact, I was never here today. I was downtown looking for vintage CDs. Stuff that's never made it onto iTunes. Got it?"

"Got it," Elliot said. Somehow, the laptop was related to Bobby's connections among his old techno-buddies in the intelligence community. His caution was understandable, to say the least. "So let's run down the process again for us non-techno types," he suggested.

"It'll work like this," Bobby said. "You hit the space bar and speak into the microphone here on the machine. You have to make it short and sweet. It'll only chew on a few sentences at a time. What you say gets translated into Malay—don't ask me how—and then comes out through the speaker."

"How will we know if we're getting a good translation?" Christie asked. "I did some PR work in Europe and Asia, and sometimes that became a major problem."

"We won't," Bobby answered. "But I can assure you that no expense has been spared to make it the very best."

Christie looked down at the dog and gave her a pat.

"And what if she won't respond to anything but a live human?"

"Then we've got a big problem," Bobby replied. "For now, I suggest that we just think positive."

"What about the other direction, when she talks back to us?" Elliot asked.

"First, I record her panting into the computer, which converts the Morse code into words, all Malay, of course. Then a little magic happens and the computer says it back to us in English. So, who wants to start?"

"I will," Christie said. The dog sat at her feet, quiet but alert. Bobby turned the laptop toward her so she could hit the space bar. "What's your name?" she said into the microphone.

A moment later, a Malaysian voice came out of the speaker. The dog perked up immediately. It panted for a brief interval, then stopped.

"Got it," Bobby told them. "Okay, hold on while we crunch this."

While they waited, an additional complication struck Elliot. They were assuming that the dog could write and spell. Without those things, her Morse code ability wouldn't mean much. No one who was illiterate could send a telegram without someone to write out the message for them. Same problem here.

The computer's speaker came to life.

Name Lyana.

Christie looked down at the dog in utter amazement.

Elliot tried desperately to put this moment into reasonable perspective. He couldn't. Nobody could.

"Wow," Bobby said softly. It seemed as good a response as any. Lyana came up on her haunches beside Christie and looked at Bobby patiently but alertly.

"Let me try one." Elliot hit the space bar. "How well can you spell?" he asked into the microphone. With only a little hesitation, the computer output his question in Malay. Lyana was silent for a moment, as though pondering the question.

"Good thought," Bobby said. "Spelling sort of defines the name of the game."

Lyana replied with a brief string of panting. She looked directly at Elliot, as though she understood the process with the computer and the translation.

The speaker came back on in English.

Spell some.

"One more time," Elliot said, and hit the space bar. "Does that mean you can spell some words and not others?" he asked. His query went through the translation process and out to the dog. This time, they didn't have to wait. She nodded her head for a "yes."

"Smart," Bobby said in admiration. "She's already optimizing the process."

"My turn," Christie said. "Where is your home?" They all waited as the question wound its way through the process and prompted an answer.

Here.

Christie's eyes grew moist and she knelt and hugged Lyana. "I wasn't expecting that." She turned to Elliot. "Ask her if she has any brothers and sisters."

Elliot asked. The cycle played out.

Don't spell.

They all looked at each other. "So what's that mean?" Bobby asked.

"It might mean a lot of things," Elliot said. "It might mean she can't spell their names. It might mean she can't spell the number to tell us how many. It might mean she didn't understand the question in the first place. We're going to get a lot of this until we know more about her."

"You're right," Christie said. "We can't start thinking of her as a human in a dog's body. That's not what she is."

"Right on," added Bobby. "She's still a dog, a very smart dog, but still a dog."

Still a dog, Elliot mused, *but a dog like no other.* He wondered if Hoffner and Stennis had any idea what they had set in motion.

He would soon find out.

———

Korvin closed the laptop and went to the counter of the Internet Cafe to pay for the time in cash. He had what he needed. It had taken only a few minutes with Google. Oakner was a partner with Hoffner and another scientist in a biotech company. Undoubtedly, the dog was somehow part of their research. And Becker had some sort of stake in whatever they were up to. A very big stake. So why had Hoffner phoned Oakner's home number yesterday? He must have been contacting Oakner's wife, a woman named Christie, according to what he'd just found online.

Maybe it was time to pay her a visit.

CHAPTER 73

"It's probably best for you to tell us what you already know," Stennis said. "We don't have any time to waste."

"Fair enough," Elliot said from his side of the picnic table. He guessed that Stennis was older than he appeared, and worked at staying in shape. He sported a tropical tan, probably from Mexico, most likely from Cabo. Hoffner, on the other hand, appeared pale and stressed, drumming his fingers incessantly on the weathered wooden surface.

"I know the two of you have a company that does some kind of stem cell work," Elliot continued. "I know that Oakner's a partner in it. I know that the company's financed through grants from something called the Xanos Foundation. I know the dog is somehow part of the deal. I know that Oakner damn near died down in Cabo, and that set off a chain of events that's brought us together here on this lovely day."

Stennis stared down at his folded hands. Then he spoke. "A few years back, I was at a conference on neuroscience in Vienna. My team's research involved the application of stem cells to various neurological afflictions."

"Brain diseases?"

Stennis nodded. "Brain diseases. Anyway, I met Dr. Oakner at this event. He introduced me to an individual of considerable wealth who had a very rare case of early-onset Alzheimer's. In fact, it was the earliest ever diagnosed."

"Who is this person?"

"It doesn't matter," Hoffner interposed. "He doesn't live here. In fact, he doesn't live anywhere anymore. For now, let's just call him our sponsor."

"So this rich sick guy was the money behind the funding?"

Stennis nodded again. "He was at this conference looking for a cure. Oakner was speaking, and afterward our sponsor approached him and talked about his disease. Oakner knew what I was doing at Pearson, so the three of us got together. It was a fantastic opportunity. We'd get virtually unlimited funding to pursue something that might be a major breakthrough in treating not only Alzheimer's, but a whole range of neurological pathologies."

"All our sponsor wanted was an equal share of the company, and the first available treatment we could develop," Hoffner added.

"And you became the third leg of the deal, the financial pipeline from the money to the lab?" Elliot asked Hoffner.

"You have to understand that there was no fraud involved," Hoffner replied. "Our sponsor knew full well that we would use part of the funding to generously compensate ourselves. Secrecy and security were his main concerns."

"Our original deal for the company produced a very

convenient division of labor," Stennis said. "I did the research, Oakner developed surgical techniques, and Mike handled the business affairs. The basic idea for what we were doing is simple, but the practice is extraordinarily complicated. You know how stem cells work?"

"Just barely," Elliot admitted. "They're cells that can grow into different kinds of body parts, if everything goes right, which it usually doesn't, right?"

"That's good enough for now," Stennis said. "The plan was to inject a special preparation of stem cells into our sponsor's brain, where they would replace the neurons destroyed by Alzheimer's. We made excellent progress in the research, and now we're in the final stages of perfecting a workable treatment."

"If the technology proves successful, it'll be a monumental accomplishment," Hoffner said passionately. "For the first time, there'll be hope for millions of people suffering from incurable brain disorders."

"But then something happened," Elliot interjected. "What?"

"Dr. Oakner developed a big problem about the dog. He went absolutely nuclear," Stennis said. "And that's when it all started to fall apart."

"The dog?" Elliot asked. "By all means, let's talk about the dog."

━━━━━━━

Korvin gazed at the reclining form of Dr. James Oakner. The doctor's eyes were closed. His mouth was slightly open. It appeared as though he might have fallen asleep while watching television on a lazy weekend afternoon.

"He seems so peaceful," he commented to the nurse.

"Yes, he does," she agreed. "They often appear that way."

"When we were little, he was constantly in motion," Korvin observed. "We were always wrestling around."

"My brothers did the same thing." The nurse smiled sympathetically.

"I'll be helping my sister-in-law with the long-term care arrangements," Korvin said as he stood up. "Is there someone here I can talk to about that?"

"Absolutely," the nurse replied.

Thirty minutes later, Korvin walked out of the hospital. His chat with the administrator had been quite pleasant. He reached for Hoffner's cell phone.

━━━━━━

The rat cautiously worked its way along the foundation's edge. Its exposed position made it skittish and pumped its senses to an elevated state of alert. The brilliant bloom of day and the open space worked against its poor vision. It preferred darkness and cramped conditions, which favored its highly sensitized nose, ears and whiskers. But the smell of the dog food up ahead overrode its normal caution.

Its ears picked up the sudden twitter of a telephone on the far side of the wall; it was familiar with this noise and found no threat in it. It moved on toward the intersection of the deck with the foundation.

"Hello?" Christie picked up the portable phone as she went to open the door to the deck for Lyana.

"Hello, Ms. Oakner? This is Branford Ellis from the Neural Care Unit at Pearson."

"Oh my God—is something wrong with Jim?"

"No, no. Nothing like that. I was just phoning to tell you I'll be in charge of his transition to long-term care. I'd like to see if I can schedule some time with you."

The rat reached the deck, put its paws on the edge of

the planking and pulled itself up to view the source of the smell.

"Of course you can," Christie said as she slid the door open and Lyana went out onto the deck. "But I need to check my calendar, and I can't do that right now."

Lyana smelled the rat and saw it at the same time. A complex array of hormonal emissions, skin odors and dank fur. Only the rodent's head and front paws peeked over the edge of the deck by her food bowl. A threat to her food supply. An atavistic reaction overcame her.

She barked, a single and authoritative bark. The rat instantly disappeared.

Korvin heard the bark in the cell phone's ear portal, and smiled. "I'm sorry, I didn't mean to interrupt. It sounds like you have company."

"Yes, I have a visitor right now."

"Not to worry. I'll phone you back in a few days and we can work something out. Nice talking to you."

"Talk to you later."

Korvin pocketed the phone and headed toward his car. *A visitor. Yes, you have a visitor.*

———

"The dog," Stennis said as he stared absently at his hands resting on the picnic table. He looked up at Elliot. "I hope you're ready for this."

"At this point, I don't think I have a lot of choice. Go ahead."

"You have to start with the idea of an animal model. Obviously, when you're developing a new treatment for a disease, you don't just jump in and try it on humans. You try it on animals. But which animal? First you consider the organ that you're targeting with the treatment, and then choose an animal where the features of this organ resemble that in a human. In diseases of the brain, this would normally be a primate, a monkey of some kind. But in our case, this proved problematic. Extremely problematic."

"Why's that? It sounds pretty much like basic science."

An odd smile came over Stennis. "The science is fine, the person is not. You see, our sponsor is not the most trusting of souls. He's very creative about binding you to his interests in ways that don't impede your progress, but also guarantee that you deliver exactly as promised.

"He understood that we have to operate under a set of ethical guidelines that all stem cell researchers adhere to. If we did otherwise, we'd be ruined professionally. Our work would be totally compromised. He also realized that we stood to profit enormously if we succeeded. Our sponsor leveraged all this in a way that I have to admit was quite ingenious.

"Somehow, some way, he found out about a renegade research operation that had produced a very novel animal model. We have no idea who they are, or why they did what they did. All we know is that he insisted we use their model instead of the conventional one."

"It wouldn't involve dogs, would it?"

"Not dogs like you'd normally think of dogs. Very special dogs. Dogs that would pass the science test, but flunk the ethics test. That was the trick of it. The dogs gave us the data we needed, but guaranteed we'd keep the results strictly to ourselves."

"So if everything had to be a secret, how did you plan on getting rich with your company?" Elliot asked. "Wouldn't you eventually have to reveal your data to the FDA before you could sell anything?"

"The deal with our sponsor took that into account,"

Hoffner answered. "We would use the animal model based on the dogs to perfect our technology, and then treat his Alzheimer's. Once that was done, we would use the perfected treatment on a conventional animal model, like a monkey. It would proceed very quickly because we would already know what we were doing. We would then use that data to get FDA approval for clinical trials and market the final product."

"But then Dr. Oakner had a problem with the dog. Why?"

Hoffner glanced nervously at Stennis. "I hope you're a fairly open-minded person," Stennis said to Elliot.

"I'd like to think so."

"Well, we'll see about that," Stennis said. "To ensure the integrity of the research, our sponsor had to fully disclose the provenance of the test animals. It started with stem cells extracted from a frozen human embryo. These cells were then cultured in a laboratory until there was a large population of them. A special bit of DNA was added to the cells for experimental purposes to help with the research.

"Then a surgery was performed on a Labrador retriever two-thirds of the way through her pregnancy. The fetal pups were very carefully removed from her womb with the placenta left intact so they could be put back in to finish their gestation. While they were out of the womb, the human stem cells were injected into the ventricles of the pups' brains. These are hollow cavities inside the brain, so there would be no damage to the brain itself.

"The surgery was completed and the pups continued to develop in the mother's womb for their last trimester. During this time, some of the human stem cells integrated themselves into the pups' brain tissue."

"Wow." Elliot couldn't think of any other response.

"Strictly speaking, this work would have been within the general guidelines of the research community and regulatory bodies in many countries. Similar procedures have been done with other animals. It opens the door to some extremely productive research. And the number of human neurons that actually integrate into the animal brain is extremely small, maybe one in a million. The animal brain is completely unaffected by their presence."

"So what was different this time?"

"It seems that a very large number of stem cells were injected into the pups' brains. Enough that they altered the final brain structure at birth."

Lyana, Elliot thought. "So let me guess," he said to Stennis. "You wind up with some very smart doggies."

"You might be right," Stennis admitted. "But we don't know that for a fact. We never had any direct contact with the animals themselves. We were only given data on the physical structure of the brains. The way it worked, we developed the stem cell cultures here, and then shipped them to our sponsor, who gave them to the lab with the dogs. They would surgically insert them into the animals' brains and do imaging of the results, which would be shipped back to us for analysis."

"How many of them were there?"

"Seven. Only one of them is left now. The rest were eventually euthanized to allow microscopic examination of their brain tissue. I was assured that this was done humanely and in keeping with current guidelines."

"And the one that's left? It's the one that wound up here and got loose?"

"That's right. It's a different case than its siblings. All the others were injected with a stem cell culture that induced a condition that mimics Alzheimer's. This allowed us to study how well the therapy worked when it was applied to them. This last animal received an injection that *lacked* the Alzheimer's condition. This guaranteed that it would survive for the duration of the project."

"And why did you bring that dog here to Pearson? Why didn't it stay with this other lab?"

"It was part of our agreement with our sponsor. His surgery would be done at a private hospital here in the city. The last dog would be injected with precisely the same cell culture that we intended to use on the sponsor himself. It would be a precautionary measure. If the dog had an adverse reaction, we would postpone the sponsor's treatment until we figured out what had gone wrong."

Stennis stopped and shrugged. "Of course, all this is just speculation."

"Why's that?" Elliot asked.

"Dr. Oakner's comatose, we've lost the dog, and our sponsor's Alzheimer's has beaten us to the punch. His disease has progressed to the point where it's highly unlikely that the treatment will help. His brain tissue is probably compromised to the point where it can no longer be reconstructed."

"I'm with you on all this," Elliot said, "but I still don't understand why Oakner was so bugged about the dog. Didn't he know about it all along?"

"Yes, he did," Stennis answered. "That wasn't the problem."

"Then what was the problem?"

Stennis and Hoffner exchanged worried glances once more.

"You really want to know? It won't change anything. And you might not like what you hear."

"I'll take that chance."

Stennis spoke. Elliot listened. The park glowed green in the bright overcast. Sparrows darted in and out of the nearby bushes. Traffic rushed and hissed out on the street. Stennis finished. Without a word, Elliot rose from his seat and started off across the park.

He had no idea where he was going.

CHAPTER 74

Korvin slowed as he drove by the big house of ashen stucco with its terra-cotta roof. A frontal approach was risky, too risky. The front door looked massive enough to resist a forceful break-in. The element of surprise would be lost. An alarm might be issued. Picking the lock was also out. A security camera peered down from above the door, its digital gaze scanning for intruders.

He drove on past and wound down a steep and wooded grade devoid of housing. Near the bottom, he turned onto a short service road. It terminated in a pumping station surrounded by a Cyclone fence and a perimeter of loose gravel. He walked behind the station and peered up the hill. The house leaned out slightly over the treetops high above. This would be the route. No one would expect an entrance from this side.

He tucked the scabbard holding his knife into his belt and started toward the slope. A train whistle sounded somewhere in the distance far below. He reached the underbrush and started to climb.

Everyone in the house would have to be exterminated, except for the dog. Simple enough. That done, he would secure the animal and defeat the front camera. Then he would trace his path back down the hill, get in the car and drive back up to the house front, where he could quickly load the beast. Finally, he would retreat to the woods once again, and phone Becker. This time, his price would be substantially higher.

His foot came down on a dead limb and snapped it, generating a sharp cracking sound that radiated outward among the trees. It reached a crow perched in a fir high overhead. The bird peered down and caught a trace of his movement. It opened its beak and cawed.

Lyana lay on the deck and wallowed in the dry perfume of the planking. Her flank rested on a folded blanket supplied by Christie, and her belly swelled with premium dog food. The day was bright and dry and pleasant. She idly counted the flowerpots that lined the far side of the deck. There were seven, and they held four plants of one species and three of another. Did four and three equal seven if all the things were not the same? She wasn't sure. She would need to find out.

The caws of the crow interrupted her speculation. They came from below, down the hill. She processed their pitch, their timbre, the spacing of the intervals between them. She sorted the pattern against many such patterns she'd learned in the woods. This particular sequence signaled the presence of a large, ground-based predator. It warned the crow's peers to avoid descending to the forest floor.

She raised her head and cocked her ears, listening for

more. None came. She brought her head back down and let the world drift into soft focus.

━━━━━━

Elliot walked slowly back across the field. Stennis and Hoffner had left the park. The picnic table stood empty. A robin alighted on it. The bird surveyed the grass, saw nothing of interest and flew off. Elliot took its place. His world was slightly askew, like a ship taking on water to starboard in a storm. The effect was worse sitting, so he stood and fished for his car keys.

━━━━━━

Lyana caught the man's scent through the crack in the decking by her nose. It bore an unmistakable signature of musk, perspiration and elevated adrenaline. Its presence startled her and she leapt to her feet. She knew immediately that it came from below and trotted to the deck's edge. She peered down through the tree canopy thick with the bloom of spring foliage that hid the ground beneath. She sniffed vigorously and analyzed the vast store of odor. The man's scent was growing stronger. It kept rising ever higher above the aromatic noise level of the woods. She turned and headed toward the open door to the house. She must tell the woman, the sweet woman who touched her so nicely.

Christie sat at a little desk inset off the kitchen. She copied a list of Malay words off her laptop and wrote them neatly on a legal tablet. She intended to construct a Rosetta stone of sorts, and use it to teach Lyana English. She stopped writing as the dog trotted in from out on the deck. Lyana ran to her, sat at her feet and began the encrypted panting.

Lyana could see the woman look at her with great curiosity. She seemed to be straining to understand.

"What are you trying to tell me, girl? What is it?"

Bad man here.

"Are you still hungry? I just fed you a ton of food."

Bad man now.

Lyana rose and whirled toward the sliding doors. She stopped at the entrance and looked at Christie and continued to pant with great urgency. She stared out onto the deck, then back at Christie.

Christie stood up. "You want me to see something outside?"

Lyana skittered out onto the deck. Christie followed. Lyana stopped at the deck's edge and peered down into the foliage. She looked back anxiously at Christie. She could now hear the man as well as smell him. The sonic ghost of his motion floated up out of the woods.

Christie looked down over the deck railing. "Sorry, sweetie. I don't see anything. We'll try again a little later. Okay?" She walked back into the house and headed down the hall.

Lyana looked on in frustration. Words wouldn't work. The woman couldn't understand her. She quickly surveyed the objects on the deck.

She saw a solution.

———

Korvin stopped at an old metal T-post, part of an ancient fence now long gone. He walked on past and stood at the base of the support structure for the deck. Its wooden columns sat in concrete foundations and rose up to the deck, forty feet above. A system of cross-bracing stabilized the structure. It also provided a way to climb to the top. He grasped the first brace and began to climb.

Lyana nudged her water bowl over to the big pot nearest the house. She thrust one of her paws into the bowl and soaked it. Then she removed it and poked it into the soil in the pot. She repeated the process several times and created a muddy mash. She pulled her caked paw out and ran toward the sliding doors.

Christie's phone rang. She stopped her search for a new legal tablet in the study and answered. "Hello."

"Hello, Ms. Oakner, this is Branford Ellis from the Neural Care Unit at Pearson. How are you today?"

"I'm fine." Christie felt a surge of alarm. The voice was different. This was not the same person who phoned earlier.

"I just wanted to follow up after my meeting with your brother-in-law."

"My brother-in-law?"

"He seemed very nice. It's good you have someone to help with all this."

"Yes. Goodbye." Christie sprinted down the stairs toward the kitchen.

Korvin thrust himself up to the next level in the structure. He examined the detail of the decking above. Surprise would be critical.

Christie burst into the kitchen and skidded to a stop. The sliding glass door displayed a figure built from mud smears and paw prints. A stick figure of a human. A crude yet powerful icon born of dirt and ingenuity.

Lyana stood next to the figure. She looked up at her drawing, barked twice and twisted to face the deck.

"Oh my God!" Christie exclaimed. *The gun!* She turned and ran toward the stairs.

Lyana puzzled over the woman's retreat. Did she understand the message? Was she running away? The dog's ears continued to pick up the man's exertions under the deck. Her nose confirmed his agitated state. She moved out onto the deck. She needed to protect the woman from harm.

Christie pulled the pistol from the bedside table, a big automatic of some kind. It felt heavy and cool. Jim once told her it was armed and ready to fire. She could only hope he was right. She bounded back down the stairs and then slowed as she approached the sliding door. She couldn't see the dog, but she could hear it out on the deck.

Korvin grabbed the middle railing and vaulted over the top. He pulled the knife from its scabbard as he landed on the decking and caught sight of the dog. The animal was circling and growling. Its ears hugged its skull. Its tail shot straight out. It stared directly into his gaze.

He caught a flash of chrome and snapped around toward the source. A woman in a doorway pointed a pistol at him, a 40mm automatic. His focus traveled instantly from the gun to her eyes. She would shoot him, yes. But she lacked purity of intent. Few had it. Civilization dictated otherwise. He had just enough margin.

"Don't shoot!" he yelled. "I'm a federal agent."

He reached toward his coat pocket, as if to extract some identification. The woman's eyes tracked the movement of his hand. They failed to see his other hand bring the knife up and back. At this range, its velocity at impact would be catastrophic.

Lyana observed the swing of the man's arm and his grip on the knife handle. From her time in the woods with him, she knew his intent. He would throw the knife at the woman with deadly force.

The dog launched into the air. Her jaws intercepted the wrist and palm of the hand holding the weapon. They closed with enormous pressure that sank through flesh, sinew and muscle, and clamped to bone.

Korvin fought to control the shock of the bite. The pain was horrific, and burst in molten pulses from his stricken hand. The power of the beast's bite was almost unbelievable.

Christie watched as the dog's momentum caused the man to stagger backward and drop his knife. The intensity of their struggle held her transfixed.

Korvin overcame the shock of his injury. He transmuted pain into rage, and rage into action. He leveraged his great strength to make the dog's tenacious grip work against her. He picked the beast up off the deck and flung her in a brutal arc.

Lyana held tight as Korvin propelled her through the air. Her teeth remained solidly entrenched in the man's hand.

The violence of it all overwhelmed Christie. She had forgotten about the pistol in her hand.

She didn't even notice Elliot, who suddenly appeared alongside her.

Korvin spotted Elliot as he brought the dog around toward a railing post. He knew that the cop wouldn't hesitate to shoot him.

Lyana saw the post coming up in her peripheral vision. She understood what would happen. She would be shattered by the impact. She opened her jaws and flew free.

Korvin instantly took advantage of his released hand. He fell into a roll, grabbed the knife on the deck floor, came up and pitched himself over the railing.

Lyana landed on her back, rotated and returned to her feet just short of the sliding door. She spun toward Korvin, just in time to see him disappear over the edge of the deck.

Elliot took the gun from Christie as Korvin disappeared from sight. He rushed over and looked down. All he saw was a rustle of brush. He jumped over the side in pursuit and landed heavily on the sharp angle of the slope. Christie appeared above him. "Send the dog around!" he yelled. He started downhill through the brush.

Korvin made his way down the slope. Pain shot up his leg. Most likely, he'd broken his ankle in the jump off the deck. Elliot would most certainly pursue him. And at this pace, the cop would overtake him before he could reach his car down by the pumping station.

Elliot turned to a rustle in the brush behind him. Lyana. He faced her and pointed down the hill. "We have to find him." Lyana nodded and moved ahead and on down the hill. Did she understand? He could only hope so.

Elliot would assume he was headed straight downhill,

Korvin decided. He turned left and struggled laterally across the grade on his bad ankle. If he could cover enough distance, he could find a place to hole up, a place to regroup.

Lyana pursued the scent. She moved with caution. She knew the man was armed with the knife and could cause great harm, even at a distance. She'd seen him kill. The scent trail turned left. She followed.

Korvin found the spot he sought, a small open space followed by a dense stand of brush. He moved into the stand and crouched. His ankle pulsed with pain, but he ignored it. His right hand throbbed and bled from the dog bite, so he shifted his knife to his left hand. He could throw, slash or stab with either.

Elliot moved cautiously down the hill. The woods had gone silent, with no sound of hurried motion. Lyana was somewhere up ahead. Korvin either had beaten him to the street below or had concealed himself. All he could do was wait and take his cue from the dog.

Lyana followed the scent into the open space and froze. The strength of the smell told her the man was very near. She peered straight ahead into the dense stand of brush.

Korvin watched the animal from behind the thick foliage. She had tracked him here. Could she see him? He doubted it. A searing wave of pain shot up from his ankle. He shifted his weight slightly to alleviate it.

Lyana heard movement. She saw just the slightest rearrangement in the pattern of the brush up ahead. She had found him. She weighed her next move carefully, and then casually sniffed the ground in front of her.

Korvin watched the animal put its nose to the ground, then turn and trot off the way it had come. He suspected she'd seen him, but he didn't care. She would show Elliot where he was, and the moment the cop appeared in the little clearing, he would rear up and throw his knife. The range would be short. The force would be lethal.

Elliot spotted Lyana trotting back up the slope to him. She stopped and gave him an urgent look. He pointed to the direction of her travel. "You want me to follow?" She dipped her head in confirmation, then whirled and headed back down the slope. Elliot checked the pistol as he followed. The safety was off. A round was chambered.

They continued cautiously on down the slope. Then Lyana abruptly turned left and followed the contour of the hill. She slowed and moved forward in a slight crouch. Elliot did the same. What was the dog up to? Was she putting them in harm's way? Their opponent was supremely ruthless and extremely clever. Was she any match for him? One way or the other, he would soon find out.

Korvin's ears picked up their approach at the far periphery of his hearing. His training and experience dissected the sound. The cop and the dog were walking together. They were approaching from the expected direction. Good. He adjusted his grip on the knife handle. It wouldn't matter that Elliot was armed. The knife would be buried in his throat before he could even take aim. The man was a small-time cop. Korvin was a world-class practitioner of applied violence.

Lyana stopped, turned to Elliot, then sat on her haunches. There was no time for nuanced communication. She could only hope he understood. With her right paw, she scratched an indentation in the dirt and then made a biting motion at it.

Elliot got it. She was referring to the bad man, the one she bit.

Lyana's paws dug indentations on either side of the original one. She looked up at Elliot expectantly. He thought he understood, but how could he confirm it? His mind raced. He pointed to himself at one indentation, and then to Lyana at the other. She nodded energetically. Then he traced lines from the two outer indentations to the middle one. Once again, Lyana nodded vigorously. He had it. They would come at their prey from opposite directions.

He nodded back to Lyana. She took off up the slope. He crept slowly ahead. He could hear her out in the woods, moving in a big semicircle. Ahead, the brush began to thin toward a small clearing.

Lyana ran as fast as she could to get into position. She had communicated as best she could, but the timing was all up to her. She had to complete her part of the encirclement and begin her final move before Elliot walked into the open alone and exposed himself.

Korvin heard the dog crashing through the brush, making no effort to conceal itself. What was going on? Suddenly, he understood. A pincer movement. He was being entrapped in the most fundamental of military maneuvers. The dog was now running at him from directly behind. A sudden burst of barking confirmed it.

Elliot heard Lyana bark. The direction of the sound confirmed that he was on the right path. He brought the pistol up. He moved ahead.

Korvin saw one last option. He put aside his pain, rose out of the stand and moved forward into the clearing. He wouldn't be where they thought he was. When Elliot entered the clearing, he'd be right in front of him. Maybe even in stabbing range. The dog would arrive a few seconds too late.

Lyana bounded through the undergrowth and caught

sight of the alpha man leaving the stand and moving across the clearing.

Elliot cautiously parted the brush with his pistol. Lyana was no longer barking.

Lyana reached the stand and leapt into the air. In the longest leap of her life, she sailed all the way over it.

Elliot parted the last strands of brush, and there was Korvin, only a few feet from him. The man's throwing arm was cocked and holding a knife.

Lyana bounded across the open space and pounced on the alpha man from the rear. She sank her teeth into his neck with all the strength she could muster.

Elliot watched as Korvin staggered under the assault. Still, the man continued toward him, eyes ablaze with murderous intent, even with the dog hanging off his back.

Korvin brought the knife into a stabbing position. "You're dead!" he screamed at Elliot.

Elliot brought the pistol up but hesitated. He might hit Lyana.

Korvin made his final lunge. Elliot sidestepped. Korvin crashed to the forest floor.

With the alpha man down, Lyana had leverage. She shook her head and neck to maximize the damage inflicted by her clamped jaws. A vicious growl came out of her as she did it. Korvin went limp. The knife slipped from his hand.

Elliot picked up the knife and tossed it away. He put his hand on Lyana's back. "It's okay now. You can let go." Lyana opened her jaws and backed off.

Korvin lay on his side, and Elliot looked down at the neck wounds. It appeared that the dog had crushed several vertebrae. Her teeth had shattered the discs and severed the spinal cord, the lifeline to the body. It seemed an amazing feat of strength, even for a dog. But then again, this was a dog like no other.

Lyana stood a short distance away, panting heavily. This time, there was no code in it.

CHAPTER 75

Elliot tamped the last of the dirt with his shovel. Only a chipmunk bore witness. The light was nearly gone. The forest had entered the hush of twilight. A trickle of sweat ran down his side. He had to leave soon, before he lost the light entirely.

He rested for a moment on the shovel's handle, wheezing. The grave was shallow, but Elliot didn't care. The corpse had no real identity. A citizen of nowhere. If discovered, it would become a John Doe in the morgue. The wound on the neck would generate some temporary interest. An autopsy would be performed. An investigation would be launched. No leads would emerge. The investigation would sink to the bottom of the bureaucracy and stay there, never to resurface.

He lifted the shovel and started back up the slope. The chipmunk noisily tracked his departure and then scampered off into the long shadows, which would soon drown in the dark.

Becker sat quietly in his wheelchair. He wore a mono-grammed robe of Mongolian cashmere. The nurse turned him toward the window, away from the attorneys, who conferred in hushed tones over the disposition of his vast empire. Factions had already formed. Power was polariz-ing. Litigation would ensue.

Becker looked down upon Lake Geneva through va-cant eyes. His hands hung limp and lifeless over the edges of the armrests. His mouth was slightly open, as though he was trying to form a word.

He wasn't. He was gone.

———————

Lyana watched the woman who sat cross-legged in front of her on the deck. She now knew the lady's name was Christie. They had established this after a long discourse during which Christie read Malay words off a legal pad. Christie had accumulated just enough vocabulary to com-municate simple concepts: *Name Christie. Home here. Lyana hungry?* Lyana panted back at her, even though she knew Christie couldn't decode it. Lyana understood that this was simply the first step in a learning process, that someday they would share thoughts and feelings at a much more profound level. The love was already there. All else would eventually follow.

Elliot looked out at Christie and Lyana on the deck, then over at Stennis and Hoffner at the kitchen table. Lyana had shocked them into a state of intense delibera-tion. They knew in advance that she would exhibit some intelligence; they were completely unprepared for what they had just witnessed.

"So, what do you think?" Elliot asked.

"We want to talk about it a little more," Hoffner said, "but I don't think we want to take the animal."

"She's clearly in a class by herself," Stennis said. "She presents all kinds of ethical considerations. We really don't want to get bogged down in that kind of thing. If we take possession, we take responsibility. I don't think we want to do that."

"We'll simply do what we were going to do anyway," Hoffner said. "We'll repeat our testing with conventional laboratory animals."

"Sounds good to me," Elliot said. "That leaves us with just one question."

"What's that?" Stennis asked.

"What do we tell her about her brothers and sisters? The ones that grew up with Alzheimer's and died for the data?"

Elliot expected they would pause and consider. They didn't.

"Ever heard of ataxia-telangiectasia?" Hoffner asked. "It's called AT for short."

"No, I haven't."

"You have a newborn child," Stennis said. "A beautiful baby. You bring it home and feed it and love it and play with it. It becomes your world. Then around eighteen months, something seems wrong. The baby can't walk right. You have it examined. It appears to be cerebral palsy. It's a big shock, but you adjust. You still have your baby, you still have the love, you still have hope. Then your baby becomes a little child, and more things start to go wrong. The child's eyes twitch and won't track right. They become permanently bloodshot. It chokes when it swallows. Its speech is slurred. It gets chest colds all the time. It has a weakened immune system, like someone with AIDS. It struggles to keep walking, even a little, but its legs won't let it.

"Finally, they figure out it's AT. You discover you're living with a death sentence. Your baby will die in its late teens, and you will watch the entire process, month by month, year by year. And AT doesn't affect the intellect. The disease leaves your child with full knowledge of what's happening to him. He knows that there's nothing anybody can do, not one damn thing. So, you get the idea?"

"Yeah, I do." Elliot looked out at Lyana, who was sitting beside Christie on the deck. This remarkable animal and her departed siblings had made a contribution to humanity that defied all forms of valuation.

"I can't guarantee that our work will cure AT, but I can guarantee that it's a very big step in the right direction. So you take it from there, okay?"

"Point taken," Elliot said. "There's just one other thing."

"What's that?" Hoffner asked.

"I want my job back."

Hoffner thought for a moment. "That may be a little difficult."

"But not impossible. You're higher up the food chain than the Chief. And the Chief has always been very responsive to those who can eat him."

———————

Elliot walked out on the deck after Hoffner and Stennis departed. "We're done. The dog's yours," he told Christie.

Christie smiled and stroked the dog's neck. "Lyana's not anybody's. She can live here because she wants to."

"I hope she understands that she's got a very good deal," Elliot said.

"I think that's a pretty safe assumption," Christie replied. "She's definitely seen the other side of life."

"Yeah, I guess she has." Elliot sat down on a bench. He put his hand on Christie's shoulder. "There's something I want to know."

"What's that?"

"You told me that you and Jim had a fight down in Cabo on the night that he gassed himself. You said it was personal."

"It was very personal."

"And I respect that. I really don't have any right to ask you about it."

"Then why are you doing it?"

"I want to put all of this behind us. All of it. Once that's happened, we can see what's left for us to work with."

"Not much, I'm afraid. Not much."

"Maybe, but maybe not. There's no way I can know unless you tell me."

Christie continued to pet Lyana while she spoke. "I was doing quite well before I met Jim. I had a great job with an international PR firm. I was put on a team that had a very odd assignment. We were charged with keeping someone out of the media instead of in. Our client was extremely wealthy, which made him a prime target for journalists. We couldn't make him poor, but we could make him boring, which worked quite well. The media couldn't find a hook to make him interesting, and his coverage was minimized. There was only one problem."

"What was that?"

"I fell for him. Head over heels. I left the agency. I lived with him in huge houses scattered all over the world. I flew with him in private jets. It was great fun—for a while. But then I began to wonder where it was all going.

He wanted babies, but he was extremely paranoid about marriage. He wanted to be the king and produce an heir, but without the benefit of a queen. I resisted, but it was hard. I loved him. I wanted to be with him, and I really did want a baby. I'd put it off for a long time, and I was more than ready."

"So what did you do?"

"I caved in. He made me an incredible offer that would set me up for life, regardless of what happened to us. And our baby could stay with me until it was grown. The whole thing was spelled out in this incredibly complex legal document. So it was set. Only it turned out he wasn't so good at making babies. He had a very low sperm count. So we turned to in vitro fertilization. You know how it works?"

"A little. They remove some eggs from you and fertilize them in the lab, then put one back in you."

"That's basically it." She paused and petted Lyana softly. A sad smile made its way gently over her face. "We went ahead with the first step and had some of my eggs removed and fertilized with his sperm. We had a busy schedule, so we postponed the transplant step, and the embryos were frozen, so they would be ready when we were. This turned out to be a very good thing, because I started to realize I was making a huge mistake. He was almost fanatically obsessive about secrecy and security, and I saw that I was going to be yanked completely out of circulation. No friends. No social life. Just a baby and splendid isolation."

"So you backed out."

"I backed out. I thought he would be livid, but he wasn't. Then I understood why. He had the babies, our frozen embryos. They didn't need to go back into me. They could go back into someone else. I read the fine print of our agreement, and sure enough, ownership of the embryos stayed with him. He could now produce an heir at his leisure.

"Anyway, we lingered on for a while. But something was wrong with him. I don't know what it was. He wouldn't say. Whatever it was, he became distracted. He developed a consuming interest in medical research. I thought maybe he had cancer, but he said absolutely not. We were at a medical research conference when I met Jim, who was there as a speaker. I didn't start dating him until later, though. I may be a lot of things, but I'm not a cheater."

She doesn't know, Elliot thought. *She really doesn't know.* "So your fight with the doc down in Cabo was over your old boyfriend?"

"No. Jim knew all about that when he married me. What he didn't know about were the frozen embryos. There was never any reason to tell him, so I didn't."

"That's what the fight was about? The embryos?"

"He wanted to have a baby. After everything that happened, I was all through with that idea. Jim got very insistent and emotional about it, and that's when I let him have it. I told him that I already had a stash of frozen babies from my previous relationship. I told him I didn't want to make any more. That's what put him over the top."

She stopped and reached for Elliot's hand. Her eyes were full of tears. "I shouldn't have done it. It was very nasty. I was so angry. It changed everything between us. He was never the same after that."

Of course he wasn't.

Elliot said nothing. He looked out over the railing at the view of the valley. The world was far more beautiful and brutal than he could ever grasp. Everything she said fit with what Stennis and Hoffner had told him yesterday in the park about their partner. But it was only half the story.

Elliot now had all the pieces. Elliot put it all together, just as Oakner had done, down in Cabo. The final revelation was what Stennis had told him in the park at the end of their meeting. It concerned the source of the stem cells.

Oakner knew all about the dogs, about the stem cells injected into their fetal brains, about their immense value to the project. What he didn't know was where the stem cells came from in the first place. Their sponsor had told him they came from "an anonymous donor." Oakner's final blowup with Christie suggested otherwise. It suggested a very disturbing possibility to him. It suggested that one of the frozen embryos, her joint creation with their sponsor, had produced the stem cells that settled into the canine neural tissue.

It suggested that the minds of all seven dogs bore the imprint of his wife and her former lover, Lyana included.

Oakner had driven over to Stennis on his boat and confronted him. Stennis knew the truth. He was the only one who did. He had no choice but to tell Oakner. DNA testing would have confirmed it anyway.

No wonder Oakner wound up roaring drunk. Had he also tried to kill himself? Or was it an accident? It no longer mattered. The answer was locked forever in the doctor's comatose brain.

Elliot looked down at Lyana, who lay quietly beside Christie. She was a beautiful animal, with her sleek coat of black fur and eyes of brown and gold.

"Elliot? What are you thinking?" Christie asked.

Elliot smiled. He wouldn't tell her. Not now. Not ever. He reached over and gave Lyana a pat.

"I'm thinking maybe the three of us should go for a walk in the park," he said.

Lyana wagged her tail once. Did she somehow understand? Was she already picking up some English? There was no way to know. At least, not yet.

About the Author

Pierre Davis (aka Pierre Ouellette) is the author of two previously published novels, both dealing with the intersection of science, technology and humanity. Early in his career, he worked as a lead guitarist with several nationally recognized pop and jazz groups. Later, he was the cofounder of an advertising and PR agency focused on high technology, and served as the creative partner. He has also produced and directed a number of short films and documentaries. He resides in Portland, Oregon, where he is at work on the sequel to *A Breed Apart*.